"Haunting. Riveting. Filled with hope. *The Lost Melody* is all these things and more. Author Joanna Davidson Politano delves into the dark world of Victorian mental health, and it's the reader who comes out the winner after being enchanted by this tale of identity lost. After you read the last page, the characters will live on in your mind. Truly a fantastic read!"

Michelle Griep, author of *Lost in Darkness*

"Joanna Davidson Politano's stories go on my bookshelf as a favorite! The stories she pens entice my Gothic-loving senses, thrill my literary soul, and inspire the dark romantic inside my spirit. I cannot emphasize enough how strongly I adore each story from this vivid and insightful author, and how badly I wish for all readers to experience her tales!"

Jaime Jo Wright, author of *The Souls of Lost Lake* and Christy Award–winning *The House on Foster Hill*

Praise for *A Midnight Dance*

"Politano writes beautifully, evoking the magic of ballet and the theater from the opening turns to the final curtain, leaving readers applauding for an encore."

Booklist

"If you're looking for mesmerizing historical romance, you need to read this book."

Interviews & Reviews

"Politano's latest novel, *A Midnight Dance*, is a true work of art that encapsulates ballet in the Victorian era."

Box Office Revolution

"With an ability to create characters who pirouette right into our hearts, Politano has written a story that is at once deeply atmospheric, yet grounded in the universal ache to belong and be loved. A gently charming romance seamlessly weaves through Ella's quest to unravel the mystery of her past."

Kimberly Duffy, author of *A Mosaic of Wings* and *A Tapestry of Light*

the
LOST
MELODY

Books by Joanna Davidson Politano

Lady Jayne Disappears
A Rumored Fortune
Finding Lady Enderly
The Love Note
A Midnight Dance
The Lost Melody

the LOST MELODY

A NOVEL

JOANNA DAVIDSON POLITANO

Revell

a division of Baker Publishing Group
Grand Rapids, Michigan

© 2022 by Joanna Davidson Politano

Published by Revell
a division of Baker Publishing Group
PO Box 6287, Grand Rapids, MI 49516-6287
www.revellbooks.com

Printed in the United States of America

Library of Congress Cataloging-in-Publication Data
Names: Politano, Joanna Davidson, 1982– author.
Title: The lost melody / Joanna Davidson Politano.
Description: Grand Rapids, MI : Revell, a division of Baker Publishing Group, [2022]
Identifiers: LCCN 2021062755 | ISBN 9780800736910 (paperback) | ISBN 9780800742201 (casebound) | ISBN 9781493438747 (ebook)
Classification: LCC PS3616.O56753 L67 2022 | DDC 813/.6—dc23
LC record available at https://lccn.loc.gov/2021062755

This book is a work of fiction. Names, characters, places, and incidents are the product of the author's imagination or are used fictitiously. Any resemblance to actual events, locales, or persons, living or dead, is coincidental.

Most Scripture used in this book, whether quoted or paraphrased by the characters, is taken from the King James Version of the Bible.

Scripture marked NIV is taken from THE HOLY BIBLE, NEW INTERNATIONAL VERSION®, NIV® Copyright © 1973, 1978, 1984, 2011 by Biblica, Inc.® Used by permission. All rights reserved worldwide.

Baker Publishing Group publications use paper produced from sustainable forestry practices and post-consumer waste whenever possible.

22   23   24   25   26   27   28   7   6   5   4   3   2   1

The light shines in the darkness,
and the darkness has not overcome it.

John 1:5 NIV

This story is for my wonderful grandfather,
the musician who "saw" everyone and loved them well.
Miss you, Grandpa.

FIRST MOVEMENT

And those who were seen dancing were thought to be insane by those who did not hear the music.

~Friedrich Nietzsche

HURSTWELL ASYLUM

One day in late May of the year 1886, I found myself imprisoned in the Hurstwell Pauper Lunatic Asylum. This was unconscionable— I had *never* been a pauper.

I woke in a damp little room, and the music of the place was entirely wrong. I'd fallen asleep in a Beethoven sonata, white and airy, wrapped up with silky delight, and woken in the dark heart of Berlioz's eerie *Symphonie Fantastique*, my head thudding with deep bassoon, the echoing rhythm of rain hitting stone. As my mind surfaced, I scrambled to collect the memories of the place, the bassoon solidified into a voice—one quite near the foot of my bed. I did not open my eyes to check.

"Don't go too near. She's moving."

"Waking?"

"Not for several hours. Involuntary muscle spasms, most likely."

Indeed. They'd overestimated whatever drug they'd injected into me. Or they had, as people often did, underestimated *me*. An odd thing happened when one carried a giant weight of troubles all her life—she built up a great deal of strength.

"Will we keep her?" A light timpani voice contrasted with the first.

"I'm not certain yet. It's a rather odd case, and she's already proved volatile. We cannot let her go free."

I had fought, hadn't I? My mind swirled with memories—an urgent need to escape. The failure to do so. Yes, I remembered. This is what came of trusting one's best friend. I may not even marry him now.

"Has she a name?"

"Cora . . . Cora something."

No. No, that wasn't right. I wasn't Cora.

"I've forgotten. Her last name is of no consequence. She doesn't belong to anyone."

Ouch. A pin into a live pincushion.

Scribbles on paper. "What is her condition?"

"Delusions," came the deeper voice. The bassoon. "She hears music."

"Rather a nice malady to have, isn't it? Hearing music?"

"Not when there isn't any."

"Right, of course. Any other details?"

"We've only to decide if she's acute or chronic—and that depends on her."

"Well, her committal was . . . *oh*."

"Yes. Oh."

What? "Oh" what? my mind cried out. I recalled my childhood, my father, my home. Pianofortes. Performances. But the recent events, the details of this place, eluded me. Shrouded in the thick mist of the moors.

"Well, well. Look at this," said the lighter voice.

Papers rustled. I wanted to snatch them and see for myself.

A frantic rapping just outside interrupted the meeting, and the door squeaked open. A breathy female voice inserted itself. "Pardon, Doctor. It's the man in the male long-stay ward—he's suffered another attack."

"Very well." After a blustery exhale, footsteps shuffled, then the door slammed shut.

But it did not lock.

Did not lock.

My heart pounded, three beats for every second that swept on silently, drawing those men and their footfalls farther from my cell and its unlocked door. My skin grew clammy, a line of moisture gathering along my legs where they lay cemented together. No one came.

I slowly activated my stiff muscles and pushed up on the bed, swinging my heavy limbs down and feeling about the cold floor for shoes as I fought the oddest sense of imbalance and heaviness. I could feel the blood recirculating, as if I'd lain comatose for a week.

Maybe I had.

Whiteness closed in around the edges of my vision as I lifted my head a bit too quickly. I saw two of everything, then four, then two, then back to one again, and the air felt thick. I forced myself to stand, holding out my arms for balance.

I could do this. I could. The woman who played an entire piano concerto without a scrap of music, who drew more listeners than her male counterparts, who survived a man like my *father*, could certainly stand up and walk out the front door of this rotten place. Especially since no one had a valid reason to keep me here.

They didn't.

Stretching my neck, my legs, I eased myself up, preparing for whatever would come.

"You're getting on quite well." A voice to my right slid under my skin and chilled my bones.

I turned on wooden legs to see the bassoon-voiced doctor, who had apparently sent his partner on, remaining to observe me from against the door.

Thornhill. This was Thornhill, the superintendent, and a shadowy fear began to overtake me. Why, though? I couldn't remember the details. The gears of my mind groaned into movement. Such fog, clouding what I needed to remember. "Where . . . Who . . . ?" I worked my mouth, but there wasn't enough voice to come out. My throat was dry. A cotton-lined tube.

"Hurstwell Asylum, and your father."

"My . . . *father?*" I clutched the back of a wooden chair. I began to shake. Impossible. *Impossible.*

Now I knew for certain this was all a catastrophic mistake. He couldn't do this to me—not anymore.

1

I carry a deep sadness of the heart which must now and then break out in sound.

~Frantz Lizst

THREE MONTHS EARLIER, MANCHESTER

I was playing a piece by Berlioz the night my father died, the second movement of *Symphonie Fantastique* with arpeggios smooth as a horse's gallop. Footsteps stopped and a figure hovered in the doorway, and I knew what was coming before our maid even spoke the jarring words. "He's gone, Miss Vivienne."

"I see." I did not smile, for that would have been wicked, but I did relax, more than I had allowed myself to in many years.

Her steady footsteps crossed the carpeted room past where I sat, and she threw open the drapes on every long window—drapes that had remained drawn for years to keep my father's headaches, and his resulting temper, at bay.

It was dark outside, still very early morning, but so many hours had passed in the waiting. The maid turned, those wise old eyes cast my direction. "Night is passing, and day is soon to come for you, Miss Vivienne."

We shared a solemn smile. Then she gave a brief curtsy and left me.

A breezy emptiness infilled my soul at the sudden silence, a sense of unfettered spring air blowing through hollow places. Gone were Father's company and his uncanny business sense, but so were the sting of fresh lashes across my fingers as I practiced, that voice bellowing through the halls, the silent fight always knotted up in my belly with nowhere to go. Suddenly, it had all gone slack. It was over, and I was alone in the world.

I grieved the man, but I couldn't say I was unhappy. I looked over the vast spread of pianofortes that awaited restoration laid out before me with a new sense of ownership, of delight. It was *my* repair shop now, and darkness would have no place here anymore. *God, you are the master of this house now. The master of me. No one else shall ever be.* I felt his heady presence with the coming dawn and I welcomed it.

After several deep breaths to acknowledge the passing of a soul, I lifted my fingers to the ivories in the flickering candlelight and began the piece again from the beginning. The song was the perfect end to our tumultuous years together, powerful dissonance brimming with deeply textured tones that climbed to a rich climax as the dawn crested, colorful light brimming through the room, then simply stopped at the obvious point of conclusion, and the room was empty. Quiet and peaceful in morning's rosy glow.

Within the hour, familiar footsteps—masculine ones—sounded somewhere in the foyer, and my breath caught. I kept my fingertips poised on the ivories, feeling the oddness of Richard's presence in this house. Things were shifting already.

I continued playing as his footfall entered the room and crossed to me. He stopped at the pianoforte and sat beside me, the bench creaking under his weight. The slight bump of Richard's shoulder as he slid close was all that passed between us, but it was plenty. I paused, for I suddenly couldn't remember what came next in the piece.

Oh, how Father would hate this.

I almost began to play again, but Richard's arm came around me, solid but cautious. I felt every inch of its gentle weight. We'd known each other all my life, and this was the first time he'd ever dared. I looked up into his face, and he smiled down at me—a solemn, affectionate look that expressed every word he didn't need to say. The regret for my loss, the relief at my freedom, the uncertain hope of what was to come between us.

I played on for several minutes, and he listened without a word, as he always did. The song came to a gentle conclusion and I sat motionless, fingers still perched on the keys. The enormity of his masculine presence nearly undid my calm. What would happen now? Father was gone. There was nothing stopping Richard from . . . well, anything. I could feel his keen scrutiny on me. Deciding.

I looked up at him, and he leaned nearer, those familiar crescent-shaped eyes and clean-shaven chin, and laid his forehead on mine.

I ran my tongue over my lips that had gone dry and met his gaze. "So, now what?"

His hand lifted to my cheek and stroked it. "Everything's different now, isn't it?" A gentle smile. "What will you do with your life?"

I closed my eyes. "Oh, I have a few ideas."

His finger came down the side of my face and teased my lips. "Anything that includes me?"

"Perhaps." I looked up. "How are you at handling horses? I've been meaning to hire a driver."

His look was amused and sympathetic all at once. Oh, how I adored this man. "Better than handling certain redheads."

I smacked his arm, and somehow it relieved the night's tension. Filled the cracks with a bit of joy.

"I bet I can guess your plans." He leaned back. "After your mourning period, you'll go out and continue to perform, maybe even better than before, and with a newfound joy that no one will truly understand. You'll appear in concert hall after concert hall

all over the Continent and amaze your audiences . . . then come home to a quiet house and live the simple, uncomplicated life you were always meant to have. One you fully deserve."

I gave a polite smile but said nothing to contradict him. I'd known for years what I'd do with myself when I finally possessed freedom, but I dared not shock Richard with it. Not yet. I'd at least let him kiss me first.

"You'll have your pianoforte shop, perhaps a few students, and your friends. Modest and simple and delightfully musical, a life of high quality is what fits you best."

Few people actually knew me, as it turned out. I was a Chopin nocturne—surprising, complex, and impossible to master.

Many tried. I'm happy to report that they had all failed.

Well, nearly.

2

They probably think because I am so small and young, nothing of greatness and class can come out of me; but they shall soon find out.

~Wolfgang Amadeus Mozart

HURSTWELL ASYLUM

I stared at the asylum doctor who stood between me and freedom, listening to my explanation. My mind swam in the medicinal pea soup the longer I sat upright, but it latched on to one fact. "So you see, it wasn't my father who brought me here. It couldn't be."

"I suppose not, if he's dead." The doctor, a bulldog of a man with a heavy face resting upon the cushion of his broad shoulders, availed himself of my vacated bed, perching on the edge and sinking it quite low. "Well, then. Perhaps it was another man who signed for you." He lifted page after page on his clipboard, scanning the lines. "I just assumed. I was not here to meet him, of course. It was late when the papers were signed. Rather an emergency situation, you understand."

"Who *did* sign me over to this place then?"

He scribbled on his paper, not even allowing me the dignity of eye contact, then came the instruments from his brown leather satchel. First, the listening device, its cold metal horn shoved down the top of my oversized asylum gown. "Hold still."

I shook my head, trying to clear the remaining fog. "You will release me, won't you? Once you've examined me and I'm proved fit?"

"I'm afraid not." The cold metal found a new spot. "Wouldn't you like to be well again? To stop hearing music and be like everyone else?"

I pinched my lips and looked down. "If I stop hearing music, you'll let me out?"

He blinked, as if the notion of my leaving had never occurred to him. "Perhaps." His calm smile had a numbing effect. Not the disarming sort, but the way one's leg feels after its owner has been lost in a book too long and forgotten it was tucked under the body. "We'll just wait and see, shall we? Now, Miss Fletcher, we'll start with the routine information and get you admitted."

"Fletcher?"

"Do you prefer Cora?"

I frowned. Cora Fletcher. Who was she? Not me, that was for certain. I wasn't sure if it would help my case to mention it or merely solidify my diagnosis.

The doctor worked through a series of questions—address, sex, age, hair color—as if I'd be an inmate here long enough to need a record.

"Living conditions?"

I glanced about the place with a grimace. My head ached. "Deplorable."

"At home, that is."

"Lovely." My voice took on a tone as distant as my normal life.

"Parents' mental state?"

"Quite at peace in their graves."

His lips twitched beneath his beard. "I meant, when they lived. Siblings similarly afflicted with—?"

"None."

20

"Other relatives?"

"Deceased."

He jotted. It didn't take long, for the entirety of my family could be summed up in one word: *dead*.

"If you would only let me send word to—"

"Your condition is of no concern to anyone outside the asylum. It is a private matter."

Chills climbed my spine, although I couldn't say exactly why. "Allow me to send for my manager. He'll—"

"Out of the question. We don't allow contact with friends or relations—it's bound to excite, and we can't have that, can we?"

The chill deepened. No letters. No contact. He scribbled a bit more as I began to sense the quicksand into which I'd fallen, drawing me into a pit I would not escape without a fight.

Very well, then. I knew how to do battle.

"Occupation—none, I assume?"

"I am a concert pianist. And my name is not Cora Fletcher, it's Vivienne Mourdant." I edged my chin up. "You'll find my name on the local playbills."

He sat back with a steady gaze upon me. "I'll warn you, we don't indulge delusions at this institution."

"I'm not delusional." I looked him in the eye.

"I've heard witness from several people here at Hurstwell that you hear music playing at night. Nocturnal hallucinations are, in fact, delusions."

"My life is full of music because I'm a concert pianist. I'm surrounded by it all the time, and it has become part of my subconscious."

"I see." His look of pity soured my belly. "Now then, let's talk about your true occupation, shall we?"

"How, pray, can you possibly know that I'm not what I say?"

"Because you are Cora Fletcher. Many people know you as such. A great many more than you can find to say you are someone else." He lifted my hand and I snatched it back, holding it close.

"I don't believe you."

He said nothing of my being in a madhouse, my logic being unreliable. With a firm look my direction, he took my hand back, guiding it toward him with gentle tugs and turning it, palm up, to touch indents on my fingertips. "Callouses. Signs of hard, physical work. Not signs of a concert pianist. If I were to guess, I'd say you are employed at a loom. I've seen similar indentations on other patients. And there has been a girl missing from the looms over Menston way." The doctor set my limp hand back on my thigh and his face folded in gentle pity. "We're here to help you, Miss Fletcher. Institutions aren't what they used to be, and I'm not your enemy. Just remember that."

I tucked my cold hand against my body. The gentle pity—it was anything but comforting.

He peered into my eyes with another tool, his fingers so close I caught the scent of lye and talcum, but his touch was not harsh. "Well, now that you've given up your hope of leaving . . ."

Had I? Would I ever?

"I'll have a nurse show you to the wards."

As he ushered me into the hall, my lungs filling with fresh air, my reason returned in cool waves, and the details of recent days—the ones at Hurstwell—began to take shape. Most of them, anyway. The long stone corridor glowing with oddly distorting gaslights . . . this was familiar. I'd walked here, had conversations here, felt frustration and ire in these shadowy halls.

But Cora. Cora Fletcher. Where did that name—

Oh. Yes. With a shock of awareness, I recalled why I was actually here, how I'd come . . . and who, of all people, had been behind it all.

It had been me.

Music is like a dream. One that I cannot hear.

~Ludwig van Beethoven

THREE MONTHS EARLIER, MANCHESTER

Richard remained all day on that first morning without Father, and I had not rushed him out. Especially since he still had not kissed me.

After the undertaker had come and gone, we sat side by side on the rickety bench of an old pianoforte I was restoring for a client, my fingers tripping lightly over the keys along with our conversation. The door opened and we jumped apart, an instinct born of many years.

"Pardon, miss, but your father's solicitor is here to see you." Sarah, our upstairs maid, stood in the doorway, her cool face surveying the scene.

"So soon? Can he not wait a few days?"

"He was quite insistent you meet with him today, so I've put him in the study." She offered a quick curtsy and left.

I rose and excused myself, going to meet the man.

The mustached solicitor sat at Father's desk in his ill-fitting gray wool suit and laid out my future. "I do apologize for adding strain to your grief, but I thought you should know as soon as possible," he began after a few cursory sympathies. "There are many notes due in full within thirty days, or the estate must be sold, and the profits forfeited to pay your debt."

"*His* debt."

"Which, unfortunately, is now yours." He shrugged awkwardly.

I fisted my hands in my lap. Father still had power over me—even from the grave. "By the estate I must sell, I assume you mean this pianoforte shop? My home?"

He folded his hands over the giant stack of papers, appearing appropriately grave. "I'm sorry to say, that is the only viable asset your father retained amidst all his spending."

My face heated. "He wasn't taking students at the end, of course. His income was severely limited." In fact, most of it had come solely from my performances and the few pianofortes I had restored myself. A bout of apoplexy had left him bedridden for over a year, and I'd watched the funds dwindling. "The debts shall be seen to."

Yet the man made no motion of standing to leave. "There is one other matter, Miss Mourdant. One of a slightly more sensitive nature." His fingertips traced the edge of the papers he still held.

I smoothed stray hairs off my warm face with an impatient hand. What could possibly be more sensitive than the mountain of unpaid notes with my name attached to them? "Very well, what is it, then?"

"Well, the matter of guardianship."

"I am already of age, Mr. Finley."

"Of course. It isn't your guardianship, but that of your father's ward."

I blinked. "There's a child? Whose is he?"

"She." He centered his gaze on my face with a frown. "You aren't aware of her?"

"Obviously not." I tamped down my temper, clutching my hands together to keep them still.

"She is a grown woman, actually, and I regret I have few other details on the matter. I have only . . . well, this." He slid a scrap of paper across the desk to me.

The ward's address explained the reason for his embarrassment. "Hurstwell. She's in an asylum?"

"I'm afraid so. She's been deemed unfit to care for herself, so her guardianship now passes to you."

"But . . . who is she?"

"Rosamond Swansea. She was your father's ward, and now she is yours."

My mouth hung a mite slack—rather unladylike, but I was no actress. I was shocked and could not mask it.

"I assume you'll want her arrangements to remain the same?"

I blinked, searching my mind. "Why . . . yes, I suppose. Yes, that would be best."

"The next bill to Hurstwell is due in just a fortnight, but that is one account your father managed to keep current all these years. I suppose you could let it lapse for a time if you need to attend the more pressing notes . . ."

I rested my forehead on my fingertips, blowing out a breath. "I'm sorry, but how is this woman connected to us?"

"Your father didn't share those details with me, but I do have this." He took an unfinished yet striking ink sketch from his folder and slid it across the desk.

One look and I sucked in my breath. It was *her*. That ethereal face, the gently angled jawline, the rich hair piled atop her head . . . all my spinning thoughts stood still. I sat straighter. A choking sense of dread came over me. Prickles and chills that climbed my skin, right into my hairline. Richard was waiting for me, notes had to be paid, but all of it melted away as I stared at the face of the woman whom I hadn't thought of in many years.

Impossible. This is simply not possible!

Yet there she was, perfectly portrayed with those sweetly imploring eyes that resonated in my mind, a hauntingly beautiful face resurfacing in my memory after all these years. This . . . this was the mysterious ward? It was uncanny. Unsettling, even. I knew those laughing eyes, that tilted head resting on her hand in just that way, but it couldn't be the woman I remembered. Couldn't possibly.

"I'll leave the matter to you, Miss Mourdant. Her fate is now in your hands." He handed me the asylum's address and rose to leave as if he hadn't just tipped my world off its axis. I stared down at that image, fighting panic.

There exists in most of us a small, hidden fear that we are secretly mad and on the verge of being found out. Mostly I had lived with the niggling worry in the background, in the quiet part of my brain that admitted I was odd and slightly music obsessed, synthesizing every ordinary collection of sounds into a personal symphony. But those dreams I often had—odd and vivid ones, and always with music—had the maids looking at me as if I truly was mad when I dared speak of them. They'd felt so very real, and I'd thought, until the maid had set me straight, that they truly had happened.

Perhaps some of them had. Like the dream of this woman. A specter who played the same haunting song on Mother's old pianoforte while she smiled at me, wordlessly welcoming me to join her. It had been one of the more pleasant of my dreams, and the memory of her face had become a comfort to me in those days.

But that had been so long ago. I'd been a child, a lonely, isolated one, and my understanding of reality so very immature.

There was, of course, some simple explanation for it all. Of course there was.

With a shake of my head, I pulled my pen and blotter close and dashed off a letter to Hurstwell Asylum, inquiring as to the details of the woman for whom I was now responsible. The one I'd always thought a figment of my imagination. I did so without telling them of the guardianship that was switching hands, or letting on how little I knew of my actual connection to her, admitting silently I was merely appeasing my conscience on the matter.

I slid the image close again and studied her face, the roundness of her cheek against her fingers, and the dusting of curls along the nape of her neck. There she was, just as warm and inviting as I remembered. I looked back to the address, that lost melody resurfacing in my mind after all those years, then I crumpled the thing in my hand.

Madness. Somehow connected to us. To me.

Confused, tired, I moved back into the front room to find Richard still waiting for me.

He rose to greet me, hands outstretched to take mine. His fingertips found the little paper still curled in my palm. "What is it?"

I hastily swept the paper away from him, clutching it tight. "Nothing that need concern you." Warmth poured over me as I realized what that little scrap would reveal. What it might change between us to have my family connected to someone at an asylum.

I moved the scrap behind my back, and he dove for it playfully. "Truly, it isn't!"

I held it high, and he jumped, grabbing it from my hand. Alarmed, I snatched it back. My face heated even more. One glance at that address and his look of adoration would melt into something else. Something I'd never wanted—pity. I tightened my fist around that small wad of paper.

He frowned and stepped forward. "Everything of yours concerns me, Vivienne. I want the bad with the good." He reached behind and threaded it firmly from my grasp . . . and I released it to him, stepping back.

I held my breath while he flattened it and read, frown deepening. "Asylum? What—"

My chin edged up. "A matter of the estate."

Richard stared down at the paper containing only an address, as if he might derive more information out of it. "He has a fortune holed up in the place, does he? An investment, perhaps."

I sighed, going for brutal honesty—on one matter, at least. "There's no fortune, Richard. No inheritance save the shop. You should know that first and foremost, if you have any intentions concerning me." The notes to be paid were plentiful, and the income was not. That much I knew. The strain of it had contributed to Father's illness.

He looked at it again, then tossed it on the lid of a Chalmers upright. "I expected as much. He had little to offer you in life, either. Pardon my speaking ill of the dead."

I turned away, silent for a ghost of a moment as the chill of recent death once again passed over me. "It was not easy living with him, but he did give me music." I walked to the window, looking out into the sunlight. "That is all the inheritance I need."

"You're right. What do you need with a fortune, anyway?" He came to stand behind me, his solid presence giving me heart flutters, and laid his hands on my arms. "You'll marry and settle down with some fine bloke, and what's his shall be yours. That's how it usually works, anyway, and how it should be. All you have to do is coast. Keep up your performances to maintain the shop, then marry and allow someone to take care of you for a change. And if I know you, you'll put this business with the asylum aside, elegantly folding it into your father's past to be forgotten along with the rest, and go on with a most splendid life."

I shivered. He was right about one part. I had no intention of pursuing this matter and uncovering uncomfortable details of my father's history.

At least, not yet.

Every difficulty slurred over will be a ghost to disturb your repose later on.

~Frederic Chopin

Frederick Harford first stepped into my life several weeks after Father's passing. It was at an evening performance at an estate on Hanover Square, and everything seemed rosy. Effervescent in the sparkling light of crystal chandeliers. It was the one small parlor performance arranged before entering mourning, and it would make a tiny dent in the debts. It was bad form to be seen out in society so soon, but a terrible disservice to cancel positions I'd already agreed to take, I had reasoned. The hosts were counting on me. Most people in London didn't even know of my father's recent demise, except my manager, Marcel Beauchene—whom I had not told of this performance I'd arranged myself. I had decided not to even dress in mourning, and there had been no one about to disagree with me.

I moved through the opulent room, watching Richard from a distance whenever I dared, and noticing his attention on me as well.

At one point, though, I looked for him and instead locked gazes with an older man staring at me quite openly from across the room. He stared as if he knew me, with the boldness of one too old to care about propriety. Not leering, but intensely interested. Curious. He had something to say. I could see it haunting the windows of his eyes.

A tap came on my shoulder. I spun with a smile meant for Richard, but it was another man—the Marquis D'auberney. I'd seen him about London here and there but had never made his acquaintance. Nor did I wish to, for he was a fugue in some minor key with awkward arpeggios and heavy-handed high notes. I returned his look of interest with a polite one of disdain.

Which he apparently took as an invitation. Of course he would. Let him try—he wouldn't get far with me. He bowed, and I caught sight—thank heavens—of Richard just beyond. Our eyes met over the marquis's shoulder and understanding passed between us. My wonderful longtime friend sauntered near, hands clasped behind his back, offering greetings in passing but keeping his eyes on me.

"You must excuse me," I said to the marquis. I couldn't abide the thought of standing so near to him that I could taste his breath. "I'm afraid I've emptied my glass." Meaningless banter irked me, and I suppose that was another of my oddities. I turned my back on the marquis to take a fresh glass from a passing waiter, hoping the man would find another guest to bother.

Instead, the foolish man remained and raked me with a look. "How is it I don't remember encountering you among this company before? You've a rare look of intelligence in your eyes, and that hair . . ." He stopped just short of fingering the dark red tresses curling over my shoulder. "I don't often encounter such a lady."

I leveled my gaze at him, polite smile in place. "You only attract what you are."

His face split in a silly laugh. He thought I was joking. Flirting, perhaps. "I believe it would be more pleasant to talk in the gardens. Won't you join me?"

"I'm afraid this isn't the time," I said. Richard was closer now, just over the man's shoulder and a few yards back. Listening. Watching from the corner of his eye. Another sip as I waited.

"It's an ideal time to escape. They're about to start the music."

I frowned, lowering my glass. "You've something against the pianoforte?"

"Heavens, no. Not when it's played by a musician of some quality. Tonight, unfortunately, we're burdened with the dubious talents of a Miss Vivienne Mourdant. You've heard of her, I assume?"

Richard cocked an eyebrow at this and fought a wicked smile. It was contagious and I dropped my gaze to keep from rupturing my composure. "I have."

"I won't regale you with the details, but let me assure you she's a second-rate performer who has elbowed her way into the music world on the strength of her connections. Quite amateurish as a performer, though."

"Indeed? Is that what they're saying?"

He leaned close. "She's been seen sidling up to wealthy gents at events like this, and I'm certain that's how she manages to secure performances."

My skin chilled. "Well, now. It seems the woman has no redeeming qualities."

"Quite as I see it." A smile curled the ends of his mustache. "Pray tell, what's your name?"

"You won't like the answer to that." I placed my now-empty cup on a passing tray and glanced toward the pianoforte. Almost time.

"It's no matter what your connections are or aren't. For such unusual beauty, I can forgive the lack. Would you welcome a call from me sometime?"

I pressed my lips together. "I'm afraid you won't like the answer to that, either."

His look of confusion behind his terrible white smile made me want to laugh.

Just then the crowds hushed, and the host, a noble older gentleman with several medals decorating his black cutaway coat, stood before his guests to announce the night's entertainment. His dramatic introduction culminated in the mention of my name, and there was applause.

Worries slipped off my shoulders as I approached the mahogany pianoforte, a stately Erard with smooth, polished surfaces and gold lettering. I let my fingertips trail over the ivories with a little shiver. *Hello, beautiful.*

I perched upon the fringed stool, positioned and ready, and delighted in that one perfect moment of quiet anticipation. Then the music found me, curling my fingers and compelling them over the keys. Everything fell away in a swirl of sound for the next twenty minutes, and I forgot the very troubles I'd just been pondering.

At the conclusion I rose to applause, fully revived and at peace, my heart filled with the great creations of genius composers who'd come before me.

The first face I saw in the crowd as my heart floated back to earth was the marquis's. My instinctual politeness drummed up a cool smile in return to his stare, but he averted his eyes and melted into the crowd, never to accost me with his attentions again.

At this, I smiled for real.

Until I saw the older man again, the one who'd been studying me, approaching from the left. I spoke to a few more people on the way, but soon I turned to him and drew up a most charming welcome. "Begging your pardon, but have we been introduced?"

"Not formally, but I've already received all the introduction I need." He fluttered one hand toward the pianoforte that still vibrated with the concerto's dramatic conclusion and returned his steady gaze to mine. Something about the unusual sparkle in his eye suddenly made the man seem far from innocent. "You," he said, in a slow, intentional way, "pierce the darkness with light. Did you know that?"

I laughed, fingering the beads at my throat. "That's certainly the most original compliment I've received." How could he know to say such a thing? He'd not seen the child version of me hunched and terrified in the dark larder over and over again, clawing at the door, desperate for light. I shivered at the memory of Father's wretched punishments that still made an odd, lonely chill come over me in the dark.

"It's something Schumann said—the duty of every artist, he called it. A light such as yours should be taken into the utmost darkness, you know."

I held my breath, unable to relax. A light in the dark. Yes, that's precisely how I saw my future—the daring plans I'd only begun to concoct in secret. *Make today count.* I rose with that notion on my lips every morning, and soon I'd be able to act on it. A new day, a new rescue for one lost soul suffering in the dark as I once had. As my mother had before me. I'd even been tempted to blame her death on my father, on his merciless control over her until the very end, but perhaps that was taking things too far.

"Your light is wasted here in the sunny parlors of the ton. Might I suggest a new, more significant outlet for your music?"

That stare of his continued to penetrate my layers of poise with an unsettling knowing. I studied him back. "Forgive me, but are you certain we haven't met before? I feel as if I should know you."

His face lit with an instant smile. "Quite true, you should. I've been hoping to make your acquaintance since I first heard you make a showpiece of a Brahms minuet in Lisbon, and I've been to every performance you've given in England since."

I raised my eyebrows, my heart straddling pleasure and unease. "How you flatter."

He smiled tenderly. "Even your voice has a musical quality, smooth and rich like honey." Then he broke the stare and shook his head as if he'd forgotten himself. "I beg your pardon, Miss Mourdant. I should at least provide you with a name to go with my ramblings, shouldn't I? It's Frederick Harford, man of the cloth, amateur poet, and psalmist, lately of Westminster Abbey. Ah, and an associate of the Royal Academy as well."

Royal Academy? He'd have known Father then, most likely. I accepted a small scone from a passing footman, a glass of water from another. "My manager handles the long-term engagements." Yet my curiosity wouldn't let go just yet. Perhaps it was what he'd said about being a light. "What sort of outlet did you have in mind?" I nibbled the edge of the flaky pastry.

"I've been working in hospitals around the country, experimenting with music in the wards, and the results have been quite pleasing."

I eyed the man, looking for the jest in his expression. "Truly, a hospital?" I wasn't keen on giving up a great deal of time to create a musical spa treatment of sorts for invalids laid up in hospital. *Lord, forgive my uncharitable spirit.* "What are you hoping to accomplish?"

"Why, healing of course. Music opens up what we once believed lost. It penetrates, influences, and restores like nothing in a bottle can. Lost memories resurface, peace invades pain . . ."

I breathed in deeply, plunging through his rambles. "And who pays for such a thing? Surely not the patients." I loathed to tread into the unpardonable topic of compensation, but neither could I afford to work for free. Not now, anyway.

"Why, I'm hoping for donors, once I have established my methodology."

"Sir, if it's a donation you seek from me—"

He opened his palms before me. "Not at all. My aim at this moment is to conduct a clinical study to attract potential sponsors. When minds are open, pocketbooks follow. What I need is a true musician to open those minds and demonstrate what may be accomplished—a performer who has enough light to pierce the darkness." That tender smile returned, and my heart quickened. "You see, my dear, I only want you for your music."

My back stiffened. "I don't recall any of London's hospitals having a reputation for being particularly dark, Mr. Harford. Had you a specific one in mind for me to . . . pierce?"

"Actually, where I wanted to take you and your music is the darkest place in all of England—the county asylums. Hurstwell, to be exact."

I spit my water into my glass to keep from choking, then held gloved fingertips to my lips. "I beg your pardon?" Normally, I wasn't one to believe in coincidences—not when I'd personally experienced God's remarkable sovereignty. Yet I couldn't explain this any other way.

"You've not seen darkness until you've experienced the despair at such a place, Miss Mourdant. There is nothing it needs more than a little light breaking through. It's a dead end with little comfort, no hope."

My heart pounded as I searched for polite responses, and I offered what I hoped was a passable yet vague regret.

Ten minutes later I was standing beside Richard at the fringes of the room, screened by the fronds of a tropical parlor plant, relaying the entire conversation to him in whispered tones. "What is it about me that makes that man believe I'd willingly go to an asylum? Heavens above!"

He laughed, eyes sparkling. "At least he isn't suggesting you go as a patient."

I cringed, highly aware once again of my connection to the asylum—the one I still kept from him. One I didn't fully understand myself.

"So what did you say to him? It wouldn't surprise me to hear you'd agreed to one or two visits."

I blew out a breath. "For what purpose? To perform for a band of hopeless inmates?" I stopped the indelicate flow of thoughts, but Richard was eyeing me, openly judging my words. "Oh, leave off. You know as well as I and the rest of England that madness is a disease without a cure. What good would it do to play music for them? They're broken in a way no one can truly fix." I'd been arguing this point with myself in the privacy of my bedchamber for weeks now, every time I thought about that mysterious ward

. . . or met her smiling eyes in that sketch. "I don't give myself over to futile tasks, you know."

He shrugged. "The Vivienne Mourdant I know always seemed drawn to the helpless and needy, even to the point of endangering herself. Much to my chagrin at times."

I looked at this man with new appreciation, feeling warmly *known* by him. "You're right, that is true." Perhaps he wouldn't be shocked by my secret plans for the future. "Richard, you mentioned changes in my life. The plans I had. I do want to aid the helpless and needy, it's true." I swallowed, growing brave. "But not those in asylums. People who actually can be helped—people with a future."

"Oh?"

I'd spent months—no, years—preparing for this, planning and arranging things in my mind, waiting for the opportunity. Only in the weeks after Father's death had I begun to put anything on paper, to consider my wild scheme a possibility and to let myself dream of it.

Make today count. That had become my motto, the thought I woke with every morning, and I could scarcely wait to see how it would play out.

I leaned close, glancing through the fronds to be sure no one lingered near. "Richard, there are countless numbers of women in England—in Manchester alone—trapped in abominable circumstances, practically owned by men who are meant to protect them but who do exactly the opposite. Good, kind women. Clever ones. And they cannot do a thing about it, the way the law is. Their money, their children, even their own bodies legally belong to husbands or fathers or guardians, and they can decide nothing for their own lives. No one sees or pities these women because they're wealthy, materially provided for, but they're broken and poor in spirit. Crushed by the men who have charge over their lives."

"And what do you propose to do about it, break them out of their gilded cage?"

"Why . . . yes, actually."

He puffed out a breath, hand on his forehead. "You've no idea what you're suggesting. That requires finding them respectable lodging. Positions. Possibly a way of escape, and a great deal more support along the way. Not to mention the legal and moral battles you'd face . . . inquests . . ."

I straightened. "Why do you believe that because a thing is hard, I cannot do it?"

He sobered. "I'm certain you are capable of doing a great many things, and perhaps you could become a fine friend to these women, if nothing else. What you're suggesting, though, would take a great deal of the one thing you, my lady of many talents, do not have—*money*."

My fingers stiffened on the palm frond.

"Forgive the vulgar topic, but I'm merely trying to be realistic. I think it's a fine ambition, but not for you. You're a young, unmarried woman without resources or protection."

"But with a great big God," I whispered, looking out at the happy facades in the room. The practical always overlooked that resource.

"I suppose so." He blinked. "You've never spoken this way before. I had no idea you had such leanings."

"I've always attended church. You know that."

"So do most people. But they do not speak that way about God."

I averted my gaze. How did I explain my relationship with God? I couldn't think of him as a father, for the word had always made me cringe. He began more as an imaginary friend in my childhood, his undeniable presence filling that cramped little larder every time Father locked me in, and I one day realized this imaginary, always-present ally who sat with me in the dark was quite real. And that he'd come looking for me. I'd leaned on him in the privacy of my heart ever since.

Yet how did a full-grown woman put such a relationship into words?

He sighed. "I simply don't know why you'd go to such effort. Why you care so deeply about women you don't even know, whose troubles are none of your concern."

Because up until recently, I had been one of them. And years ago, so had my mother. It weakened her in the end, of that I was certain—it had cost her so much, including the chance to enjoy her newborn daughter. No one else would see it that way, though. No one who had not lived there, watching it all occur.

I looked away and swallowed back the words I could not voice, even to this longtime friend of my heart. Some shadows were so deep, one never even thought of opening them up to the light of another's scrutiny. Instead, I put to him the question that had long been on my heart. "Does it not bother you that women are suffering under our very noses? That no one steps forward to help them?"

"I'm not saying it's right, but I don't see what can be done about it. What goes on within a man's home is his own business, and we cannot simply insert ourselves in another family's affairs. Especially without a great deal of income to back up a rather outlandish scheme. When it comes down to it, they're about as hopeless as those inmates of Hurstwell."

I chewed the edge of my lip. But then a line from my neatly printed brochure, the one I'd meant to slip into the hands of hurting women, came back to haunt me. "There is no such thing as a hopeless case," I murmured, then looked through the fronds to that odd man—that Frederick Harford—and saw Rosamond's face. Her sweet, smiling face. "No such thing. Only those who have lost hope."

Richard crossed his arms, leaning in to study me. "You're thinking of going, aren't you? To the asylum, that is." He shook his head. "You're actually considering taking that position so you can dig around in your father's affairs at Hurstwell. Admit it, you are."

I shook my head, willing my heart rate to steady. "Oh, Richard. Aren't you listening? I have other plans."

"How much has the man agreed to pay you, anyway? It must be something princely to drag you near such a place."

"Don't be ridiculous. No, I won't be going there. You couldn't force me. I haven't time to waste on such things, and it's probably a ghastly place." I spoke those words with firm conviction, meaning every one.

This is the mark of a really admirable man: steadfastness in the face of trouble.

~Ludwig van Beethoven

I was right—it *was* ghastly. Hurstwell Pauper Lunatic Asylum stood at the end of a long, rutted drive, a great, menacing giant of timber and rock crouching amidst the trees.

The matronly nurse held the hem of her skirt up out of the muddy drive. "Welcome to Hurstwell, Miss . . ."

"Fletcher. Cora Fletcher." I'd signed on for a lower staff position with the most nondescript name I could conjure at a moment's notice, neatly tucking away my true identity. No sense in announcing who I was, if I meant to investigate matters.

And investigate I would.

I'd meant what I told Richard when I'd rejected the idea of coming here, but the rudder of my thoughts had swung the other direction when an unexpected response from Hurstwell arrived at the house:

There seems to be some error. I'm sorry to inform you that we've no record of a patient by that name at this establishment,

*and never have. Perhaps you have the wrong asylum and might
inquire at others.*

Yet it was Hurstwell that had received Father's payments every
month for years. I checked the records twice. And the sketch—that
face—I *knew* that face. But only under the oddest circumstances.
In a recurring dream that evaporated by morning, complete with
a haunting melody heard only by me.

Every time I saw that shy smile in the sketch, in my memory,
something weakened in my core, and I couldn't erase the image
from my every waking thought. *Come find me,* she seemed to be
saying. *Don't let me be forgotten.* I'd requested the solicitor to
look into it at first, but all he'd done was report a likely paperwork
error and request that they stop the payments. I'd pushed him to
find more, and he'd offered me the card of a private investigator
and the oddest look of concern for my sanity.

Yet when I studied that inked portrait, that shy little smile full
of warmth . . . well, I knew the bumbling man in the ill-fitting suit
simply hadn't been clever enough to get to the truth. He never
would. And I needed the truth.

That night I'd dreamed of her again, so clearly and memora-
bly. I watched her draw her song from the keys, that lilting tune
stretching from major to minor, wrapping itself around my senses.
It intoxicated. Lingered. Then she'd looked right at me.

When I'd woken the following morning and said, "Make today
count," I knew who I would help, who needed me the most. The
only one I had the ability to rescue at the moment, the one who
had no one but me to help her.

And the one who absolutely would not leave my mind. All my
pressurized zeal turned her direction, and I was eager to rescue.
To pull her from whatever darkness had swallowed her.

No record. There was more to this story. No mention was made
of the payments received over the years for this ward, but the
solicitor assured me no more would be requested of me. Not to

be put off, I'd written a second time, and they'd promptly and firmly replied that I was to stop inquiring. They'd done a careful look and found no evidence of such a patient ever having been at Hurstwell. They declared the past payments a mistake, or a possible case of fraud from a third party, for truly, no such patient had ever been there.

Now, looking up at the place, I could see any number of things being lost in the great old rambling dungeon. How could they possibly know she wasn't there somewhere?

I shivered, slowing my step as we approached, realizing I would be expected to go inside. This was probably a terrible idea. There was a simple explanation that would make me feel foolish in the end. Yet every time I'd spoken to God about Rosamond Swansea, expecting a release from the odd tangle of curiosity, it had only intensified.

I'd felt prompted to dig. To find truth. A sense of going after a single lost sheep, as he had once done for me in the dark larder of my childhood. God had filled my heart with a nearly tangible longing to work out the secrets surrounding this mysterious woman and to honor her with the truth.

My time was suddenly quite free too. All my scheduled performances had been canceled. Word had spread of my father's death, my manager had refused to book engagements during mourning, and life had ground to a halt—all except the debts I must pay and their deadlines. While every other rescue I wished to do would cost me money, this one would earn me a small income. So now, weeks after my release from darkness and shadows, I was tramping right back into them. Only this time, it wasn't a larder and there was no Father locking me in. I had come by choice, and I could leave the same way, whenever it suited.

Truly I could.

I clamped my hat onto my head and hurried to follow the dough-faced nurse up to the front steps that were covered in petals. The last cherry blossoms swirled around our feet, blowing in a gentle pink cyclone against stone. Nurse Branson's flaccid skin, however, told the story of what lay inside. It was a black hole, this place, wasn't it? A cave without sunshine. A person rarely left once they set foot in it. Even the staff.

She knocked, then a man swung wide the heavy doors to admit us. It was cold and still inside, without benefit of hearth or fire. Even though the day outside was pleasant and warm, the place was a wintering old soul inside, glowing with garish lights that dulled the senses in an eerie way. Yet I did not feel afraid. "You have gas lighting here."

She brightened for a moment. "Bit of a surprise, out here in the country, I suppose. It does help to have the place always lighted, never running out of candles."

"It certainly changes the whole look of it. You see everything differently." I took in its vastness. The lit portions were seen more clearly, the dark corners more obscured.

"It's a helpful little boon in our line of work. There are some things it's best the patients don't see. Some shadows best left dark. And we can dim the whole place at once, when we need to, with the turn of a valve. Softens the harshest edges, don't you know."

I shivered, wondering what occurred when the gas was dimmed.

I removed my hat and ran fingers over my hair, taking in the staircases that twisted to unseen heights, the recessed arches and neat stacks of old books. I should be terrified, but somehow the monstrous old place invited me deeper, arousing my curiosity, boasting deep violet shadows plump with secrets they were willing to offer anyone bold enough to explore them.

"You say you're from Manchester, miss? You look hearty enough. The superintendent'll be right glad to have you. There's too many of them, and not enough of us." The woman's voice echoed in the large entry space barely warmed with rugs over stone floors and narrow shafts of natural light slanting down from high windows. "You'll want to put up your coat and hat, then I'll show you about. Hopefully it don't scare you off."

It was a place of closed doors, locks and bars, countless rooms of so many forgotten things. And I'd never wished to explore a place more. "I'm quite determined to take this position." I had just as much confidence in my remaining as I had when I'd told Richard I'd never come here.

I clasped my bag and took in the echoes, erratic screeches, and moans that bounced off the walls so one had no idea from which direction they came. I shifted in the scratchy wool suit I'd bought from the rag-and-bone man and caught sight of a handful of patients clustered together as they hurried up the stairs with two aids. "They look so hungry. So . . . pitiful."

The woman's lips pinched into a narrow line. "We does what we can for them, but there's only so much of the staff to go 'round." The woman with steel-colored hair was brusque and efficient now, even in the way she walked—I struggled to keep up.

"Of course." As we left the large, open entryway, the thick walls of the corridor muffled everything, and it was all oddly silent, with hanging lights casting swinging shadows. "How many patients are there?"

"Near to three hundred altogether. A hundred or so on the women's side, twice again as many on the men's."

"And the staff?"

"One superintendent—that's Dr. Thornhill, of course—a handful of attending doctors, a few nurses, and maybe ten or fifteen women to see to things, depending on how many have left or come on board that week."

"That isn't many."

Her face was grim. "Like I said, we does what we can."

We turned a corner, and down the corridor to the left stood a pair in heated discussion—a tall, dark-suited doctor and the nurse he towered over.

I braced myself to keep from rushing to her rescue, so like my father the man seemed. "What is he doing?"

"That'd be Dr. Turner. He has a lot of opinions. Strong ones."

Nurse Branson tensed as we moved on, crossing her arms. "Duffy," she called, and the little nurse broke away, hurrying toward us from the shadows.

Face white, eyes wide, the young woman approached, obviously straining for composure. "Yes, Matron?"

"Show this woman around, won't you? She's the new aid."

"Yes, ma'am." She dipped a curtsy, her face still pale, and some primal urgency in me surged to the surface. A need to escape. And to rescue the nurse, of all people.

Still flushed and unsettled, Nurse Duffy frowned at me. "Well, come along, then."

Distant cooing sounds echoed about the walls. Birds? No, voices. Residents. Humans. Short little screeches followed, and those echoed. They were jarring.

I looked about, memorizing the place as if drawing an escape map for when I'd have need of it—the arched doors with heavy metal locks, the raftered ceiling, two high barred windows at the end. The entire building made a U shape, with the large entryway and main living and working spaces forming the base of the letter and two identical wards—one for men and one for women— branching northward from it.

The woman called Duffy paused at a narrow linen closet and rummaged about inside, coming out with an armload of gray uniforms and whitish aprons similar to what the other staff wore. "You'll need these. Won't want to soil your own things." She looked only about thirty, a bony little thing, but seemed aged already. "Now, this way. I'll take you to the kitchen."

"Perhaps you can simply leave me in the file room for a while. I can see you're all busy, and I'd like to familiarize myself with the patients and their conditions."

Her glare was anything but welcoming. "Those are private. Only Dr. Thornhill sees the patient records, and they aren't none of our business." She kept walking, near sprinting, and expecting me to follow.

46

"It's just that I've never been in a place like this, and—"

She spun on me. "See here, I've no time for your needless chatter, unless you'd like to clean up the vomit on the third floor and dress wounds in the infirmary. That's what you're keeping me from." She spun back with a long-suffering sigh.

"I beg your pardon." I increased my pace so I could walk beside her and catch her eye. "By the way, who was that brute of a man? I'm sure you didn't deserve whatever he said to you."

She slowed her steps and her shoulders slumped forward, a bit of tension leaving her. "That's Dr. Turner. Dr. Mitchell Turner of the women's chronic ward. Only doctor always on staff this side of Hurstwell—the rest float between the wards."

"Is he always so surly?"

"Only when a body won't do things to his liking—and there's a lot that's not to his liking. He's particular and stubborn, wretched man. Stay out of his path and you'll manage."

"Perhaps he should be the one locked up."

The woman gave a short laugh. "Everyone here's locked up."

We paused before a cluttered, oversized kitchen, and she waved a spindly arm about. "This is likely where they'll put you, unless you don't suit. Then it'll be the dayroom with the invalids or the slaughterhouse."

"They have one of those here?"

"Hurstwell takes care of itself. Everything done right here on the grounds, from the meat to the dairy and the farming. Even the graves are dug by the patients in the men's wing."

"*Graves?*" Perhaps they simply dug them for a local cemetery. A parish service to earn their keep.

She waved me down another hall and jabbed one long finger at the window. In the bleak light of dusk, stones rose and fell like crooked teeth protruding from the rolling green hills that stretched on forever. Absolutely forever. There must have been hundreds. "Got to have somewhere to put the bodies, now, don't we?"

I squinted, wondering if I'd see the name Rosamond Swansea

on one of those stones. It was the most likely explanation, but one that sunk my heart. The moment I'd recognized that face, the porcelain skin, dark hair, and gentle eyes, I had ached to find her. To rescue her as she'd once rescued me, in a way.

"You'll help with bath day for the long-stay patients—that's Tuesdays—and you'll want to wear your oldest uniform for that. It can be messy, especially for the ones who don't want to go in."

"Only once a week?"

She threw me a bitter look. "You're free to bathe the wretches on your own time, if you can find any."

As we wound through the humid laundry space, now empty of workers, and out into the fenced courtyard beyond, I barely heard Nurse Duffy's explanation of how things were run, how to manage the patients, until she pointed out the tower ahead, with the words, "It's forbidden." My eyes snapped to the tall, slender structure with a worn slate roof in the receding light. Bare vines climbed nearly to the top, intent on strangling the thing. "What's in there?"

She frowned up at it. "Can't say. Never been up there. I value my hide."

"You mean, it's something dangerous?"

"There's danger up there, or danger in getting caught. Don't care to find out which."

I did. Intensely so.

"They threaten us within an inch of death for going up there. They call it the lost tower. Don't sound too promising to me."

I swallowed a lump rising in my throat, looking up at the windows near the top. The sound of clanking, metal on metal, drifted down from somewhere in that old tower. "How terrible."

She shrugged. "Better than being attacked by whatever's up there."

When we'd finished our tour of the place and I'd helped her clean up in the infirmary, she showed me the three floors of the women's wing separated from the main building by thick iron gates. This was what she called "the wards" and told me my duties tonight would be here.

"It's where they sleep, and it's kept locked up tight at night. Gates are shut, locks are secured. That way we don't need staff on watch all night over the whole building. Just the wards, patrolled by the new ones—like you."

"How delightful."

"We all take our turn at it. The new ones just get more. The rest of us get to sleep in our shared quarters in the attic, take a shift once a week or so. You'll start with every other night."

"So what am I to do on my turn?"

She shrugged. "Help them bed down, sit in a chair somewhere to watch the corridors, and try not to fall asleep. Another nurse will relieve you at four, and you'll sleep until seven. You'll have to walk the corridors three times a night, all three floors."

"Why are there so many floors?"

"There's the acute on floor one, infirmary and epileptics on two, chronic on three. You'll get used to it. Here, we'll start you out easy, with the acute ward." She stopped me in the open doorway of a long chamber with green-glass windows at one end and two dozen beds bolted to the floor, occupants milling about in various stages of undress as they readied for bed.

I walked in to the sound of their voices, all tuned to the different melodies locked within each individual and creating a cacophony of noise. It was like no symphony I'd ever heard, but it was, oddly enough, exactly like the orchestra tuning before a performance, each musician preparing fingers and minds for what was coming.

Only for these people, there was nothing coming. No beautiful performance, only the endless noise of preparation. I let my gaze pass over the women—scowling, staring, whimpering, drooping, shaking.

I shut my eyes to the sight. Two or three days, a week at most, and I'd be away from here. Hopefully with some answers. Then a door opened and a soft melody struck my senses, distant and echoey as if from the heavens, slipping through the oddness and shadows. I blinked the illusion away, breathed deep, but it remained—high, pinging notes bouncing off the walls.

I looked to another nurse as she jammed a corner of the sheet under a thin mattress nearby. *Do you hear it?* I stopped just short of voicing it. I'd often heard music at night in my childhood, but I'd stopped asking the maids about it when their odd looks made *me* feel odd. Yet it always came when I needed it most, this music that softened the darkness, and apparently I needed it again.

Nurse Branson hurried across the room to us. With a grunt, she tripped over a small figure bent near one of the beds, and a dark-haired lad of maybe eight or nine shot straight up. Laughter and giggles sounded as the women turned to gape at the stumbling nurse.

"Away with you, clumsy sod!" She rose and lifted her hand to box his ears, but I was after her like a hawk, spinning the boy away to shield him from her hand.

"What are you doing?" She hissed. "Know your place, girl. You ain't in charge."

She shoved me aside and smacked the boy on the shoulder. "Go on, get on with you, Lew Wiggins. You should be long done with the pots."

"Yes, ma'am." He scrambled, grabbing for an empty bucket on the way out. But when she moved deeper into the room, he slipped back in, looking me over with concern. "You're not hurt, are you, miss?"

"Thank you, I'm quite well." I looked him over, this scrap of a boy with a man's solemn eyes. "You don't belong here, do you?" My voice was gentle. Did they stoop to locking up foundlings now too?

"No, ma'am. I'm the slop boy."

The chamber pots. This chap emptied the buckets of women who saw soap only once a week at best. "Are you, indeed?"

He held up a clean pot, then slipped it under one of the beds.

"What a noble lad. Thank you."

"*Out,* boy!" Nurse Branson came through with a swinging hand, and the boy scrambled.

I rose and leveled a look at her. "A simple 'thank you' wouldn't be completely out of place."

She merely cast a hard stare at me before moving on into the room. She may have authority here, but she seemed to sense she was otherwise no match for me.

"Lights!" Nurse Branson called, turning down the gaslight valve near the door, and there was a scrambling for beds, as if the ward was one short.

All except a slight, middle-aged patient who wove absently toward the far wall of cloudy windows, hands on her chest. A nurse grabbed her by the shoulders and spun her around.

The patient yanked away. "I open the curtain!" Her voice was low and gravelly. Frantic. They grabbed her again, and she flailed. "Curtain! *Open the curtain!*"

No curtain graced their greenish glass—only bars.

Another aid came running and they yanked the woman off her feet, pulling her, with heels dragging, to her bed as she moaned and thrashed. I could only stare in the meager light coming from the corridor and hope my mouth wasn't hanging open. The minute she touched her mattress, the poor woman sprang up and the incident was repeated. The aid knocked her off her feet, then slapped her across the face, shoving a finger near her nose as the other held her down. "Don't make me fetch the corset."

The curtain woman crawled into her bed, curled into her stained sheets, and lay still. Others around me began to whisper and point.

"Hush up, the lot of you!" Nurse Duffy stood guard, arms folded over narrow chest, and the aid wove between beds toward the door.

As mattresses creaked and twentysome women settled into beds, we all made our way toward the door.

"Open the curtains. Just open . . ." The wretched woman's voice was muffled, as if she sobbed the words into a pillow.

My heart wrenched as I heard my own childish voice crying into a pillow, knowing there'd be trouble if I was heard. With a sigh I moved toward her bed and tried to whisper. "There aren't any, you know." Protectiveness leaked from my heart and gentled my voice. "It's best if you just lie still. There are no curtains to open."

The frantic woman leaped up again, yelling about the curtains, and a pillow sailed across the room from one of the other beds, striking the back of her head. Still she scrambled until the aids charged over, one pulling her arms, the other dousing her face with a glass of water. I heard her collapse into a puddle of frantic tears on the floor, then there were footsteps in the corridor—slow, steady ones.

The door creaked open farther, a triangle of light spilling over the scene, and in a beat everything quieted. Even the aids turned to watch as a tall, straight figure carried a glowing candle into the dark room. Footsteps approached, then that voice, firm and low like a finely tuned cello, washed over us all. "Mary Jo? What seems to be the problem?"

"Dr. Turner, she's causing a—"

"Begging your pardon, Nurse Duffy, but I'm asking Mary Jo."

Dr. Turner? *This* was that surly Dr. Turner, the brash man with all the opinions?

He turned toward the trembling woman. "How about it, will you tell me?"

"The curtain. I need the curtain opened."

"All right, then." He set the candle down, striding over to the windows. When he passed, I caught a glimpse of his face—strong and fresh and framed by dark hair and long sideburns, with an ocean of gentle intelligence in his eyes. His kindness came naturally, as if he possessed a lavish supply and used it often—he was Bach's masterful cello solo, Air on the G String, that enters with gentle strength and warms a room as it swells to a quiet climax.

The room held its collective breath as he reached up and drew back imaginary curtains and pinned them on nonexistent hooks, latching the stays, and something clicked within me. "There now, curtains opened." It was brilliant, really.

That posture, his manner, his candle lighting away the shadows . . . a light in the darkness. *He dances to the same music.* I could feel our melodies tangling and dancing opposite each other in a way I'd never sensed before with another human being.

As those nurses stood like fenced bulls ready to charge, Mary Jo padded unhindered to the window behind the doctor, where she leaned on the wall with a shuddering sigh and stared out into the sky. "That's better." The silence lasted endless moments, then a few light clicks sounded, and that mysterious music came again from some distant place above, a muffled scattering of notes that made my heart pound. Mary Jo tipped her face up toward the moonlight and lifted her arms into a rounded, graceful hold and began sliding them back and forth in perfect rhythm with the tinny music still echoing in the distance.

Violin. She was playing a violin. My heart pounded in the realization that she heard it too—this madwoman heard the same music I did.

Nurse Duffy huffed. "Doctor, this is—"

"Simple." He cut off the nurse with a curt word, and I suddenly had some idea of the nature of their disagreements. "It's a simple favor we can do for one in our care."

"With all due respect, Dr. Turner, we cannot leave her here all night. It isn't safe." Nurse Branson, the one who'd shown me in, moved past him and gripped the woman's arm. "Come along, now."

Panicked, Mary Jo twisted away. The doctor moved to intervene, but the patient fought them both and landed in a tangle of nightclothes and limbs on the ground. They struggled to help her rise and held firm to her on each side.

I moved closer, gathering courage. "Here." I pretended to scoop papers off the floor, holding them out to Mary Jo, who was now locked between nurse and doctor. "What if I hold the music for you?" She stared, and no one moved. "It's all right, I'm a musician too."

She watched, her one eye focused on me while the other wandered off to the side, and she smiled, spreading the tight triangle of her nose. She straightened and attempted to lift her imaginary bow, and when they released her arms, she began to play.

Dr. Turner watched her, then he turned his gaze on me with warm, steady approval. At close range, I noticed a trace of whiskers spread over his pale cheeks, a slight bump in the bridge of his nose. Everything about him breathed welcome and authenticity. We stood facing one another, several feet apart as the woman played on. Yet it felt for all the world as if we were waltzing together, his Bach cello solo paired with my Chopin piece, right there in the ward—which was suddenly not so dark.

When the odd music faded, Mary Jo stroked the imaginary instrument lovingly, and then, to the shock of us all, she thrust it toward Dr. Turner. "You play, Doctor."

"Very well." He turned his shirt cuffs up as if he took this quite seriously, and lifted the violin and bow, positioning them in a manner not entirely awkward for a novice. Then he moved his hand back and forth across the invisible strings, drawing out a song one could almost hear.

The room fell quiet, watchful faces turned toward the man in the center, drinking in the music he exuded without a sound. He had an otherworldly bearing, this man—someone who had one foot planted on earth and one in heaven, with an equal number of beloved people in each. I didn't know what to make of him.

Mary Jo had sunk into calm, eyes closed, body swaying along with the doctor's music.

At last, the silent concert was interrupted. "Dr. Turner," whispered Nurse Branson, with a look of deep significance. "I think it's time for a move."

The man's expression was strained, but he gave a single nod and turned to the patient. "Mary Jo, I've a friend I'd like you to meet. She loves music too. Perhaps you could move to a bed closer to hers."

Something jiggled in Mary Jo's neck, then she swallowed and stepped forward, head bowed. "Long as she don't mind fiddle playin'."

"She'd like nothing better."

"Come along." Nurse Duffy stepped forward, reaching for Mary Jo, but the woman pulled away.

"Perhaps we'll have our new friend go with us instead this time." Dr. Turner looked directly at me as he lifted his candle. "If she's willing, that is."

I blinked. "Me? Of course."

6

Music expresses that which cannot be put into words.

~Victor Hugo

We stood on either side of a trembling Mary Jo and led her right past those nurses, who stared with wide eyes. Nurse Duffy's gaze was aimed directly at me, shooting fire and metal, as if we'd been battling and I'd won.

"Doctor, this is highly unusual," she said at last.

"Good."

"I'll be forced to report this to Dr. Thornhill."

"Please do."

Thornhill—that was the superintendent. The head of Hurstwell.

Nothing stopped us, though, and soon we were moving out the door, into the gaslit corridors, and toward another set of stairs where the pinging music I'd thought I'd imagined came again, echoing even louder. I looked at the doctor's silent face, that pale countenance that was tired and worn into gentleness. *Do you hear it? Please tell me you do.* But I swallowed my question and breathed in the fresh air outside of that overfull room.

Then the doctor turned to me with a smile. "I'm deeply in your debt, Miss—"

"Fletcher. Cora Fletcher." I smiled. "And think nothing of it."

His return smile was deep and genuine as he guided us down the hall. Mary Jo seemed subdued now, even compliant, as she followed along, looking about at the corridor with grave curiosity.

"How are you getting on here? It's quite a place."

"It's like nothing I've ever seen. Whatever I expected . . . it is more." We stepped in echoey silence for a moment before I braved the next question. "Dr. Turner, might I ask what is kept in the lost tower? There seems to be a person up there. A patient."

His shoulders hitched, his step hesitating. "Yes, patients. The ones who are considered beyond help—the lost causes."

Hence the name "lost tower."

We walked several steps in silence. "I'm not certain anyone deserves to live out his days in such a place. Surely there must be something you can do, if a person still breathes. At least to make him fit to live among the other patients."

His face remained grim, and he did not answer.

We climbed the steps and entered a door on the third floor labeled *LONG-STAY WARD*. Then I understood the heaviness in the doctor's expression when the move was suggested—it was a sort of death sentence for poor Mary Jo. Yet with this man at the helm of that ward . . . a spark of hope. Of possibilities. Of music when necessary.

A quick series of clicks echoed in the hallway, and that distant plinking music started again, louder this time, just beyond the door. He opened it, and the sound narrowed to a single point, a withered skeleton of a once-tall woman with long, slender hands wrapped around a wooden box with an opened lid.

A music box. A real one. At least I wasn't mad. Not yet.

"I'll just leave the gaslights off so we don't wake everyone," he said.

I exhaled and nodded as Dr. Turner guided Mary Jo to the woman with the music box and made introductions. "She loves music the way you do, Anna. Perhaps you should become acquainted. Mary Jo, Anna here worries during the storms. Perhaps that's when you should play for her."

The older woman looked up, a lost look dulling her countenance. Something rattled in the distance, and Anna hunched forward, cranking that box, then curling over it and melting into the sound. Mary Jo approached, placed a hand on the woman's curved back, and they shared in the music together.

Another rattle, and a bang that echoed deep within the bowels of the old place. A figure lurched up from a bed with a loud cry and bolted through the room, frantic. I jumped aside, but her body collided with me, knocking the candle from Dr. Turner's hand, and suddenly with a clatter the dismal little room was dark. Closed in like a larder. The frantic woman clutched my gown, groaning desperately into my face like a demon. I jerked away, but she held with a vise grip. A wild screech sounded in the darkness nearby. I froze, my blood coursing in thick pumps. Moisture soaked through the front of my dress from the woman's clammy skin as I stood there, frozen within a nightmare. Her panic seeped into my bones.

My vision adjusted and I saw her face. Two dark spots set in white eyes focused on me, imploring. Begging without words. Sharp, snapping with unspoken thoughts. I couldn't catch my breath—long dark hair and fine, porcelain skin. Gown askew over a slender frame.

Dr. Turner pulled her away. "You're all right, Victoria. You're all right."

I stared at that face as it melted into the shadows. Darkness again wrapped itself around me, tightening. Oddly chilling. I felt my aloneness.

I gripped the end of that Anna woman's bed, drawing strength from her music box just as she did, clinging to what was solid. She wound it again while Dr. Turner likely put the frantic patient back to bed, then he came for me, leading me out with one hand to my back.

Light. A small glow along the corridor. I could see again, had a sense of what was around me. I took a few breaths as the world settled back into normalcy. Stones, wall lights, rows of doors.

But that face. Those wild eyes.

My legs began to tremble. No, convulse. I could not steady them. Alternating hot and cold prickled my skin, and I grabbed hold of a shelf recessed into the wall, propping myself up.

Dr. Turner swept me upright like a limp rag, searching my face. "What is it? What's happened? Are you ill?"

Oh, the tenderness. The warmth in his look. I shook harder. The memory of low groans and distorted features along with bright, intelligent eyes pierced my composure, and I stumbled, shaking with silent tears. He caught me, and I leaned heavily on him. If he moved, I'd fall.

"You're afraid." He laid a hand on my back, and calm radiated from the spot where it lay. "I shouldn't have taken you there so soon. It was too much."

I didn't fear the woman, actually. No, not at all. I recognized that intense sense of desperation, the sharp terror, and I feared *becoming* her, trapped forever in darkness once again. I'd come here as one separate from them, pitying them. As I'd stared into her face, so terribly afraid, the line between us had thinned and all but disappeared.

I smoothed my hands over my face, pushing back my hair and forcing a smile. "I'm afraid I have a rather irrational fear of the dark. Truly, I'm fine. It's childish, really."

He eyed me, unconvinced. I didn't add any words to my explanation—I'd already admitted too much. I was glad of his closeness, though. Darkness had never been like this—so alive and full of mystery.

"Dr. Turner." A voice sliced through the moment, and the solid chest jerked away. "The superintendent would like to speak with you."

I stumbled forward, catching myself on the wall. Nurse Duffy stood tall and resolute several yards down the hall. Her hard look centered on me through the shifting light from the wall sconces that made her face seem harder. Older. Almost stony. "He's waiting in the office."

"Of course," he said quietly. "I'll be down presently."

The nurse paused, looking from one of us to the other.

Turner crossed his arms. "Perhaps you should take him the message."

"Of course, Doctor." She lowered her gaze and hurried off, shoes clicking on tile as her uniform fluttered around her legs.

I covered my heated face with my hands. "What will she tell him?"

"Hopefully nothing much."

I peeked out at the firm lines of his face and sensed he wouldn't make some false excuse if the nurse did describe how she'd found us. And for that, I couldn't help but respect the man even more.

My first stint of night duty, three days into my time at Hurstwell, left me longing for the lumpy little cot in my shared room rather than sitting awake in the thick darkness that cloaked the place. Those enchanting corners and blue-violet shadows turned cold, with movement drifting across walls and sounds for which I could not account.

Propped up in a straight-backed chair in one of the acute wards with a cup of warm tea beside me, I drifted into a restless half sleep between rounds. I dreamed, as I had in childhood, about the pianoforte playing at night in the forgotten old rose room, the lost melody once again drifting up to me. My childhood self walked down the stairs as I'd done so many times to find the ethereal woman with her distant smile playing at my mother's pianoforte.

Only this time, I had a name to go with the vision. "Hello, Miss Swansea," I said, and she turned, beaming a smile of welcome, now tinged with a lovely sort of wistfulness. Her head tipped to the side just slightly. *You know me*, her look seemed to say again. *I can count on you, can't I?* She laid her slender fingers upon the keys, and her smile grew, the welcome warming. I wanted to join her. I'd done so before.

"Where are you?" I asked, but my voice whipped away on a breeze. "Where?" I said again, louder.

But she merely faced her lovely instrument and sank into the music, into the act of playing, as I so often did. She never spoke to me in these dreams, somewhat disconnected from my world as if we didn't quite share the same one, and I was a specter to her as much as she was to me.

The song swelled until it filled the room, then tapered off, she and her music fading together. Growing distant. A sense of desperation—an urgency—along with the sucking sensation of being pulled forcibly from the dream. From her. "Wait! Where are you?"

Then a harsh whisper cut through the scene, finally jarring it loose. I blinked in the dim light. It wasn't her voice, though— wasn't Rosamond. Wasn't familiar. *Don't drink the tea*, it said. As I shivered and strained to hear the ghostly pianoforte music that wasn't there anymore, the voice inserted itself again into the remnants of my dream, slicing like a knife through its tapestry, and I was awake, blinking and cold in the dark.

"I said, don't drink the tea."

My mind inched out from beneath a heavy weight as I blinked the room into focus. Beds. Rows of sleeping women. Cold hearth. My mind found solid ground and began taking baby steps forward into clarity. "What on earth—"

"It's the tea." To my surprise, the voice came again, clear and distinct. "But you'll soon be right as rain," it said, with the airiness of a lady nibbling tarts in her front parlor. "You didn't drink it all."

The stony gray world pulsed in and out of focus along with my exaggerated heartbeat as I sat in that chair, gathering fragments of my scattered consciousness. "Heaven above," I mumbled. "What was in that wretched cup?"

"A bit of tincture to make you sleep. Oh, it's meant for the patients, but they have an old under-the-tongue trick, and I'm afraid someone dissolved their capsule into your drink."

I rotated my head toward the bed beside my chair where the cheery voice came from and studied the unfamiliar round face there. "You're real."

"Much as you are, love." There was a rustle of sheets, and a rosy face appeared, propped up on one fist. "I don't suppose you sing, do you?"

I gave a shaky laugh, rubbing my head to clear it. "Not well."

The woman gave a dramatic sigh. "Pity. I dearly love to sing, and I haven't found another soul here who does. I heard you say you were a musician . . . The place needs a bit of lively music, don't you think? I'm Clara, by the way. You can call me that."

"Clara." I eyed the pale countenance with smiling lips, bright eyes. "Why are you still awake? It must be nearly half past two." It was obvious by her pert expression that she had been awake for some time.

Another deeply layered sigh. "I almost never sleep, love. A curse and a blessing. I never miss a thing that way. I adore knowing things, especially what I shouldn't."

I raised my eyebrows in the dark. "You know a great deal about Hurstwell, then."

She shrugged and gave a nod. "Same with every place I live. I used to be undercook at Edenwold Estate in Manchester, and I sampled every scrap of gossip worth tasting." She sat up. "You're a bit of a snoop too, aren't you? Saw you poking about with your eyes when you thought no one was looking."

"Merely looking for someone I thought I knew." I'd hardly realized I was doing it, but I had been studying faces, peering into rooms as we passed, ever on the alert. "There's a patient I've heard is here. I cannot seem to find her, though."

"There's a lot of us here, you know. Just look about at mealtimes."

I had. I had looked, every day. Every face. No one resembled the flower-like creature with the endearing head tilt who'd played Mother's pianoforte in my dreams.

"It's easy to live in this place for years and never meet half the women here."

"You've been here that long?"

"Long enough."

I shifted on the chair, looking her over again as my mind settled onto solid ground. "Forgive me, but you don't seem to . . . belong. Here, I mean. Especially for so long." Awkwardness clogged my throat. "The others seem sickly and quiet and terribly . . ."

"Melancholy? Yes, I suppose they are." She sat upright, eyes shining in the dark. "There's no sense in joining them now, is there? Especially when one can bring life and sparkle to a place with a bit of good humor, and it doesn't cost a farthing." Her voice seemed to bounce from word to word, even at a whisper.

I smiled in spite of myself, feeling the tension melt from my body. "How right you are. I admit I'm not keen on being here myself, but perhaps I shouldn't show it so much."

"Not a bit of it, love. None of us wants to be here, staff or inmate. We're all of us flotsam floating downriver, caught in the rocks and stuck there unless some kind soul pulls us loose."

"If it's not too bold, how *does* a body end up here?"

She giggled. "There are as many stories as there are faces about the place." And like a flower unfurling colorful petals, Clara began to tell me of the various women in the ward, and how they'd come to Hurstwell. The stories were sad, terrifying, sometimes humorous—but all so unique.

I began to picture individual faces—a young, overworked newly-wed; a woman whose children—and purpose—had left; an out-spoken vicar's wife with ideas that didn't align with his; a great-grandmother who couldn't recall the names of those she'd raised, and then Clara slowed. "I ought to save a few stories for the other sleepless nights, I suppose. You'll be awake much as I will when you're on duty, and we might as well keep ourselves entertained." She shifted again and her smile widened, until I couldn't be certain of what I thought I'd seen there before. "So you don't sing. Can you play a fiddle?"

"I play the pianoforte. My father was a music tutor."

"How grand! Say, we had another one who played. What a lovely way she had with music."

I straightened. "Where is she? What's her name?"

"Wouldn't you know, I don't recall her name." A flicker of fear shadowed her face, but then it melted into her chummy smile until I wasn't certain I'd even seen it.

"Couldn't you introduce me to her? Point her out to me? I should enjoy meeting another musician."

"I couldn't." Clara hesitated. The guarded look again streaked her features.

"Why not?"

Her lips pinched, eyes darting down. "I've been better at keeping my mouth shut, you know. If I'd done it before, I would never have been locked away here a'tall."

It wasn't fitting, this distress nestled deep within the sunniest of people, and I suddenly wondered what had been done to her. And by whom. Digging into her story, however, felt an invasion. "All right then, what did she look like, this musician?"

Clara's expression eased. "She had long, pretty brown hair—they usually cut hair, but not hers. She wouldn't let them. White skin like alabaster, and a lovely little face so perfect and soft—all except a little mark." The woman poked at her lip. "Right about there. Aside from that, she was a beauty. She stood out here, she did."

The odd feeling turned inward, chilling me to the core.

That birthmark. I knew that birthmark. I looked away, feigning disinterest even as questions surged to the surface and my skin tingled. It couldn't be. Just couldn't.

7

The music is not in the notes, but in the silence between.

~Wolfgang Amadeus Mozart

I discovered one marvelous benefit to the darkness at Hurstwell—it allowed me freedom. The sort I needed to explore where I wasn't meant to go. After completing rounds at three, I slipped through the locked gates of the ward with my key and ventured out into the night through the laundry courtyard. I had one hour until the next aid came to relieve me.

I rounded the building to the lost tower, hand shielding the tiny flame of my candle. Only the very distant crunch of wheels on gravel came to me, giving me a sense of where the lane was and which direction I was headed.

The lost tower. These were the only patients I hadn't yet looked over, whose faces I had yet to glimpse. There would be a familiar birthmark among them, I was certain. She was nowhere else in Hurstwell.

Wind sucked at my uniform as I paced on, pulling me farther out toward the tower and the pitch blackness of the moors just beyond. It sliced through trees, whipping and moaning in a way

I could only call *ghostly*. Forcing my way through it, I reached the tower and flattened myself to it, praying the wind would die down. I fumbled through the key ring. Surely there was something here that'd work . . .

A skeleton key. I jiggled it around in the rusty old lock, and after several jerks and a metallic squeak, it gave way. It wasn't the key that was meant to fit here, but it was enough to release the ancient mechanism. I pulled the door and it groaned, shrieking its protest into the night.

I froze. The whole place must have heard.

Heart galloping, I shot a glance at the main building. A light appeared inside the second-story window of the wards—infirmary and epileptic—flickering there for some moments. I shoved my candle inside the cracked-open tower door to hide it and waited until the glow left the upper window. My left arm holding the candle began to shake. I couldn't drop it—the darkness would consume me, and I'd never find my way back.

Deep breath. Slow movements. I shifted my slender frame through the narrowly opened doorway and left it open so the squeal wouldn't announce my intrusion again when I left. I edged deeper into the musty space and blinked, willing my eyes to adjust to the dimness. Rows of dim gaslights illuminated stone and emptiness, small puddles of moisture. There was nothing here—no sign of life.

A few more blinks, my eyes adjusted, and I found I was wrong. Deep in the shadows, three faces stared out at me from behind the iron bars of a cell, the whites of their eyes illuminated by the bouncing light of my flame as I drew near. A few more stirred behind, rising up to sitting positions on pallets. They moved about and simply stared at me, watching with mild surprise from their side of the bars just as I did from mine. "Hello. I'm . . . I'm looking for a woman. A patient here. What are your names?"

Blank stares.

"Rosamond? Rosamond Swansea?" I scanned each gritty, sun-starved face, skin laid down directly over bones. Eyes framed by red circles peered back at me, staring as if they didn't understand.

None of the faces looked familiar.

I left that cell and walked toward another, voicing the same name. No response, so I started up the cracked stone steps that twisted deeper into the heights of the old tower, taking me into the shadows above. I stopped at each cell, peering in and repeating the name.

I paused a few times, staggering under the weight of what I was seeing. Flesh and hair and features—humanity, faces, and forgotten names, with histories and talents and beating hearts that tied them still to this earth. Yet they were no longer a part of it.

Why would God create these people and weave the tangled thread of madness into their lives? Make it so the only life they could have was one of constant darkness? My firm idea of God as ultimately *good*, the kind God who'd rescued me in my childhood, began to slip. A sense of something in a minor key wove through this place, and I heard not a single note of hope on the air. Felt no rescuing presence in the dark.

Why, God? Why come into the darkness then, in that larder, and not here and now?

As I peered into their faces, the only answer that occurred to me was, *I must have imagined it.* I'd simply made it up in childish desperation.

My breath shuddered, air coming thin and meager. I couldn't bear the magnitude of that possibility, of the God I so dearly loved not truly existing, so I shoved it away and refocused on the search.

Near the top of the tower my head grew light and airy, moist wind whipping in from the moors and stealing beneath my bulky uniform, chilling my clammy skin. It wasn't right, this tower. My being here. None of it. And now I understood why. These were things I wasn't meant to see—things most human hearts could not handle. Mine included.

I forced myself, even as I trembled and grasped the bars, to look into every face. Every stare that was turned out at me, and those still sleeping on the mats. There was no one familiar. No one.

Thank goodness.

Then a low groan sounded above me. A large metal door, I thought at first, but no, it was a voice. A human voice. It banished any desire I might have had to reach the pinnacle of that tower, for the noise vibrated like the roar of a beast. One I did not wish to meet.

Nearly falling back down those stairs in my haste to escape, I was soon standing outside, gulping lungfuls of fresh, clean air. How good the outdoors felt now, despite the chilly darkness just beyond the little glow of my candle. I leaned heavily on the wall, my heartbeat slowing with each deep breath.

Hand feeling along the fence to steady my steps, I held out the candle and made my way back toward the laundry and the main building. Yet when I'd crossed half the blue-black yard, there was another light. It glimmered and flickered through the knotholes of the fence.

Moving toward a two-inch gap in the boards, I settled my face in the crack and peered out over the sloping property. In the small circle of a distant light, a single figure stood still as a tree in the cemetery, the only life among those dead stones, holding a lantern over one. He was tall and suited, with a familiar bend to his broad shoulders. I watched the silhouette of Dr. Turner as the wind moaned low across the expanse, a long draw of bow against cello strings.

My body remained leaning on that fence, breeze playing with my loosened hair, but my heart traveled out to be with him, to stand beside him in his secret grief as I only wished the rest of me could. What other doctor felt as he did about the patients at Hurstwell? Who else grieved the loss of any life here? He was a man among men, a solo who could stand on his own in a very dark world. Yet he deserved, more than anyone, to have a light-filled harmony to counter his somber melody.

8

Give me a laundry list and I'll set it to music.

~Gioachino Rossini

An odd little song arose on Clara's voice from somewhere in the steamy laundry, where I found myself on staff on my fourth day there. Night shift had left me tired, but a heavy dose of curiosity kept me alert.

"Keep 'em in line, and don't take no for an answer," Nurse Branson said as she installed me in the new position. "And here, you'll need this." She handed me an empty bucket.

"Am I to do laundry too, then?"

"Sure. You see a uniform standing still, you douse it with cold water—along with the poor sot who's wearing it." She turned to go, but narrowed her eyes at me, as if reading the distaste on my face. "It don't do no good to pity 'em, you know. Most come from the workhouse or the streets. Thieves and the lot. Hard work and plain living is the best thing for 'em."

Clara's bright face, red and mottled from the steam, appeared between the damp hanging sheets strung up around the room. She looked to me, in this place, like a trapped songbird. "We've got us another musician, Nurse Branson. Grand, isn't it?"

I cringed, lowering my gaze. I hadn't thought it through when I'd announced to Mary Jo and the entire room that I was a musician. Word was getting around, especially among the patients, and my true identity was bound to come out.

But Nurse Branson was busy grimacing at Clara, who tossed a wadded sheet high in the air and burst out in a surprisingly resonant voice. "The water is wide, oh waly waly. I cannot get over. Nor have I wings, oh waly waly, with which to fly."

Branson sent her eyes heavenward with a sigh of long-suffering but did not stop the woman. There was great freedom, it seemed, in being thought mad. "Don't encourage them," Branson commanded with a finger point my way, then she spun, striding around the great hissing laundry vats toward the exit.

Nurse Duffy stared openly in my direction from a few tubs over as she carried several stacked baskets of pins, no smile gracing her pallid face. She made no secret of her wariness as she looked me over, stopping before me. "I did warn you about the lost tower, didn't I? Not to go there?"

My fingers gripped that bucket handle. "Quite thoroughly."

Another glance up and down. "Why are you here, really? What sort of trouble are you trying to cause?"

"I'm here to work and earn my pay, same as you."

Her eyes were wide and bright. "You don't know the first thing about me."

My starched collar felt too tight, her face too close.

Clara giggled behind the nurse, and Duffy turned on her, a glare toward both of us. The nurse spun and stalked away. Clara laughed harder, a release of pressurized tension, which earned her a resounding *thwack* from a wet towel.

"You old codger. Can't you keep still?" This came from Kat, a bitter old broomstick of a woman on my left, who had, according to Clara, been sent here by friends when she'd collapsed at the steel mill in Leeds. Poor woman had worked nearly fourteen hours a day—*after* helping her father dip and hang candles to sell. She'd been used up the way a rag-and-bone man eked every bit of life out of limp old cloth, then turned it inside out for more. I'd begun putting faces with some of the stories and recognizing the women as Clara pointed them out. "Did you play in front of people? Great crowds?" Kat asked.

I shot a glance at Nurse Duffy's back, only one laundry vat away, but she wasn't listening. With great clouds of steam enveloping us, I turned toward Kat, keeping my voice low. "I never noticed who was watching when I played, I suppose." Vague, but truthful. "And it was different every time. Always wonderful, though." I had been clinging to my anonymity like a shield, but I was an anomaly to these women, most of whom never had the money to set foot inside a theater. Symphonies were as foreign to them as silks and hot water pumps.

"Were your gowns quite lovely? Did you have your hair done up and oiled?"

I shot another glance at Duffy.

"Oh, don't fret over that one. She's sore at everyone prettier than her. It's on account of her betrothed leaving her years ago, just so he could take up with someone else. She writes him letters. Every night. Although I don't think she posts them."

I stared at the woman's slender back swathed in a too-large uniform. She turned her face, and in the sunlight her profile seemed softer—more vulnerable beneath the thin veneer of bitterness. How those gaslights changed the look of everything.

"You look exactly like the woman he left her for—red hair and all. She was telling Branson that once. I don't suppose you *are* the other woman, are you? It would be uncanny—"

"Aye there, music lady, I need some more pins." It was a female voice across the room, direct and loud but friendly around the edges. A wiry inmate named Bridget Hurley waved me toward the back, where clothesline was strung above our heads like webs.

73

I found the baskets of pins neatly stacked and brought her one. She took a few with a nod of thanks and jammed them down onto a few garments. "They'll chew your ear right off now, won't 'ey?" She nodded with a wry smile toward the women. "Thought you might do with a rescue."

"It isn't so bad. After the night shifts in this dreary place, their voices are like a symphony."

One dark eyebrow shot up. "Wouldn't pay to hear that sort o' music. The song of the insane."

"I don't believe they all are. Clara, for instance." I looked over at the woman in question, who was scrubbing grayish linens with a cheerful vigor. "I believe someone's put her here because she discovered their secrets. She's a terrible gossip, you know." I thought of Rosamond, of the possibility that someone had put her away and she mightn't even be mad, either. "Is such a thing possible?" I held my breath, looking away so as not to seem overly eager for her answer.

Bridget dropped a handful of pins on the table before me and paused, studying my face from a proximity no lady would have tolerated. "Irish, are yeh? Must be, with hair like that." She was staring at me, and her eyes held as much sanity as Clara's.

I touched my long red hair tucked back in a knot as I watched her fly through her work, those large dark eyes standing out against white skin. "My grandmother was Scottish."

"Come along then and help me carry this." She hoisted a basket of wet, wrung-out linens, and I grabbed one end, wicker digging into my arm as we moved toward the far corner just inside the open doorway to the fenced-in yard.

It was more tranquil here, cotton and linen softness without the steam pumping in one's face and the clatter and bang of machines. I mopped my forehead with my sleeve and looked to Bridget, who'd already poured her abundance of energy back into digging through the sheets, then sweeping them up to pin.

I'd noticed Bridget about the asylum. Shrewd and agile with

dark, wavy hair and more practical sense than all the staff of Hurstwell combined, Bridget was hard to overlook. Her internal rhythm seemed a bit faster, a tad heartier, than the rest of them.

I handed her a pillow cover and she snatched it away. "Sheet next. *Sheet.* It goes sheet, pillow cover. Sheet, pillow cover."

"Of course." I handed her a sheet, shaking out the crumpled thing, and she took it. "So how *did* Clara end up here? I don't suppose you'd know, would you?"

"Moral insanity." More pins jutted onto the line. "Caught kissing the master's son in the butler's pantry late at night. Or *being* kissed by him, no one's quite certain which."

"That's a terrible reason." I peeked through the curtains at the rosy-faced young woman who endured what had been done to her with remarkable good humor and aplomb.

She looked me over past the clothespins jutting from the side of her mouth. "How did *you* end up here, then? Don't seem the type, either. Even for staff."

"I'm only keeping myself out of the workhouse while I wait for what comes next. My usual place won't have me until I'm out of mourning—for my father, that is. I lost him a few weeks past."

"That so. Well, you can have mine if you want him. He ain't doing me a lick of good."

She had an oddness about her, in the abruptness of speech and the things she chose to say, but it wasn't unpleasant.

I held the end of a pillow cover as she pinned. "You've a father?"

She eyed me, jabbing a pin down. She was always moving, this one, always buoyant and perfectly logical. Even in the dining hall with nothing to do, I'd seen her twirling her long, dark hair around two fingers. "Came from somewheres, didn't I?"

"I meant . . . still. *Still* have a father. I couldn't imagine a father allowing his daughter to be taken here. Or is he who put you in?" Now that I'd had a taste of people's stories, I wanted more. I wanted to understand. I'd never before thought how a soul ended up in a place like Hurstwell, but the more I spoke with each woman, the more I saw strands of normalcy mixed in with terrible fortune and tragic turns, and sensed the wrongness of it all.

She shrugged, waiting to answer until she'd once again emptied her mouth of pins and turned to sweep up more wet laundry. "I always was a lot of trouble. A real nuisance, just like me dearest Paul." Her eyes sparkled.

"Who's—"

"Can't keep me mouth shut, you know, and he had the very same affliction."

I smiled. She was different, perhaps. But *good* different. So was her so-called affliction of not keeping her mouth shut. "I rather like that you don't."

She stared at me with that keen look of hers, head cocked a bit, as if I had calculations on my face that must be reasoned out. Then she turned back to work. "You'll play for me sometime?"

"Of course, the moment you are free of this place, I'd welcome a call from you. I could teach you too."

She eyed me again. "Won't be easy."

I wasn't sure what she meant. "I've never been one for 'easy.'"

Her full lips curved in a flash of a smile, and she was, with that accessory, quite lovely. It was easy to like Bridget, kind and affable and wonderfully forthright, and I almost wished I could take her with me when I left.

I watched her work for a minute. "So what really happened? To put you here, I mean? There must be more to it."

There was no answer at first, only swift movements and the muffled echo of clanging and yelling, the whooshing of steam. "Because I cannot ignore that things ain't right." She yanked another basket off the line and started pinning again. "No woman in her right mind can't get out of bed and care for her own babby. I'm broken, always been, and this is where you go for that kind of thing."

"I was told that once, you know. That I'm odd—broken."

She eyed me skeptically. "That so. What for?"

My governess had been the one to say it when I'd tried to get her to catch the enchanting cadence of music in the gentle blend of outside sounds that seemed so clear to me. Music had always woven in and out of every part of my conscious mind, whether a formal instrument played or not. "Because there's music that lives inside of me. And apparently that isn't where it belongs."

She didn't laugh, this girl with the pert face. She was quiet a moment, then said, "I do envy you."

I blinked at the unexpected response.

Nurse Duffy whipped aside the damp sheet hanging before us and scolded me with her eyes. "There's a whole roomful to be watching out here."

"Of course." I sprang out from our little corner and hurried back into the chaos, slipping a few times on puddles and catching myself on the sides of giant metal tubs.

Duffy caught up with me and held out a large basket with great wads of sheets tied up in packets. "Make yourself useful. These go to the linen shelves in the men's wards. Second floor. I'll take over here. Come back for more when you're through."

I accepted the basket and propped it on my shoulder—which ached a surprising amount—and wove through the women toward the doors.

Up in the empty wards, I sank into a muffled quiet. The dim glow of gaslights hid everything except the small circle around me, giving the gentle sense of being alone at last. In these moments of quiet, with daylight streaming through high windows, I didn't mind this place. Not at all. Dropping the basket before the closet, I stretched my arms, circling my shoulders, then began stuffing the tied bundles onto the shelves, along with the other white-gray linens already there.

But a closed door across the way caught my eye. It was on the left side and it led to an office of some kind. I could see the edge of a desk through the window. Pulse pounding, I finished the bundles quickly and slipped over to it, peering inside. It was the men's ward, though. I'd find nothing on Rosamond here, but I couldn't resist. Couldn't turn off my curiosity.

Very little daylight streamed through the barred windows, but I could make out a small kidney-shaped desk and two cabinets for paperwork. I stepped in and peered around, then slid open the cabinet drawer that was eye level to me. A mess of papers. Letters. Little notes. I dug through, my eyes scanning the variety of handwriting.

A *bang* in the corridor shot panic through me.

I darted out and nearly collided with a small, dark-haired boy toting a bucket. One glance up at me and he dumped the liquid contents on the floor between us.

"Aye, now see what you've done!" he called out loudly, dropping the bucket on the mess and raising his hands. "Watch where you're going, why don't you?"

That little face—it was the slop boy from my first night. "What are you doing?" I hissed. Ungrateful wretch.

"Ho now, what's the problem here?" A tall doctor in a suitcoat emerged from the shadows just down the corridor and stood before us, arms folded.

I froze. How had I not seen him?

"Taking care of slops, Doc Carpenter, and this here lady knocked me bucket over."

"You're new." The alienist eyed me from his great height, without welcome or malice. "Well then, help him clean it up. You'll be on slop duty with the boy until he's done, and maybe next time you'll remember to look where you're going."

"I didn't—"

"What part of those instructions weren't clear, Miss . . . ?"

"Fletcher. Cora Fletcher." I clenched my jaw.

"Very good, Miss Fletcher. I appreciate your cooperation." His gaze snapped between us. "I shall inform your charge nurse. Branson, I assume?" He sidestepped the putrid mess that was beginning to consume the air before I could confirm and continued down the hall.

I blew out a breath and looked at the boy, frustration mingling with relief. "I suppose that was your idea of a rescue."

"Did you want that doctor to catch you in there? It's not like you heard him coming."

"I was only looking about."

"You was snooping."

"You couldn't even see what I was doing in there." With a grumble, I got down on my knees and helped sop up the mess with a rag he'd dropped over it.

"Enough to know you was doing it wrong."

I grumbled more as the boy began whistling through his teeth, getting on with his work as if it were some pleasant task. "What do you know?"

"Alls I know is, there's a wrong way to snoop, and a right way." A jangle of heavy keys had me snapping my gaze back up, looking at the proud little face. A large ring of keys dangled from one finger. "One good turn for another, I says."

I was speechless.

"Aren't nothin' worth seein' in that little office. No one uses it just now. But Thornhill's office . . ."

The head of the asylum. The superintendent. "You have a key to it?"

"And now, on slop duty, no one'll be hanging about to see you. Help me real fast so's you have time to run down before Thornhill finishes rounds. That's usually in about half an hour from now."

My throat was tight. "What's in his office?"

The boy shrugged. "Whatever it is you're looking for, guaranteed." He swept the rags up with a dry one and dropped them in a wheelbarrow nearby. "About time someone cared to check up on things. Right glad to help whoever's bold enough."

I rose. "What do you mean?"

He shook his head, wiping his hands on another rag. "Things ain't right here, and if I could read, I'd already know what it was. So now, here's your chance to do it instead." Then the whistling began again.

I stood, shocked and awed. There was a light at the end of the tunnel—or, as they say, perhaps it was an approaching train. I wasn't sure which, but serious-faced little Lew Wiggins was the first ray of hope I'd had in days.

———

It would be practice, this clandestine operation. Practice for when I had a chance to sneak women out of their homes one day and smuggle them to safety. Richard's reaction to my whole plan had planted the seeds of doubt in my mind—doubt about whether or not a sheltered pianist with no experience could even accomplish such a thing. This would be my proof to myself. A test of my abilities. And I was certain to find something in that office that would change the direction of my current search—something.

Night had fallen as we made our way downstairs. Lew glanced around as we entered the wide-open entryway and lowered his voice. "Now's your chance, if you're gonna do it. The guards have gone for the night, patients all locked up in the wards."

I swallowed, staring at that heavy oak door. It was always kept locked, and that meant it was protecting something. Guarding secrets. I couldn't begin to guess what I'd find in there.

9

What will come of all this, heaven only knows!

~Ludwig van Beethoven

I slipped in as the hush of evening fell over Hurstwell, and the entryway stood empty. I closed the door behind me as softly as I could, even though it insisted on squeaking.

Fresh lemon on leather—that was the first thing that struck me about Dr. Thornhill's private office. Also that it was oddly quiet—muffled. Tufted leather and wood dominated the furniture, and everything seemed impeccable and well-oiled. I shielded the little candle I'd brought, hoping it wasn't too visible under the crack of the door, then held it up for a better look about.

File drawer. The first one rolled open when I pulled, and I riffled through *S* for Swansea and *M* for Mourdant, wondering how long I had.

"It's not there," said a voice.

I jumped. Hot candle wax splashed onto my finger, and I clutched the burning spot, gritting my teeth to keep from crying out.

The large leather chair spun, and Nurse Duffy watched me

with a pert smile, her slender figure swallowed up in that chair. "Good evening."

Picking remnants of wax from my fingertips, I straightened. "I'm looking for a patient file. I needed to verify some information."

"But it wasn't in that drawer, was it?"

I stood still as stone, watching her without offering up a word.

"Why not try the desk?"

"I don't think you could possibly know which file I came to find."

"You're right, I don't." She pushed the rolling chair back from the desk and tapped the bottom drawer. "But I would bet it's in these files. No one's ever looking for the patients in there." She tossed her head toward the large filing cabinet through which I had been riffling.

Narrowing my eyes, I approached the desk drawer and pulled. Locked. I searched through the keys on the ring, but Nurse Duffy slid open the top desk drawer, producing a smaller key, and fit it into the lock. The drawer slid open, and there were loads of files, all marked with names—and a red letter *D* beside each.

Deceased? Delusional?

Heart hammering under her stare, I skimmed over the names as I hovered the candle over the tabs. There near the back was the name that made my blood pulse—Swansea. I reached for the file but pulled back without touching it. I didn't dare reveal so much to the woman watching me from the chair. It was enough to know it was here, that I had the right asylum—and that Rosamond *did* exist.

Just before I closed the drawer, I caught sight of the file behind "Swansea" that stopped me cold. It read "Thornhill, Thomas." I stared at the dark ink on that tab, hardly daring to breathe. There was a hole in my lungs, and the air was escaping. My head felt light.

"Well?"

I shook my head, firmly closing the drawer. The less she thought I knew, the better. "I suppose I was mistaken. The file . . ." What, doesn't exist? Is too revealing? "I should go. I'm needed in the wards for bedtime."

I turned to leave, keeping my poise, but she grabbed my skirt, yanking me back so hard my hip hit the desk. "Either you're here for good or evil, but it isn't merely for the work." She hissed in my ear from behind. "Don't think I'm ignorant. Don't *lie* to me." She let go and I fell forward, stumbling into the wall. Without a glance back at her, I darted out the door, slipping around the dark corner and down along the corridor and away from that office, my mind a whirl of confusion. I ran aimlessly through the dark until I nearly collided with a man.

"Whoa there."

I threw out my arms, forcing myself to a stop, and looked up at the stranger emerging from the shadows. A tall, suited gentleman, solid and craggy with a face not unkind, held out a hand between us to keep us from collision. His voice had the deep intentional tone of one in charge, and my immediate thought was, *Thornhill.*

He lifted one eyebrow. "Are you lost?"

"Yes." I dared not glance back in the direction of the office. "Yes, I believe I'm in entirely the wrong place." I looked up into his face for a longer look, and I felt certain it was him. "I'm Cora. Cora Fletcher, new aid at Hurstwell."

I was all too aware of how alone we were. I'd heard no trace of Nurse Duffy since I'd left her.

How he towered over me.

"Welcome." He gave a nod. "Superintendent Thornhill." There was gravity in his face—solemnity mixed with the tiredness that comes with age. "Might I direct you somewhere?"

"Slops. That is, slop duty. With Lew Wiggins."

"An unfortunate task." His sad smile was fleeting, and I strained to see the possible madness behind his mask, but it was only calm. Extremely so. "I believe I saw a slop boy down by the kitchen, but take your time. A moment to compose yourself, perhaps? Hurstwell can be a frightening place at the start." Father Christmas—that's who he reminded me of, big and stocky, only without the jolliness. "Come, I'll walk that way with you."

An aid hurried through the corridor with a patient in tow, a woman who sobbed and stumbled along. I shivered.

Thornhill looked me over, hands behind his back. "They can catch you off guard, can't they? Broken shards buried behind such seeming normalcy." His voice was low and private. "We try to patch them up, but the cracks always come unglued eventually." His steps slowed. "A broken vessel can never truly be fixed—first this crack, then that one comes loose, no matter the glue one uses. But we do try."

He looked me over again, as if reading my every thought.

I forced my mind to be blank and smiled up at him. "Have you worked here long?"

His sigh was huge. "Too long." A few more steps. "I'm afraid a body never grows used to it. They always have the ability to shock and unsettle you." He paused, tipping his hat. "Well now, you're off this way, and I must attend to some paperwork. Best of luck to you, my dear." With a nod, he turned and strode back in the direction of his office.

Had I locked it? Had I even closed the door?

Duffy. How would she escape?

Another pause to compose myself, and I hurried down the narrow corridor, following the faint sound of whistling in the distance. I caught up with Lew outside the kitchen and was only the littlest bit jittery, the way I felt after a difficult performance.

He caught sight of me and smiled. "Find what you needed?"

I kept my eyes down and knelt beside him, taking an empty bucket. "More than I bargained for. Definitely not what I expected."

"Glad it was something, I suppose."

I gave myself over to the work, scraping food bits into a larger bucket with rope handles. The exertion worked out my nerves until I was quite myself again. Then I remembered I still had Lew's keys and handed them back. I didn't release them when his hands reached for them, though. "One day I'd like to repay all your kindness. I shall find you good, clean work away from this dungeon." What a small boy to live in the shadow of such a place. If he only knew the danger at the helm.

His pale face stilled. "Thank you kindly, miss, but I won't be leaving. Ain't such an 'orrible place, you know." Yet his face always wore a slightly haunted air. Worried, perhaps.

"Perhaps it's more wretched than you can see on the surface." We veered down a narrow hall, carrying the now-full bucket between us, and stepped outside a side door. Maybe I should tell him—confide in him about what I'd found. But what could a small lad do about it? We dumped the load in a ditch out in the yard. "Didn't you say that it felt off here, that something was amiss?"

He shrugged, dragging the empty bucket behind, then stowing it in an old butler's pantry just off the kitchen. "The work is honest and they let me sleep by the stove. I don't ask questions."

"Really, there must be better positions for such a hardworking chap."

He guided us up the stairs to the wards then, his expression firm. "Thank you kindly, miss, but I'll be staying."

I scrutinized that sunken little form. "What hold do they have over you, Lew Wiggins?" It was a trap, this place. It didn't let a body go. *He* didn't let a body go, that Thornhill. "How did you come to Hurstwell, of all places?"

He shrugged, his oversized shirt hanging crooked on his narrow frame. "Da is gone, Ma owns a bawdy house, and I was nothin' but trouble at the foundling home. Had to go somewheres." Yet his deeply shadowed face seemed as if it had materialized from the old stone walls and crevices of this place. As if he belonged here, whether or not he chose to.

Lew lifted the end of his wheelbarrow without a word.

"Your whistle. Is it a signal of some sort?"

He shrugged. "Just helps, I suppose. Me Da used to sing a lot. Made me feel better when I was afeared of the fights on our street, or the gunshots."

I watched his slender muscles work, shifting that cart down the rows as we alternated emptying the chamber pots into it. "You must have loved him very much."

He kept on, looking at the ground as he worked. "Fine man. Made the house feel full, even when the larders were empty. It were a bit rowdy at times with him there, but I wish he'd come back. Always knew I was safe with him."

"He's alive then?"

"He's aboard an East Indiaman. Midshipman." Lew straightened before the last word. "Only two years of service instead of three to get there. He was that clever."

"Seems a shame to lose him."

"He isn't lost," he hurried to correct. "He wouldn't have left me at that foundling place, neither, but he didn't know. Mum spent all the money he sent on absinthe and tonics, and the rent was due. It weren't so bad, though. Got regular meals and a roof at the foundling home."

"Could you not send word to him?"

"Already done, miss. Just waiting to hear back." He carted the load to the end of the hall where he dumped it through a chute to somewhere outside the asylum. Then he came back, his whistle echoing through the corridors. "It takes a bit for the post to catch up with him, you know." He squared his narrow shoulders, and my heart sank.

"Lew." I paused in the corridor, looking at him. "If I haven't said it already, thank you for helping me."

He shrugged, pushing his cart again. "There was a woman at the foundling home. Terrible cook, that one, but she was kind, doing for me every time she could. I remember how good it felt, and it's nice to make someone else feel that way at times. Like they have someone on their side."

I swallowed. He still needed helping, this man-child. "Just so you know, Lew Wiggins, you have someone now too." I put a hand on his shoulder and felt it relax. His smile followed.

Restless, unwilling to risk closing my eyes, I paced the corridor on each floor during my next night shift. I closed my eyes and saw Thornhill, that placid face and imposing frame. My heart pounded as I neared each shadow, imagining what surprise it might hold for me. I didn't know in whom I should confide, in a house of madwomen and unwelcoming, overworked staff, so I forced my tingling body onward, keeping alert, defenses up.

I jumped when a door creaked open a little farther down the acute ward, but soon a familiar face appeared. "You're here. Where have you been?" Clara's voice came from the dimness.

"Trying to keep awake." I hurried to dry my face with a handkerchief where perspiration had collected and smooth my frayed hair back into its knot. "I've had a long day."

She walked over, wrapped in a thin blanket. "An exciting one, I hope." Her eyes sparkled with interest. "You look as though something's happened. Did you find your patient?"

"No, I didn't. But certainly she'll turn up. Come, let's get you back to bed." I guided Clara into the room and helped her into her cot. I took the chair beside her again and gazed into the dark while she settled, pondering all I'd discovered.

She didn't sleep, though. "Something *has* happened. I see it on your face. Oh please, tell me what it is. It's the only bit of excitement I get in this place."

"Nothing, really. Just a more thorough glimpse of Hurstwell, I suppose." I left out the part about my breaking in, and about finding Nurse Duffy. "I happened upon some patient files."

"Oh, the *patient files*! You saw them! No one ever sees them."

"Shhh, we mustn't be overheard." Our voices were so low I could barely hear them myself, but my nerves were on edge.

She lowered her voice. "What did you see? Anything exciting?"

I shrugged. "There are many odd things at this place. Things a body would never expect to see. Things I probably wasn't meant to see." I stopped there, remembering her penchant for gossip.

She hugged the sheet to herself. "It's like my very own penny dreadful."

"You'll have to wait for the next installment, then. Tomorrow's my half day off." It hadn't come a moment too soon. I found myself starved for home, for a night of escape from deep shadows and mystery. From uncertainty around every corner, and the gaslights that showed so much—but hid even more.

"That's when most of 'em disappear, on their half days. They simply don't return. You won't do that, though, will you?"

"Wouldn't I?"

"You're not like the others, and I know you won't just abandon us to this place. To this deplorable trap."

"Trap?" I frowned, watching the shadows play across her face. Her hand—was it shaking?

Her eyes widened, and I knew there was more, a cavern of story below the one I'd heard about the stolen kiss.

"What are you afraid of? Tell me what it is."

She turned away, but the haunted look across her features only deepened. "Who says I'm afraid?"

"You thought of something. Just now, there was a look on your face. Won't you tell me what it is?"

"I cannot say." Her eyes shifted about the room. "One never knows who's listening at Hurstwell. Especially in the dark."

"In daylight, then?"

She twisted the sheet in her fingers. "Maybe." Then she shook her head. "M-maybe."

10

Without music, life would be a mistake.

~Friedrich Nietzsche

I sat on the stool of a lovely refurbished Bösendorfer, hands in my lap as the sun warmed my back through the windows. "I think it's time, Marcel."

My longtime manager, the erratic Frenchman who'd set out to manage my career and apparently my personal reputation, looked up at me with raised eyebrows. "And why is that?"

I'd come to his studio first upon leaving Hurstwell, determined to make him begin scheduling performances again in spite of my mourning period, but I'd forgotten how hard it was to make Marcel do anything. I shut the lid over the keys with a sigh. "I'm not truly mourning—I never was. You know that more than anyone. There's no reason I shouldn't return to performing as soon as possible."

He looked at me over the edge of the *Manchester Chronicle*, spectacles slipping down the bridge of his nose. "Would you believe, there's a run on blue thread. No one wants to pay for it, and they've slowed production, even in London. Who'd have ever thought—"

"Marcel."

"Mm?" He flipped out the paper, lowering it a tad more, his gaze placid.

"I want to play again."

"So play." He waved toward the pianoforte. "Nothing's stopping you."

"I mean on the stage. In the halls."

"Vivienne, dear, that simply isn't an option just now. Perhaps you should use this time to practice, to polish your skills."

"I'd rather perform. That comes with pay."

He blinked at me. "Do you need the pay?"

My face warmed. "I've had to take a position. But . . . I want out. Soon." I said the last words quietly, troubled faces under garish lights swimming through my mind.

"Perhaps a little change is good for you. A small break from the strain of performing." He didn't look at me as he said it. That meant he was avoiding something—or hiding it.

I narrowed my eyes at the man's newspaper shield. "What aren't you telling me, Marcel?"

He shook it again, his face glib and his eyes not fully meeting mine. "Oh, you always were a sensitive one. Why would you think I'm hiding anything? I merely believe a break will do you good."

"I love playing. Music *is* my break." He knew that too. Normally, no one pushed me harder than Marcel—not even Father. If there was an empty stage, he wanted it filled with music. If a city hadn't yet heard me play, he wanted to introduce me at the first chance. Breaks had never been part of Marcel's priorities before, and come to think of it, neither had societal niceties like mourning periods. I leveled a look at him. "Please, Marcel. Be reasonable."

"This is quite reasonable. The answer is no. You're not playing."

I banged the side of the pianoforte. "And you'll not go telling me what to do."

He met my gaze for just a moment. "Won't I?"

"You're fired." I stood, staring down at him.

"Of course I'm not."

"I mean it."

"You don't, and you know it." He didn't even glance up this time. "You'll do what I say, just as you always do. How will you manage without me? And right now I say, you wait."

Why did it suddenly feel like my career was hanging in the balance? Like whatever secret he kept meant the end of everything as I knew it? I stared into his face, but he did not look up. Not once. "I should go."

Finally, he flipped the page away from his face. "Vivienne, if you've agreed to work at this asylum, you should see it through."

"Why? I'm a pianist, and that's what I should be doing. It isn't as if I planned to keep this position forever."

"Perhaps a little change will be healthy for you—stretch new muscles, open new avenues. You never know."

"Just a minute. How did you know about the asylum?"

He blinked at me over his paper. "You just told me. The position you were obliged to take."

"I didn't mention where it was."

"Of course you did." His gaze flicked back to his paper. "Now get on with it, and we'll begin again in the fall. Or later, if you find yourself caught up in your work there."

This little investigation at the asylum had begun voluntarily—almost in defiance—but now it seemed that once again my life was still being controlled and I was merely riding downstream on the currents others had created for me.

I was shaking. Without another word, with not even the slightest acknowledgment from Marcel of my hard stare at him, I left.

Within an hour, I'd taken a hackney out of Manchester to Seaton Hall, the home of my late grandparents—and the residence next door to Richard. It had remained open to me for visits, even after my grandmother's death, and for that I was grateful.

The distant cousins who now owned the hall were in London for the season, so I'd sent word to Richard earlier that we'd meet there tonight.

I had been dreading the meeting a little, but now I craved the familiar sound of his voice. The scent and look of him. No one calmed me as he did.

"You're not going back, are you?" That was the first thing he asked when I admitted to him where I'd been. I immediately wished I hadn't.

"I don't know." I answered with half a mind, the other half on the sonata I was playing. How good it felt to have silken ivories under my fingertips again. "I suppose I have to. This is only a half-day break, and they expect me back by morning." What was it that made me so contrary? This refusal to be told what to do, even if both he and Marcel were telling me opposite things.

He sighed, leaning on the edge of the instrument. "If only you could hear how utterly ridiculous this sounds. You, working in an asylum? It was one thing to go as a pianist, but Vivvi, what if people hear of it?"

"They won't. I've signed on under another name."

"Suppose someone sees you going in? Someone you know?"

I gave a short laugh. "No one I know would be within throwing distance of that place."

He eyed me with a look that said I was only proving his point.

"I won't work there a moment longer than necessary, but with Father's debts, what did you expect me to do, sit at home?"

"Well . . . yes. That is, I hoped you would. Or perform, as you always have."

"You'll have to take that up with Marcel Beauchene. He's the one who will not let me perform until I'm out of mourning." I gripped the stool beneath me, and my thoughts kept returning to Hurstwell. The strangeness of the place lingered even now, a slight dissonance to the usual melody of my little world.

Richard laid a gentle hand on my shoulder, and I fought the

urge to pull away. "What is it? What has he left at that place to make you feel the need to go there?"

I looked at the rug, at the gold swirls against dark red.

"I know it isn't just about the pay. That can be had so many other places. Why are you letting him control you still?"

"I'm doing it for me, Richard. It's something for myself."

He stepped back. "So you're going back, then."

"I didn't say—"

"I don't like the idea of you in danger. There are men there who are stronger than you, and unpredictable to boot. Volatile."

"Fortunately, I work in the women's wards."

"You're telling me they're not just as mad, just as dangerous?"

I tipped my chin down, pondering this. Their faces ran through my mind, one by one. "No, I don't think they are. At least, not most of them."

He studied me as he leaned on the pianoforte again, chin on knuckles, several creases lining his brow. "I can see how you might be good for them, I suppose. Why it's tempting for you to go back." His frown told me he still hoped I wouldn't. "Just don't forget, Vivvi, you cannot save everyone. And you needn't worry about pleasing him any longer, whatever he's set you to do. It isn't worth the risk."

"Even if I don't return, I have other plans that are just as risky. Perhaps worse." I looked up into his face. "Richard, there are so many . . . what? What is it?"

He leaned back on his heels with a long breath, hands in his pockets. "From one mission to the next, is it?"

I looked down at my gown, resting my hands in the folds of my skirt. We'd arranged this meeting to speak of our future, and I'd said not a word on it. I lifted a look of apology toward him, tipping my head with an expression that implored him to accept.

His tension visibly melted as our eyes met. Then with gentle hands, he guided me toward the couch and sat beside me, our knees touching and his nearness engulfing my senses, and I was utterly his in that moment. "Richard. How I've missed you."

Relief spread over his face, along with his smile. "I'm glad to hear it." He sighed. "I do love the way you care for people. There's truly no other woman like you, but I've always known that. I'm merely being selfish, wanting you to myself. Wanting to keep you safe." He moved closer. "Forgive me?"

My eyes fluttered closed as a smile teased my lips. "I suppose." When I opened them again his face was near mine, his eyes intent on me, on what was about to happen, and I felt it all the way to my belly. Without hesitation, I lifted my hand to his smooth cheek and invited him in, sensing the taste of him just before his lips met mine and he kissed me gently, savoring, then with growing abandon.

His arms slid about me and pulled me into the kiss. I surrendered, lost in the familiar smell, the sweet, gentle scent of him that I never knew I could miss so much. For now, there was only me and the man I'd adored since he'd first looked at me with that crooked smile and told me my hair was far too red.

When I leaned back with a small sigh, he was smiling. "That's better. Now, what were you saying about this mission of yours?"

My senses swam pleasantly. "I believe I've forgotten."

His smile widened. "Good. Now, perhaps we can have that conversation."

I cleared my throat, moving back on the couch to bring clarity to my head. "I'd like to pay my father's debts before anything, so I may go free and clear into whatever awaits."

"Fair enough. As long as it doesn't take more than a week."

I laughed. "And I'd like to decide something about the future of the pianoforte shop. I'll either have to sell and give it up or put my all into making a go of it. That might take a bit longer, though."

"It needn't take any extra time. Once you've decided, I'll help you with whichever direction you need to go."

I laid a hand on his arm. "Richard, you truly are good to me."

"Someone ought to be."

I brushed my fingertips along his cheek, drawing forth another smile.

"You're not going out again tonight, are you?"

"I shouldn't think so. Why?"

He shrugged. "You're alone now, so I only wanted to make certain you're looked after."

"I do appreciate it, Richard, but I'll be right as rain."

"Even at the asylum?"

"I'll slip out under the cover of darkness if I ever need to."

He rose, lingering in the doorway. "Don't depend too greatly on the cover of night, Vivvi. A girl like you with that copper-bright hair and fair skin . . . you nearly glow in the dark."

I pinched my lips together, looking down at my lap. "So I've heard."

When he'd gone, I moved through the quiet house, with only the hushed footsteps of servants as company. It was rather nice, visiting when no one was about. Perhaps I ought to give up the position and stay in my own quiet home, as Richard had suggested. Only, I soon wouldn't be able to keep it.

I ambled up the stairs and through a gallery, hardly looking at anything, until one small portrait caught my eye and made me freeze—it was her. Rosamond. Several years aged from what I remembered, but it was that same familiar countenance, head tilted with a secret smile on a sweet face. Had it been hanging here all along? Or had I never ventured into the gallery before now?

I stood before the painting, studying her every gesture and feature, running my fingertip along the colors. She posed looking back over her shoulder, long brown hair piled loosely, with curls about her face. I touched the oil paints of her face, those laughing eyes. I hadn't ever seen them this way—she'd always been so shy and wistful.

I'd begun to believe she didn't exist—that was why I'd wavered about returning, wasn't it? But now her eyes held me captive, even when I looked away from them. The memories, the familiarity, were undeniable. She was there, somewhere. Here was her portrait in my family's gallery. There was a file at Hurstwell with her name on it.

I thought of that face on the whole carriage ride back to Manchester. Once, a long time ago, those lovely dreams of her and her music were all the beauty I had in a very dark childhood. They saved me, in a way. Now, the tables had turned, and I was meant to help her. And considering the limited options for one as poor as myself, I was the only one who could. My other plans paled every time I saw that face again, thought about her missing in that wretched place.

Words from the Gospel of Luke floated through my mind, nudging me. Convicting. *What man of you, having an hundred sheep, if he lose one of them, doth not leave the ninety and nine in the wilderness, and go after that which is lost, until he find it?*

People didn't simply disappear, and there was much more to her story. To Hurstwell, and everyone who came within its grasp.

At home, still rattled from a bumpy ride in a hired hack, I sat down at a refurbished upright in the shop and, eyes closed, tried to summon a Chopin piece. When my fingers didn't cooperate, I moved to Mozart. Even that highly accessible melody escaped me. I restarted several times, and it was like my fluid, natural skill had been broken. I didn't work anymore. My music had begun to splinter apart, as if Hurstwell's shadows had come home with me, magnifying my uncertainty with each passing hour. I sat with fingertips on the keys and let the sound of the wrong notes fade away, but the frustration didn't ebb. Not until I left the shop altogether and climbed the stairs to my own space.

There was a sacred spot in my bedchamber's bay window, overlooking the streets of Manchester. I climbed onto the thick sill and closed the curtains around me—enough seclusion to resemble the larder where God had always met me, but with open views from the window to keep me sane. There I laid my heart bare.

Almighty God, won't you come into the darkness of this situation? Won't you bring this woman to light? I know you can make such a thing occur, even when it seems impossible. Please, Lord, I need to be away from that place. And so too, if she lives, does Rosamond.

I rested my heart in his presence, shoring up strength for whatever came next, then opened my Bible, letting the familiar words cascade over me.

I returned to Hurstwell in the morning without a word to anyone, halfway believing my prayer would be heard, and my way would be blocked or some answer would come to light. I was unhindered though, and soon found myself in the laundry again, monitoring the hardworking patients. A nod from Bridget, a smile from Kat, and life quickly settled back into the routine I'd begun to learn.

But then, out in the corridor after lunch, I saw Clara. She saw me and darted my way, visibly trembling.

I haven't understood a bar of music in my life, but I have felt it.

~Igor Stravinsky

"Please, you must make her leave." Clara clutched my arm, yanking me into the shadows of the dim hallway. The sunny, buoyant light of Hurstwell was terrified. Shaking. "She heard us talking about her the other night, and she hasn't let me alone since."

"Who? Who won't let you alone?" But I knew.

Clara's fingertips skittered over the cloth of her skirt, the wall behind, her sleeves. This was a side of her I hadn't seen—or expected. She forced the normal cheery smile onto her pale face, but it wore like an ill-fitting mask. "She always did like me best, because I believed her. I believed what she said about why she was here, and that she wasn't mad. I knew how easy it was for a perfectly sane person to be trapped here."

Goose bumps rose on my flesh, a deepening awareness of what I'd begun to sense about this place.

"I couldn't save her, but perhaps she believes you can avenge her. Set things to rights."

I tipped my head with a frown, watching her expression. "You make it sound as though this person is a specter."

Her lips clamped into a tight line. "What *else* would she be?" Her voice was a hiss now.

It took monumental effort not to roll my eyes. "Truly, a specter—?"

"She is, I tell you, whether or not you believe it." Her dancing fingertips sped up, her face pinched. "She used to walk about, but she hardly spoke, not to anyone. She's been gone an awfully long time, but then last night . . ."

I eyed her. "Sounds like the stuff of legends." Yet the echo of that ghostly song from my own dreams pierced my doubt just a little.

"One you won't tell anyone. Not *anyone*. Please, you must keep quiet about it. Only . . . ask her to leave me alone." Clara's soft voice became a strained whisper.

"I'm afraid I haven't seen any specters."

She looked at me with wary eyes that seemed to promise, *Oh, but you will.*

Movement down the dim hall caught my attention. Heat slammed my chest. I blinked, adjusting my vision—it was only an aid, tall and willowy with a gray gown and somber face, gliding across the adjoining corridor.

This was silly. Ghosts, of all things. I forced out a breath, trying to clear away the silken cobwebs of fear.

"No one speaks of her anymore, and it's as if she vanished. Not even a mention." Her voice grew agitated. Desperate. She looked up at me as if pleading with me to believe her. "I remember her, though. Her name was just as lovely as she—a perfect name for a specter—*Rose.*"

I froze. It was close. Too close. "I thought you couldn't remember her name."

"It escaped my memory, but now it's come back. It has all come back. It's forbidden to speak of her, and now most everyone's forgotten."

"Why forbidden?"

Clara fidgeted with her sleeve. "Don't make me say. It'll have you in trouble, too, knowing that part of Hurstwell's secrets. Please don't make me say it."

I frowned. "Perhaps she isn't dead, just moved to another part of the asylum. And sometimes . . . sometimes she's able to wander the halls. Was she—is she—a patient here?"

"She used to be—not terribly long ago. Epileptic ward, even though she wasn't epileptic."

"Come, I'm certain—"

"She told me she was here because she fell in love with the wrong man. A duke named Santiago, and she was only a musician." She would not, it seemed, be dissuaded from her recitation. The words spilled out like a waterfall too long dammed up. "She carried his child and went mad when the babe died. Well, at least she thought it died, but I'm almost certain they merely took the child away. I heard it cry a few times after they said it died, but perhaps it's just as well. A woman cannot raise a babe in a place like this, and the duke wasn't about to let her out. Then after a time, she vanished. I believe she was killed, and the killer never faced justice. So ever since, she's stuck here, waiting . . . waiting . . ."

I lowered my lids and forced myself to listen quietly to the outrageous tale. To tread gently. "I'm afraid I have nothing to offer this specter, if in fact that's what she is. It isn't as if I was even here when—"

"If you don't believe me, go and look her up. The records of all the patients who've died are in the cemetery gatehouse. You'll find her name, as sure as I stand here."

I was seized with a panic, a deep unexplainable dread, that her words might be true—that Rose was Rosamond, and that she was dead.

"I just thought . . . I thought someone should remember her." Clara's fingers twisted in the fabric of her skirt. "Someone should know her story so she didn't simply vanish." Her voice was quiet.

"No one deserves that—not even the people here." She sucked in a breath. "But I shouldn't have said anything. I always do that, always get myself into these scrapes." Moisture glistened on her skin.

Her fear, at least, was quite real. That made her stories harder to ignore. "How . . . how did she die?" I couldn't force my mind to wrap around the possibility. This wasn't the end of the story I'd hoped for. Not at all.

"She became so violently mad in the end, after the babe, that they locked her up in the tower and we never saw her after that. Then, according to an aid, she fell to her death from a window— some say she did it herself, others say she was pushed by someone the duke hired. Or perhaps . . . by Thornhill."

My gut twisted.

"So now she walks the halls, looking for escape. Trying to get out, to be free again."

I shivered. That part wasn't real, of course—the ghost part. "Everyone here looks like a ghost. How will I even know which one she is?"

"You always know when she's about, because you hear her song in the air. Haunting, it was." Then she began to hum, eyes closed.

It was the song—the same one I'd always heard in my dreams. The lost melody that even now was returning to me in odd ways.

"Please. Won't you help her?"

I swallowed, afraid to promise anything. Afraid to face another night in the dark.

In the transition of patients for the second lunch shift, I snuck away and slipped out the front doors with a nod to the guards. I lifted my hem from the rain-soaked ground and looked about for a gatehouse, anyplace the records Clara mentioned might be stored, but there was nothing. Only the oddly placed tombstones jutting from the hillside at every angle. I thought for a fleeting moment of Dr. Turner, standing there alone with his lantern, and wondered how he fared.

I returned and asked the guards about the records.

"That room over there," said the stoutest one, with a little wave toward what I'd always thought to be a closet. I nodded my thanks and hurried over, an eerie fear in my stomach. Crates and boxes of files lay shoved into recessed shelves and scattered across a rutted old table. I dug through everything, file after file, a little sick at how many there were. Yet Rosamond Swansea was not among them. Not even a "Rose."

I smoothed my hair, my skirts, and ducked out of the little room into the now-empty hallway. How much time had passed? Had I been missed? Voices echoed from a distance, and I hurried toward them, but in the corridor, the whisper of skirts, a soft footfall. A small noise.

I turned, half expecting to see the ghost.

It was Nurse Duffy, her face sharply accented in the gaslights. "There you are, you idle bones." She grabbed me by the flesh of my upper arm and dragged me along the corridor, away from that file room.

Shaken more than I cared to admit, I stumbled after her without a backward glance.

"You'll have double duty, you know. Seeing as you have so much time to spare."

"What, you want me in two places at once now?"

"Two rounds of night shift. You're on again tonight . . . and tomorrow." She huffed as she paced down the dark hall. "See if that leaves you all fresh and pretty."

Pretty?

She turned to stare into my face. "All this effort, and he'll never even notice you. Not after a couple nights on rounds."

"Who?"

"I know what you're after. Turner isn't what you think he is, and it's best you stay away."

Then I saw it, clear as day. She had been this way toward me ever since the run-in. The one with Dr. Turner in the hall. What I didn't understand is why she cared so deeply.

But I suppose I should have known that too.

I looked her over, wondering how long she'd been taken with Dr. Turner, and to what lengths she'd already gone to catch his attention.

The second round of night shift in a row was tolerable, but after a week of erratic sleep on top of it, the third night left my head buzzing and my legs twitching. After a second cup of tea that I had made extra dark to startle my senses awake, I strained to see into the distance as the hour neared four, but no one came to relieve me. At five, I walked the wards again to keep awake, to avoid a fitful dream in these echoing halls, but I heard no footsteps, saw no other staff member.

The gaslit corridor of the third floor seemed alive. Lights pointed up toward the ceiling, casting shadows over the walls, giving them a life of their own. Creating movement and dancing figures that were not there.

Warm calm washed over me as I lowered my tired body into a chair, but after a few bleary moments I realized the reason for the calm—music. Not the tinny sounds of the old woman's music box in the long-stay ward, but a languid, beautiful sound that could come only from a pianoforte.

I sank into it with a smile, nearly giving in to sleep—but wait. This was not home. I was not above the shop with Father below-stairs, trying to drown his disappointments in Beethoven. There was no Father here, no pianoforte.

And there should be no music.

The sound wove through my foggy senses, muffled and distant. Another vivid dream? I forced myself to rise, shaking my senses alert and moving down the hallway. I peeked in each ward, scanning for empty beds. I reached the stairs—the music had stopped. Just now? or minutes ago? I descended the stairs on shaky legs, again looking for empty beds. For anyone moving about. After a walk down the corridors of the second floor, I moved to acute on the first and paused in the familiar room where I always sat, willing it to ground me in reality.

"You're still here." Clara's voice reached me with a rustle of covers.

My gaze snapped in her direction. "The music. What is it? Where?"

She blinked at me in the darkness, and again I felt the leaden pressure of my oddness before she even spoke. "What music?"

Of course it had stopped—or its muffled tones didn't reach this room. I sighed and shook my head, waving her back to bed. It had been so clear, though. Very soft and almost faraway, but distinctly piano music. I moved back into the hall, placing my hands on the wall to still my spinning senses. The music faded in and out, like my grasp on reason.

Hadn't Clara claimed to hear it too? Hadn't Rosamond's song once reached her ears? Or had that been someone else? Things were fuzzy.

Perhaps the music was meant only for one person at a time, whoever the ghost . . .

No. This was preposterous. I was tired beyond reason, and that's all it was. Auditory hallucinations happened when one lacked sleep.

Kneading my temples with a long sigh, I moved farther down the corridor to keep awake and silently cursed whoever had not shown up to relieve me. The music continued to echo in my skull, almost a ringing sound, and as I paced, I began to plan for how I could steal a small sleep the following day. I was growing desperate.

Shadows shifted. Wind howled like the moans of an old woman. I blinked bleary eyes, half expecting the promised ghost to walk out of the darkness and beckon me. The only result was dry eyes and jittery nerves. I moved up and down the corridor, mind growing numb.

Then a shuffling ahead jarred me to alertness. My night shifts so far had been uneventful, but now it sounded as if a scuffle were going on. Then, a woman's muffled cry. I hurried toward it with a pounding heart but saw no one. "Hello?"

A tri-folded letter lay open on the ground just outside the locked ward gate. I reached through the bars to pick it up and a flutter of dried pink rose petals tumbled out as I lifted it. Hand shaking, I drew the page in toward me and flipped it open. It was old, yellowed sheet music—a page of a Bach concerto on one side, distinctive handwriting on the other.

Please help me. I have enemies even now, and I cannot escape. Only you can help me, and you know it. Don't leave me here. Do not abandon me. You may not believe in me, but I believe in you.

I have every confidence you can find me, if only you'll look in the right places.

The writing was spidery. Light and wispy. I blinked, lowering the page as a faint echo of pianoforte music sounded in the distance, and I wanted to cry. It was happening again. The dreams—the vivid dreams. Shifting shapes on the window, low moans—my imagination fired like a steam engine.

The line between truth and imagination, laced with exhaustion, grew fuzzy. I'd flown like a bird from the tall clock tower of this place when I'd dozed the night before—that had been a dream. But the music—that seemed real. So very real. I still heard it when I stood still enough.

I swayed. It was time to force their hand, to make someone stand in for me. At least for a few hours. Climbing up to the second floor, I was surprised to find the corridors empty. But there was always someone on second, right? Epileptics needed extra attention. Even at night. Shoving the note into my apron pocket, I curled into a night shift chair against the wall and forced my thoughts to march in a straight line. The woman. The note. She needed help. So did I. Someone should be coming. I'd wait here, just rest my eyes.

Rose. The ghost.

Music.

Her music.

No, stay awake. No dreaming. Awake.

Awaaaaake.

12

My heart pounds sickeningly and I turn pale . . . I seem to be losing my mind.

~Robert Schumann

I jerked awake as dawn was about to crest the horizon. I'd lost the battle over sleep sometime between six and seven. I exhaled and forced my stiff limbs into motion, sitting upright and looking over the rows of beds. My head had settled back onto my body, but fog still thickened my thoughts. I blinked at the lumpy form of Clara on the bed, and everything seemed to normalize.

Wait. The epileptic ward. Second floor. Hadn't I sat down to wait up there?

"Wash and come help with breakfast," said a voice to my left, jerking away the last of clinging slumber.

I twitched and blinked at Nurse Branson, who looked even paler in the cool light of dawn. "No one came to relieve me. I've been on rounds all night. And the two nights before."

She yanked sheets off a bed and balled them up before moving to the next. "There's nothing for it, I'm afraid. We've had another orderly quit, and we're all down there making gruel and slicing bread." She tossed a bundle at my lap. "At least you caught a bit of sleep, it would seem." Her stare was hard. Accusing.

"Nurse Branson," I said. She turned, fist on her hip, and I grabbed for a sense of grounding. Of sanity. Someone had left me that note, had played that music, and it hadn't been a ghost. I had one guess who. "Where is Nurse Duffy?"

Branson sloshed water into the washbasin. "How should I know? I'm not her keeper, am I? Now get on with you."

"I heard music playing. It was here. At night. I believe she did it." The sleep-laced words tumbled out of my mouth. I was on edge—slightly desperate. "She wants to scare me, I think. To punish me. You cannot let her do this—I need to sleep. Need—"

The woman slowed, eyeing me with caution. "Is that so?" She flipped out a towel and laid it by the washbasin, then stood watching me, hands on her hips. "Come down when you're able, and we'll see what we can do about finding you a little rest later."

I slogged down toward breakfast by sheer force of will, did what I was told, then moved into the day. A little strength returned to my body the longer I stayed in motion. A hastily downed bowl of gruel helped, then I went through the motions. Kitchen, laundry, dayroom.

It wasn't until after dinner had been served and the sun went down that the dizziness hit again, and that's when it struck me—perhaps I should be one of those aids who quit. So many did. In my haze, I couldn't remember what had possessed me to return after my half day.

The position at Hurstwell was quickly becoming more work than it was worth. Mysteries be hanged. I could find another position too, just for the summer, and set a different solicitor on the matter of the disappeared ward. Yes, I could go home to my own bed and be done with this place and all its gaslight and ghosts.

It was like whiplash for the senses, this lack of sleep, and after three nights of it I craved a bed and quiet. Yes, it was time to leave this place of leaping shadows and constant intensity. I only had to make it down the lane, and . . . what? How did I find a conveyance out in the forgotten woods this late at night?

I wound my way to the kitchen, where steam and yells filled the air, and staff hurried about making giant kettles of tea to accompany the medicine that would keep the most erratic patients asleep for another night. How wretched it all seemed now. I approached Branson, who was making up trays. I untied my apron and met her gaze. "I'm afraid I must—"

"Yes, I know. Here, help get these out, then we'll see about the arrangements. It's been a wretched day."

I blinked. Staff truly must leave every day. She seemed to take it all in stride. I pushed through the tedium of carrying armloads of trays up to the dayroom as patients filed in, making their way toward the benches.

Bridget touched my arm as she passed. "You're well?" Her frown told me she didn't think so.

My mind hummed with a thousand ways to say goodbye, but faced with the sheer exhaustion of uprooting myself, of explaining everything, I simply said, "Yes. I'll be all right." A small tug of regret made me hesitate, but my spinning senses urged me forward with the decision. Some were built for night work, for the asylums, but I was not one of them.

When I reached the kitchen again after delivering the trays, someone handed me a bowl of stew, and I wolfed it down, realizing how little I'd eaten that entire day. Likely that was part of the problem.

Before I'd finished, Nurse Branson was whipping off her dirty apron and scurrying over. "I've managed a reprieve for you. From now until breakfast—a full night. Hopefully that'll be enough, yes?"

"No. No, no. What I meant was, I must leave. Go home."

She eyed me. "The beds here will do quite well for a quick rest."

"I mean . . . for good. I'm resigning."

Her frown made my stomach flip. She took me by both arms

and steered me to a stool. "I'm afraid we cannot let you do that."
Her eyes searched mine. "It's just a temporary hold, until your
mind clears. Then you may go if you wish, I suppose. Besides, it's
nearly nightfall, and it looks like a storm is coming. You cannot
leave now anyway."

Quicksand. The place was quicksand, and it began to pull me
under. "What sort of hold?"

"Well, it seems you've been a little out of sorts—said a few odd
things. It's probably just a little overwork, and a rest'll fix you right
up." Arm looped through mine, she guided me toward the door,
pausing to nab a cup of steaming liquid from a sideboard. "A bit
of special tea, a nice night of sleep, then we'll see how you feel."

"I'm perfectly well. I don't need any hold, or special tea, just my
own bed and home." I felt jittery clear through to my fingertips,
my stomach alarmingly weak.

She dropped my arm and looked me directly in the eyes. "Nurse
Duffy was not about last night. In fact, she was serving in the
men's wards with me, filling in for someone else. And there was
no music."

"Perhaps she was lying. Or she got other people to. One never
really knows about a person."

She bristled. "I've been here long enough to know my staff. I'm
not like the rest, you know. I stay in a place when I says I will, and
I know who I can trust and who I can't. I saw her myself most of
the night, and there's no way she could have done what you said.
I doubt anyone else would have taken the time, either."

"You think I'm imagining it."

"I've seen it happen—folks believing they have some enemy,
someone out to get them." A hint of maternal concern flickered
over her features.

"Come, I'll show you." I shoved a hand into my apron pocket.
"You'll know the handwriting, I assume, if you know the staff
here as you say."

With a tightening frown, she waited as I pulled out the tri-folded paper with lines of music on it. There, I wasn't imagining things. Wasn't dreaming it all. I flipped it open with trembling hands, but there was no writing. No scrawled note. I blinked, turned it over and back again.

Branson lifted her eyebrows.

"I . . . I must have . . . it was dark. Very dark." I couldn't swallow. I folded it up and stuffed the paper back into my apron pocket.

Branson leaned near and looked me full in the face, getting a read. "As I've said, you're long overdue for some rest, Miss Fletcher."

"I just need to go home." My skin was cold with perspiration. I turned and took long, decisive strides away from her, but she caught up and held my arm, guiding me back downstairs in her no-nonsense way. At the row of offices on the main floor, she knocked on one and urged me in. "Here she is, Doctor. She won't rest, though."

"Very well, send her in."

A small clock ticked on the desk, and the man sat, arms crossed over a narrow chest. It was the one who'd set me on slop duty after nearly catching me snooping. He waved me toward a seat. My senses felt unnaturally leaden, much like when I'd taken that tea on my first night. I could barely think.

The tea. Yes! Someone must have slipped the same powder in my food. Or in a drink. Something.

I stiffened against the wall, refusing the proffered chair. A stern glare compelled me, so I complied—and nearly fell over the chair as I came around it.

The doctor's eyes narrowed.

"Someone must have added . . . you know, a little sleeping powder to my supper," I said, my mind struggling to form the right words. "I assure you, I'm quite well, just in desperate need of a little rest."

"I've gotten word of your behavior this morning." The clock continued its ticking as he set his papers down on the neat desk. "We looked into your background today, and it seems you have a history of erratic behavior. Friendships with many men, in and out of positions, drifting about, violent bursts of temper."

"But that's absurd. I've never—"

"We've found a great deal of information on you, Miss Fletcher, and none of it points to sanity."

I laughed, high and awkward. "Yes, well, here's the thing. I'm not Cora Fletcher. Whatever you found about her . . . I merely gave the name to avoid using my real one."

He raised one thick eyebrow. "And that is?"

"It's Vivienne. Vivienne Mourdant."

The eyebrow lifted higher. "The pianist?"

"Yes, I play the pianoforte. For the theaters." My brain slogged along, pulling words out of the mud still filling my head. "I've played the Alexandria. Here in town. Also on the Continent. Mozart, Haydn, Chopin is my favorite." My mind spun.

"It appears you've been this way since the death of your mother and brothers."

"Oh but—"

"They are dead, are they not?"

"Yes, but—well no, I don't have—"

"Well then." He frowned and dipped his pen, then wrote on the paper before him. "We'll place you on light duty for now, day shift only in the laundry, but under the circumstances we cannot permit you to leave." He looked up to me with a sigh. "You'll still be expected to work, but you'll be under our care for the next few days until your . . . condition improves."

"But Cora Fletcher is completely fabricated. She's not—"

"She's quite real, and so is her reputation about Liverpool. Now, I'll have to ask you a few questions, Miss Fletcher."

I stood, back stiff and legs shaking. My body ached from prolonged tension. "No, you must listen. I'm not Cora Fletcher. I truly am Vivienne Mourdant. Whatever you found on this Cora woman is about someone else entirely. Let me bring someone here to vouch for me."

His bland look told me how useless my suggestion was to him. "This Cora. It's just a name I made up. I tell you, I'm Vivienne Mourdant."

"Very well then, *Miss Mourdant*." He rose, waving me toward the door. "Come this way and we'll let you have a rest. Then we'll talk again and see what's to be done. First, a little tea."

"I don't want tea."

He paused, eyes like steel. "I don't recall asking a question."

Father had said similar words. So often. I clung to the back of the chair, heart pounding in my chest, then followed the man out of the room. I needed air. Space. My heart drummed out a rhythm of fear, a desperate sonata.

I didn't belong here. I was a pianist, with a heart for hurting women. I had a mission and a purpose. Freedom. I wasn't one of them, the patients here.

"We've a nice quiet space where you can rest. They're making up some tea, and you'll get all the sleep you need."

Alarms rang in my fuzzy head.

"A handy little cot in the larder should do nicely."

"Larder?" I breathed out the words as dread set its weight on me.

"Dark and quiet, with not a soul to bother you. We'll have to lock it, though—you understand."

Sweat moistened my skin, gathering in every ridge and crevice. We rounded the corner into that opulent front hall, and he passed me off to a nurse. Panic buzzed with each step, and all I saw were the front doors standing open to the wide outdoors beyond. A man—a large guard of some sort—frowned at the looming storm as he held the doors open for another man struggling under the burden of several crates. Lanterns hung along the drive like arrows lighting the path to freedom, but the rest of the world was dark.

I didn't mind. Let the dark swallow me. It couldn't be worse than this place.

Walking behind the nurse, I reached for a heavy candlestick, the only object around that would make a nice distracting clunk when I threw it down the hall, and let it hang in the folds of my uniform. I gripped it tight, watching the door, watching that oblivious footman. There were ten paces between me and the outside world. Eight. Now six. Time slowed, focus narrowed. I held that candlestick tighter and wondered, in a tilt of vertigo, if I'd be desperate enough to use it as a weapon.

With only two steps between me and freedom, fear lifted in the breeze of the storm, and I saw only hope and necessity.

13

An unmarried man, in my opinion, enjoys only half a life.

~Wolfgang Amadeus Mozart

Dr. Mitchell Turner blinked in the dim recesses of his dungeon-level quarters, forcing his eyes to concentrate on the paperwork spread before him. It was likely just the storm, but something felt off tonight. Lightning popped bright through the high, narrow window, and he covered his eyes, then a crack tore through the night. A banging echoed down along the pipes, followed by a low wail. That would be Anna—third floor, second block—afraid of the thunder.

Turner blinked again, tried to focus, but the wailing grew urgent. He shoved his hands through hair that was badly in need of a cut and sprang up with a sigh. Not bothering with the outdated frock coat hanging on his chair, he blew out his little oil lamp. He'd be spending the better part of an hour up there, if it was anything like the last storm.

Half the patients in this asylum looked to him for hope, for wisdom in the midst of their confusion, but often it seemed he didn't have much to give. Some days, like today, he had little more than an empty body to stand with them through a storm, and he felt like a fraud.

He tucked his disheveled cravat into his shirt rather than fiddling with the knot and took the stairs to the third floor two at a time, turning down the hall to the long-stay ward. Striding down the rows of beds in Anna's block, he gathered the old woman up with all her moaning noises and rocked her, crooning the sacred songs she loved until the panic was replaced with a frenzied submission, eyes darting. *Amazing grace, how sweet the sound.* He reached for her music box balanced on the water pipe by her bed and wound it. *That saved a wretch like me.*

Then the box took over. Its familiar notes plunked into the whimpers and babbling, drawing a blanket of calm over the room. Anna grappled to climb close to him, as if clinging to a life raft, and hummed along with the box in that low, gravelly voice until her trembling slowed. She buried the top of her moist head into his shoulder, and he did his best to balance against the force of it. He continued singing the old hymn to the music box's tune. *I once was lost, but now I'm found.* Her body relaxed, muscle by muscle. Then came the sobbing.

He spoke quietly to her, routine assurances, and eventually helped her collapse back on the mattress, limp as wet hay. With a sigh of relief, he covered her. At least he hadn't had to drag out the corset—she'd settled quickly this time. She peeked out, two wide eyes with double bags beneath them, but said nothing. She rarely did.

A voice came from the next bed, muffled by blankets. "You were asleep, weren't you, Doc? I can tell by your hair."

"It *is* nighttime." He ruffled the offending mass, turning toward the bony woman in the next bed—Alice. "But I wasn't asleep, actually. Not yet."

"Your Dahlia's been asking after you, Doctor."

Pain sliced clean through his midsection, unbalancing him. He grabbed the metal bedpost.

Dolly.

"Mayhap she's afraid of the storm too and she thinks you've forgotten her. Have you forgotten her?"

Not likely.

He forced in a breath. "I haven't. Thank you, though." He rose and stretched the kink in his back, but it only intensified the low ache in his gut. A foolish thing it had been to tell this woman stories about his wife, thinking it would be cathartic to him and meaningless to her, with her mind that leaked like a colander. What harm could come from telling her?

A lot, as it turned out.

Funny thing about Alice—she had a few stray pieces of flypaper somewhere in that leaking mind of hers, but only certain facts stuck. The lovely parts of all the Dahlia stories were captured in her head and often repeated, but other parts had fallen through the cracks. Like the part about Dahlia's death. She never remembered that.

And he never forgot.

"Another night, Alice. We'll talk about her another night." It brought him tired relief to say those words.

As he gave Anna's little box one more wind, a distant scream jolted through his painful haze and drew him bolt upright. It was a hysterical sound. Animal-like and entirely foreign to his ears. It must be the new intake. He'd heard about her, the young delusional who'd been brought in a near-vegetative state, so full of sedatives they had to check her pulse to be certain she shouldn't go straight to the morgue.

So this was why. This was what she became when she was awake. Rising and moving toward the door, he shoved his fist into his shoulder and rotated his head to stretch his stiff neck. Oh, how he craved bedtime. And dreaded it. Perhaps he should—

Bonggg. Metal on wood. It echoed deep in the asylum and he tore down the corridor toward the main stairs where the yelling had been. From the sounds of it, she was trying to escape through the front doors.

119

When he reached the second-floor landing and looked down, three or four figures struggled in the distant shadows below, then one broke away and bolted. They apprehended her again and wrenched her arms behind her back, lashing them with something. He hurried down the stairs as she fought, every muscle in play.

How wildly out of place she seemed in this sterile old building, with its stone walls and dull chill. The effect was electrifying, and he couldn't stop staring as he approached, drawn to the rare display of strength. Although he wasn't certain who he should help when he reached them. Would the lasso win? Or the creature?

One more flight of steps. It was dark, but their forms were growing clearer. Lightning blazed in the windows, and suddenly there she was—turbulent and wild with great masses of deep red hair flying about her shoulders.

Crash. More thunder, then the lightning illuminating the space. This time she was still, chest heaving and head down. Resigned.

Then she swept aside the great curtain of burnished red hair, lifted her glowing countenance to him, and it was her. Not a new intake, but *her*. The musician who'd reached Mary Jo, who'd studied him with those snapping bright eyes. Yet she was here. In captivity. A patient? How had he mistaken her for an aid?

Her body had stilled, but her face, those flashing eyes, radiated a turbulent look that was quite spectacular, and he knew her strength was only reined in, crouched and waiting.

She twisted away and a nurse struck her face, the sound ricocheting through the emptiness. She cried out, which earned a slap from the on-duty guard as well.

Jolted, he sprang from the shadows and shoved the nurses aside. The guard raised his hand, and Turner slid between the man and his prisoner, accepting the blow on his back with a grunt.

The man instantly recoiled. "Dr. Turner. I wouldn't . . . that is, I didn't . . . I didn't mean to strike you, sir."

Turner bent down and lifted the young woman to her feet, holding her steady. "But you did mean to strike her."

Her knot of hair now lay in long, wild tresses about her face, framing the passion there with a sense of banked fire. Something clenched in his chest as she stared at him, expressing respect and thanks and a bit of curiosity. Somehow she said a great deal without a word.

Turner forced back his shoulders. "Carry on, but with a bit of civility, please."

One of the nurses grimaced. "Treat her like a delicate kitten, then?"

"Like a human."

The captive woman straightened, her keen eyes still focused on him, then the little group collected themselves and moved on with her in their midst. He stood and watched until they were out of sight. Something about her left him in angst—as if he should warn someone of what he saw in her, protect people from the eruption about to occur—or protect something fragile and beautiful within her.

A rigid voice from the shadows jerked his attention away. "Doctor, what do you think you're doing?" It was Superintendent Thornhill, six feet of grimace and authority, towering behind him in the shadows.

"They struck her—twice."

"Out of necessity." He folded his arms. "Is there any doubt she's mad? You had no right to impede them."

"I'll not apologize, if that's what you're waiting for." Turner held his jaw tight and watched them lead her around the corner at the end of the corridor, that defeated wild creature taken to the cage where she'd lose all her strength, her will to fight.

It had always seemed both a bad and a good thing, this loss of will. There was a succumbing to calm . . . but also to deep despair. They lay in these wards until they grew brittle and stale.

"Do not forget your place. I am your superior." When Turner

didn't answer, he lowered his voice. "You've found the pills I left for you?"

"I have, thank you. I won't be needing them."

His voice gentled. "You're far more useful to me as a doctor here than a patient. Find a way to get some rest."

"It'll just take time."

Thornhill put a hand on his shoulder. "What is it, a year now?"

"Two, sir." And three months, two days.

He heaved a sigh. "You're not the first, you know. Life deals in bitter blows. Every one of us reaches some sharp point in life, like a painful nail stuck in the thread of our story, pivoting everything that comes after it. See that you manage the direction it pivots you, yes?"

"I'll do my best."

"Tomorrow, then? Meeting in my office?"

"Nine o'clock."

He gave a stiff bow and turned toward the passageway that would take him back into the bowels of this place, a tomb-like darkness where he might find a fitful bit of rest. Yet those wild eyes, the lips half parted over white teeth, glorious hair flowing over her shoulders, the whole untamed look of the captive lingered around his senses and made him anxious to do something. To at least see what became of her.

Perhaps her remarkable face would be the reason he'd toss and turn tonight, rather than the usual. Yet when he entered the dead-end darkness of his room, his head hit the pillow and he only thought, with aching bitterness, of Dahlia.

SECOND MOVEMENT

So it was that I woke in a cell after a drug-induced sleep with two doctors, the bassoon voice and the timpani, talking over me, and I officially became a patient at Hurstwell Pauper Lunatic Asylum. I'd tried to escape, but who wouldn't? It was akin to kidnapping, what they'd done to me—how could I not fight back?

Dr. Thornhill looked me over after completing his examination and snapping his bag shut. "Now, Miss Fletcher."

I didn't correct him this time.

"I'm afraid we'll have to put you through the normal routine of a new patient, even though your case is somewhat extraordinary, having been on staff here. You'll start with constant supervision—you understand, of course—in scullery duties or perhaps the laundry."

"How long until I'm evaluated again? I'd like a chance to prove my sanity."

He straightened the cravat straining to encircle his neck. "There are hundreds of patients in this institution, and we are painfully

123

understaffed. You cannot expect me to personally attend you on a regular basis."

My eyes were dry. Fixed. "*When?*"

He looked at me directly. "I aim for an annual consult with each patient."

Annual. *A year.* I swallowed the bitter news, shaky hand brushing hair off my face, and tried not to weep. A year without Richard, without music, without freedom.

It was all starting over again, wasn't it? Father was gone, but I was still trapped. This man was my captor now. Thornhill—the sight of his name in thick, dark letters on a file came to mind. Think . . . think. Where had I—

Patient file. He had a patient file.

The fear came surging back.

I'd thought it had been that awful nurse—what was her name? Duff or something. I'd thought she'd put me up to this, leaving the note and arranging the music, but it must have been him. He knew now that I knew. Somehow.

I glanced back to his face, craggy and shadowed, with new eyes. "You cannot keep me here."

He clutched his bag, rising from the chair and looking me over. "The law says I can."

No laws would bind me, though. Not this time. Slipping from his grasp was all that mattered now.

14

How sad it is that these great gentlemen should believe what anyone tells them and do not choose to judge for themselves! But it is always so.

~Wolfgang Amadeus Mozart

Humblest of apologies, dear Byron. I cringed as I ripped the page from the back of his book of poems in the now-empty dayroom. My heart pounded with anticipation. After four days, my head had begun righting itself. I remembered everything, and I had my reasoning back.

I'd been handed over to slop duty with the amiable Lew Wiggins once again. It had been his idea, he'd told me, and it was a good one. Then when we were alone, he'd suggested I write a letter. "I'll even deliver it myself," he'd offered, and relief had poured through me.

I hastily scrawled two notes in the empty room as fast as my hand could scratch out the words and dropped the pen on the blotter. I tucked the notes into the frayed belt of my asylum gown—the blue gown of the acute ward—and hurried on with a steadying breath.

I caught up to Lew in the first corridor, where he was emptying pots into his rusty cart. "I have them." I kept my voice low.

"Wait till my hands are clean. Help me finish."

I nodded and bent to scrub the first chamber pot, instinctively holding my breath. I watched the boy work, agile and good-spirited. "You deserve so much more, Lew Wiggins."

He popped up beside an unmade bed. "Who's to say any of us deserves anything? I got a full belly and dry bed. A man can't ask for much more."

"Won't you let me take you away from here? Someone will be coming for me, and I can take you along—help you find better work."

He straightened, fisting his back with both hands. "I don't ask nothing to make a few deliveries, miss. You don't owe me nothing."

"But life can be so much better than this, and I can help you. Please, won't you let me?"

"Who'm I delivering to?"

"I may have to go and kidnap you then, if you'll truly be that stubborn."

Fear flashed in his eyes.

"I mean no threat, Lew. But life outside of this place can be grander than you know. I mean to prove it to you, whether you let me or not. They cannot threaten you into staying, no matter how afraid you are."

He moved away and knelt to grab another pot. The contents sloshed into his wheelbarrow, then he went to work scrubbing. "I've a sister." He spit out the words without a glance my direction. "They're not always good to her, and I'm all she's got left."

"She's a nurse here?"

"Patient."

That single word realigned everything. "I see. Tell me about her, Lew."

He sighed, bending to place a clean pot in place of the one he'd picked up. "Her name's Violet, and she's just as pretty as her name.

Like a flower, she is, but they won't treat her that way, you know. They don't see the point in her stayin' alive, stuck in a chair like she is, with her mind 'alf gone. They don't know what a gem she is." His face shadowed as he spoke of her. "Or how fine she used to be, before she got sick and disappeared into herself."

I shuddered. "Oh, Lew."

"She never left me, even when me ma did for days at a time. She'd sit and croon over me, kissing me and tucking me in. I can't leave her."

"No, I see that. You cannot leave Hurstwell." I handed him another clean chamber pot, and he placed it under the next bed.

"So where am I delivering?"

Right, the letters. "It's only two. The first one goes to a Mr. Marcel Beauchene of Lowergate, the other to Richard Cartwright of Devon House. Can you remember that? Richard Cartwright."

He gave a nod and paused to wash his hands in the basin. "Beauchene, Cartwright."

I'd only intended to write to Marcel, but the man fairly pulsed with the erratic strains of Liszt's *Hungarian Rhapsody No. 2 in C-sharp Minor*—volatile, surprising, with periods of dramatic trills offset by low, heavy notes I knew to avoid. He'd been nearly heroic in his protection of me throughout my childhood, but whenever I did anything *un*reasonable—such as finding myself institutionalized under a false name—well, he was quick to wash his hands of the situation. Even if he had been the one set on me continuing here in the first place. I'd never been able to predict the man's actions, so I included a letter to Richard as well, instructing him to ask for Cora Fletcher as soon as possible.

I wiped my hands on an old rag when we were done and extracted the letters, holding them out. He reached for them, but I snatched them back. "You'll truly deliver them?" It was quite a trip from the asylum. It was a big request . . . and my only chance.

He shrugged. "If I can."

I despised that word "if." Especially now.

It was only after the boy had disappeared with those two small life rafts that worry set in again. He'd hardly asked anything about how to find them. Perhaps he only intended to turn them over to Thornhill. A sick fear snaked through me, souring my stomach.

I spun on my heel with a sigh and froze. At the other end of the chronic ward stood its master, tall and distinguished with a guarded look on his face. We stared down the length of that emptiness, and again I had the sense of low, beautifully played cellos sweeping through the silence, warming the shadows with understated strength.

I couldn't look away, couldn't take a step forward or to the side as I waited for his gaze to release me. He pressed his lips together, seeming to study me with questions all over his countenance— was I an aid or a patient? Sane or mad? I swallowed, tempted to go to him and throw myself at his mercy. To confess everything and beg him to believe me. Yet I sensed there were certain lines the man would never cross, rules he wouldn't break, and I had a pretty good idea which those were.

"Miss Fletcher, isn't it?" He approached, yet seemed to hesitate, and I did not confirm or deny the name.

He reached me and simply stared for an unsettling length of time. I wasn't certain what he saw. "I was glad of your help before, with Mary Jo."

"Think nothing of it."

"You have such steadiness in you. It's a rare quality."

I had the sense he was evaluating me, looking for something. "Sometimes when you live among storms, you become a rock to endure the waves."

"It was bad, then, after your family died?"

He must have been reading my file—or speaking with Thornhill. "With my mother it was very sudden, I believe, like glass shattering. Father and I both felt her lack immensely. She was only twenty-nine and I a mere babe."

"It seems a waste when they are gone so young, doesn't it? I'm afraid I understand all too well the shock, the way the pieces never quite fit together again."

I gave a simple nod, and we shared a moment of solidarity. We were silent, but I was, for once, not alone.

"Well then, thank you again, Miss Fletcher, for your assistance, and for lending your musical abilities. You're quite an actress."

"Actually, it wasn't acting. I *am* a musician—a concert pianist." Hope buzzed along my skin. "And my real name is Vivienne Mourdant."

His face clouded and he seemed to retreat into himself, as if suddenly aware of the very "otherness" of me, the huge chasm between us. "All the same, I'm grateful."

My heart withered, and I gave a nod, but he did not leave. In fact, he continued staring.

"This music you hear. Is it . . . all the time? Or just certain days, perhaps when you are most tired?"

I pictured with absolute clarity the way he'd taken that invisible violin to chin and played with such precision, to the tempo of an unheard beat. *You hear it too, don't you? You hear the music.* I balled my hands to keep from asking it aloud. *Don't try and tell me you don't.* "It's more that I *feel* the music. Deeply. It's in the air everywhere." I watched for a flicker of agreement, of understanding, but he merely continued to stare, as if waiting for me to make sense.

Why couldn't I explain it? Didn't he sense the rhythm pulsing through the whole earth, the very order and symmetry to everything? The way two different people, a doctor and a musician, could work in parallel, playing different parts but ultimately linking together in the song of service to the weak? "Is it so wrong," I whispered, "to have a life brimming with music?"

"Most people don't go about hearing music that isn't there. It's as simple as that."

"Most aren't listening."

He shifted, shoving hands into his pockets. "It isn't so bad here,

Miss Fletcher. You'll see soon enough. We're trying to help you. Just relax and let us do our work."

A pull. A quicksand, everything nudging me farther into it, encouraging me to accept my fate and be swallowed by this place.

I would not. Neither would I cease to be who I was. I looked up at the doctor and spoke with a whisper-soft voice. "It's a far cry from Vienna's Theater auf der Wieden, but I enjoyed the concert you gave for Mary Jo all the same. And . . . my name is Vivienne."

Four days it took to know whether or not Lew had delivered my letters. I'd been assigned to the laundry, since I already knew the work, and on one of the trips out to the yard I heard a voice.

"*Psst.*"

I nearly dropped the bucket of dirty water. I stood, scanning the tall fence, the empty yard. With a huff, I shifted, positioning my arms a few different ways to get around the container, and sloshed the metal tub full of grayish water farther out into the yard. Arms trembling as I neared the fence, I stumbled and the basin tipped, releasing all that sludge in a big whoosh over hard-packed ground . . . and my shoes. I groaned, hand to my face as wetness soaked through. Then I heard tapping.

"*Psst.*"

More tapping.

I peeked between my fingers. My spine straightened like a fox looking for the hound, but I saw nothing. No one. Then the tapping was near, just on the other side of the great wooden fence. The thing was so tall, I couldn't see over it, though.

"Vivvi!"

I dropped to my knees on the water-soaked ground and put my eye to a knothole in the wood. Two inches from it was a striking blue eye with smile lines folding around its depths. I knew those depths.

"Richard." I breathed out the name, and the taste of it on my lips drew all the oddness of the past weeks into sharp focus. At once my floundering soul was grounded again. "What in heaven's name took you so long?"

"I came as soon as the chap brought your note, but they sent me away. Do you know, you aren't allowed visitors? I even remembered to give them your false name—then I tried your real one. Still, they wouldn't let me see you. What sort of position is this, anyway? So by Friday I figured I ought to make my own way in. Had a frightful time trying to lure you over here."

"So that's why no one came. I wrote Marcel as well."

"You won't be hearing from him, I'm afraid. He's left for the Continent."

"So soon? I thought that trip wasn't until—"

"Listen, we haven't time." He twisted to look behind him, golden hair taking the place of his eye in the hole, then turning back. "Guards are on the grounds. Tell me what's going on so we can get you home. The shop's in an awful state and you have creditors looking for you."

"I've no idea what's happened, but someone's set me up—made them think I'm mad. I tried to get away, and now they've admitted me."

"You're a *patient?*" I couldn't tell if he was angry, doubtful, or annoyed. He definitely wore the I-warned-you glare he'd mastered in our childhood.

"Look, there's something odd happening here. Notes. Music. A patient they claimed was never here has vanished, even though her stay had been paid for."

"Vanished. You mean, kidnapped? Run away?"

"I have no idea." I blew out a breath and laid everything on the table. "Father had a ward, someone at Hurstwell, and now she's passed to me, only no one knows where she is. The office claims she was never here, and they know nothing. They only know how to charge for her keep, apparently. Father has been paying her way at Hurstwell for years."

"Who is she?"

"I'm not sure, exactly."

His stare was steady. "You're certain she's real? Perhaps he's been scammed into paying for some made-up relation."

"She's real. Richard, I recognize her. I've seen her before. I thought it was a dream at first, when I saw her years ago, but maybe not. Go look for yourself—her portrait is hanging in the gallery at Seaton Hall, second from the end in a little oval frame. She's real, Richard, trust me—and somehow she's connected to my family. Only, no one can tell me where she is or anything about her. I can't do a thing about any of this until someone breaks me free of here. Oh, and listen to this—the head doctor has a *patient file*. Meaning, he might be a patient here. Or was one. I saw it myself, with his name. Look into him—his name's Thornhill. Thomas Thornhill. I couldn't get a look inside his file, but I saw it. I know I did. You have to tell them who I really am and get me out of here."

"I already mentioned your name, and they didn't seem to believe it."

"Because they already know. Or don't care." I shook my head. "Someone's set me up, and they have no plans of letting me go."

"I'll look into it."

"No! Richard, there isn't time. Something's amiss and I'm afraid of what they'll do. Someone here—*someone*—is out to get me."

He frowned, working his jaw. "Very well then, I suppose we'll have to sneak you out. But I'm not helping you chase down this missing ward."

"Agreed."

Thus, our escape plan began. In two days' time I would find my way to the cellar as the sun went down and hide in the morgue under a sheet. When it grew fully dark, Richard and Lew, who'd apparently already offered to help when he'd delivered the note, would sneak me through the ventilation system that led to fresh air—and freedom.

"I can't believe I'm about to do this." He heaved a sigh. "Wait, yes I am. It's *you*."

"I owe you, Richard."

"Yes, you do. But even more so now." A wicked smile gleamed in his eye. "Good thing you're worth the trouble."

I relaxed into a small laugh and felt myself at last.

"It's good to see your smile again, Vivvi."

I closed my eyes, letting his voice wash over me. Dear Richard, who sounded like the music of home. "Thank you for rescuing me, Richard."

"I'll do my best." He moved back and patted his chest over his coat, digging out a few small items. "Here, take this and hide it, just in case you're stuck." He wrapped the items—a set of matches and a small folding knife—in a handkerchief and passed the little packet through the crack. "It should help you get to the morgue if you hit a snag. Now get going, and don't raise any eyebrows for the next two days. Can you manage?"

"No promises." Footsteps crunched over dry ground somewhere behind me. I spun, tucking the little packet in my belt.

"Just . . . be in that cellar."

My relief was indescribable. "Done."

I slipped back toward the laundry with fresh hope and new strength.

A scream split through the clank of machines, jerking me into alertness. I darted for the door. Bridget crouched on the ground between a tussling Clara and Kat, crying out over and over, banging fists on her forehead. Whistles blew as two nurses pulled the chaos of limbs apart, yelling above the hiss of steam, and Bridget launched herself up, flinging her arms about and striking a nurse.

I dropped my bucket and ran to Bridget. "What is this? What happened?"

No one answered me, but when they had Bridget standing, arms twisted behind her back, her dark eyes met mine and her gaze was steady. She gave a slight nod. Then they spun her and hauled her away.

"What's happening?" I whispered to Clara.

She shrugged. "She goes to the stacks a lot—solitary. Can't abide when people ruin her patterns, and some folks can't abide her bossing them." She looked me over. "You're the lucky one, aren't you? They were about to go see who was standing around out in the yard. Could have been you instead."

Lucky, indeed. I watched that wiry frame disappear through the doorway between two nurses, recalling her secret look, and knew my near miss had nothing to do with luck. "How long will they keep her?"

Clara shrugged again, little pink lips pinched. "A day, most likely. She's in there so often they daren't keep her longer or she'd never see daylight."

"What if it's longer? Is there a way . . . could I go and see her?"

She frowned. "In solitary?"

"No, perhaps just a message. Clara, would you give her a message for me?"

"Tell her yourself. It'll only be a day or two."

"Right. Of course."

I exhaled and rested my fingertips on the little packet tucked in my belt. One day in there, and I'd be able to thank her before I escaped. Another, and I'd have to choose.

15

I will seize fate by the throat; it shall certainly never wholly overcome me.

~Ludwig van Beethoven

How easy it was to sense music now, as if home was close enough that I might hear my pianoforte from time to time. Squeezed between several women on a long bench in the dining hall, I looked over the great open space of peeling green paper and heard the *symphonie de la dine*, a collection of voices mingled with the aroma of meat, a most unusual concerto.

And I wasn't sorry to leave it. Tonight was the night, and I'd been watching every clock I passed, counting down the minutes as the small hand neared eight. It was a quarter after seven now, and the tension built in my chest toward the grand crescendo. I hadn't seen Bridget yet, but I focused on the memory of Richard's tender smile over me. That was my rainbow at the end of this storm.

"How fast did your fingers move?" Clara's high voice was jarring. "Could you play any song you wanted?"

"As fast as the song required. There's nothing like letting one's mind and fingers take over and sinking into the melody."

"Who taught you to play?"

"My father, I suppose. He was a sought-after tutor who gave lessons out of our home." I grew antsy. Could I handle the escape, fuzzy as my mind still seemed to be at times? I was weak. Malnourished. I hardly slept, with a lumpy bed to cradle me and that consuming darkness all around. Over the weeks as both aid and patient, the glowing gaslights and pitch-black shadows had dulled the edges of my reason.

"Do your fingers ever grow tired?"

I took a deep breath as the soles of the aids' shoes pounded the wood floor, scurrying about to drop tin plates before us. My stomach lurched at the aroma of solid food—meat. "Not often. In fact, they're energized by playing." I curved my fingers in my lap. *Soon. Very soon.* And my soul began to calm. "My hand cramps at times, though. That's when I know it's time to stop."

The meat was dropped before me and the aroma, the very sight, interrupted my thoughts. I cut into it and was daunted to find it tough and slightly spoiled. Yet I wasted no time tucking into it, for if I didn't, someone else would.

"It must be quite lovely, to surround yourself with music any time you want."

I slowed my eating as I neared the end of the small slab of broiled beef. "It's the most glorious taste of eternity. It brings the chaos of the world into order and rhythm and harmony. It's calming and exciting, quiet and loud at the same time."

My head swam with desire, my fingers longing for the silk of ivory keys—then I surfaced and realized my supper companions had fallen silent. I smiled at them.

"It's no wonder you hear music," said Clara. "After living so long in such beauty, who'd ever want to go without it?"

I smiled at her and she returned it. How odd that here, of all places, I should find like-minded souls, yet it was the only place in all of England protected from the influence of society's disapproval. It was too bad, really, that I had to turn down that

Harford man's offer to bring light into these dark asylums after I escaped. There was something precious here that I couldn't bear to walk completely away from . . . yet I wasn't sure I could ever return.

"Well, I for one would give my last farthing to hear you play a single song." The voice came from behind me, and I spun.

"Bridget!"

I stood and hugged her, and she stiffened, patted my back with awkward movements. She received my thanks with her good-natured shrug and a smile as she squeezed in between Clara and me. Her responses to all my questions were vague answers, her natural spark dimmed by that day in solitary.

"Why risk yourself to help me, Bridget?"

"We're friends now, aren't we?" So simple, so honest, so very Bridget. I'd gotten the chance to see her once more, but leaving her behind still felt like a betrayal.

Before I knew it, the most warm, inviting display of colors stretched across the sky just outside the barred windows of the dayroom as the nurses turned up the gaslights. My heart pounded hard enough to give me away beneath the ugly gown that I'd soon be able to burn in my lovely oaken hearth at home. Until then, though, I was a jumble of nerves.

When no one watched me, I reached deftly under the bench where I'd hidden the packet of knife and matches. My fingers spidered along under the lip of the wood, searching, but they found nothing. Chest tightening, I double-checked my location on the bench and stretched out a bit farther, and my roving fingertips met with, not the packet, but paper.

I picked it out of the lip and held it scrunched in my fist until I was certain no one watched. Then with eyes up to keep guard, I smoothed it out on my palm and glanced down. It was a scrap torn off a yellowed Haydn piece. Just a few words were scrawled in the familiar spidery writing from that mysterious note I *hadn't* dreamed up after all.

    I never escaped.
    You won't either.

A small rose embellished the bottom of the scrap instead of a signature. I fisted the note and forced my mind to get around it, to keep moving forward. I didn't need the little packet, and this note meant nothing. I could step on a stage and play a Chopin piece from memory, could command the attention of audiences without a word. I could make it to a lousy cellar.

"Bridget." I dared whisper to her as the two aids spoke with each other. I meant to utter a friendly goodbye, a thanks for our brief friendship, but looking at her pale face I decided against it. It would go better for her if she knew nothing.

She waited, eyebrows raised.

"You have music too. You simply have to recognize it for what it is."

She offered me a full, warm smile that reached her black Irish eyes, but then it dimmed. "It's always easier, you know, to simply accept one's fate. To not pretend."

"Always easier, always easier," chanted a woman named Lizzy Potts, as if chastising us as she rocked forward and back, hands tangled in her gown. "Eeeeeasier."

But then I brought my tea to my lips and inhaled deeply, and a slightly bitter tang that was growing all too familiar met my senses. Sleeping tincture. I looked to be sure—there in the bottom of the cup swirled those now-familiar little flakes, ready to spin my senses and knock me flat so I couldn't go anywhere but bed. It looked to be a double dose, even though sleeping tincture— even a standard dose—had never been part of my regime. Even as a patient. I blinked, glancing from one aid to the other. Chills climbed my arms and I set the cup on my knee.

It was coincidence. Merely coincidence. I'd been given the wrong cup, one meant for the volatile patients who took the tincture every night. I looked them over again—Duffy caught my gaze and held it, just for a moment.

Clara's bright eyes were focused on me, and she smiled when I looked up at her. Bridget was watching too. Her eyebrows raised in question. Were they all staring at me? All aware of what I'd planned for that night? Of what was in my cup?

Or was I truly losing my mind?

I kept my head down. It suddenly seemed far easier to stay. To not risk being caught. Surely someone would find a way to come fetch me, and I could leave the right way.

But when?

No, it was time to go—now.

In carefully timed intervals, I dumped the tea into the potted plant on the sill near me as backs were turned, pretending to sip when they looked my way.

I could barely breathe over the pounding of my heart. It only grew worse as the turn of the hour neared. I looked out the dark window and became aware of the strangeness of the property outside these walls, the suffocating darkness that would surround me. Would Richard bring a candle? I couldn't bear the dark.

It occurred to me that I'd never told him why. I'd never spoken to him of the locked larder. Nor would I want to speak of my time at Hurstwell.

Then I saw with panic how low the sun had sunk—how dark the sky had grown.

It wasn't until we headed single file toward the wards that I realized I hadn't concocted a plan. Was it too late? I had no way to reach the lower level, and I hadn't time to devise anything foolproof. That meant I'd fail. I always botched the performances when I skimped on practice, when the piece wasn't memorized completely. I couldn't ever rely on my wits.

We turned into the dim corridor on the way to the ward, that dead-end, soulless room where I'd end every day until I forced something to change.

And if I'm free . . . perhaps I can help her. I watched Bridget's narrow back as it moved ahead of me. We were helpless here—all of us. I wasn't any good to anyone unless I braved an escape. Right now.

Careful to keep the dull look pasted over my features, I fell toward the back of the moving herd, away from most of the nurses. As we approached a corner, I slowed more, and when they disappeared down the next corridor, I bolted to the left. I pedaled with all my might into the near darkness of a north-facing hall, hoping to find stairs or a doorway.

Anticipation thudded in my chest. Freedom was close. They hadn't locked up the chambers for the night yet. I could still get out.

A yell, then two sets of footsteps pounded down the hall behind me, ordering me to stop. I lurched forward just as someone caught my gown, and I collapsed, the side of my face bouncing off the floor, sharp pain riding up my jaw. I trembled with fear, with desperation, as the unseen nurse hauled me to my feet, bruising the flesh of my arms with her grip.

It was Duffy. "You fool girl. How many times—"

I threw my head back and screamed.

She yanked my hair until I saw twinkling little snowflakes. "Shut up, or you'll get worse."

My trembling intensified. I could use this. I was desperate enough. I gave in to panic, let it seethe through me, take over my being. My body shook uncontrollably. "I'm having a spell," I breathed. "A spell. I just want to sit down and—"

"We can arrange a nice long sit, your ladyship." She yanked me by the neck of my gown.

I coughed. Swallowed what shot up into my mouth. The light outside was fading, along with my chance of escape. Richard—would he wait? How long?

"Let's see what Dr. Thornhill has to say about this."

A river of nausea streamed through me. I hurried along beside the woman who made no concession for my stumbling stride, and we turned left down another hall, away from where we'd been going with the masses.

Away. That was a start. There was hope. We neared the end of the corridor and there were many doors, some cracked open. Yes. Yes, a spell. I had to have a spell. I gave myself over to the trembling, the sheer terror that gripped me, and let it utterly consume me. I could almost smell it.

Passing a window that seemed even darker than the last, I threw myself on the ground, biting clean through my lip as I hit. I tasted blood. I added jolts and spasms, magnifying everything. Then I went absolutely limp, hair splayed over my face and limbs askew . . . and I waited.

She screamed, that wretched nurse, and I almost felt sorry. She tore off down the hall, yelling for the doctor, and I lay still as death.

The second her footfall turned the corner, I scrambled up, reining in fear as if I was walking onstage to perform and bolted, holding my sleeve to my bleeding lip. I dove through the doorway at the end, happily discovering the most beautiful sight—*stairs*. I flew down two flights, trying to soften the clunk of my footfalls in those awful hard shoes they'd given me, wondering how long it would take. How long until I reached the basement, or until they found me. Whichever came first.

The stairway opened into the main floor in the back hallway, which led to the kitchen. I paused in a wondrous state of calm. I was alone. Halfway there. Which way was the lower stairs? One more level to go. I yanked off those treacherous old shoes that kept tripping me and hurled them deep into the kitchen and ran on bare feet—my first taste of freedom.

I skidded to a stop as a shadow bounced over the tile at the other end, growing larger. I ducked into an open door—a vacant office. I put both hands over my heart to still it.

A nurse's frantic voice echoed off the walls, then that deep bassoon voice joined it. "Come, I heard something this way." The voice came into the hall. "She can't have gotten far, and she isn't leaving. The place is locked up tight as a drum."

They moved closer, opening and closing doors. I moved farther into the shadows of the room and looked about for a place to hide. The sound of doors grew nearer. There was nothing to hide me—a narrow bookcase, a tabletop on a stand. I stood frozen in the center, waiting for light to penetrate my hiding spot and for them to pounce. I held my breath, rooted to the rug. I was a fox, cornered by the hounds, too terrified to run. I clapped a hand over my mouth and forced myself to remain still and silent. *God save me.*

"Doctor, this way. In the kitchen—it's her shoes. She must have escaped out the back."

I bit my knuckles. My shoes. Those blessed, horrible shoes.

Three sets of footsteps thumped over the tiles and grew fainter. Crescendo, finale, and then . . . stillness. I pushed out my chest and breathed again, forcing steadiness into my body.

Sliding out into the shadows of the corridor again, I looked both ways and moved toward the end along a thin red runner. Down one hall and up another—I'd never find my way out of the maze. I happened upon a series of doors, the last of which opened into the cellar steps. With a small cry of glee, I plunged down into the dark, feeling along the chilly walls to keep my bearings. For once, darkness equaled freedom.

A never-ending climb down, and I was there. Free. In the same part of the asylum as Richard. And I had only to find him.

He'd rescued me from a roof once, where I'd climbed onto an enticing-looking gable to write some dreary correspondence. What an inspired view it had been . . . and terribly hard to leave, especially in long skirts. I'd looked behind me and, lo, there was Richard, climbing the angled roof, hand outstretched to me. I could still see his face, earnest and good, and feel the relief rush through me.

Soon I'd clasp that hand again and be ushered back to freedom. Tears warmed my eyes.

Yet as I slid along the torchlit passageway, oppression hung heavy in the air, and I could scarcely breathe. I slowed and blinked to focus. There were bars down here in long rows, cast-iron and cold. They moved. No—just the creatures trapped behind them did.

People.

A giant of a man with long, ropy hair sat hunched on something, staring out at me. Another was a younger lad with open flesh sores, watching me with gaunt eyes.

"Which way to the morgue?" My voice jumped about the emptiness, echoing back louder than I'd meant it to be.

No one answered. They looked at each other, then at me. Silence carried on endlessly until a scratchy voice a little ways down called out a reply. "Never heard of anyone *wanting* to get there."

"Please, it's important."

"You're mostly there." Another voice rang through the dark. "Straight ahead and curve to the right, follow the light. You'll see it."

The light. Of course, in the darkest moments one must always look for the light. Jittery and chilled, I moved that way and indeed found the orange-yellow glow ahead. The sight of it washed over me like the warmth it surely spilled, and I moved swiftly, eagerly, full of expectant victory down the long hall that still stood between me and that light. But voices echoed behind.

Had I closed the cellar door?

I curled against the wall and couldn't escape the smell—that noxious aroma that, although I'd never been in one, clearly belonged to a morgue. Breathing through my mouth, I walked into the room that in itself felt like a tomb—insulated from the activity of Hurstwell by thick walls. I could no longer hear the echoing noises, or the voices. Just . . . nothing. White-sheet-covered surfaces were spaced about the room, with metal drawers and an opening to a chute on one end. What on earth went down that chute?

With a final quiver, I lifted a folded sheet from the pile and lay down on one of the empty tables, covering myself fully and settling in for a long wait. How eerie it felt beneath that shroud, my nose tenting the material over me. I tried not to let it puff upward with my breath. My nerves thrummed in my neck, vibrating through my body as I willed myself to relax. Wait, and stay quiet. Perfectly still.

But then I heard Richard's sure, steady footsteps coming directly toward the morgue, and I nearly sobbed with relief. This leg of my journey was coming to a close, and now the longer, more difficult part began—proving my sanity, clearing my name. Rescuing the Hurstwell women I'd promised myself I wouldn't leave behind.

But first, a gushing display of gratitude to Richard. Perhaps even a peck upon his cheek.

He entered and soon the sheet was lowered from my face like a cage door opening, and I drew in a cool, grateful breath, my mouth full of words—but it was Dr. Thornhill looking down at me.

The sight was a sickening punch to my stomach. Dread and anger poured through my veins. Lew, that wretch. Thornhill had obviously known exactly where to find me, with those certain footsteps, which meant that little rotter had told him.

No, it was my fault. My fault for trusting a stranger. A small boy who would do anything to look out for his sister and himself.

He shook his head with a long sigh. "You had me believing in you, Miss Fletcher. Believing you would only be here a short time, that you might come round . . ."

I pressed my spine into that cold table, cowering away from that pillar of control, the man who held me captive without a single physical restraint. "*I . . . don't . . . belong here.*"

The lines around his eyes curved down in that signature look of pity. "You worry me, Miss Fletcher. How long will it take for your brain to absorb reality, I wonder? Another year? A lifetime, perhaps?"

I curled my long fingers into my sides. "I am who I said I am, and nothing you say will change that."

His face softened into fatherly concern. "They're called delusions of grandeur, Miss Fletcher. Illusions that have been mistaken as reality. It isn't your fault, though, that you believe yourself something of a great performer. Even the most outrageous dreams can be cataloged as memories by your brain, and you cannot be expected to sort through it all without help. Not to worry. We'll do whatever it takes—for however long—to help you sort fact from fiction."

Electrified, I sprang off that table. He lunged and grabbed me, twisting my arm behind my back, and a sharp pain shot up into my neck. I kicked like a wild stallion, reckless and terrified, landing several solid hits into him.

He jerked me back, my head against his puffy face as he anchored me to him with a warrior's grip. "You want to endanger everyone you love? Look at you. *Look at you.* No one in this state is fit to be around people. Not even the ones in an asylum."

Panic and despair rushed through my veins, for I knew what was coming.

He spun me by my hair to look at him. I dared not move. One turn, and I'd see that fistful of hair hanging loose from his hand. His face had an eerie calm, and I had the sudden sense that he was the madman, hiding behind a mask of sanity. "I'm beginning to lose all hope for you, Cora. Any hope that you'll recover." He let go of my hair and drove me forward, his fist gripping my wrists and digging into my back.

"Vivienne. It's *Vivienne* and I can prove it. Fetch my manager, and he'll tell you—"

"Beauchene, isn't it? Marcel Beauchene." His voice was weighted with calm. "He's already been to see you, the night we had to sedate you. Yes, we checked into your claims before admitting you."

I spun and slapped his face with all the force of my frustration. "Liar."

He yanked me away from him, holding me at arm's length with a sharp look. "Once fractured, always broken. The shards fall apart again, ready to stab the flesh of anyone who comes near."

"I've never hurt anyone."

"How can a broken mind ever see the truth, though?"

I looked into his eyes, now fixed and hard. No Father Christmas. "I'm not the one who's broken."

"We all have natural instincts. A penchant to lash out in violence, to preserve and survive. Only, when we're broken, there's nothing holding back that instinct. Nothing to keep us from hurting anyone who gets in our way."

My skin crawled. "I'm not like that. I've been set up. I have enemies—"

"The only enemy you have right now is you." His words slipped out, the smooth calm of a blade. "Look what you do to yourself."

I bolted, and he yanked, his grip tight on my hair.

I cried out as he pulled me, dancing about on my toes to keep my hair connected to my scalp. He urged me on and I stumbled up the stairs, and my gaze darted about—desperate, searching. Richard should be somewhere. The farther we went, the harder it would be for him to find me. Could he break me out of solitary? Would he try?

Yes, he would try. Richard would always try. And I would be ready.

16

The essence of the beautiful is unity in variety.

~Felix Mendelssohn

Dr. Mitchell Turner stood, arms crossed, in the shadowed corridor. Through narrowed eyes, he watched his superior slip noiselessly from a padded cell, sliding the door closed behind him. "What are you doing in my ward?"

Dr. Thornhill swung around, blinking in the dimness, then turning to quickly latch the door and bolt it. "What I must. I have need of this room. It's—"

"A relic of darker times. At least that's what you promised me once."

"Some inmates—"

"*Patients*." Turner's insides turned rock-hard.

"Some *patients* exhibit behavior that necessitates a return to more . . . barbaric methods."

How warped humanity had become—a beautiful, imaginative creation of God tainted by this world, born into sin and chaos for thousands of years and devolving over time into this. "I cannot condone this practice."

A good-natured smile smoothed over the man's features. "Well then, it's a good thing you're not in charge."

"You act as though the patients here are one step away from the beasts in our fields." He couldn't get past the image of poised, intelligent Cora Fletcher pretending to hold up the music for Mary Jo. Extreme humanity and kindness had poured from her, making her seem more solid and grounded than even the superintendent standing before him. He'd seen her wild and frantic the other night, but even then there'd been lucidity burning in her eyes. "Chaining them up this way, like animals—"

"Like *children*, which is what they are. They must be made to understand that their circumstances at Hurstwell depend largely on their own actions." He sighed. "Certain people, Turner, are simply born a burden to those around them. It is up to us to keep that burden off the family, to keep them safe, however we can. This is our mission." He gestured toward the bolted door. "This is what we do for them—for the families. For the rest of the world."

A burden. Yet Mitchell saw traces of their Creator wrapped up in each intricately designed patient, and he had the intense feeling that locking them up deprived this asylum—the world at large—of the blessing of them.

"I'll thank you to let me do my work and trust the method." He puffed out a breath, smoothing back his oiled hair. "I'm not above hearing your ideas, Turner, but I'll only implement what I believe is best. Something with scientific evidence to support its use."

Turner ground his teeth. "Where's your proof on the efficacy of these restraints?"

"It's the only way to administer the medicine she needs most— sedation . . . and truth. Hard, pointed, black-and-white truth that will puncture her delusions and set her free. And I cannot administer either while she's fighting me." He gently poked at a red mark on his cheek to prove his point.

Mitchell stood his ground, afraid of what he'd do if he stepped forward. "Do you honestly believe this will cure anyone? Has it yet?" He pictured the wild creature with the flaming hair and fiery spirit and wondered if it was the delusions that held her captive—or this man. "I daresay I'd fight tooth and nail if someone tried to keep me in that place, Doctor. Would she even attack without being provoked?"

"I don't care to find out." The man's look was pointed. "What if I left her free with a mere slap on the wrist and she grew bold—attacked another patient? What then? I'm not willing to take that risk. She has been admitted, and I'll do what I must to ensure she—and everyone else—are kept safe."

"We'd do better to aid them, Doctor, rather than defeat them. They are not the enemy. They're *fighting* an enemy, and we must be on their side."

"And what good do you see coming of that, Doctor? Have you heard any happy endings come from this asylum? From any across England?"

Indeed, what good? He forced himself to look away from that shadowed end of the hall where the last door remained closed, and remembered—or rather, quit trying to stop—the memories from flooding over his being. *"This is our fight, Dolly, and I'm going with you to that place."* He could hear his youthful voice vowing it. *"Where you go, I will go. What you face, you'll face beside me."*

Dahlia's relief had been instant and messy, tears pouring down her face as she had melted into him. She'd been so relieved, so grateful for his promises, believing them just as much as he. Within months, she was begging—*pleading* with him—for freedom. It had been a mistake, she claimed. All a mistake to come here. She wasn't mad. She didn't need confinement, just a little help—and no one would believe her.

And then she was dead.

Turner locked gazes with his superior. "What exactly is her diagnosis?"

"Hallucinations—hearing music—and delusions of grandeur.

She believes she's a famous concert pianist and she's late for her scheduled tour."

Mitchell stared at every crack running up and down the door before him. He swallowed and forced his mind to remain in the present. "Well, she certainly seems to have some background in music. Perhaps she is a pianist."

"She may play in her little parish church or some other such business. There's always a little truth to what most of them say. Surely even you know that, Dr. Turner. Yet they have no grasp on reality. A competency or obsession with music does not equate to professional talent."

"What if her hallucinations are temporary? Right now she looks as though she's merely lacking sleep and good nutrition. There are so many other explanations."

The man sighed, his bushy gray eyebrows lowering, and placed a hand on Turner's shoulder. His voice was gentle. Gravelly. "There's something built in all of us that wishes for a happy ending. If they can have one, we believe, then maybe we will too. Yet we live in a broken world, where happy endings are rare—especially in our profession."

"Perhaps no one is trying hard enough. Everyone gives up on these people before offering them half a chance. Provide her some decent food and rest, a little compassion, and see where it gets us."

"I appreciate your charitable spirit, Dr. Turner, but this case runs deeper than poor health. As you've likely seen in the report, Cora Fletcher lost both her mother and two brothers in a fire about a year back, and she's not been right ever since."

"She told me she was a babe—with her mother, at least."

"Deception is among her traits. Repainting stories to suit her purposes, and that's only the surface. Unstable, erratic, and overly driven by instincts as an animal, her neighbors say."

Turner bit his lip.

"And it has come to my attention recently—this not yet being on record—that she's regularly hallucinated a woman playing the pianoforte who's been dead for many years. A woman she never could have met. So you see, Dr. Turner, she is truly unwell and always has been. And even in her moments of lucidity, we must not lose sight of that. As I told her, broken vessels may be glued back together, but they will always be cracked and prone to break again."

Turner shifted his weight. What was the truth?

Only one thing was certain. She was orphaned and alone. Struggling through grief. Turner glanced at the heavy door with the impossibly tiny window, caging her in. Yet she had lived caged before, he sensed. Suffering placed thick walls around a person that no one ever wanted, bars over a window that allowed them to merely look out at the sunshine so many others enjoyed every day. Many sat there in utter silence for years too—not because they were afraid to call for help, but because their voices were already hoarse for trying.

Perhaps that, in the end, was what broke them so completely.

Thornhill lowered his voice. "She isn't Dahlia, Turner. You mustn't fear everyone will come to the same end."

Mitchell studied his superintendent, the swoop of saggy skin under his eyes, long white hair forced over thin spots on his head, and a wall of bitterness rose between Mitchell and this man. If only Thornhill wasn't his superior. If only the man had any clue of what Mitchell had gone through—how very unclinical it was. "What happened to her does make me think twice about what *should* happen to Miss Fletcher. She has suffered a great loss and has long endured affliction over it. It's time someone actually helped her."

"A long affliction." Thornhill stood with arms crossed over his chest. "You sound as though you're making a case for her to move into long-stay. Is that your professional suggestion?"

Long-stay. She'd be in his care, and he'd be able to shield her. To help her. What was Greer's research he'd come across about the effects of severe trauma on the brain? He could help her, perhaps ease some of the wounds she'd borne. She was worth saving. They all were.

But long-stay also meant exactly that—a stay so long it never ended. He looked up at his superior and weighed the two terrible options before him.

17

Imagination creates reality.

~Richard Wagner

I lay hurting and bruised on the floor of the solitary confinement cell where I'd been tossed. They had called this unknown Cora Fletcher erratic and violent, and everything I'd done recently only proved that. Even Dr. Turner himself, who had tried standing up for me, had witnessed my worst. No wonder they thought me mad.

Maybe I was.

Then I'd never leave.

Oh heavens. I pushed up onto all fours, stomach lurching with such force. I lunged for the chamber pot and missed, emptying my stomach onto the floor.

I used to look at the other patients around me and feel out of place, starkly different amidst unstable insanity. But now I could taste the anger, the metallic desperation I saw in some of their faces. How delicate the line was between sanity and madness. The longer I existed in these gray halls, the less confident I was of which side I belonged on.

This place was wrong, all wrong. One set of footsteps retreated,

Thornhill's staccato limp echoing down the hall, and a sudden panic gripped me. The file. The patient file on Thornhill. I had to tell someone. Had to get help. I was being held by a madman. I rose up and banged on the door. "Dr. Turner!" *Bang, bang.* He'd believe me. He would. "Help!" *Bang, bang, bang.*

The door jerked open, knocking me back, but it was Nurse Duffy who squeezed in, hand in her apron pocket. In a flash I wondered if she too had been a patient here. I flew at the cracked-open door, and she slammed it shut, grabbing my arm and twisting it behind me. Pain jolted with surprising intensity. "A right sore spot of trouble you are." A stab in my thigh and a coolness spread through my leg. "Learn to keep quiet," she hissed, and her face was bleary. Underwater. "And things will go better for you."

I pictured Rosamond's smiling face as the injection dulled my senses, forcing the dreamy image of her into clarity. Re-creating that lovely calm I always had when I saw her. White and airy. Beautiful.

Long dead. They'd said that. About her. A woman long dead is who I'd seen.

But she wasn't. She played. She smiled. Roses and music.

I lifted higher, weightless, off the ground and peaceful. Detached.

Rosamond. I always felt her playing before I heard it, vibrating the furniture beneath me. It was the same song, that ghostly rhapsody easing from major to minor, seeping through the walls to find me in my quiet little chamber in the east wing, and I swam in it. Lay in the cushioned feel of it.

I rose in silken movements, letting the music soak through the soles of my feet, and padded toward my wrapper. I was nine again, my delight unpolluted by adult wisdom. I knew the way by now, down the stairs and through the gallery to the rose room just below, where my mother's great Collard & Collard lay exposed to the moonlight that fell through long windows, the dustcover drawn back so the visitor could play.

She was a splendid creature in white, with soft waves of glistening chestnut hair down her back. Perched on the flowered stool she played, fingers flying over the ivories. Then she stopped, lifting those porcelain hands, and turned to look at me. How ghostly her face—white and drawn, yet crowned with a celestial glow. A perfect round birthmark near her full lips curved up when she smiled her welcome. Even her imperfections made her beautiful.

I hovered in the doorway until her invitation came—a gentle pat to the empty chair beside her—then I crossed the great room, sliding close and placing my hands on the higher keys, two octaves above hers. The moment was not ruined by words—we simply sat beside one another, two pianists lost deeply in music, and enjoyed it together.

I closed my eyes and felt her prelude as she began, a dramatic lead-in that invited my higher notes in response, then we were playing together. Brahms. Chopin. Rosetti.

When the sun shed its garish light over this house, she would be gone, the pianoforte covered again, and no one else would have heard the music. That's how it always went. Why did no one else ever hear it? Why was all this beautiful playing for my heart alone? They'd call me an odd little thing if I mentioned her and get that look in their eyes.

Yet none of it could steal from me this sacred moment, the feel of her cold, smooth arm moving gently against mine, the sound of our music mingling into one song. Not even Father, who stole most of what mattered, had a right to this small, secret part of my life.

I smiled, languid and peaceful, willing myself to remain forever, but then the tingles started. First in my fingertips, then up my arms and tightening through my chest. Flashes of awareness. Reality. The dream was ending far too soon, and I fought the wakefulness, swam back to the depths, but the more I forced it, the faster the fog lifted, drawing me back to the heaviness of Hurstwell.

I groaned, oddly sore upon the bed, but I was not in the cell, nor was I in my chamber above the rose room. I lay with leaden limbs and stared up at the curtains swept back from the pillars of a tall walnut bed. I blinked my eyes and my mind was clear. More so than it had been in a long time. Everything was still, chaos had quieted, and I was myself again. I lay on the softest cloud of sheets and pillows, enveloped in comfort.

Vienna. I was in Vienna, at Herr Strasser's home with birds chirping outside the window and *I was not mad*.

It had all been a dream.

The odd old man at the party, the ward, the failed escape, the entire asylum—it had all been a wretched, soul-searing dream I never wanted to revisit again.

Well, most of it. There was one single bright spot in that nightmare—the young doctor with a gentle strength of nature so pure that it could only have been imagined. Hope had radiated from him when I'd given up on humanity, lighting the darkness with which I'd begun to see the world. If only he was real.

I closed my eyes and thought of Bach's cello suite, pictured his easy smile. The rest of his face had faded already in the way of dreams in broad daylight, but the song and the smile, the memory of him bending low to comfort a madwoman, were enough.

I breathed deeply and let it out. Of course I find someone whose melody could impact souls . . . and he's a dream. Yet now, at least, life made sense. That reality had been far too dark, too painful, for God to have truly brought me into it. Only my own imagination could conjure up such evil, apparently.

I sat up and rubbed my face, hair tumbling over my shoulders, and looked around the lavishly appointed blue room. It seemed like I'd slept a year. There was a cushioned quiet to the mansion, a thick silence that I appreciated.

Herr Strasser always insisted on hosting me when I played in Vienna, but never before had I come in without thanking him and his wife profusely for having me. Last night, for some reason, I had. They must think me terribly uncouth.

I groaned at a rap on my door that I felt in my head. I shoved stray hair off my face and shielded my eyes that suddenly seemed terribly allergic to sunlight. What had I had to eat and drink the night before? That foolish marquis must have given me something—but what? Never had I slumbered so hard or succumbed to so vivid a nightmare.

I'd barely wrapped myself in a robe from the end of the bed when the door burst open and the indefatigable Marcel Beauchene marched in. With wild curls running rampant and a blue smoking jacket wrapped around his torso, he appeared far from ready. "Ah, at last the sun has deigned to make her appearance."

I groaned and collapsed back onto the bed face-first, clutching a pillow over my head. I heard the swish of luxurious cloth as he slid the curtains open, felt the penetrating light from the window even through my buffer.

"I had to cancel last night, with the condition you were in. Someone must have slipped something into your drink. I do hope you're better now."

I sat up, flinging the pillow aside. "You canceled *Die Josefstadt?*"

"You know me better than that, Vivienne. No, I was forced to cancel your special appearance at the Ungers' dinner party. They were terribly disappointed. One of them in particular."

I heaved a sigh and crawled back under the sheets. "I have no regrets about disappointing Florian Unger." Marcel was the world's most catastrophic matchmaker. With the brain of a mad scientist, his dearest pastime was shoving two things—any two things—together to see what sort of reaction he could achieve. The more explosive the reaction, the more delighted he was with his experiment. Self-indulgent yet agreeable, he often managed to have his way.

Except this time. Poor Florian. His company was almost desirable compared to the apparently drink-induced nightmare I'd endured instead, though. Feeling the chill of it again, a shiver overtook me that made Marcel blink. It had seemed so real. Too real.

"You are well, I hope? You're scheduled to play."

"Quite." Not that he cared terribly how I fared. I was his machine that he must keep well-oiled so I could continue to bring the world what was of most value to him—music.

"Come, get yourself dressed and we'll think no more of it. They're sure to have food waiting for us on the veranda. I hear the lilacs are out."

Lilacs. My favorite. A minuet for the senses. "Very well. And Marcel, you'd better select the gloves for tonight."

I looked at the man's back as he rummaged through my box. I fought him on nearly every decision as my manager, for I hated to be controlled, but I did allow him this.

"How about these, with the little pearl button? You've not worn these since Florence."

"Marcel." I sat up and clasped my arms around myself, glad to feel the worst of the headache receding. "I had a terribly strange dream last night." I fumbled about in my mind for the name of the fictitious asylum. Something with an *H*.

He spun, grasping the pearl-buttoned gloves. "Do leave off talk of that ghostly music woman today, will you? I cannot bear it."

I stiffened. "How did you know of *that* dream? I've never told anyone."

"Of course you have," said another, deeper voice from the shadows of the open doorway. Who was there? "Don't you remember? You told *me*."

I strained to see the tall brown-tweed figure in the shadows. Such a familiar angle to his frame. Familiar stance. "Who's there? Who are you?"

But the new man didn't step into the light. I couldn't quite see his face.

I rose to go to him and felt rough fabric against my skin. I looked down, and it was not my silk wrapper around me but the odd-fitting asylum gown tied with a rope. I scrambled back into the bed to stop my head from spinning and lifted my fingers to ensure they were real. *I* was real.

Red lines on my fingertips. Signs of hard work—the looms, he'd said. Telltale indents that made me more Cora than Vivienne. A breathy sense of panic filled my lungs, and I looked to Marcel, but he had vanished.

I took in the blue damask furniture on my left, but when I looked to the right it was a flat surface two inches from my face, stained and smelly. A padded asylum wall. I jerked my gaze back to the other side, but the generous damask was replaced by a heavy studded door with bars over a high window. The airy setting of that room in Vienna was sucked away, leaving the heavy reality of the asylum sitting on my chest. I tried to shake this dream off too, head moving back and forth on the pillow, but the gray walls refused to dissolve, to give way to my reality of home and safety— because this *was* my reality and I *wasn't* safe. I'd fallen asleep and dreamed Vienna. Dreamed Rosamond.

My heart pounded. I lay there, still and panicked, my senses limp with an unnatural sleep and the haze of dreams. I felt my tenuous hold on reason slipping.

My shoulders and back were stiff, and a painful pressure chafed at my wrists. I strained to see what held me—leather straps. I was chained to this awful bed that reeked of vomit and stale moisture. Frantically I took in the whole of that square confinement, the small cell of my nightmare. A dreadful purgatory. I turned my face to the side and wept. *God, what has happened? Why have you left me here? You knew what they'd do—why didn't you stop me from coming back?*

I began to shake.

I planned to do more with my life than simply my charitable Christian duty. So much more. Didn't you see? I'd planned to give my whole life to helping the weakest ones. To rescuing women. You'd have done the same. Why do you repay me this way? Several deep breaths, then out poured the question I'd managed to shove down through years of motherless solitude, a lifetime of living under my father's cruelty—*Why me?*

18

Truly there would be reason to go mad were it not for music.

~Peter Ilyich Tchaikovsky

I lied. The moment that bland-faced aid opened the door and asked if I was ready to cooperate, I lied. But the deception earned me release from that wretched box and a harsh scrub in icy water. Both of these felt necessary to the continuance of my life. The aid, whom I hadn't seen before, tugged me along with an air of annoyance into a dark room with loose and broken tiles and several metal tubs lying in wait, grumbling about the mess I'd made of my clothes.

I stood, cold and shivering as I stripped, with elusive truths whipping around my tattered mind. I knew what it was to drown then, for I nearly did. Plunged into the dirty water and held there, then yanked by my hair, sputtering and gasping, I was chilled enough to believe I'd never be warm again. "Say you're not a pianist."

"What?"

"Doctor's orders. Say it—*I am not a pianist.*"

"I will not lie!"

Down under the icy water I went, hair floating around my face, until I forced my head above water again and drank in the air.

"Say it."

"It's not true."

Down I plunged again, bubbles escaping my mouth, which had barely closed after my angry words. Seconds ticked. My heart thumped. Panic tightened. I tried to force my head up, but her wiry arm held it down. Finally she pulled me up, and I gagged and coughed on the sting of inhaled liquid.

"You're making it harder on yourself, girl. Say it and I'll be able to let you out."

"How dare you—"

With a grunt she shoved me back under and held me there until I scrambled, clawing and scratching for air. I came up spitting mouthfuls of water. It was inside me too. Every cough tore through my lungs and made me need to cough more. I couldn't catch my breath.

"Say it, or I'll hold you longer."

"You'll kill me!" I sputtered and gasped.

"People die all the time." But a flicker of doubt shadowed her features. Perhaps she was new. Not fully evil, but one who followed orders. Just as controlled and confused as many of the patients here. The fight went out of me as I caught a few breaths of steady air.

"Well?"

She made to shove me down and I clamped onto the sides of the tub. "I'm not, I'm not."

"Not *what?*"

"I'm not a pianist." How odd those words tasted, dulling my very soul. Pulling me down into the pit of this place like mud around my ankles so I might never leave.

She narrowed her eyes. "Again. Louder."

My whole body shook. "Please. A towel."

"*Louder.* We need to know you mean it." She wiped a bare arm across her forehead. "It's for your own good."

I was angry for her. For me too. This place was a trap. I sat straight and spoke from down low, and I felt those words even as I quaked, teeth chattering. "I am not a pianist." Water dripped from my hair. Moments passed. Then she nodded and dropped a towel just outside the tub. Relief smoothed through her features, but I felt more twisted up than ever.

I was fully aware as I stood naked and shivering on the floor a moment later that I had nothing, not even a scrap of my own clothing. Barely an identity and, after what seemed like several rounds of sedatives in that cell, a delicate grasp on reality. I grabbed for the towel, and my head swam, half-formed thoughts skittering through my swampy mind. I knew only one thing, and I clung to it with the tenacity of one going under. *I have to escape.*

I perched with wet hair on a hard, straight-backed bench in the dayroom with icy water trailing down my back and scanned for a cracked-open window, a door ajar, a hole in the system through which I could slip, but there was nothing. My fleeting attention turned to the patients, these yellow gowns who needed extra monitoring, but my heart sank. They sat wilted to chairs and benches with vacant stares, hope deflated from their bodies. These were the ones not even fit to work. Bodies lived there, but spirits had decayed inside. There would be no help from them.

Nurse Branson set paper, pen, and inkwell before me. "You are lucid?"

I nodded.

"Can you read and write?"

I fisted my hands on my lap and kept my voice even. "Of course."

"Copy the line at the top until the page is full." She had the air of a mother, but one whose maternal nature had dried out. My heart urged me to appeal to her, get her to look at me and see something worth nurturing, but she turned her back and left.

I am not a concert pianist was scrawled across the top of the page. I dangled the pen above the page until a splotch of ink dropped onto it. I was being restrung, the way pianofortes were when the old strings grew brittle and weak. Every morning and evening, I was placed in the dayroom with a paper and ink and asked to write out some statement, and thus release my grip on truth. I numbed my mind against the words and wrote and wrote, until those evil lines swam before my eyes. I drank the tea every night, swallowed pills in the morning, and moved through life, doing what I was told.

I prayed lavishly in those days with each breath in and out, begging, pleading with God in half-formed sentences and scattered utterances. The strong, silent presence of the Almighty, which I had often felt beside me like the warm glow of a hearth, had brought me through the years with Father, but I'd always had my music then too. This prison was stripped of music. My life had been interrupted—stolen from me—and now there was nothing. Only silence.

But then . . . there was Richard.

19

The man that hath no music in himself, Nor is not moved with concord of sweet sounds, Is fit for treasons, stratagems, and spoils; The motions of his spirit are dull as night, And his affections dark as Erebus. Let no such man be trusted.

~William Shakespeare

One week after my release from solitary, I once again saw the face of my would-be rescuer, Richard Cartwright. The nurses were herding the yellow gowns—and me—on an outdoor constitutional, one big mass of circling cattle, when Lew Wiggins appeared, his clean-scrubbed little face popping into my vision on the left.

"Where you been?" His voice was the merest whisper.

I nearly lunged at him with days' worth of pent-up nerves. "What's happened? What have you done?"

"Ain't done nothing." He backed away, frowning. "Your friend's here. That Cartwright fellow."

I blinked. "Richard? Where?"

"Gots to go. Working out in the cemetery today."

"Wait, Lew!"

But the boy was gone, sucked back behind the moving mass of bodies.

Soon, as we filed back inside, Nurse Duffy clamped a hand on my shoulder. "Visitor. Come along."

The simple words electrified me, hastened my steps. I moved toward the main double doors, and that's when I saw it. How had I not noticed before? Richard's trap parked there in the drive. My knees weakened as I stepped over the threshold, but I forced myself forward, chin up, and into a little office. The door closed promptly behind me and Richard's familiar voice was arresting. "Vivvi."

"Oh, Richard." I turned and crossed the room and sank into the chair opposite his, before a big desk.

"I'm sorry I missed you a few days ago. I—"

"Perfectly all right, Richard." I reached for his hand. "It was I who was late, anyway. You're here now. And I'm here. We—"

"You know me, Vivvi. I never go back on my word—not usually."

I pulled my hand back to my lap, looking up into his face. So familiar, that perfectly waved hair over his forehead, the smooth jaw that jutted forward with confidence. Light glinted off a few stray hairs along his jawline. His valet had missed a spot while shaving. I even knew his porter's name was Raoul and that they sometimes argued. Yet I sensed this man, my dearest friend, was suddenly foreign to me. Removed, even though present. My stomach tightened. "What do you mean?"

"I tried to send word, but the boy said he couldn't find you. I'm relieved to come here and find you well."

"I'm *not* well." I began to shake. "They've—"

He took my hand in his again, so warm and strong. Large. Long fingers, perfect for playing the pianoforte or wrapping around the neck of a violin. He never played, though. Richard had no music in him. I'd never sensed that more acutely than I did now. "I don't change my mind often, you know."

"But . . . ?" My heart pounded.

He gave an awkward laugh, and I wrenched my hand away, all the prisming pieces of my memory shifting into focus. I'd been standing at the fence in the laundry yard, letting down every shield.

Telling him everything. *"She's real. Richard, I recognize her. I've seen her before."*

Richard. It was Richard I'd told about seeing Rosamond. Richard standing in the shadows in my Vienna dream. How could I have forgotten? He was the only person in the world I'd ever have told, anyway. The only one I trusted.

Past tense. I would never trust him again. Yet it couldn't be that he was betraying me—that he *had* betrayed me in our escape.

"I think it's best you stay here for now, Vivvi."

"Richard?" I felt faint.

"It's what you need right now."

I bolted up out of the chair, staring at my dear friend who had managed, for the first time in his rather predictable life, to be utterly surprising. "And what about Thornhill? The madman who—"

"*Isn't* a patient here. And wasn't. I looked into it—his name is Timothy Thornhill, and the patient name you gave me is Thomas."

"That proves nothing. He locked me up when I'm perfectly sane. So many patients here are. There's something wrong happening, and I need to prove it."

"All this talk of enemies, some mysterious force after you . . ." He stood and took a step toward me. "Vivvi, I found that portrait. The one of the woman you said you saw."

"Don't you believe me, then? Richard, she's been here and we have to find her. She exists."

He dropped my hand, rubbing the back of his neck as he looked away. "I don't know how to say it, but . . . well, you can't have seen her. And she isn't here." He looked about the hall, then finally at me. "She's dead, Viv. I know she is—I saw her, went to the funeral and looked down at her in that narrow little coffin. You were only three weeks old, but I remember it."

"What do you mean? How do you—"

"It's your mother, Vivvi. Your mother in that oval portrait, second from the end."

Heat slammed against my chest. *My mother.* Rosamond was my *mother?*

"All this about seeing her in your home at night . . ."

"I didn't make it up, Richard. I didn't." My voice was soft. Breathy. "There's some explanation, I'm sure of it. I was thinking that I must have dreamed it, after all. I do that sometimes, you know." It sounded so flimsy though, even to me. I remembered with instant clarity the way the maid's face had looked when I'd described the woman I'd seen playing the pianoforte at night, after the first encounter. *"What an odd little thing you are,"* she'd said, and went on to explain what dreams were. "Yes, it was only a dream," I tried again. "A silly dream after I saw the portrait as a girl. Of course I couldn't have seen her." Which meant she wasn't here. Wasn't in need of rescue.

But now, because of chasing her shadow, *I was.*

What on earth had I been thinking?

A thought struck. "Father's been paying her way. Paying for this ward. She was here—I know it! Someone's hidden her. Or hidden what happened to her. And Richard, there *is* someone setting me up. Playing music at night, leaving letters, making me believe I've gone mad."

Pity stretched his face taut. "Eat well, be healthy, and I'll be round to see you when they say it's time to come home." Those beautifully chiseled lips came near to brush my cheek and I jerked away, feeling his warm breath on my temple. His arm stiffened. "Very well, then." His voice was a whisper, his expression firm. "Hate me if you like, Vivvi. But this is best."

My chest heaved in and out, neck tense clear down to my shoulders. How I wished for a pianoforte that I may bang out my anger upon its keys and let it be felt throughout the house. None of this made sense. None of it. But he should be helping me sort it out. Believing in me. "Richard." I gave him one final chance, standing poised and tall in my rope-belted gown. "Please tell me you're joking. That this is part of some alternate escape plan."

His gaze turned on me with pity. Sheer, sickening *pity.*

"What of our future? All those things you said? We can't have those things if . . ."

He stood for a moment before answering. "You've always had your eccentricities, but I overlooked those for the good traits—your sensible, decent ways. Intelligence. Passion. You were a woman I could respect." He shook his head. "I'm beginning to realize I shouldn't have written off those quirks."

"Are you saying—"

"I don't know." His voice was quiet. "There's never been anyone for me but you. Not ever. But . . . I'm not certain what to think. What I should do."

Nurse Duffy knocked and entered. "Time's up."

I walked backward out of the room with her, and Richard followed, his ever-steady gaze unsettling me. The nurse paused, presumably to allow for final goodbyes, and I pleaded with every ounce of my strength in that look. A hot tear budded in the corner of my eye, and Richard's mask slipped for a brief, vulnerable second, angst creasing his features, then it was back up, decision made. He bowed his head and turned his back on me, leather boots thudding on the front hall tile as he strode toward the door without another glance. Without me.

I fisted my dress and screamed in my head. I fought the tears so hard I shook as I watched his tall figure stride out those doors, then Nurse Duffy was poking my back, urging me along. "It's longer than we allow most patients. You aren't even supposed to have visitors, you know. You ought to be grateful."

As his shadow disappeared out into the sunshine, I wrapped my hands around my upset stomach. We crossed the rug of that great entryway.

Duffy sighed behind me. "Sometimes people who love us do what we need them to do, not what we want." Her words came out in clipped tones with an odd hint of warmth softening the edges.

I forced my spine to straighten and matched my stride to hers.

I'd never been the harmony to his melody, had I? He'd merely sat back and enjoyed what he heard, a song he liked the sound of without really understanding all the little nuances, the complexities and depth of tone. Nor did he care to.

All my eccentricities. As if I was myself in spite of those things, not because of them.

"Bodies are broken at times, and so are minds. Broken people belong in hospital."

I felt numb. Clammy. We headed toward the dining hall. It was lunchtime now, but my insides felt too tight for any sort of food. "I need to use the water closet, if you please."

She veered to the left and paused before the door, shifting her weight. "Be quick about it."

I ladled a spoonful of stew but dripped it back into the bowl before me.

"Buck up now, will you?" Bridget whispered as I sat beside her on the bench that evening at supper. "You survived solitary. You're free now, aren't you?"

I stared straight ahead. "I've never been further from it."

She slipped me her half piece of bread. "Of course you're not free, if you try and escape the way you did. Running only makes them lock you up tighter." She leaned over her potato, lifting knife and fork to saw it into perfect little cubes. "Heaven knows what you were thinking."

"Don't you long to be out? Aren't you desperate for escape?"

She thought about this, chewing slowly as she stared ahead. "For some, there's no escaping what binds us. Whether here or there."

I looked her over, this woman who managed to be content in an asylum. It was as if she chose captivity, because true freedom was beyond her comprehension.

"Perhaps some of us are simply trying to make the best of our circumstances, rather than wasting energy trying to change them.

Me dearest Paul had a way of doing that. Making a home of any place he was."

"I will never stop trying to escape. Never. And this place will *never* be home."

She ate in silence, stealing glances at me. I had no mirror, but I saw reflected in her guarded expression how truly wretched I'd become. I fingered the long strands on my shoulder. Pale and frantic with trembling fingers, I almost didn't blame Richard for leaving me here.

"Bridget," I said softly. "Do you often recall your dreams?"

"Sure, sometimes. Until I get out of bed, of course. Then they're gone."

"And are they . . . very realistic?"

She gave a short laugh. "Not a bit. Winged creatures and falling rocks and a voice that don't work when you call out for help. That's the sum of it usually, and thank the stars, it's nothing like real life."

When they herded us into one massive bare-floored room—the waiting area for the weekly drownings in metal bathtubs—I perched on the edge of the bench along the wall and looked about. There had to be a chink in the armor, a cracked-open window or a misplaced key on a table. "What if I hid in the laundry one afternoon, in those great big piles . . ."

Bridget eyed me with a pitying look and defeat settled over me. Life was suddenly an unfamiliar melody and I was expected to play it.

The music box began again, right beside me this time. The lanky older woman in a lace cap curled around the box each time it played, clinging to it like a life raft. The entire left side of my body was pressed up against hers on the crowded bench, but she didn't even seem to register my presence. She stared straight ahead and saw nothing outside of herself.

She hummed deep in her chest where the remainder of her lived. That was her only sound. No voice, no laughter, just a quiet melody. When some patient screamed in a distant ward, she wound that little crank frantically, then bent over and melted into the music as if she needed to drown out the sounds of Hurstwell.

I understood.

Richard had proposed to me once—or nearly proposed. He'd been the only man who'd truly appreciated me, who'd known me forever. But now he, of all people, believed me mad. Which made it harder to believe I wasn't.

When the dayroom matron had placed the paper before me with a pen and inkwell, I stared down at the words. *I am not a concert pianist.* I took the pen, bracing myself to write the lie again, but all I could think of, with jarring dissonance, was Marcel Beauchene and the odd way he'd put off my return to performing. And the fact that it was my father who'd talked him into taking me on, arranging my engagements, forming my career—and that had ended as soon as Father was no longer alive.

I wrote the line once, then again. Dropping the pen, I curled my fingers into my lap and quietly sobbed. The tears had been pressurized all day, ever since Richard, and now they burst forth in messy paths down my face. I quivered from the force of keeping silent up to now, thankful the orderly's back was to me.

But as I clung to the edge of that bench, a warm hand slid over mine, smooth fingers in a gentle clasp around my shaky ones, the sweetest human contact I'd received in a great while, and it flooded my heart, making a bridge to the island of my lonely soul. I looked over at her, but silent and elegant Anna stared straight ahead with the vacant countenance of a feeble mind.

Within that worn-down body resided a spark of instinctual nurturing. She was a mother—or had been once. And though her mind was shuttered, her heart knew how to mother still.

My heart warmed, a momentary balm over the deeper, lifelong hurt of motherlessness that never seemed to go away. The woman's face was wreathed in a calm smile directed out at the room at large as her fingertips pressed their way over every knuckle and vein on my hand with tender knowing. *So this is what it's like.* I felt every move of her fingers, the serenity flowing from her to me, and I soaked up her mothering hungrily. Greedily. I did not let go until they called for me.

When they shuffled us all into our beds, I almost wished I could be in the long-stay ward so I could listen to Anna's music box and fall asleep in her warm presence. Silence was the loudest sound when one was trying to lay a chaotic mind to rest, and I couldn't stop thinking about that lost old woman, and about Richard, with a pang of agony.

I lay chilled and tearless on my mattress that night, not believing I'd ever fall asleep again, but eventually a leaden tiredness overcame me and I sank into it.

Much later, a hand clamped over my mouth and I woke. I shot up in bed, struggling against hands that seemed to be coming from everywhere in the sleep-hazed darkness, but they overpowered me, my mouth still firmly covered. Before my mind had fully righted itself, I was being hustled out of bed and toward the far wall, stumbling over the cold floorboards.

20

You believe happiness to be derived from the place in which once you have been happy, but in truth it is centered in ourselves.

~Franz Schubert

It was impossibly dark. We had somehow melted into the paneled wall, which opened in one spot, and now I was stumbling between my faceless kidnappers through a dark, short passageway. I bent over to keep from hitting my head, and they hurried me along with whispers and shushing until I thought I'd scream for want of answers. "Where on earth am I?"

A woman's voice answered. "Priest's hole. There's one in most of the great houses, you know." It was Bridget, off to my left.

"They found a skeleton here once," said another high-pitched voice nearby. Clara.

"Oh, leave off. They did not," hissed Kat.

"Sure they did. Put one of them priests in hiding, then something happened, and they couldn't come back for him. Got trapped here."

"Oh, that's just a rumor. Any man could have gotten out if he'd wanted to."

"Yes, but he wouldn't—not if he'd been threatened on pain of death to stay put."

"Hush up, the both of you," Bridget said. "We've no idea who can hear us in this old tunnel."

I breathed dusty air. "Why are *we* in it? I'm no priest."

"You'll see."

The other ladies laughed, and we shuffled forward. At last the corridor released us through another door into a wide-open room with moth-eaten curtains and dusty crystal chandeliers filled with drip-laden candles. Moonlight fell in silver streaks across a check-ered floor . . . and highlighted the most magnificent rosewood pianoforte I'd ever seen.

I could almost feel the music vibrating off the paneled walls, a nocturne to capture the wonder of nighttime in a forgotten old room. I held my breath and approached the great instrument, a full grand pianoforte, in the glowing moonlight, as if nearing the royalty who must have owned such a piece. I ran my palm over its surface, appreciating its rich finish and perfectly curved sides. What would it sound like? Perhaps deep and throaty to match its regal bearing, but the smooth wood and finely crafted inlay spoke of a gentler side too.

I turned back to Bridget, who stood with arms folded between half a dozen other patients all watching me eagerly. Bridget cocked a small smile. "Perhaps you can think of it as home—at least for now."

With rock-hard pain melting into tenderness, I strode back to her and embraced the slender woman. She tensed instantly, and I whispered "thank you" near her ear as she responded with stiff, awkward pats. I stepped back to look again at the pianoforte, then at my kidnappers. Tears budded as I looked across each pale countenance brimming with smiles, and all I could do was stand in the center of that dusty room, hands over my face, and sob.

A soft voice broke the moment. "Why don't you give it a play?"

"I think it's sufficient simply to stand here and stare at it." How hungry I'd been for such beauty.

"Isn't it a good enough one?" Clara's round face was pinched with concern.

"It's the most exquisite thing I've seen in forever." I walked over to it again, my bare feet sweeping clean spots on the dusty floor. "A six-octave, triple-stringed Broadwood with a metal plate, brass inlays, and fine matched ivory keys." I lifted the lid, propping it on its stand, and ran a hand over the strings, surprised they were in decent condition despite the neglect. Dusty and loose, with hammers that were nearly bare, but present and whole. Someone had cared for it not long ago.

"Broadwood. Is that good?" Clara leaned forward eagerly.

I smiled. "It's said that Beethoven, who owned an Erard, treasured the richly textured sound of his Broadwood even more."

"Then why not play a bit for us?"

I glanced through the tall, barred window streaming with moonlight. "They'll hear me. I shouldn't like to make trouble again so soon."

Bridget shook her head. "This is the east wing. An addition built onto exterior walls at least four feet thick. Come now, give it a try."

Despite her assurance, I closed the lid to quiet the sound, then walked around to the keyboard. Resting my finger on one ivory key, I felt the weight of it against my touch and shivered, unable to voice the unreasonable fear churning inside. A simple hymn rolled from my memories to the keyboard: *Rock of ages, cleft for me. Let me hide myself in thee . . .*

The familiar notes plunked gently into the room, despite the gentle jar of a slightly out-of-tune and run-down instrument, and I delighted in the sacred piece. A shiver rode up my arm at the last note, and I pulled back, looking up at the women huddled together in silence, drinking in the modest melody.

"Now play something more," urged Clara. "Something you'd play in one of those important performances."

Performances. A sickening uncertainty returned as I recalled Marcel's words and that evasive look. *"Perhaps you should use this time to practice, to polish your skills."*

And the asylum copy work, papers filled with the words Marcel seemed to know but I could not grasp: *I am not a concert pianist. I am not a concert pianist.*

Fraud. I was a fraud. It had all been a sham and I was nothing.

Fear tightened about my throat, and I rose from the stool. "Another time, perhaps. It needs a thorough tuning and so much repair—"

"And you need a project." Bridget smiled at me. "Now you know how to come here if you're awake at night. Can it be fixed?"

I ducked under the lid again, feeling the strength of the strings that could easily bear the weight of a tuning, checking the board for cracks or weakness. "It appears solid in all the important ways. But I haven't tools or—"

The worn groove in my fingertip caught, supposedly the result of working at a loom, but it was not. It was this—restoration. Pianofortes. I'd never seen a loom in my life. With a smile I fitted all five fingers over those strings, feeling the familiar grooves and running my hand up and down the length of them. It was who I was. No matter what they said, or made me write, I was still myself and they were wrong about who that was.

I turned back to the motley little group and smiled. "You have given me the most lovely gift I've ever had in my life. I don't know how to thank you."

"You can start by bringing it back to what it should be," Bridget said with a matter-of-fact smile.

I nodded. "I'll see what can be done about it. Seems such a waste, leaving it to rot." I lifted the lid again and settled the stand back inside, resting the lid onto the case. As I did, the clock in the tower bonged once, twice, three times.

Bridget's arms shot out to the side and she froze. "Shhh."

The women quieted and my stomach flipped.

"Twelve, three, and six, twelve, three, and six," Bridget mumbled, wringing her hands. "Every three hours they check our ward. Twelve, three, and six."

I swallowed twice. We stood in the shadows and waited, listening for sounds from the main house. The candle Bridget had lit flickered over the paneled walls as we waited to be caught, but no one came.

"Just keep out of sight if you hear someone, and remember the pattern," Bridget whispered. "Twelve, three, and six. When you hear the clock strike, stop moving and stay quiet. They'll check the wards, then it'll be safe again."

"Should we go back? We should go back." Clara fidgeted with the fabric of her gown.

"Here, help me get it covered again." Bridget fetched the sheet rumpled on the floor, and together we spread it over the grand instrument. "Had a cover when we found it, but we wanted you to see it straightaway all uncovered."

"Someone loved it once." I turned my attention back to the great instrument and ran my hand over the wood as we drew the cover over it to put it to bed.

"Place used to be a conservatory. A boarding school for musicians and the like. They built this addition just to house the instruments. A shame what it's become, all quiet and dull."

I inhaled and laid a hand over the covered instrument, feeling the warmth of friendship around me, and gave a wobbly smile. "There's still music in these walls."

My fleeting thought as we left was of the very distant music I'd heard on that sleepless night on duty. There *was* a pianoforte here. Perhaps I hadn't imagined the music after all.

But who had played it?

———

Bridget pulled me back in the dark tunnel while the others went on, and we turned a different way and up a few rickety wooden steps. "The priests used this as a lookout to see when the sentry seeking them out had gone and it was safe to come out of hiding." We climbed up directly into a high clock tower that was open to the night air. Four clockfaces as tall as me stood sentry over the vast moors beyond. I watched the clock mechanism click and turn, driving the hands around.

Bridget looked over the ticking gears in the center of the room, relaxing as she watched all the wheels turning each other and the rods leading up to the clock. "I like it here." Bridget settled herself onto a bench, body slumped against the wall. Her foot tapped the rough wood floor in the slow, steady rhythm of the clock. It seemed to have melted her nervous energy.

"Surely if there's a priest hole, it leads to an escape, doesn't it?"

Bridget shook her head, eyes closed. "The tunnel has a door on each floor, and it lets out in that music room. Used to be a tiny little space for him to hide, barely a closet, but it was knocked down and expanded by the conservatory into that great room. And there's no exit from there except the main doors into the front hall, but those are locked up tight."

I heaved a giant sigh and settled back against the wall.

"Before you go making any more excuses, there are tools up here to work on the clock. Plenty of them. You can help yourself, then bring them back when you're done."

I sat still, delighting in the steady beat resembling the metronome of my childhood practices, taking comfort as if leaning against a mother's heart.

"How did you find this place? The addition, the tunnel, the passageway to the clock tower."

She shrugged. "I stare at the paneling in our ward. Isn't much else to look at when you can't sleep. The paneling was all fifteen inches by fifteen inches except that one—it was thirteen and a half by fifteen. Not quite square. Anything that doesn't fit the pattern is special."

I looked over her bright face, closed up here at Hurstwell like a candle in a closet. "How very true that is." I shifted on the rough wooden seat. "How is it that you all know about these tunnels and the staff does not?"

Bridget leaned her head back and closed her eyes again. "Because they've never looked. They come and go as they please. But we are left to claw at every space and wall for a moment of relief from our lives."

"You've given me that tonight, you know. Relief."

She angled her face toward me, smiling and leaning back on her elbows. "So've you."

"I've given you nothing but extra trouble. I saw what you did for me that day in the laundry."

She blew hair off her face, thoughtful for a moment. "I'm broken inside, like a clock missing a single gear, and nobody lets me forget it. But you look at me like I was a whole person already. Even if I never get fixed."

"You're not broken—just put together differently." I looked at her troubled face. "Who else would have seen patterns in the panels? If not for you, I'd be suffering miserably, one wall away from the most beautiful instrument I've ever seen, never knowing it was here."

She flashed a half smile my way, then dropped her gaze. "Also had bouts of melancholia."

I stared at this woman, trying to wrap such a word around her being.

"Dodged it off and on me whole life, but once I had me that babby I always wanted, one of me own, I couldn't move fast enough to dodge the wave. Socked me like a load of feed." She shifted under the weight of what she'd silently carried for so long.

"What's it like? Having melancholia, I mean."

She stared at the floor. "Heard talk of the seaside once. It's something like that—a wave that sucks you down, then eventually it lets you up again. Doesn't matter what you believe about the Almighty or anything else. You can't climb out. No one can pull you out. Just has to roll over you till it passes, then you stand up and keep going. Until the next one. Then, one day when me body felt better, that wave wouldn't let me up. Just set right here on me chest and stayed."

"Couldn't you remind yourself of all the times the wave has passed? Look forward to what was to come?"

She shook her head. "When the wave hits, you're underwater. What's true suddenly doesn't seem so true anymore, what you used to love isn't the least bit lovely, and you could vow the world had gone flat. The air is weighted, keeping you down on your bed, and you have to push the weight off you just to get up and start the day."

"I never would have guessed it. I don't see a bit of melancholy in you. In fact, you've always seemed quite the opposite."

"Those that have it the worst, we're the ones fightin' against it the hardest. Only, we lose the fight on the inside."

"I'm so sorry, Bridget."

She shrugged again in her affable way.

I looked down, laced my fingers up in the fabric of my gown. "I think I understand a little. The silence here, the lack of music . . . it has been heavy on my soul. How I wish there was music."

"You've got music wherever you go, Vivienne Mourdant, inside your being, and you'll come out all right. Music's the enemy of melancholia. Your freedom."

"Sometimes." I wrapped my arms around myself. "Other times it lands you here."

Bridget smiled as the wind tickled her face with her hair. "There's music even here. You have only to find it—or make it for yourself."

21

Off with you! You're a happy fellow, for you'll give happiness and
joy to many other people. There is nothing better or greater than
that!

~Ludwig van Beethoven

You should marry again, Doctor.

Those words hung in Mitchell Turner's memory as he strode
out to the gardens in the early morning. Somehow Nurse Branson,
head matron of the wards, saw him as a sort of patient himself,
and this, his remarriage, the mark of his cure. Nothing else would
prove to her with any certainty that he'd healed from what had
happened to his wife.

Missing her had been crippling at first, and his regrets were still
a heavy weight, but time had mixed a sweetness with the pain too.
Sweetness that had begun to eclipse much of the hurt on the good
days. To be around Dahlia was to experience delight, for she was
full of it, and her joy was contagious. That's what he thought of
now when he remembered her, and he smiled faintly to himself.
It faded only when a wave of regret followed the sweet memories.

He plucked a little purple flower and turned it over in his fingers.
How he adored the way she'd always tucked a little sprig behind

one ear—elfin, it had seemed. Lovely. She'd woven these longer sprigs into her waist-length hair. He wished he could do so for her now—or that he'd stopped to do it then. So much that had seemed small and unimportant then was now all he valued. It felt as though they'd been spinning in a chaotic waltz, and when it came time to dip her back, he'd dropped her.

He ambled through the garden, carefully selecting blooms one by one, lingering over the feel and scent of them to be sure he had the right flower each time. *In honor of you, Dolly.* They were, after all, *her* flowers. She'd convinced him that gardens would be a grand idea, a taste of what she'd left behind in their little hamlet. "Perhaps they won't even grow here," she'd said as she threw handfuls of seeds about the marshy soil. No one else had bothered to tend the yard before, but she had insisted the patients be allowed to grow something so the work of their hands might bring about life. She had an insatiable hunger for beauty, for flowers, as if she were at home among her own when around them. "How lovely it'll be to wake up in the springtime and see what has chosen to grow. It will be a most wonderful surprise."

He looked toward the bed of azaleas, and he could see her. See her crouched before the dirt, turning her hands in the soil, toiling over flowers she wouldn't live to enjoy.

He left a long sprig of wisteria on her grave just outside the gardens, then he carried the rest up to the third floor. It had become a Friday ritual, a calm spot in his week and the joy of the patients'. *I think you'd approve.*

Up in the long-stay ward where he reigned over his tiny kingdom, Mitchell walked into the dayroom to the sound of happy chittering and excitement over the bundle in his arms, and he made a great show of delivering each flower to the right woman. A daisy for the quietest one, a complexly petaled rose for another. Anna received a sweet little viola, which she tucked with a pleased smile beside the others inside her music box. "That's nice, that's nice," she mumbled absently, then drifted back to wherever she'd lost herself.

On down the rows he went, saving the hardest for last. He then handed the bright and open zinnia to the silent patient huddled to one side in the wheeled chair, hoping the flower would inspire her to resemble it. "Good morning, Violet. You should sit by the window and have some sunshine."

No answer. He wasn't expecting one. The mere sight of her, vacant and disconnected, fractured his soul.

"They tell me you had a bad night again. Nightmares, is it?"

Her muscles flinched beneath her dress, but she said nothing. This patient had him by the heart more than most—perhaps because of her flower name, like Dahlia's. Or maybe because of the many other ways the woman resembled her. She was so young, so helpless, with that very same wistful little-girl look Dahlia had possessed.

"I trust you'll have a better night tonight, Violet."

He placed the offering beside her as he always did, and she glanced at it, looking up at him, and then away. Neither the man nor the flower held any meaning in her distant world, but he did it as if making an offering to Dahlia.

No one—*no one*—would be abandoned in this place. Not ever again.

Before Mitchell's arrival, Violet had been isolated for so long that she'd forgotten how to talk, how to be human. She'd been animated and troublesome once, even frantic he'd heard, but that was in the distant past. Now she had fits of panic in which she rocked passionately back and forth, sometimes screaming in horror as if someone tried to pull her soul right out of her body . . . or she sat in this dejected, eerie silence. There was no in-between.

Staff had taken to locking her up alone most days, seeing no benefit of having her amongst the others when her unpredictable outbursts disturbed them, but Mitchell wouldn't have it. Her eruptions were relatively contained, not injuring anyone, and isolation wasn't good for a soul. Yet the small freedom of being out in this room only seemed to make her quieter—even more edgy and withdrawn.

Delicate, withered Violet was one of the few patients who'd ever made him wonder if some were incurable. Which in turn made him question the usefulness of spending his life in this place, of whether or not he was doing any good at all by remaining. Nothing penetrated her dulled mind, and she was nearly feral. No amount of effort on his part encouraged her more human side—and indeed, Thornhill had insinuated she hadn't one. Yet he couldn't bring himself to give up on her. Perhaps the day he did would be the last before a breakthrough was about to occur.

Today was not that day.

Heaving a sigh, he turned back to his patients. Such unique people they were, so wholly themselves at every moment. A thought flashed through his brain—Dahlia never would have given up on them. Not even Violet.

Then as he made his way into the corridor, turned the corner past the dayroom and wards where he had taken Mary Jo with that woman Cora Fletcher, another thought dawned. *Neither would she.* The flame-haired musician had swooped into this place, igniting in him what he hadn't even realized was still there to light. She couldn't help but do so.

Yet neither she nor Dahlia could help the patients at Hurstwell. Not anymore.

He turned, forcing himself to walk toward the end of the corridor and the farthest solitary confinement cell. An unexplainable force had always repelled him from it, as if a ghost lingered there.

Dahlia hadn't been well at Hurstwell—anyone could see that. Her pink flesh had grown ashy, the singsong voice tightened to desperate squeaks and pleas. *"Please listen, Mitch. I'm not mad. I just need to be free of this place. Please. Don't let me die here."*

But Thornhill had convinced him this was best. That treatment was necessary, that everyone begged to leave at one time or another, but a cure would be impossible if he gave in and removed her from Hurstwell. Thornhill had made nearly the same argument just a few days ago, when he'd made use of the isolation chambers once again. As Mitchell now stood in the narrow shaft of light before that closed door, skin clammy with sweat, anger swelled up in him. Anger at so many . . . including himself. Regret pooled in every quiet place of his soul, burning hot as lava.

He made a hard pivot and walked stiffly to the supply closet. Gathering wood and hammer, a small bucket of nails, he marched back through the corridor and slammed a board across one of the isolation ward doors. With nails clamped in his mouth, he anchored the wood in place and hammered all his anger into it.

Man had come up with many wretched ways to punish one another, and this barbaric entrapment had to be one of the worst. In the depths of pain, nothing served the sufferer less than being alone. Life had become a race, with those who were able-bodied pushing those who weren't out of the way so they could get on with it.

He'd secured two cells, then a presence approached from behind and the hairs on his neck stood up. He froze, lowering his hammer.

"I used to be like you once." The low voice of his superior bounced off the walls as he neared. "I thought I'd save the world and completely overthrow a broken system. Trouble is, there's nothing to replace it with."

"Anything is better than this."

Dr. Thornhill came to stand before him, shadows making dark half-moons under his eyes. How aged he looked. How worn from years of asylum work. "Even small liberties in the wrong hands can actually be a severe cruelty in the end. A risk."

"You've stopped seeing them as people, Thornhill. To you, they've become mere bodies to maintain and control, nothing more."

"Believe me, I see them as far more. Which is precisely why I operate this asylum as I do."

"How can it possibly be best to—"

"Because it is!" The snapping words echoed down the hall. His jaw was taut. "Someday you will stand back and survey the wreckage of what was, the utter devastation caused by a patient who only the day before seemed perfectly sane and deserving of every liberty he'd been given. Then you too, Doctor, will question your instincts and each drop of compassion you ever showed, and you'll start to look at them the way every other alienist has learned to do—as broken and beyond repair. Disease to be mitigated and contained." He was trembling as he spun and marched back down the hall, disappearing into the stairwell at the end.

Mitchell pictured again, like a flash of lightning, the trapped creature fighting her captors. Yet she'd seemed so slight in his arms when she'd collapsed there. These piles of stone and grayness were crushing her as they'd crushed Dahlia, extinguishing her beautiful life without a thought to its immense value. He shivered. "I don't think I'm capable of seeing them the way you do," Mitchell said to the empty corridor where Thornhill had stood, and left the boards in place over the first two chambers. Sunlight streamed down onto the gray floor from the high window, a single bright spot in a cavern of shadows.

22

Ah, it seemed impossible to leave the world until I had brought
forth all that I felt was within me.

~Ludwig van Beethoven

"A message for you, music lady." Bridget marched by in the laundry
with a basket of wet clothing balanced on her hip. "From the slop
boy. He says to tell you, 'End of the year at the earliest.'"

I lost my grip on the crank and stumbled back. "December?" It
was only June now. Perhaps early July. I clutched my gown, counting the weeks. Months. Panic rose like the tide, swirling around my
neck. I'd sent Lew Wiggins back to Marcel Beauchene's house to
find out from his staff when he was expected back, and this wasn't
the response I'd hoped for.

I'd been counting on his rescue. Waiting for it. Marcel Beauchene
had rescued me once before, and it had been, as everything he did,
a memorable affair. Because of a misunderstanding, I'd been left
shivering and alone at the age of eleven on the steps of Théâtre du
Palais-Royal on a gusty, rainy night. The driver believed I would be
returning with Marcel, and the second cellist had mistakenly told
Marcel he'd already seen me leave with the driver for a celebration
afterward, so there I stood, wondering why no one had come for me.

A rather soft-spoken, kindly man had approached me, speaking in languid French and pulling me along by the hand as if I should be going with him. Surprised, confused, I'd gone along, half thinking he'd come in place of my normal driver. We hadn't left the glow of the flickering streetlight when Marcel Beauchene, who had at last discovered the oversight, came flying out of the shadows with a savage growl, cape fluttering and fist leading the way. One hit and the Frenchman was scrambling to escape, leaving Marcel to put his arm around me and march me toward the rented barouche with all his usual grumbles.

"I didn't think you were coming," I said when we'd been seated in the coach.

"What do you take me for?" There was a snap in his words as he jammed the lap blanket tight around my legs. "Of course I came for you. Don't I always?"

Warmth seeped around the chill inside and drew forth a smile. It was the first time I was truly aware that he cared about me. That he'd be there to swoop in and rescue me, the way a father might.

But now . . . December. I shifted from one swollen foot to the other, mopping my forehead with my apron. I'd never grow used to the way the fabric scratched my skin. Never grow used to so many things at Hurstwell.

Bridget puffed out a breath, bobbing for gowns in the basket and pinning them to the line. Her rhythm was steady as a metronome, clicking off the beats. "It's no palace, but this isn't the worst place to be for a time now, is it? You're safe and fed. And you have a pianoforte," she added with a whisper.

"You don't understand. I have a life outside of this place, an entire mission yet to be started, and a whole host of people who need me." I took a deep, shuddering breath, thinking of all the women I had once planned to rescue. "I must get back to it, Bridget. I've been waiting so long for the chance. It's what I was meant to do."

"Not right now, you ain't, because you're here. And nothing happens without the Almighty's say-so."

A note of dissonance in my heart. "I cannot understand, Bridget. Why would he ever want to stop me from serving? From rescuing?"

"He hasn't stopped you at all. Just relocated you."

"To a rathole." I yanked on the crank, spraying water on us both.

She wiped her face with her sleeve and untangled another gown to feed through. "What good's a candle out in pure daylight, then? You tell me that."

I froze, hand stiff and sore on the wooden handle.

"A light such as yours should be taken into the utmost darkness, you know." That odd little man from the parlor gathering had said that. About asylums, no less. An odd prickling sensation climbed my skin. What had he to do with this? Nothing, most likely.

Yet I couldn't shake the memory of his face.

Bridget pushed my hand aside and put all her weight into turning that crank. "We alternate so's no one gets too tired."

I gritted my teeth as I leaned down for more wet laundry, still fighting in my spirit against her words. "I'm not bringing any light to Hurstwell. All I do here is laundry."

She shrugged. "That's your choice." Scooping up a handful of pins, she began throwing the wrung-out linens over the line and stabbing the pins in place. "Alls I know is the dark has lasted far too long here. And you have daylight bottled up in you."

I smiled faintly. "Bridget, where'd you come by all your wisdom?"

"Me dearest Paul, that's where. He spent more time locked up than I have. Good enough fellow, though. Writes the best letters."

I blinked. "Your wise friend is . . . at Hurstwell?"

"Prison. Well, not anymore. Hard to be in prison when you're dead."

"Oh." I squeezed a tunic and shook it out. "I'm sorry. How long has he been gone?"

She stared at me like I was mad. "About two thousand years. But you'd know that if you read the Bible."

I pinched back a smile. Ah. *That* Paul. Dear Saint Paul of the

New Testament. Never had I heard a body speak of him in such personal terms, as if he still lived. "No wonder you're so wise, learning from him."

"He's my favorite. Always writes his letters the same way, greeting, truth, closing. Righteousness. Love. He had his patterns, the same as me. Fine man, he was. Full of fire and passion . . . and imprisoned."

"And an encourager, all the while." I threw her a meaningful smile.

She shrugged. "There was only so much about Paul a person could lock up. He was still Paul, and you're still you." She turned from her linens and looked me in the face. "Make your music for us, Vivienne Mourdant."

I swallowed, pausing in the silence. How odd it was to finally hear my own name.

I turned back to my work and Bridget eyed me. "You don't think we're worth it, do you? Admit it. You believe there isn't any point to improving our lot because we're paupers. Mad ones to boot."

"I've nothing against anyone here."

Yet my own words returned to strike me with a powerful blow. *"Why would I ever want to waste my time playing for an asylum?"*

I shivered and looked at the face of my friend but found the lack in myself—not her.

"I wouldn't even know how to begin helping all the patients at Hurstwell. I'm a musician, not a doctor."

She looked ahead, her face drawn. "What's it like, to have a gift like that? To be able to give it to the world anytime you please?"

I watched the longing etched into her face.

"Don't have anything to offer that sweet babby, when it come right down to it. Not a thing. What if babby girl was a mite touched in the head, like her ma? Couldn't bear to watch her walk through it. And if she isn't, what would she want with a ma like me? But I'd give her beautiful music if I could. A little something to express what's inside me, so's she knows how I feel about her when I haven't got nothing to say."

My heart stretched in endless directions, a longing to connect this woman to her dream. To spark a bit of light in Hurstwell's darkness. It wouldn't take much, really.

December. That was an incredibly long time to sit still here doing nothing. We worked silently for a while, alternating at the crank, then I heaved a heavy sigh. "I'll need an abrasive sponge and some water, maybe a few wrenches for tuning. And plenty of rags."

She cocked a smile. "I can manage that."

———

I started slipping out by myself after two nights of restless sleep, feeling my way along that passage and coming face-to-face with that glorious Broadwood bathed in moonlight. I brought candle stubs and the items Bridget had filched from the kitchen and perched on the bench, tracing the gold lettering across the front of the piece.

A Broadwood. The case was miraculously intact on all sides, and there was no detachment from the base or shrinkage of the baseboards. The bracing under the soundboard seemed whole and firm. Blessedly, John Broadwood built pianofortes that were simple in design but superior in craftsmanship. Besides that, someone had cared for it in recent years. Someone who knew how.

I lifted the lid, marveling at the way each piece fitted together so perfectly as if it were all hewn from the same piece of wood. That's when I saw it—a hand-carved signature just inside the casing with a flourish of flowers around it. *J. Broadwood*, it read.

Signed!

A rarity indeed, yet here it sat to rot away in this place where value was so often miscalculated and beauty misunderstood.

On the most torrential days with Father, the maid named Jessie used to sneak me a small cup of fruit while I was locked in the larder, and I'd never tasted anything so sweet. I delighted in those few bites, in the fact that no matter what Father did to me, he couldn't take away my delight in that fruit in that moment.

That's precisely what the pianoforte became for me in those long summer days at Hurstwell. It grew more manageable to sit straight and quiet on those hard benches, to walk about with my head down, to swallow the slimy cabbage and old bread without complaint when I knew I could return to the candlelit room at the end of the day and slowly draw out the beauty of an old, forgotten relic. Several nights a week I slipped into that room for an hour or two, gingerly scrubbing rust from the strings and cleaning dust and grime off every crevice I could reach.

It breathed life back into my gray soul, watching this thing of beauty be uncovered and restored to brilliance. In time, rotted spots on hammers were replaced by carefully filed-down scrap wood, the cloth under the key levers was cut out and paper spacers put in its place to level the keys. I'd used a small wrench to carefully tighten each pin and bring the strings into tune, grateful for the exacting father who had taught me to tune nearly perfectly by ear, and thus I sank quite easily into the simple tasks that had made up so much of my life before.

Things were different than I'd envisioned for my life, but I'd let circumstances paralyze me for too long when before they had always mobilized me. Inspired me to act. My heart still wished to pursue normalcy, freedom, and my idealized set of circumstances, but this was my locked larder now, and merely enduring it would be a waste of life and heart.

Summer became fall, and in that abandoned wing a sense of normalcy returned, an undercurrent of music stirring within me. I hummed that enchanting forgotten melody from my dreams as I worked, picturing Rosamond's sweet face, head tipped with lips pinched in a secret smile that made her eyes shine.

Those days many of us were shuffled outside to clean up the gardens, collecting leaves and trimming down roses. There was a great deal of freedom in this work, for the yard was Dr. Turner's domain and the nurses did his bidding outdoors.

I watched Dr. Turner across the short hedge of roses, present among us yet somehow absent too. Lost in his own troubles. How familiar that figure seemed to me now, yet I knew him so little. Only through his actions, his bearing toward the patients, could I catch a hint of his melody.

I felt disloyal to Richard at first, focusing thus on the doctor, but then I stopped and realized how much time had passed—how much life had been lived since he'd been there. And how I felt a different person now anyway, with scales falling from my vision week by week, and a heart softening in new ways. I closed my eyes and breathed in the air spiced with autumn and spoke to my companion. "It seems like an eternity since I've come . . . and no time at all."

Bridget stood, wiping her arm across her brow. "Comin' round to the place, are you?"

I shrugged, tossing another armload of leaves onto my basket and stuffing them down. "For now. I've become used to it, but I cannot help but think every day about what I'm missing out there." I looked down at my hands, cracked and dry. How removed my former life seemed, how surreal. Just another of my vivid dreams.

Nurses appeared at the asylum doors, opening them and ushering out the long-stay patients, who limped, shuffled, and stumbled out into the grassy expanse for their airing out. They marched in a large, odd-shaped circle with the slower ones on the inside, the more able-bodied ones rounding out the edges. Something softened in me when I spotted Anna wrapped around her music box as she shuffled forward, a lost look upon her face.

Bridget swept up another armload of leaves from beneath an ancient beech tree and dropped them in the wheelbarrow. "Did I ever tell you about my Michael? A widower with four of his own when I met him, and not a woman in five parishes would have him because of it, until me. We've been wed nigh on eight years now, and he's a good 'un."

"You've not said much about him." I didn't push—Bridget had a way of unraveling the facts as she talked if a person only let her. "Do you miss him very much?"

"Of course I do." She paused to shove the cloth back onto her hair and sighed. "That man can melt me from the inside with a look. He has me heart on a platter. But it weren't always that way. He were a disappointment at the start, you know."

"Was he terribly difficult?"

"Terribly quiet, is all. Well see, he ain't me big brother. He's no fiddle-playin', knee-slappin', big-laugh man full of life and fun. Such a disappointment, and never once in those early years did I look him full in those chocolate eyes and feel their own unique magic. Fool thing it was, wasting the first six years mournin' the way I thought things should be. Nearly missed the blessin' of what was." She leveled a meaningful look at me. "It's like they say—clouds don't stop the sun shining, just you from seeing it."

But what sort of blessings can a person find in an asylum? I paused to look across the gardens to where Anna plodded along, her hunched back to me. One step away from the catacombs, they'd said.

The catacombs, that wretched cellar level of Hurstwell where they kept the volatile ones—anyone who might escape or who disturbed the healing environment too greatly. As they claimed Anna did when she couldn't be soothed quickly enough. They were afraid of what she'd do to those around her, they'd said, and how her panic affected the entire ward with every storm.

My chest squeezed at the notion of this lacy little woman shoved out in the dark where no one would hear her cry out when she was afraid. I still felt the flicker of warmth where her hand had rested on mine, knobby fingers tracing along my knuckles.

As I stared, Anna bumped into a nurse and the woman spun on her, barking something. Anna cowered and wound her box, but the nurse wrestled it away and smashed it on the flagstone walk. Anna shot forward with surprising strength, a guttural scream erupting from her chest as she fell onto the grass and wept, sweeping up the pieces of the splintered box.

I moved toward them, but the nurse yanked Anna up by the arm and propelled her to a bench and left her cowering, a fawn without its mother. Anna fell onto the bench and stared at that smashed music box, sitting forward as if compelled to go to it, to save it, but not moving.

When the nurse departed, I knelt before the shaking woman and held out the little bouquet of wildflowers I'd gathered. She looked up, blinking as she registered the gesture. She took them and I wrapped my hand around hers to form a gentle fist around the stems.

Her chin trembled, and her voice sounded distant. "No more music. No more." For a moment she held my gaze, tenderness mixed with sorrow. All at once the sweetness of the dream, of the way that woman—whoever she was—had looked at me as I entered the rose room, washed over me with delight. But then in a flash it was over. "Too bad, too bad." Anna's attention drifted away, and the absent, slightly troubled look settled over her face again.

Her other hand came around mine and she began that gentle probing of my hand. She stared off into the distance but continued her skilled caress, learning the contours of my hand by feel. She moved up my arm, then to my face, touching my cheek and smoothing my hair away from my eyes. Then she took one of the small purple flowers I'd given her and tucked it with a sad, distant smile behind my left ear and patted my cheek.

I smiled, just a little. Bridget was right—there were blessings even here. Small drops of goodness not to be found anywhere else. In no other place had I ever known what it was to have a mother.

I rose and went to collect the shards of her music box—a little spinning dancer on her mechanism, a littering of dried flower petals, a cheap paste ring, and two folded papers. I swept them into the skirt of my gown and brought them to her, depositing them on the bench and fingering each piece. The box, however, was beyond saving.

And despite my desire to make use of this time here, I felt just about as useful to her. *I can do nothing for her, Lord. Nothing.* She leaned forward and her feeble old fingers poked at the pile, sorting through and feeling each object. Then her feet jolted out to stop her forward fall—long, swollen feet that were dirty, as if rarely washed. I caught her and steadied her back on the bench, and that's when the odd thought came into my head—*wash her feet.*

I stared down at them, spilling out the tops of worn slippers with the sores of old age marring doughy skin. They were scabbed and weathered, and a rim of redness traced the outline of her shoes.

I had nothing to wash them with. No water, no rag. And when she caught me staring, she tucked them swiftly under the bench, her asylum gown curtaining them.

Something else, then. Some other way to encourage her. I grabbed one of the papers and opened it. "Would you like me to read this to you?"

It was a hand-copied poem by Longfellow, a fanciful piece about dancing daffodils, but she only gazed ahead and fiddled with the fabric of her gown as I read it. I opened the second—a letter. With a smite of conscience for eavesdropping, I skimmed the lines about holding tight to the memories of "us," and not letting the tide pull them away from her, then I read them aloud. I looked up at the weathered face, where stories and triumphs and losses lay buried.

It was toward the end that a line caught my eye and I slowed to read it again:

> *I beg you to tell them who you truly are. Let people re-member the real you. I will no longer call you Anna, for that is not the woman who has my heart.*
>
> *Philippe*

Another look at the woman's face, but she seemed unfazed. What *was* her real name? Who had she been? "Do you know this Philippe?"

She blinked, as if waking up, and her eyes focused on the grass at her feet. "Philippe? Here?"

A man yelled across the field, and Anna startled, feeling about her lap for the box to calm her. Heartbroken, I grabbed her hands and began humming. Humming, humming, the first melody that came to mind, and it was *her* song—the lost melody from the dream. How easily it resurfaced in my memory once begun. Anna began rocking to the rhythm, her face easing just slightly.

I *could* be of some use. It wasn't my life purpose, but while I was here . . . well, kindness was never a waste of time. Then her hum joined mine and she too was voicing the notes of Rosamond's song. Spooked, I let my voice fade, but Anna's continued, striking each note with a soft, clear voice.

"How do you know that song?" I whispered the question when she stopped, and I stared into her face, into that weathered countenance that held no trace of familiarity. But it should—it should. That melody had been embedded in her memory when so much else had fallen out, and it belonged to Rosamond. My heart pounded, but Anna said nothing—simply looked beyond me toward the gardens. I caressed her hand as she had mine, and tried again. "Do you know me? Do you know Rosamond?"

I held my breath, but the only response was her gnarled fingers once again tracing mine.

A door slammed up at the house, and I spun, looking about to face the wrath of a descending nurse, but no one approached. Still crouched before the bench, I scanned the yard and my gaze connected with Dr. Turner's. He stood facing us across the garden, sleeves rolled up in the midst of work. He had something to say, it seemed. I set the papers in Anna's lap and rose, holding his gaze.

But he didn't speak. Poised as a white stag he studied me, and all I knew was how wild and windblown my hair was, how silly that little flower tucked behind one ear, which is exactly where his stare centered. I touched the purple bloom, my skirt gently tickling my legs in the breeze, but could not bring myself to part with that little bit of color. We stood that way, staring across the low shrubs and dying roses, and he seemed to be looking at me, but also at something that did not belong to the present. I wondered what he saw.

He approached with long, loping strides, hands in his pockets, and stopped before us. "Once again I find myself in your debt, Miss Fletcher." A quick nod toward Anna. "I wish there was some way I could repay your kindness."

"No need." He repaid me in droves with that tender look, the open approval on his face. Yet there was a hint of angst there. He wanted to ask something of me, or tell me something, but for whatever reason he held back.

He crossed his bare forearms over his chest and studied me, as he always did, but tension swelled between us in the silence. Mighty restraint. He lowered his voice. "I'm never certain what to make of you, Miss Fletcher." His eyes strayed often to the flower tickling my ear. It almost looked as if he wished to touch it—which was madness. How fitting.

I shrugged. "I'm not certain anymore, either. But it's Vivienne. Vivienne Mourdant."

He dropped his gaze and heat washed over my skin. I hadn't played in months now, and it had stripped something from me, erasing a large piece of my identity that I'd always taken for granted. Instead, the rhythms of Hurstwell now formed the backdrop of my days. I was becoming part of it, or it part of me.

He cleared his throat. "Anyway, you'd do better as an aid than a patient, the way you are with her, no matter your name. It's a shame you cannot be."

"If only it were up to you." I swept a few more flowers up from the grass, touching their velvety petals.

"You know where to come if I can ever help, ever make things a little easier for you."

I looked up at him, at that earnest face. "Actually, there is something you can do for me."

"Oh?" His face shuttered, withdrawing. Regretting.

I sighed, twisting a tendril around my finger. "Boot polish."

He blinked. "Boot . . . ?"

I smiled. "I'd be ever so grateful for a mite of linseed oil, if you've any to spare."

23

The language of music is common to all generations and nations;
it is understood by everybody, since it is understood with the heart.

~Gioachino Rossini

The deep bassoon of rolling thunder was the night's background music, and I listened to the storm's symphony from beneath the lid of that old Broadwood, feeling my way along the soundboard. *Crashhhh*. It was a noisy storm, pounding staccato against the windows accentuated with deep, booming rolls of percussion through the moors. *Boooom*.

I had lit only one candle stub, for I'd begun to run low, so I operated largely by memory and waited for flashes of lightning when I needed to see some small detail. I worked Dr. Turner's borrowed boot oil into the crevices by feel where the pedal post met the soundboard, easing its movement. Next I'd polish the entire wooden case of the great instrument, bringing it to a fresh shine. I exhaled and dust puffed around my face. I pulled out of the pianoforte and froze as the sound of shuffling footsteps in the priest's tunnel echoed, like mice. Large ones.

Twelve, three, and six o'clock. It was none of those. Not even eleven.

It was Clara's face that appeared in the meager glow of my candle stub, her worried little countenance, then Bridget and a few others. Finally, two women hustled a blanket-wrapped figure in, guiding her into the moonlit room and unwinding her cocoon. It was Anna, a tall, angular creature pale and hunched with fear. She huddled around the empty space near her middle where her music box belonged, and I felt a new wave of revulsion for the nurse who'd smashed it that afternoon. Anna fell into convulsions outside of the blanket, then the thunder rumbled, and she screamed, scrambling for the door.

The women caught her, wrapping her in the blanket again, covering her mouth. As my heart twisted, the thought came again. *Wash her feet. Serve the least of these.*

"She needs music," Clara said. "You're the only one who has it. Her music box is gone."

"I still haven't finished—"

"Well, it'll have to do." Bridget propelled the wrapped-up woman toward the pianoforte, pushing me along with her. "Unless you want to send her to the catacombs. That's her next stop if she carries on this way, and there's no coming back from it."

Another flash of lightning, and the woman writhed and screamed, dissolving into sobs as the storm cracked through the sky. Hang those wretched storms that crept over the moors all spring, summer, and fall. I swung toward the ivories, rounding my fingers over them.

But I began to tremble.

I'd polished and tuned and oiled, yet in all those weeks I couldn't bring myself to play. I wrote the words *I am not a pianist* nearly every day, and they had begun to melt my reality, reshaping it completely. I'd begun, in some hazy way, to place my pianoforte days in the same category as my vivid dreams where I saw some nonexistent woman playing and heard music that wasn't real.

Now, sitting over those keys I felt nauseous. A heady fear swept over me at the thought of playing. I wasn't ready to release that part of who I was—to find out it was an illusion. The silent old instrument beckoned me, begging me to dignify it with music, but what if . . . *what if* . . .

"Let me assure you she's a second-rate performer who has elbowed her way into the music world on the strength of her connections. Quite amateurish as a performer, though."

I swallowed as that odious little marquis's words echoed back from a lifetime ago. They harmonized in an awful frenzy of notes with everything I'd heard since then. It grew into a cacophony and I couldn't think straight.

I couldn't seem to remember a single reason that I knew myself to be a true pianist except that my father had been the most famous teacher from here to Leeds and I was his daughter. And I had always played.

Thunder cracked, and somewhere a great tree splintered and broke, groaning as it fell. Anna cried out, sending the women scrambling to tighten the blanket and hustle her over to the side of the pianoforte. She clung to my arm and quaked. The blanket edged down, and I felt her racing heart against my shoulder, a wild tempo of fear, and closed my eyes.

Music was at the core of all humans. A rhythm. A steady beat. And there was a song to match every beat.

I rummaged through my mental collection and chose—Schubert's Impromptu in A-flat Major, op. 90. Frantic, urgent, the staccato beat of falling rain, of someone sprinting through it. I tried out a few bars, letting their sound plunk into the room. With Anna's heart beating against me, I found the hurried tempo with surprising ease, and my fingers stepped into it, tripping through a trill in the higher octaves, answering with the left hand in the melodic lower ones.

Soon my fingers were searching for the notes as if they had a mind of their own, a horse given its head. The music was fresh air and birdsong, a cool ocean in summer. I swam in it, letting the current carry me through my fear. High notes raining down, low notes answering, her heart pounding against my arm.

I pleaded silently with her internal rhythm to calm, willing it to slow, and that determination found its way into my fingertips, moderating my tempo. It was almost imperceptible at first, slowing my arpeggios until I reached the midsection and the notes stretched into an almost languid pace. I had no explanation for what happened next.

Thudthudthudthud. Thud. Thud. Thud . . . Thud . . . Thud. The heartbeat against my shoulder slowed, beat for beat, coming down off its rapid peak and into a steady largo tempo along with the music. I kept on, inventing a bridge at the end and playing across it directly into a Mozart adagio, Piano Sonata no. 17 in B-flat Major, a more relaxed rhythm, which sank deep into the room as everyone quieted, listening. I lost myself—utterly lost myself—in the most beautiful thing my hands could create, and it filled me to the brim, spilling out in tiny tears that I blinked away.

I felt the steady rhythm of Hurstwell's "hopeless case" against my arm, and I again saw the bold letters across the top of my own little brochure: There is no such thing as hopeless cases. Only those who have lost hope.

Warmth seeped through the arm of my nightdress, and the living heartbeat of a woman. I had such big plans before Hurstwell—plans to rescue and to help those who had no one else. But perhaps I'd lost sight of my main aim.

No hopeless cases. None. Not even here. Only those who have lost hope—and need to be brought back to life.

"He hasn't stopped you at all. Just relocated you."

All at once the swell of peace I'd experienced grew clear—it was his presence, there all along. Waiting for me to step into it. To acknowledge it for what it was—a blessed sweetness permeating the cold stone walls, the bars, the discouragement that had polluted my heart. I was me, even in this place, because I was his more than I was anything else. His pursuit was the constant in my turbulent life, even now.

I drew the song to its tender finale and left my fingertips atop the keys, the song still pulsing through every inch of my being. I felt more fully myself than I had in months.

Another glowing light appeared somewhere to my left and a boot scuffed on the floor—someone had come through the locked main door. I wasn't afraid, though. I closed my eyes and suddenly had the calming sense of Bach's cello solo in the emptiness behind me.

Beauty still exists, even in the midst of playing wrong notes. Finding it, taking notice of it, might be your saving grace. Or it might be the point of the disruption all along.

~Vivienne Mourdant

Fading notes vibrated through the air as Mitchell Turner stood in that abandoned old room of shadows and tall windows, stunned into silence as he stared at the back of the trim little figure who had somehow produced the most magnificent sound. Then he brought the oil lamp closer to her, and she turned toward him, that great mass of flaming hair down her back, face still flushed with the passion of her creation.

That arresting stare held his as always, inspecting and challenging, yet demanding nothing. He let the stare linger, assessing her and never quite able to take her all in at once. It was his own fault she was constantly surprising him—he should know to expect the unexpected from her by now. Yet it was rather thrilling to feel so turned about every time he encountered her.

All he could do was set the lamp on the closed pianoforte lid and extend his hand to her. "Miss Vivienne Mourdant," he said with wonder. "A pleasure to make your acquaintance."

She held up her slender hand, and he grasped it, holding on to it for a moment as he looked her over anew. Seeing things as they truly were. It was so fitting—her slender form at the piano, those long white fingers drawing out the melody that seemed to come from who she was. Who he should have seen all along.

"I know I shouldn't be here. I was just—"

"You're right. You don't belong here." He looked at her tense face, then at Anna, with soft white wisps around her calm features. No, Vivienne Mourdant shouldn't be in an asylum. Yet somehow, oddly, this woman was exactly where she belonged.

After settling a more subdued Anna back in bed, Mitchell found Vivienne Mourdant in the clock tower where Bridget had said she'd be, propped against the stone wall with one leg dangling off the bench. "I owe you an apology, Miss Mourdant." He wouldn't be able to sleep until he gave it. "What I assumed . . ."

Her profile was perfected by the shadows, her features soft in the glow of his candle. She tipped her chin down, the only acknowledgment of his apology. "I'm beginning to doubt any of us in this place are truly mad. Or perhaps madness isn't what we think it is."

"You've not seen all of Hurstwell."

"I've seen enough." Even in that oversized asylum gown, she was draped in elegance, just like her music. "What I'm beginning to realize is that this place is filled with people who need help . . . but the point is that they are *people*, broken or not."

He couldn't stop staring at those long, slender hands wrapped around the edge of the rough bench. They had created a miracle of sound with little apparent effort, music that had penetrated his pain-dulled heart and leaked into Anna's unreachable mind where no one else had gone—or cared to go.

"You see it too, don't you?" His voice was raspy, but his soul hopeful. Almost alive again. "That spark of humanity in the people here." Most simply didn't. They were busy. Overworked and tired.

In answer she simply looked up, that vibrant face beaming directly at him in that shadowed old tower, the lights of her eyes making it suddenly hard to breathe. Music was here, she was right. There was no place where it could not seep through, even the place of his deepest pain, and since she'd come it had invaded, ringing from those old gray walls and waking lost souls.

Their exchange in the chronic hall echoed back to him. *"Most people don't go about hearing music that isn't there. It's as simple as that."*

"Most aren't listening."

He was. He was listening. He settled on another bench near her and leaned close. "Tell me about it. About this music you hear."

She looked down and thought for a moment, then spoke candidly. "The music . . . it haunts my heart and mind, and I invite it to, because quite frankly it is far more welcome than many other things trying to invade my thoughts. It's like an echo, a reverberation after spending so many hours in the midst of sound and rhythm and song." She closed her eyes, face turned up in the enchanting moonlight pouring through the translucent clockfaces above them. "And I can feel it. I put my hand on the pianoforte when someone plays, on the wall of this place when there is no one playing, and there's a rhythm to everything. An undercurrent to the atmosphere."

He swallowed, memories sweeping over him. A cloudy spring day in the hamlet, walking up the flagstone path to the cottage, and knowing, before he entered, that Dahlia was singing. He'd closed his eyes, leaning against the door, and he could feel it—the gentle vibration of the music within.

She looked away. "I must sound even more mad to you now."

He cleared his throat, raking fingers through his hair and shaking away the residual mud of regret sucking him down. "Well, it is quite extraordinary, hearing music the way you do."

She looked at him with that bold, steady way she had. "Is it?" She rose and wrapped her shawl more tightly about herself, eyes turned toward the clockface, and swayed with the tempo of its ticks and thunks, skirt dusting her bare feet as she smiled up at him with a wry smile. "Perhaps we're all a little mad in our own way, no? If this is my madness, I see no reason to be sane. Music is at the core of every human, in a most basic way." She placed a hand over her heart. Then, eyes closing, she lifted her shawl-wrapped arms and bounced them lightly as if conducting.

She'd come into herself tonight, playing the pianoforte. She'd been a cogwheel out of alignment, shifting back and forth against its mate, but now she'd locked into position, teeth fitting as they should and turning together. No matter what this place told her, in this moment she knew who she was.

He swallowed, watching her lithe form given over to the tempo of night music. The water pipes thrummed, gurgling and clicking as they surged to life, the clock thunked in the background. The woman of magical melodies spun in slow circles, encompassing all the sounds, drawing them all into the beat of the clock with her feet until it all merged together into the symphony of Hurstwell. The chaos of noise synthesized into order. Rhythm. Auburn-haired music with lovely freckle-spattered white cheeks. Elegance and color swept through the stony gray of the tower he'd visited a hundred times, but now would never forget. The peace he sensed here would linger as he left, warming his night.

The steady rhythm pounded through his chest, inviting him to break out of the grief and regret and join in. It felt instinctual. Yet he shouldn't. Already he was far too captivated with this woman— legally a patient—and it warred with the internal morality that had always been his own rhythm.

He could not look away, though. Could not help being captivated. She lifted her arms as if dancing with a partner, leaning into his imaginary arms, and continuing her waltz about the little space until her foot caught on a loose board and she stumbled.

He sprang up and caught her, the gentle weight of her suddenly in his arms. Her lovely face was so close, breath coming hard from her dance.

"I'm not mad, you know." She gripped his arms, surprising strength closing around his biceps. "You must believe me. Please. I'll die if I stay locked—"

Bonnnng! The sound from the clock shuddered through the tower, shaking the moment loose. *Bonnng.* He set her on her feet and stepped back, heart racing. Vivienne Mourdant stood frozen, feet apart and eyes wide as the clock bonged a third, then a fourth time. *Bonnnng.* After the fifth he bolted, down the staircase and through the corridors. At the door of his basement chamber, he fumbled with the lock, dropping the key three times before managing to get the door open just as the eleventh bong died out in the night air.

He burst into his flat and strode to the basin, pumping the handle up and down with his entire upper body until cold water sputtered out the end. Cupping his hands, he doused his face with the coolness and splattered it across his shirt. He shoved his hair back, then leaned on the sink, breathing hard.

"I'm not mad. Please believe me. Please, Mitch. I'll die if I must stay. Don't let me die here."

He leaned over the sink, water dripping off his hair, and shook. It was a curse, wasn't it? Regret. A curse that never went away. If only, if only, if only. And now he was starting over, the echo of what was reverberating through his skull.

This time, he'd do things differently. Starting with believing her—and with *not* growing attached.

Patience and tranquility of mind contribute more to cure our dis-
tempers as the whole art of medicine.

~Wolfgang Amadeus Mozart

"Psst."

I nearly dropped the heavy basket of wet linens as I glanced
around the yard outside the laundry. Dr. Turner stood in the
shadow of the great building, his presence increasing the tempo
of my internal rhythm. I hitched the basket higher and walked to
him. After days of silence from the man, I'd begun to wonder if
I'd imagined the entire performance with Anna and the talk in the
clock tower, dreamed it up as I had the tendency to do.

Perhaps it was because of my parents' story—I'd felt Dr. Turner's gaze on my back as I'd played, and fancied it being similar to
the way Father had watched a young woman play and forgotten
she was his student, and he her much older pianoforte tutor. Had
my father looked at my mother in that same shocked manner of
enchantment when he'd first heard her play? Blinked in surprise
as if a cloak of invisibility had been lifted from her shoulders and
he saw her for the first time?

I shivered as I reached Dr. Turner and glanced behind me to be sure no one saw.

He dropped his voice. "Come with me."

"Where?"

"Leave your basket and come."

I dropped that thing without hesitation, running to catch up as he strode around the corner of the fenced-in yard to the back. "What's this about?"

Then, I saw it—the lost tower. I stiffened.

He didn't answer until we'd slipped through a wooden door and closed ourselves into the narrow stairwell that circled up into the darkness above. He fumbled to light a candle and lifted it into the narrow passageway, the tiny flame leaping before us as we climbed the steps that went round and round into darkness above. "I'd like your help with something, Miss Mourdant."

I stared at Dr. Turner's back as he walked ahead on the stairs, at the light that created a glow around his figure. I could barely breathe the thick, wet air as we climbed. The daylight brought little illumination to the place, and it was mostly the dimmed gaslights running in long lines up the stairwell that gave any light to the place. Shadows were still deep and heavy, cloaking the faces that stared out at us on the climb.

"Under the circumstances, I've decided you will continue to be an unofficial aid, but I shouldn't like to make a scene about it. Dr. Thornhill wouldn't give his permission, and I don't plan to ask him, so it's best he not find out."

"How will he not?"

"He's away—the man is strict about keeping a six-day work-week and having plenty of distance from the place when he can. He's at his residence over in Newall, and he won't return until tomorrow. You will be my once-weekly aid, attending only to certain patients. Starting with one in this tower."

My heart nearly stopped. I nodded and we continued climbing. What might God be orchestrating in this place? For some reason,

I'd gotten it in my head that the secret of my disappearing ward, of Rose the ghost, lay in this tower. Perhaps her story lingered with a patient here.

My mind swirled with thoughts of ghosts, dreams, and Rosamond Swansea. I looked around, bracing to see a white face with dark hair peering out at me, begging for my help. Our footsteps echoed together up the narrow stone steps that were slick with moisture. Staccato dripping sounded high above us.

"He's a brown-gown patient."

"And brown is . . . ?"

"Violent. He cannot be around others."

I hesitated, leaving my foot on a step for a few heartbeats before continuing. Rosamond—was she violent? Is that why I'd never seen her among the others?

"You told me the other night you doubted madness existed, that no case was truly hopeless. Well, this one's what I call an impossible patient—nothing will reach him and he's just short of savagery."

"And what do you intend for me to do with him?" *Clang, clang.* I couldn't tell if it was the pipes surging to life or a man's head against the bars of his cage.

"Do what you do. What you did with Anna. Work your magic."

"I'm a *musician*, not a magician."

He paused on the landing, hand on the rail as he turned to me in the semidarkness. "Just give it a go, will you?"

A roar sounded above us. A primal growl, then a dull thud.

"What am I to do, drag the pianoforte up here? Because I certainly hope you're not suggesting you will release this man into the music room alone with me."

"I was hoping you could, well, sing to him or something."

"Dr. Turner, I play the pianoforte. I cannot hold a tune to save my life."

He put a warm hand on my shoulder as we approached the top. "You're more than a pianist. You're an intelligent being who sees below the surface, and that is a far cry beyond most of the people employed at this asylum. Now please, won't you see what can be done?"

I huffed, knowing I'd say yes. I could not refuse with the sound of cellos in the background of his demeanor, the look of a calm sea staring out at me. "Very well, but he must be restrained, and you must stay close by. What do you know about him?"

"He was found wandering on the moors many months ago and brought here when he displayed some rather savage behavior, yelling nonsense like an animal. He seems to have simply appeared from the wild moors themselves. No one knows who he is. He attacked Dr. Thornhill upon arrival, and few have dared go near him all this time."

We climbed the final steps in silence, and I knew coming had been the right decision when the most horrible smell assaulted us. Suggesting a clean room was one thing I could do for the poor bloke, easy enough. I stood on my toes to peer through the high barred window at the lump of humanity within. Streams of light fell on a hunched figure, greasy dark hair falling over his face, sausage arms propped on his knees. Straw hemmed the cold room, mixed with all manner of dirt and excrement. No one, it seemed, dared go within those walls to tidy it.

His thick fingers shoved hair out of the way, and there was a surprising civility in his eyes, a wretched pain expressed silently and with eloquence. Yet if I had a key, I wasn't certain I'd have let him out. The door shifted against my weight with a small click. The man spun, enraged at the sight of us and lunging against his chains. I gave a cry and fell back, and Dr. Turner's chest stopped my fall. I hid my face in his shirt, trembling. I would not turn back. No. Not for anything. The doctor's arms came about me, hands splayed on my back, and their solid warmth calmed me.

The caged man's cries and groans assaulted my senses, echoing off the walls, off my skin. "Hoooooow. *Bit. Bit.*"

I shivered and turned back to the patient. No hopeless cases. No hopeless cases.

"Hill*feh*. Bitttter!" He lunged toward the door, gasping and straining, then went limp, standing defeated just outside the slices of light coming through the window. "Hillfah BIT HER!" He seemed desperate, as if willing me to understand his meaning, even though he could not get his tongue around the words properly. Helpless, restrained, he stared at me until tears warmed the corners of my eyes.

"I feel just as trapped as you." I shivered.

He blew out a breath that lifted the hair from his face, then he shoved the dark strands back. When the light struck his arm, raw, bloodied flesh showed around the chains. "Oh, Dr. Turner." My tears fell. "Mightn't you put him in something besides chains? He'll die of an infection in this terrible tower before anything can be done for him."

Horror paled the doctor's face as he saw the wounds. "Of course. We have leather straps in the long-stay ward. Perhaps that would be better."

"Much." I turned to the man and held my arm up to the window, grabbing my wrist to indicate the chains on his. "We'll fix this. Would you like that?"

To my astonishment, he nodded and collapsed back on his stool, head hanging down. He poked at the raw flesh with a frown. I left the tower with a rattling sense of dread. I carried it down the first flight of steps and into the dark corridor where Dr. Turner led me. As I sped through the shadows, eager to put distance between me and those chains and groans, he caught up to me and laid a hand on my arm. "Are you well?"

I turned, fingertips against my forehead to restore a little calm. "Quite. It's only . . . I'm not accustomed to this."

"I thought it best that you understand the full extent of what we have here. Or perhaps I wanted to convince myself that you were wrong. About madness."

I stopped under the flickering light of a torch overhead. "Why?"

"I made the mistake of not listening once, with dire consequences. I will not make it again."

Those shadows—the deep shadows over his face and being. I could picture him as he was that night in the cemetery, standing hunch-shouldered before a grave. We continued walking toward the light and a more open area ahead. "What was her name?"

"Dahlia."

"Friend?"

"Wife."

The last word jolted me into silence, an ache in my soul. "I'm so sorry," I said at last.

"Don't be. It wasn't your fault." He reached his hand behind his neck, looking away.

Broken. That's what he was. A broken and overlooked instrument capable of producing great beauty, like the abandoned Broadwood. Like the patients of Hurstwell. I'd already seen glimpses of his nature—bending low to the least of us, rich in kindness, great in strength that was spent on lost causes. Yet something had broken him. What would it take to brush the dust off his spirit and repair it to full working order?

If we were not in an asylum, not doctor and patient, I might have slipped my hand into his just to let him feel the reassurance of it, my wordless support. As it was, I balled my hand up and his hung alone at his side.

"You see a bit of her in every patient, don't you?"

He flinched, as if I'd wandered too far into a place no one had ever gone. His jaw worked, his face troubled.

My voice was low. "You've an unusual way with them—the patients, that is. I should have known there was a reason."

"I simply perform the duties of my position."

I shook my head. "It's more. You give people permission to be themselves—whatever odd collection of cracks and fissures and paint smears they have. There's true freedom in that." A few more paces, and I looked up at him. "It's a rare and beautiful thing to see potential in these people, but you see more—you see *value*."

He watched my face, as if to reason out my meaning. I couldn't tell if my words bothered or pleased him. "And you?" He faced forward again. "What is your reason?"

"Bad luck."

"I mean, the way you . . . see people. See inside and recognize the humanity there."

A smile tipped my mouth. "Still bad luck." I told him then what it was to live with Father, to grow weak and forcibly submissive under the weight of another's control, and to endure the gnawing ache of missing someone you'd never met.

"I look at the people here, and I see what I had felt inside my-self—a spark of God's created image buried under so much fear and false belief, a strength and hope and imagination no one ever took the time to recognize." It was a gift that had been a curse in the attainment, but it had shaped me. Given me an uncommon ability to rescue others. "And even being here, I find myself not as different from the patients as I'd imagined. Perhaps that's why I feared coming in the first place—the chance of seeing myself in them."

I shivered for a moment, then I told him of the vivid dreams, of playing with the mysterious ghost woman in those chilly midnight hours and experiencing tenderness, then how I'd suddenly had the ability to fly into windows and yank out children who suffered the same fate as I, and how so many vivid dreams had emboldened me in different ways. Given me a sense of protectiveness and purpose even before coming here.

"I determined years ago that I would make certain no one else would wither and fade away as my mother once had—as I nearly did, when I was locked up in the dark." I sighed. "I suppose everyone has a story like that, though, being shaped against one's will, life dealing unfairly with them. After everything I've experienced, I cannot look away from those people, Dr. Turner. That's all it is. They're as desperate as I once was."

"Your fear of the dark. It comes from that, doesn't it? From being locked up."

I shrugged, feeling the heat flood my face. "Silly, I know. Such a childish fear." I'd said too much.

"It came from when you were a child, so it isn't silly. And what shapes our adulthood besides everything that came before it?"

His casual acceptance released something in me. "Thank you. That's very kind."

Then he froze, looking at me.

No, past me.

I turned to see a nurse darting around the corner, skirt fluttering in the lighted space ahead. I closed my eyes and released a breath, dread settling low in my belly.

"I must apologize again, Miss Mourdant. I acted in haste, without giving much thought to the consequences—for you. Of course you cannot be my assistant while you're a patient here." He turned me to face him and leveled a gaze at me. "Everything we spoke ends here, in this corridor, and I vow to you I'll never ask of you what I shouldn't again." His words echoed with layers of meaning. "You must return alone, quickly, to the laundry, and I will make certain you see no trouble for my foolishness. The laundry is just around that corner, and it'll go better that way than for me to be seen returning you."

The ache in my chest expanded, ready to swallow me whole as the sound of cellos rose to a crescendo and danced quickly toward a finale. One I wasn't ready to reach.

"I'm not mad, Dr. Turner. I don't need to be a patient here."

He paused, searching my face. "I know."

Then he was gone.

Head down, I hurried around the corner, but my steps were halted by a voice down the far-right corridor.

"Miss Fletcher."

I cringed. Turning, I faced Dr. Thornhill approaching from the shadows.

"A word, if you please."

A small group of women from the laundry—where I was supposed to be—hurried past me with wide eyes.

I swallowed my fear. "Of course."

He walked toward his office in the main entrance, and I followed, pausing outside the door. "Come in."

"I'd rather listen from here." I gripped the doorframe, praying.

His eyes centered on my face for several moments. "Very well, then." He sank into his desk chair, and I fought to keep my gaze from wandering to the desk drawer where a file was stored with the name "Thornhill" on it. Was it really him? Or was Thomas a relation? Looking at the eerie calm of his face, it was easy to believe the former, despite what Richard had told me.

He shuffled through papers as he spoke. "I do hope you've come to recognize all Hurstwell has to offer—all the help and discipline, the advanced medical resources. Perhaps you even see what there is here for you."

I pinched my lips together, not having a fitting answer. Nothing polite, at least.

"But there are also things we do *not* offer at this establishment." He turned to face me, tapping his pen on the desktop. "One should not expect to find matrimonial prospects here, for example."

I clenched my hands. "Of course."

"I hope we are clear on this matter. Are we?"

"We are."

His smile was not quite friendly. "Good." His gaze traveled over me. "Nurse, will you return this woman to her duties, please?"

A shuffle behind me caught me by surprise. Duffy hurried in. "Right away, sir."

Her grip on my arm was tighter, her face pinched in some grim, contorted smile of victory.

Night fell more rapidly than usual, it seemed. The day was drained of its light, and shadows took over the corridors, dancing beneath the rows of gaslights.

"There's something that needs saying." Clara's voice carried across the beds to me, her strained face barely visible through the heavy blackness. "I should have told you earlier, but I've been quite determined to keep to myself about things. I've been doing much better, you know. Holding my tongue and such. But . . ."

I turned onto my right side, propping my head with one hand. "What is it?"

"It's about Thornhill." Her hands twisted the sheet into a worry knot. "I saw you go into his office this afternoon, and there's something you should know. About him in particular."

"That he was a patient?"

She blinked into the dimness, fretting hands stilled for a moment. "Why ever would you think that?"

I sighed, not mentioning the file. "Because the man must have *some* secret—something he's hiding."

"It isn't that." The sheets rustled, twisting again in her hands. "It's about that patient you're searching for. You cannot ask him about her—cannot let on that you're digging into that particular bit of past."

"Why should he care if I'm searching out an old acquaintance?"

"Because she was his *wife*."

My hand curled around the sheet. "Who was?"

"It's Rose you're looking for, isn't it? The patient you were hoping to find. It's Rose, the ghost."

I said nothing. Sank down farther.

"Well, she was his wife."

"What . . . how?"

"Just before my time here began. Thornhill fell in love with her, just as everyone did, and he married her even though she was a patient."

"Did *he* think her mad?"

A shrug. "Likely didn't matter to him. She was beautiful, brokenhearted, and alone. Not to mention the child."

"If he married her, then why couldn't she keep—"

"Because it was *his*. The Duke's. He couldn't raise that man's child."

I sank back onto my pillow, pondering the unfolding past. Rose . . . who *couldn't* be my mother . . . who was probably dead . . . had married Thornhill.

Yet it awakened in me a resolute certainty on one point—just as I had said to Dr. Turner earlier that day . . . *I was not mad*. This whole thing, the mysterious notes and distant music at night. Thornhill must have found out who I searched for and felt threatened by my presence. I had mentioned my real name, and he must have realized I was here for Rosamond. Whatever the reason, he'd set it up to keep me here, to keep me imprisoned. I'd become a threat.

But a sane one.

"How terribly dreadful for him. For her too." I swallowed. "You don't think . . . that he . . ."

"I don't know." Her soft voice barely reached me. "I hope not."

Thornhill was mad. Of that I was certain. But just as surely, I knew now that *I was not*.

I let that thought weight me comfortably to the bed, carrying me toward the sleep I so badly needed. I'd leave this place yet—maybe even without Marcel Beauchene's help. They couldn't keep a sane woman in an asylum. Not for long, anyway.

I breathed out a sigh and sank into the first solid sleep I'd had since arriving.

And that's when I heard the music again. It woke me, jarring my foggy mind back to Hurstwell. It wasn't just any music, but *her song*. The lost melody that had haunted my childhood.

Mama?

I sat bolt upright, feeling every spring, and shook my head. It had seemed so distant, fading in and out, so I couldn't be sure I wasn't imagining it. I must have been half dreaming. But no, it came again, and that melody was unmistakable—it had only ever come from the woman in the rose room as she played with her eyes closed, swaying with the music like no composer I ever knew.

I'd hummed a few bars once, even played pieces of it for Marcel and a few others in the music world, but no one had ever heard it before. I knew then that she had written it—the thing had sprung from her being.

Yet it played now, in this place. Just a simple melody line without the usual embellishments, but it was definitely the same song. I scanned the room, but all was quiet there.

The night fell silent, but then a few notes of the song floated through the air again, minor arpeggios catching my ear from some distant place. My muscles twitched mercilessly, and I was wide awake, staring into the darkness as the song curled around my senses, and I halfway anticipated a ghostly figure with a warm smile to slip into the room when it was done.

Scree. I jumped at the sound of scratching on glass.

Tree at the window. I exhaled.

I rose and wrapped my sheet around myself, moving toward the priest's hole. Toward the beautiful Broadwood where someone else played the song that belonged to her.

26

Sometimes all it takes is one person, no matter how insignificant, to look at the world differently. Then invite others to do the same.

~Vivienne Mourdant

I stood shaking and panting in that chilly room on the other side of the priest's hole, staring at the abandoned pianoforte. The haunting melody still echoed through my mind, torturing me with uncertainty, but no one played. No one. The lid was propped up, which must have been why the sound had carried more than it did when I had played, but now the room rang with silence.

Our maid Jessie used to hum, once upon a time. She covered all the sounds of Father's yelling downstairs with lively music that penetrated my angst, and I later realized it had been intentional. Father's emotions had swept through our house like the wind puffing a sailing ship in one direction or another, but dear Jessie had shielded me with her lively voice. With music. It had muffled the most jagged parts of my childhood.

Then when she'd gone, the dreams of the woman at the pianoforte had started, her haunting melody filling that hole left by the maid's cheery hum. So it was that music always came when things were at their worst. Those were the hardest years with Father, when he made me his showpiece, which meant I had to be perfect.

And not just on the pianoforte.

In those days my knuckles were raw from the rod and my rebellious heart burned with anger when he locked me in the larder for half days at a time. Then at night, my tortured mind often dreamed up that lilting song that drew me toward the rose room, toward those sacred moments with the woman at the pianoforte. A way to cope. I'd always pretended it was my mother, and that she'd come to comfort me.

Now, it seemed, the need had come again. Or . . . she was here. A chill swept the room, wind rattling the glass in the windowpanes. I could almost hear a voice on the moaning wind, someone wailing for help.

A *clunk* made me spin, hand to my heart. "Oh, Bridget. I half expected to see a specter."

She emerged from the priest's hole and shut the little panel behind her, wiping her hands on her gown. "Now that would have been exciting."

I laughed. Her casual voice dissipated the eerie chill that had gripped me. It was as if daylight had returned and my fears seemed foolish.

She stepped farther into the room, looking about, staring out the tall windows at the star-studded sky. "Heard you leave, and I thought how nice it would be to hear you play again." Her voice was weak.

I looked over that dimmed countenance and forced my mind to pivot fully from ghosts and mysterious melodies. "Perhaps this time we should hear you play."

"But I don't—"

"I'll teach you. Here." I positioned a chair for her beside my stool and placed her fingers on the keys, marveling at how long and tapered they were—perfect for playing. I shoved away the residual tingles of fear and focused on my dear friend, on drawing out the music that was in her.

"This is a C, in the very middle of the keyboard. Every eight keys, it repeats again at a slightly different pitch." I played all the Cs for her, stretching from octave to octave. "All you need is a melody, which I can supply, and a pattern of chords to go with it, like this."

I positioned her fingers over C, E, and G, forming thirds for a harmonizing sound. She stared, her mind absorbing the patterns of thirds and fifths and how they correlated to the melody. I showed her a few more finger arrangements and explained why they worked together, and her expression firmed, mind absorbing the system.

Then with a deep breath, I lifted my hands and played a song whose rhythm came from somewhere deep within my childhood. *Savior, like a shepherd lead us . . .*

Halfway through, Bridget formed her fingers over the keys and inserted chords with the melody, awkwardly at first, then gaining confidence. Her volume grew and so did her gladness, and a smile equaling her wide, vivid eyes that now danced. We tripped with laughter through the piece several times, stopping to try out different variations of the chord patterns, and soon she was adding her own designs.

I folded my hands onto my lap after the sixth or seventh run-through and stared down at the keys as the song faded. "I've watched many a student come under Father's teaching. Never in my life have I seen another human being pick up music so handily, as if it were a language they'd heard all their lives and were fluent the moment they used it."

She shrugged in her usual way, hands lacing in her lap. "Weren't much to it. There are rules and patterns. I just followed them."

"That's not easy for most people." I swept my feet over the tile floor, hands gripping the round edge of the stool. "It seems at times the Almighty short-suits us in some areas to give us others in spades. It's his way of balancing us out so none of us can be too stuck on ourselves." I turned to her. "You've a great deal to offer that baby, Bridget, and you're the one meant to give it to her. She's yours, and if she's put together the way you are, well, there's no one better to mother her than someone who understands."

Her hands gripped her knees, shoulders arched forward as she stared down at the keys. "When you asked before if I wanted to leave here . . . well, I do. Sometimes so much it aches. When I looked down at that little face, and me the only mother she had, all I could think was that I didn't even know how to hold her. To hug and coddle and . . ." Her arm shook, fingers working the fabric of her gown as her voice trailed off. "But it tears me apart to think of not having the chance. Of never getting better . . . or of going home and being worse."

"Give her the gift of yourself, Bridget. Of all you are, short suits and spades. Of your own sort of mothering. You've no idea how a girl longs—" I stopped as memories crested over me.

One large tear rolled down her white cheek. "Sometimes I think you were sent here not because you're mad—but to show the rest of us the way out of our pits. You were sent here to rescue us. Me, most especially."

I squeezed her shoulder with a light laugh. "You make me sound like some sacred celestial being. I'm merely doing what I was created to do, in the place I happen to be. Which is exactly what *you* convinced me to do."

We shared a smile.

I made my way back through the walls after Bridget and realized it was mere hours until morning. I climbed into my cot. Metal pipes made tapping sounds as the system rushed to life for the day, working to warm the overlarge space. Through it all, I could not sleep—those nonsensical sounds the man in the tower kept repeating nagged at me.

Hillfaaaa bit her.

Hillfa. Bitter. The sounds were familiar. Something sensible. A code, maybe. I bandied them about in my mind as I struggled to make myself comfortable on the sunken cot. Where had I heard those phrases? Hilfa . . . bit her . . .

No. No!

Hilfe, bitte.

I blinked, memories slamming one over the other of a girl in the alley just outside the Theater an der Wien in Vienna, Austria, when I'd played there two years ago. She had grabbed my arm in a moment I'd never forget, her eyes pleading. *Bitte, Hilfe. Hilfe.*

Please, help. Help.

I scrambled up in bed, blinking in the dark, weak from lack of sleep but firm in certainty.

———

Over the hiss of steam and the slap of wet clothing in the laundry that morning, I watched for Dr. Turner and waited. He had promised to change out the chains for leather straps, and I knew he wouldn't let much time pass before attending to it.

When I saw his lithe figure striding over the dying grass at half past nine, I lowered my head, gripped a metal tub of gray water, and headed toward him.

"Where are you going?" called a voice.

"Dumping water." I moved without looking up, into the leaf-strewn yard and toward the fence. I dumped it quickly, sloshing it on my woolen stockings and half boots, and turned back, aligning my path with the doctor's even as I forced myself to stare at my feet.

I hurried my steps and bumped his arm with the tub, fumbling it and letting it clatter to the ground. "Oh! I beg your pardon, Doctor." I bent to pick it up and so did he. When we leaned close together, I spoke in a terse whisper. "He isn't hopeless, Dr. Turner. He isn't even mad. I need to see him. Please."

He looked at me, blinking.

"The man in the tower. I need to see him again."

"Impossible. He's volatile and erratic, and it was foolish to rope you into it." He gentled. "There's a reason we keep the brown-gown patients separate."

"He's more than a brown gown, you know." My voice was soft.

He straightened. "Thornhill is here today. And there's no telling what that nurse saw yesterday."

"Please—"

He stood before me, forcing me to look into his well-defined face. A firm shake of his head, then he was handing me the tub and turning away. He disappeared into the tower alone . . . but I sprinted to the door and slipped a stone into it with my foot as it closed behind him.

I waited only a moment, glancing about the yard behind me to make certain no one followed, to ensure Turner could not immediately be rid of me, then I tried the door. Thanks to the rock, it gave without argument, admitting me into the dark recesses of that tower.

I climbed by feel, flinching at every low moan or clank of metal above. I kept my eyes averted from the other faces peering out at me from the tower cells, focused on what was above—one who needed my help.

"There now. Steady, man." The voice echoed down, pulling me up toward it.

More groans.

Another turn on the staircase and then the soft glow of Dr. Turner's candle just ahead lit the way. There was no gaslight at this topmost point, I noticed. I stepped onto the landing and watched the man work. He was dressing the patient's wounds, carefully smoothing a poultice over the damaged wrists. "There now, isn't that better?"

A growl, and the prisoner hit the doctor's hands away, roaring a string of nonsense like an angry bear. Dr. Turner scrambled out of the cell and slammed the door, knocking his candle into a puddle of water. He was panting, leaning against the door he'd just shut.

I stepped forward and spoke to the prisoner. *"Kann ich Ihnen helfen?"* Can I help?

The room froze as my small voice echoed through the dark, then a match was struck and the candle again glowed in the tower landing. Dr. Turner stared at me across the glow, his face hard with anger. "Why did you follow me? I told you—"

"No one else can see us." I turned back to the man and repeated the meager German words I knew. *"Kann ich Ihnen helfen?"*

The silence was taut and I could feel my heart beating. Praying I was right. The wild bear of a man shuffled into the shaft of light from the window and blinked at me from under his mess of greasy hair. I could see the gravity in his eyes. He wasn't mad—he was a very sane man gone wild with frustration, desperate to be heard in a place where no one listened.

His gravelly voice ground out the words as his eyes pleaded with wild desperation. *"Kann ich Ihnen helfen? Bitte."*

I harnessed the few words I knew in his language and asked him what was wrong. After a few awkward exchanges, I turned back to my companion. "His skin cannot tolerate something in your poultice, Doctor. Perhaps eucalyptus—I could not quite understand. The reaction will make his injury worse."

He blinked at me. "Are you certain?"

"I doubt he's lying. He isn't mad, Dr. Turner, he's *German*." Had no one at Hurstwell managed to leave our little area of Northern England, to educate themselves about other cultures and people? It was common of such rural areas, people living and dying and existing every day within a bubble unpenetrated by the world at large. This was the unforgivable result. I closed my eyes and breathed deeply, full of gratitude for my pianoforte performances and the adventures that often took me far from England's shores.

I turned back to the trapped man and asked, in halting words, where he was from and what had become of his family.

They were in Scotland, he told me, having fled Austria together after some difficulties from enemies—with the language barrier, I couldn't make out what sort. They'd been separated, and he'd found himself in Northern England, wandering through the moors. His words gushed forth in an avalanche of sound, telling everything that had been done to him, what had gone wrong, and how desperately he'd prayed for help. I could only piece together parts of it, picking up words I recognized here and there.

He believed he'd been kidnapped by his enemies and asked me what I knew of his situation. I didn't even have the German words to explain why he was here, and what sort of place this was.

At last I turned back to my companion. "Dr. Turner, would you kindly fetch me paper and ink? This man needs to send word to his family about where they can find him or he'll be stuck here for all eternity."

Dr. Turner's frown deepened for several breaths. Then he disappeared and soon returned with writing instruments held against his chest. I pinched my lips together as I accepted them, hiding the surge of victory that flooded me. I dipped the pen in the inkwell balanced on a wooden chair on the landing, writing as quickly and clearly as I could. Hopefully his poor wife could decipher my butchering of their language. I wrote the same words out in English just below, in case she had someone to translate—that missive would be much clearer.

When I'd finished, I rose and left the page on the chair to dry. "Perhaps you ought to reconsider me as your aid. There's a lot of good to be done, if only you'll accept my help." How whole and healthy I felt in his presence—I couldn't bear to give it up.

He stiffened, the wall rising between us again. We were divided, patient and doctor. "It isn't that simple. There are rules—"

"Which aren't worth the paper they're printed on. For once— *for once*—let me be more than a patient at an asylum. Simply let me be a human." I stood toe to toe with him, looking up into his face. "You seem to forget at times, Dr. Turner, that we're on the same side. We both wish to help people, no matter the color of our gowns." I willed that stone wall to crumble.

He turned away from my challenging gaze and fortified the barrier between us. "I'm trying to protect you. And you *are* a patient here legally, no matter the circumstances."

"I never asked for your protection, Doctor. I don't need it. I only want to help the people who are dying for want of it."

Something flickered in his face, a chink in the wall. He moved to usher us both out.

"Was it not your idea?" My voice was softer as I followed him down the stairs. "You know I'm not mad. You know it." I leaned forward, compelled to touch his arm, and he paused. "I've been set up, Dr. Turner. I believe it was Nurse Duffy, for she hates me, or perhaps Dr. Thornhill. I happen to know a few of his secrets."

"There's quite a lot you don't—"

"No, listen." My heart pounded and I felt the slipping of time. The immediacy of making my appeal. "Someone has set things in place—arranged things—to make it seem as though I'm mad. I need your help. Just as much as he does. Neither of us belongs here, but we cannot escape."

He stared at me for long moments. "You'd best get back before you're missed."

That was the end of it. I could feel that in his gentle words. I nodded and started down the twisting stairs again. Fear tumbled over the small ray of hope. He turned to me when we reached the next floor, and I paused to look up into his well-cut, intelligent face as he spoke. "There is one thing you can do, though, even on your own. If you would. Help Anna somehow. She needs it."

"How?" *Her feet. Wash her feet.* The compelling notion came again, squeezing my stomach at the thought of her damaged feet. Those swollen, aged feet.

He shook his head. "She's been agitated since she lost her music box. I'm afraid a simple replacement won't do, either. It wouldn't be the same and she'd know it. Besides, she's been going on about this Philippe, and I haven't any idea who that is or where to find him."

The note. I never should have read her the note.

He ran fingers through his hair. "Just see if you can find out anything, won't you? Or at least calm her. Talk to her. Do what you can. She deserves a little gentleness."

I stared at the ground.

He sighed. "I know this is hard, being a patient here, but perhaps you shouldn't focus so much on *who* has done this to you, and whatever reason they had for it. There's a larger reason you were brought here." His face was intent in the shadows. "You're so different now than when you came. Do you realize that?"

I frowned. "Am I?" It was true, I was different—more gaunt, weak, and strained than I'd been in years.

"Forgive my forthrightness, but it seems your original plans of rescuing women—fine as they were—came from anger. Toward your father, your childhood. You were bound up in resentment, Vivienne. Shielded against being controlled but also against many good things." His gaze caught mine, making it impossible to duck away. "But here you are digging into the hearts of the lowest in society and finding their song, feeling for the rhythm of their hearts. You've been stretched the way my mother used to stretch fabric to . . . to make it softer. You came with a good heart, but I've watched it stretch and soften in new ways."

I blinked, trying to swallow the lump in my throat.

"Perhaps God saw fit to break down who you were becoming and help you build back up the right way. To prepare you for something even greater."

I grabbed the wall and continued down, releasing the pull his words had on my heart. I'd had enough guilt and control in my life, and I was ready for independence. Needed it.

I knew he was right, but I could cry for want of freedom.

He caught my arm at the bottom of the tower. "Miss Mourdant. I know it isn't what you had in mind, but I do believe you are the only one who can help her. There is music beating inside you, and there is something of the same in her, too."

Yes. Yes, the same rhythm. The same lost melody. I shook as I recalled that day with her on the bench, her low voice humming Rosamond's song. That brought the familiar notes again to the surface, weaving like a ghost through my being, striking all the frenzied chords of remembrance.

He frowned at me. "Are you unwell?"

"Anna," I said. "Was she ever called Rose, or Rosamond?"

"No, not to my knowledge."

But it hardly mattered, did it? Anna's mind was a vault of decaying memories, none of which could be accessed anymore. I needed a key to get in.

A key—like a piano key.

The odd words from Mr. Frederick Harford flashed through my mind. *"Music opens up what we once believed lost. Memories resurface, peace invades pain . . ."*

Yet how? Helplessness spread through my body. Crippling helplessness. She'd hardly spoken to me, even when I'd played for her. Not a word. But I wanted many words from her. Needed them.

I hurried back to the laundry and kept my head low, slipping back into work. The tension had begun to ease from my muscles when a hand clamped onto my shoulder, spinning me around. "Out for a walk, were you?" Nurse Branson's gaze bore down upon me.

I stared back, shoulder tense in her grip.

"They was right about you." She spoke in my face, almost a hiss. "They was right, and you're a good-for-nothing like the rest. Never should have stood up for the likes of you." She grabbed my arm and pulled me along behind her. "I've a vat of cooking oil what needs cleaned out. None of the aids can stomach it, so I'll let you have a go."

That night, weary and shaking with nausea, I curled up on my cot, fully clothed, and waited for the waves of sickness to recede. When Lew came through to place clean chamber pots under the beds, I grabbed his hand. "Lew, I need you to pass another message." I propped myself up and explained what I needed, and where to find the man in question.

"You're certain he'll know what it means, miss?"

"As long as you tell him it's from me, I promise he will. Whatever he gives you, some note or instruction, you must deliver it to me without anyone else seeing. Even for a moment."

This time it was Mr. Frederick Harford I'd asked him to find, with a simple verbal message: *I find I need help piercing the dark.*

Rose was close. I could feel it.

And when I uncovered her story, this prison would come tumbling down like a house of straw.

27

The earth has music for those who listen.

~William Shakespeare

They put me in with the long-stay patients for bath night, on account of the cooking oil encounter. Acute patients wouldn't be bathing for three more days, and apparently they couldn't stand the smell for that long. Which was fortunate, because I wasn't certain I could either.

One by one they dunked the patients, dousing and soaping them with lye, scrubbing their hair, then dousing them again. I watched Anna from my perch on the edge of the bench when it was her turn, looking her over and wondering about the mysterious song that lived inside of her. Of the secrets she couldn't even remember.

Perhaps it wasn't even her who had played. Yet she knew the song.

They were undressing her, but when an aid knelt to yank off her slippers, Anna kicked the woman full in the face and tucked her feet with a whimper.

"Hey, what's the idea?" screeched the poor aid, and two others came to hold the woman down as she fought to get away.

"Don't bother," said another aid. "This one never lets us take her shoes off. Just sponge her off and move on."

But the injured aid yanked at the woman's ankles, fighting for her slippers. "They only do what you let them do."

I sprang up and approached the scuffle. "Let me try, won't you?"

Wash her feet. It had swept over me every time I saw the woman, and nothing short of the literal act had seemed to suffice. My chance had come, the conviction even stronger than the first time. *Serve her. Wash her feet.* So I would.

They all three turned to me, then backed away from the old woman, who clung to the battered chair. "Help yourself."

They moved away and I knelt before her, hand on her knee. "Hello, Anna." I spoke softly, and her wild-eyed gaze connected with mine. White frizz hung over her face. "I won't hurt you, I promise. And I won't steal your shoes. I only want to clean your feet. Would that be all right?"

She stared at me wordlessly, so I swept one foot out and peeled off the heel of her slipper that seemed to have become part of her foot. Her skin was raw around the edges, and the more of her foot I exposed, the more I wanted to stop. To back away. This couldn't be what God intended. I stared at her long, bowed legs, her swollen feet. I held the slipper and tugged forward. "May I?"

She looked about until her gaze centered on me, then the foot I held, but she did not pull back.

I pulled off the rest of the shoe to reveal the most wretched, misshapen, blistered foot I'd ever seen. Wounds old and new, calluses that turned a few toes crooked, and blister scars covered her flesh. I had to hold my breath to keep from gasping. I held that bare foot and looked up into the old woman's face. She looked directly at me for once as I held her foot, and she gently tried to tuck it away.

A dancer. She was a *dancer*! "You were a ballerina." I'd known several, shared a stage with a few, and I had learned that no other foot became as damaged as that of a ballet dancer's. "Anna, won't you tell me about it?"

In answer, she tipped her face toward the heavens with a vacant smile and started humming, as if still hearing the ballet's orchestra. In my hand, that misshapen, hard-worn foot curved, muscles activating until her toes were pointed. I dipped a rag into the basin and began washing.

She sighed. "Remember. Always remember. Who you are." She spoke it like a song, eyes closed. She hardly flinched as I ran the cold cloth over callouses, injuries, and raw skin. When I drew my rag away, her eyes fluttered open. "Where's my music box?" She spoke awkwardly, as if she'd filled her mouth with smooth stones. "My music. I cannot forget."

"Where did that box come from, Anna? What was your real name?" I held my breath.

Rose. I almost willed her to say it.

"Ann . . . ih . . . ka. Annika." Her gaze came to rest on me again, a light smile on her lips. Her words came slow and disjointed. "It was hers—the box. Ella Blythe. Little Ella Blythe." Her look grew distant.

I dipped and squeezed the rag. Ella Blythe, the famous ballet dancer? "Did you know her?"

She blinked at me, as if returning to the present. Confusion wrinkled her brow.

"What about a woman named Rose? Rosamond Swansea? Perhaps the pianoforte tutor Winston Mourdant?"

Worry creased her face further. Her left arm began to tremble against the chair and her gaze darted about, unable to settle. "Philippe," was all she said. "Philippe. He's gone." A vacant stare stole over her face as she slumped a little, eyes dimming, and the portal swept closed.

"Anna. Anna, won't you look at me?"

Hands yanked my arms from behind. "You're up."

241

I scrambled to stand as they dragged me to the tub, peeling off my gown the moment I was upright. Soon I was dunked, scrubbed, and doused, and when I emerged, Anna was gone. I sat dripping and shivering on the bench until they led us toward the wards.

Out in the corridor, I caught Dr. Turner's eye as he passed, and without a word he fell into step beside us. I kept my voice low, shoving wet hair off my face. "She's a ballet dancer, perhaps called Annika. Speak with Ella Blythe in London. It was her music box, and she may be able to help."

He dipped his head, looking forward, and I couldn't tell for certain that he'd heard me before he split from our crowd and turned left down another corridor, files tucked under one arm. My heart pounded as I watched him go, but there was nothing more I could do.

Nurse Duffy poked at my back to keep me moving, standing between me and the retreating doctor. "You go this way. You've nothing to do with the chronic ward, you know."

We turned a corner into the hallway of the room where I slept, and that's when I heard it. A shrill scream—a voice I knew. I hurried toward it, hair dripping down my back. Bridget cowered in the center of a moving mass of bodies, arms over her head as she screeched like a boiling teapot, rocking forward and back.

Two nurses surged toward her through the crowds, shoving patients aside.

"Bridget!" I dove into the chaos, jamming elbows into flesh to make a way, but I barely got ahead.

Then a hush fell over the crowd and the knot of people loosened. I looked up. Dr. Turner had returned, striding through like a river in its course, cutting its way through rock and soil. When he reached Bridget, he shielded her with his body, leaning over her and speaking low words even as she fought him.

Her shoulders heaved up and down, but her voice quieted to low sobs. Finally, he lifted his head and looked out over the crowd. "What has happened? How did this come about?"

"It shouldn't have happened." Nurse Branson's face was pained. "One of the nurses let it slip about her baby dying."

Baby . . . dying. The words sliced through me with jagged disbelief and horror. Her baby—Bridget's baby. I hugged my middle to keep myself together. I felt compelled to be near her—to offer my presence. I had to wait, of course, until the attention was turned elsewhere.

Dr. Turner's voice was dangerously low. "You're right, and I hope the nurse responsible thinks better of it before taking it upon herself to deliver such a blow again."

There were murmurs, and Dr. Thornhill strode through the path Dr. Turner's entrance had carved. "Thank you, Dr. Turner, but I can take over from here. You need not concern yourself with an acute patient."

Turner pivoted on his heel, keeping himself between Bridget and Dr. Thornhill. "I am a doctor, and anyone at Hurstwell who has need of me shall have me."

"You have your own patients, Turner, and I don't see a single one of them in this corridor." Another step toward them. "Go about your business and leave her to me. Unless you would declare her a chronic case and make her one of yours."

I shivered under my wet gown, watching the powerful display of emotions storm below the surface of Dr. Turner's expression as he rose to face his superior, the masterful way he reined them in as if he had built up that muscle over many years. "Of course not. She is needed at home one day. She'll remain in acute."

The two men stood toe to toe now, and the entire lot of us were pulled into their tension. Whimpers and sniffles were the only sounds, the patients not daring to be anything but meek and unobtrusive in this moment.

Dr. Turner released Bridget to the nurses with a pointed look. "Go easy with her, she's had a great upset."

"Of course, Doctor." Nurse Branson turned, arm around her patient, and led Bridget firmly out of my reach.

"Where are they taking her?" I whispered to a patient who stood beside me. She merely shook her head, face pale and drawn.

I asked a nurse too. She brushed me off as if she hadn't heard me. Perhaps she hadn't.

No matter. I was Bridget's friend, and this time I would help her. I would.

28

A man of ordinary talent will always be ordinary, whether he travels or not; but a man of superior talent will go to pieces if he remains forever in the same place.

~Wolfgang Amadeus Mozart

A touch of guilt followed Mitchell Turner onto the train and into town. He rode all the way to London's Charing Cross station and disembarked, looking about and realizing why he felt so odd. So very off. He'd hardly ventured into the world beyond Hurstwell since Dahlia had died. He'd had no reason. No desire, really.

His outdated wool trousers and frock coat seemed largely out of place among the cutaway coats and adorned buttonholes, the tall hats with neat ribbons. He'd been absent from the real world for too long, and it made him cringe. Both because he'd lived in such isolation, and because he didn't now deserve to be experiencing the greater world when she could not.

The light snow had turned to slush in London's busy streets, and color flew by in every direction—bright cloaks, painted shop signs, the glitter of brass on passing coaches. His inquiries revealed that Ella Blythe had been connected to Craven Street Theatre in Covent Gardens, so he began by asking about there and in the nearby inns until he found a pub where someone could point him toward the ballet studio she now operated with her husband in nearby Savile Row.

He walked to save the fare, enjoying the stretch for his legs, and soon came upon the large brown brick three-story with red trim and a swinging sign at the gate that marked the lower level a place of business.

When he rang the buzzer, a white-capped maid answered, and Mitchell asked for Ella Blythe.

"She isn't taking pupils any longer, sir." She eyed his tall form, looking past him for signs of a daughter or some other prospective student. "I'm afraid you'll have to take one of her staff members instead."

"It's her I've come to see, actually, and on a personal matter. Can you tell me where to find her?"

"She isn't seeing the public any longer, but if you'll leave your card—"

"I've no card, but she'll want to hear what I have to say. My name is Dr. Mitchell Turner. Tell her it's about a friend of hers named Annika. Do that, won't you please?"

The maid frowned, but she backed into the house and disappeared. When she returned, she beckoned Mitchell in with pressed lips and a quick nod of her head. They began in a generous entryway that was light-filled and calm compared to Hurstwell's shadows and barred windows, then climbed the wide stairs to a small receiving room on the second floor. The room had a distinctly feminine air, light and airy—perfect for a former ballet dancer.

He was seated, and when the ivory doors opened again, there stood the regal Ella Blythe, dark silver hair swept back and pinned high and precise on her head. Her lovely slanted eyes, which held a trace of youthful innocence, looked him over before she entered, then she approached and held out a hand. "How do you do, Doctor . . . ?"

"Turner. Mitchell Turner." He took her dainty hand in his. "I'm an alienist at a small asylum in the north."

She frowned, one eyebrow arched, and taking a seat on an opposite chair, came directly to the point. "My maid tells me you have word of Annika?"

"I believe so. Might she go by Anna now? Anna Michelson?"

"Perhaps." Ella perched on the edge of her chair, ringed fingers hanging off the arms. "What made you connect this Anna Michelson person to my Annika?"

"She carried a music box with her everywhere and was quite attached to it. A small box with a spinning dancer, and she told someone that you gave it to her."

"Have you proof she is truly Annika?" Caution glazed her fresh, almost youthful look.

He rummaged about his brain for some little tidbit, something she'd said . . . "She had her lucid moments, years ago. She once mentioned a story connected to the box. Something about a little dancer throwing her enchanted red shoe to save the one she loved . . . I'm assuming if it was your box, then you too know this tale."

Long lashes blinked away sudden moisture. "Yes. Yes, it must be her. So few know that story. Annika Freidl was her name." She paused a moment. "Where is she?"

He relaxed back against the chair, easing tensed muscles. "I'm afraid it isn't good news. In fact, I was hoping you might help her. Or perhaps direct me to someone who can." He told her of Hurstwell, and of what Annika had become—but who she still remained in her memory. He was honest about Anna's condition, but carefully described her gentle nature to assure his listener that the woman had not grown dangerous in her decline. "She doesn't belong in such a place, even if her mind isn't what it once was. She's only in need of some assistance in the day-to-day. Simple care and affection, a little guidance now and again. And who knows what might return to her if she's taken out of the asylum and given those things?"

The woman's fingers trembled against the gold chair arm. "An asylum."

"A pauper lunatic asylum—for lack of any other option, I'm afraid. As I said, there was no one to care for her, but her needs are quite simple."

Ella Blythe straightened, and Mitchell could see her as nothing other than a dancer, swan-like and quietly commanding, even at her age. "Has she no family left?"

He shook his head, itching to ram his fingers through his hair but politely restraining. "Records state she is married, but I'm not certain where to locate her husband. I was hoping you could tell me her background, so I might find a charitable family member willing to help her."

"She does have a child, I believe. She was only a girl of three or four when I last saw her, but quite a bright little thing. Perhaps she might help. Her name is Emily."

He took a small notebook and pencil from a pocket inside his overcoat. "Emily . . . Freidl?"

"I'm not certain. Rousseau, perhaps. She was born to Annika before she wed." Color crept over the woman's alabaster skin. "Annika did marry one of the dancers shortly after she left Craven, the child's father, I believe, but they had such a rough go of it. I don't suppose that's who she's still married to, is it?"

"John Michelson is on record as her husband."

The woman before him deflated almost imperceptibly. "She loved Philippe so."

"Philippe, you say." He tensed the fingers holding the little pencil. "This Philippe is . . . the child's father?"

"Yes, Philippe Rousseau, her dance partner in the theater. He was arrested, you see, on old charges from his earlier life, and it changed their circumstances entirely. She could no longer dance, of course, after having her children, and he could earn nothing from prison. They faced financial ruin, the death of five of their six children, and a brutal bout of illness that nearly took her life."

"What a difficult existence."

"She was fiercely happy with her Philippe, though, dear Annika." Miss Blythe's voice became dreamy. Distant. "She loved her husband with such passion and fought for his release, but she may have felt she had no choice but to marry again, if such was possible. I only wish I knew." She sighed.

"I brought her ballet students to train, gave them cast-off gowns and plenty of food, but then one day several years after she left the theater, she simply . . . vanished. She and her daughter were gone—into the country, her landlord said, but he couldn't say where." She glanced away. "So there my pursuit of her ended, and I've hardly heard her blessed name again until this very day."

"I'm sorry to hear it." Something in his chest wrenched at the story of the frail woman under his care, at the large and colorful life that had slipped from her grasp and even her memories. "I wish I had better news for you."

She straightened, as if determined to strengthen herself. "What of the music box, then? Do you have it?"

"I'm afraid it's gone too. Not much lasts at a place like Hurstwell."

Her delicate shoulders slumped.

"It was her only belonging, and she carried it with her everywhere. Cranked it up and curled her body around it every time she was afraid—especially during a storm. She is terrified of storms."

Ella Blythe's fine brow wrinkled.

"She's become increasingly agitated since losing the little box, but I don't know much about her background. I haven't any idea what else might comfort her. Which is the other reason I've come."

She nodded. "Very well, then. What can I do?"

"Tell me about this Philippe. Perhaps I may locate him, or at least some remembrance . . ."

She fidgeted with the tip of one glove. "Philippe Rousseau. Heavens, I should remember something about the man, but I cannot even seem to summon his likeness in my mind. He was principal at Craven, and . . . oh, bother." She turned to call over her shoulder. "Frannie, is my husband back in his office yet?"

"Yes ma'am, been listening in from there since I brought your visitor in."

"Has he, now?" Her eyes sparkled, and she relaxed into her Queen Anne armchair. "What a little snoop." She tipped her head back and raised her melodic voice. "Oh, Mr. Dorian!"

"It's Jack, woman. *Jack!*" The side door burst open and a hearty man with a lively countenance strode into the room, bringing an air of energy and surprising warmth, despite his good-natured outburst. "At least in my own home, eh?" He leaned down, tipping her chin up, and kissed his wife before them all.

Turner couldn't help but smile at the little exchange.

She pinched her lips in mock anger. "Now that you've heard the whole story, *Mr. Dorian*, I don't suppose you could help us, could you? Something about Philippe?"

Mr. Dorian raised his eyebrow. "Would it be crass of me to be pleased that you've forgotten so much about him?" He kissed her forehead and turned toward Mitchell for the first time.

Turner rose and gave a small head bow. "I'm grateful for you both welcoming me into your home."

He waved off the formalities and loosened his necktie. "So you want to talk about Philippe Rousseau. He was a Frenchman with a soft voice and tall build, and for what it's worth, he was actually released from prison some years ago."

His wife turned in her chair. "And why wasn't I told? Where has he gone?"

"That's precisely why I never told you—I have no idea where he went, only that he was released on bail from . . . some unnamed source . . . and he never returned."

"Unnamed source, eh?" She narrowed her eyes, pressing her lips together. "That's what happened to the six hundred pounds you never would speak of, wasn't it?"

He heaved a dramatic sigh. "Couldn't let the poor bloke waste his life away, now could I? Not after I spent so much of my energy on him in our youth."

She smiled indulgently and patted her husband's cheek. "You're a fine man, Jack Dorian." Then she turned to me. "There now, you know as much as we do. It wouldn't surprise me at all to find Philippe escaped to the country and changed his name, just as she did. Finding him will be difficult, I'm afraid, unless . . . "

"Unless he changed it to John Michelson."

She shrugged. "It's possible, I suppose." She swiveled in her chair to address her husband. "Perhaps we should see what can be found of Emily. She'd be next of kin, if Annika's husband cannot be found, and hopefully she'd be able to free her mother and point us toward what became of Philippe."

"I can do a bit of digging," Dorian offered. "It's been a while since I've tried. Perhaps she's left a trail."

"Leave me an address where you can be reached, will you, Doctor . . . Turner, was it?"

Mitchell tore out a sheet from the notebook he carried and scribbled down the address, rising to leave as he handed it to her. "I shall look forward to any communication from you, my lady, and I do hope we can help Annika. She's a good soul."

She gave a dignified nod of Annika's head. "I'll let you know the moment I find anything of value."

On the train ride back to Menston, Turner thought of Anna and her complex life, the dancer Philippe who'd been arrested, the daughter who had presumably abandoned them, and then of her husband, John Michelson. That's what had stuck with him most—that name John Michelson. He recognized it—he knew he did.

Ever since he'd seen the name listed in her paperwork, it had nagged at him. There was something he ought to remember about the name. Something he should know but had forgotten in the jumble of all the other things bombarding him every day. His mind wouldn't let it go—it turned and puzzled about, an unfinished story his brain could not let rest until it had worked the thing out.

29

My masters are strange folk with very little care for music in them.

~Johann Sebastian Bach

"Superintendent Thornhill is asking after you. Come down straightaway." Nurse Duffy's voice startled me at the washbasin where I'd flooded my face with water.

A quiet dawn stretched through the ward. Bridget hadn't been to the room to sleep. Her thin blankets were still pulled up to the head of her cot, and I'd spent a night of increasing worry. I was already prone to it in broad daylight lately, but something about the darkness of night distorted logic and hope even further.

I had gone to the pianoforte again and simply polished the wood in small, methodical circles, thinking with aching tenderness of Bridget and her desire to offer music to her baby girl.

"Come, he wants to see you in his office."

"Me?" I felt for the towel and dried my face. "I'm just washing up, and—"

"I haven't time for this." She yanked me along, and my hip rammed the stand, sending the bowl and pitcher quivering. "And Dr. Thornhill won't be kept waiting."

How noticeable my weakness was as my legs clambered down those steps, hardly able to keep up with the wiry little nurse pulling me along. She was like a tide sweeping forward, not to be stopped by my slower pace.

We finally paused before the closed office door, facing one another, toe to toe. I couldn't read what lay behind her face, her snapping gaze full of so many thoughts. "Well, now. Here you be." With a final pinch to my arm, she shoved me into Thornhill's office. The scent of lemon on wood struck me again. "Here she is, Doctor," and Duffy was gone.

The door shut and my skin crawled in the silence. I was alone with the tall tower of command in his velvet-trimmed frock coat, his eyes finding flaws on every inch of me. I'd been in this office before, but how small the place seemed with him in it.

I tried to picture this man appealing to the lovely Rosamond, him asking for her hand—what she had seen when she accepted him.

How different he must look now. The world had hardened him. Worn down his spirit and accentuated his flaws. His white hair was combed back, giving undue emphasis to the thick gray eyebrows that hovered over his sharp-eyed gaze. New circles had formed beneath his eyes, and his skin was weathered.

He turned on me, his usual calm hardened into something else entirely. "Miss Fletcher." Two steps and he was nearly on top of me, his voice quiet. "I'm going to ask you one time, and I expect the truth. *Where is she?*"

I leaned away from his face until my neck hurt, my mind working to keep pace. "Who? Where is who?"

"I know you take it upon yourself to decide who belongs at Hurstwell and who does not, but there are things you cannot possibly know. Bridget Hurley is not just under our care for mental disturbances but for medical concerns as well. With her disappearance . . ."

Bridget—*missing?*

"Are you aware that she receives a special tincture every day for her blood sugars and without it she may well go into shock? Three days is all she has without that medicine—three days. She'll go into fits, suffer permanent neurological damage, and possibly die. I'll be held responsible, yet *you* will be the one living with her blood on your hands." His eyes narrowed. "Do you realize that by helping her escape you may have also sentenced her to *death*?"

Did he even care about her, or any of them? Had he cared about his wife when she was a patient here, or had she merely been a pretty thing he wished to own? He underestimated us. All of us. I was trembling now as he leaned over me, but I looked that madman straight in the eye. "What makes you think she even needed my help?"

"You expect me to believe she escaped from a locked isolation room by herself?"

Fight flooded my veins. Pure heat. "I'm as locked up as she. How could I have helped?"

With a growl, he yanked my arm toward him and clamped cuffs on my wrists, metal digging into my flesh where my bones jutted. "I'll show you *locked up*." They were heavy. He jerked both cuffs tight, leaving a chain dangling between them, and shook the key in my face. "This is a moral institution, Miss Fletcher, and I will not tolerate liars." His anger vibrated through the room. "You were gone from your bed last night when she went missing—you, the only known friend of this Bridget Hurley. You'll face trouble for this, if she's harmed. I'll make sure of it, you wretched little—"

"It is *you* who have lost her, Dr. Thornhill. You lost her, just as you did your own wife."

The blow to my cheek was so swift it whipped my head to the right, face stinging and neck tight with pain. I caught myself on his desk. I hovered over his papers, hair curtaining my warm face. My breath came in quiet gasps as hot and cold chased each other over my skin.

The key clattered against his desk where he threw it. "There are some who are too far mad to ever be let free. They bring no value to humanity by existing within it and are naught but a nuisance. A threat, even."

I steadied my breathing. "Bridget is—"

"I was referring to you, Miss Fletcher." His face came near mine. "But I never let your sort win. What kind of world would we have then?"

I breathed hard, but I scarcely got any air into my lungs. My head was light. Those eyes—those wild eyes that couldn't focus on mine. Red veins rose along his neck.

"Until you tell me where she is, you will remain in those. Night and day."

The force of his anger rolled over me. I closed my eyes, waiting for lashes across my knuckles. A shove into a dark closet. His face hovered near, warm breath on my skin. "Also. Never *ever* mention my wife again." His voice hissed out in harsh bursts of air. "You are not worthy to speak her name."

As I braced myself over his desk, clutching the wooden edge, his cologned presence brushed past me and left the room. Two more dizzying breaths and Nurse Branson came and grasped my arm, pulling me into the entryway. That vast, airy entryway that was such a front.

Pianist was not my identity, it seemed, but *prisoner.* Ever and always. I could not reach freedom, could not help those I longed to rescue. There were always chains, always some man standing over me, forcing my direction.

But I was still me. Somehow, I would have to find Bridget. Despite the rules, the locked doors, the shackles, I *must* act. She would not die because of this place.

In the daylight of the great hall, I blinked at the sight of a poised, simply dressed lady talking to Thornhill. A veil covered her face, but I could tell by the posture of her petite figure that she spoke with great passion.

Branson slowed her pace, apparently as nosy as I about the conversation occurring before us. I looked the visitor over as we passed, and her accent struck me. It prompted images of Vienna, and the gentle old streets there.

"Please, von't you look again." Clipped and German. "I vas told I could find here my husband."

Chills raced up and down my arms—excitement, nerves.

"I'm sorry, Mrs. Schumann, but you must have the wrong institution. There are so many about England now—perhaps your Otto is in another."

Otto. That was him—the German man in the tower. It must be!

"You are quite certain? Zis is the place from vhat the letter came. It told me to come here. That he vas here." The veil shook over her face. "I know not vere else to look."

I stepped boldly forward, clutching my hands together. "You're Leizel."

Thornhill spun on me, ready to pounce. "What sort of trouble are you causing now?" He sunk his fingers into my arm, shoving me away. "Branson, take this woman."

"Vait!" The veiled woman stepped forward, gloved hand out to me.

I dug my heels into the carpet. "He's here, Mrs. Schumann. I've seen him. He's h—" Branson yanked me off my feet. I stumbled to stay upright.

"I beg your pardon, Mrs. Schumann," I heard Thornhill say as I was pulled out of the entryway. "The inmates will say anything for a little attention. You mustn't pay them any mind. She has no idea what she says."

Trapped. Ever trapped.

"Did someone check the cemetery?" I leaned close to Lew that night in the wards as the women filed into the room. I stared at Bridget's unused bed, sheets pulled up to the lumpy pillow. Night one of three was approaching. "The one in her parish, I mean. That's where I'd have gone first, if my child . . ."

"They've not buried the babe yet. I heard them talking, and someone from Hurstwell's already been to look for her."

"Her home, then. Did she make it back to her family?"

"They don't seem to know she's escaped yet. Haven't seen her."

"You're certain?"

The boy placed a clean pot and stood. "Heard Thornhill talking to some of his men. They don't want to tip their hand yet about losing her—afraid of the constable being called—but they've been asking about. No sign of her with the family or at the cemetery."

Losing Rose hadn't seemed to upset anyone. In fact, they pretended it hadn't happened. Why the concern for Bridget, the pauper?

"Oh, and by the by, I delivered your message. Your Harford bloke didn't give me anything."

I waved it off. That could wait—everything could. "Lew . . . where else would she go?"

He stood still so long I wondered if he'd heard me. Then at last, he said, "Nowhere. She wouldn't go nowhere. That's the bad news."

"And the good news?"

He shrugged. "They ain't found her dead yet."

I huffed out a breath, smoothing fingers over my hair. She had to be at Hurstwell still. Why risk escape at all if not to be with her family or bury her baby girl? And another thing—she hadn't wanted to leave. Not especially. *For some, there's no escaping what binds us. Whether here or there.*

I heaved a long exhale, shoving long hair off my face.

God Almighty, never before have I needed your help more. Free me, Lord, so I may find her. Please . . . free me. There isn't much time.

There was no miracle, no response. I was back in the locked larder at my father's house, but this time I was alone.

30

All I insist on, and nothing else, is that you should show the whole world that you are not afraid. Be silent, if you choose; but when it is necessary, speak—and speak in such a way that people will remember it.

~Wolfgang Amadeus Mozart

They formed us into straight lines in Hurstwell's large entryway, all the able-bodied patients from the acute ward. It was afternoon, with sun beaming through the windows. There was a visitor, they said, so we were lined up like cattle at auction. It was the second full day that Bridget had been missing. I'd hardly lifted my head all day and my shackles hung heavy from my wrists, a symbol of my helplessness.

I lifted my eyes and looked down the line of women, those dull countenances that I now wore too. I had joined them—maybe not in madness, but in total despair. I saw it on all their faces, that look of lifelessness, and I felt it keenly.

My gaze stopped at Dr. Thornhill, tall and confident with a look of deep-seated hostility—almost resentment—toward the lot of us. He glanced toward me for a flash as if by habit, assuring himself I was still there, then his attention shifted on.

At last the double doors opened, admitting a flood of daylight and dry chill, and a man of no great stature. I couldn't even see him over the heads of the others lined up between me and the entrance. There was a formal-sounding welcome that echoed, and the men conversed for some moments while the doors were closed and latched against the November cold.

"How'd you manage it?" Clara whispered in the smallest voice beside me.

I turned on her with a look of incredulity. "Manage what?" Surely she didn't mean—

"Bridget. How ever did you sneak her out?"

I glared. "Are you daft? I did no such thing."

She cringed, eyes wide, which instantly deflated my anger.

I puffed out a breath. "Forgive me, Clara. These"—I jostled the cuffs on my wrist—"are the most unpleasant bracelets I've ever worn."

She stifled a giggle behind her hand. "Oh but I'm sorry, Miss Vivienne. Sorry they did that to you."

"Who else might have helped her? Did she ask for help?"

"I bet it was *her*."

"Who? What do you mean?"

Clara's face pinched. "Her, the ghost. Rose. There's no one else who could have done it."

My flesh was cold. "You can't be serious."

"Walls and bars don't stop them, you know."

"Why would Rose help Bridget, though?"

Before she could answer, Dr. Thornhill strode between the rows with his visitor, slicing through our whispered conversation. "These are our acute patients. I suggest you begin with them. The others are here for the duration, and they are quite beyond help."

I flinched at the grim prognosis.

"Nonsense." The visitor stepped into our row, and I glimpsed with utter shock the only face that could yank my mind from Bridget—Mr. Frederick Harford. He looked down the row and his focus came to rest on me with the slightest smile. "No one, Dr. Thornhill, is beyond help."

I stared back at him, my flesh prickling as our gazes met and held, his lips tipping up just slightly more at the corners. I had sent for him, in a way, hadn't I? What a lifetime ago that seemed. So many things had crowded the mystery of Rose from my mind, and I almost didn't know what to do with his presence here, so very close and startling—and not what I needed just now.

"Well, then. I suppose you came prepared with your own instruments, so you may begin when you wish."

"I have a rather rudimentary collection, but I was given to understand that a pianoforte exists here on the grounds. I had hoped I might avail myself of it."

Dr. Thornhill eyed the shorter man with no small amount of displeasure. "It's been neglected for some time, and I'm afraid it's quite useless."

I dropped my gaze, but I could feel Clara grinning beside me. A few of the others snickered. I glanced up and froze them with a look. Didn't they know enough to keep their silly tongues in their heads?

"Let's have a look anyway, if you would." Harford puffed out his chest as if drinking in fresh spring air and looked about the grand entrance. "Yes, this will be a fine place for my trials, and I'll be proud to pass my findings on to the home secretary."

"If you'll excuse me, I do have a fair amount of work to do." Thornhill was irritated. "I assume you can manage on your own."

I was filled with dread, looking back and forth between their faces, waiting for the foggy unknown to become clear. Waiting for Harford to reveal the real reason he'd come. Waiting for Dr. Thornhill to stop wasting his time and find Bridget. Had I not been bound and watched like a hawk, I would have darted off to do it myself, and likely done a better job at it.

"I'll only ask a few more moments of your time, Superintendent. I'd like to introduce you to my methods and have you observe—at least at the beginning. Perhaps you can provide insight on your patients too."

Thornhill's eyes narrowed. "You don't expect to be here long, do you? A few days at most?" The man was more irritable than usual. Much more.

"If everything progresses the way I envision, I may well be staying for some time. Not to worry, though. It'll all be worth it, in the end." He leveled his blue-eyed gaze on me as he spoke, rocking back on his heels, and I hadn't any idea what he was trying to tell me. "The advancement of science, and what have you. Now then, let us see this neglected pianoforte. And bring the patients. I'd like to gauge the nature of my work here."

We were then ushered on a surreal march, two by two through the first-floor corridor to the east wing, and I walked through the forgotten pianoforte room's true entrance for the first time. A moment more and I was standing with heart-pounding stillness in my moonlit sanctuary, but with wide swaths of golden sunlight falling over the floor on both sides of the covered Broadwood. I stared at the thing with a small smile and suppressed a shiver. *Hello, old friend.*

With a whoosh, the intruder uncovered the great beauty, lifted the fallboard, and ran a hand over the keys. Daylight struck the dangling prisms on dusty chandeliers, lighting the room with dancing color I was not used to seeing here. Then he lifted the lid and propped it, inspecting the wooden frame and soundboard within. To anyone with eyes, the instrument was well-kept and even polished. I looked away as if I'd carved my own name into the wood and would soon be found out. Harford looked it over with a keen eye, but all he said was, "This will do perfectly."

Then he looked up at all of us. "I need a volunteer, if you would. Someone to play so I may interact directly with the patients and make my notes."

Suddenly tense, my gaze roamed the lines of patients, daring any of them to point me out. It was Dr. Turner who looked right at me with those unsettlingly honest eyes, watching from a shadowed corner. I could almost hear the echo of music with him looking at me that way, see Anna on the chair beside me as I spun a most glorious rendition of Chopin.

Even from this distance, Bach's cello solo was not muted. Separated by an entire room, by Dr. Thornhill and a host of patients, I felt Mitchell Turner's presence more strongly than the sun beaming down upon my back from the windows.

"Might I entice someone to volunteer? You, perhaps?" Harford looked at me directly and there was no denying who he meant. Everyone nearby looked my way. "Do you play?"

Now in the spotlight, I felt myself step forward as if I were following a script. "I do." Or perhaps stepping directly into a trap. The oddness of all this unsettled me.

"Someone else, perhaps." Nurse Branson swept forward, her nervous countenance looking to me and then to Thornhill—highly aware of my so-called delusions of grandeur that Hurstwell was not about to indulge. "That one is a patient."

"Is it your habit to restrict your patients so? I should think the home secretary would wish to rethink the funding given to such an institution."

His chin jutted with the intensity of his irritation, but Dr. Thornhill said nothing.

Ridiculous. Harford had no more access to the home secretary than I did Queen Victoria, most likely, but Dr. Thornhill didn't seem to realize that. What had the man claimed to be, an inspector from the lunacy commission?

The older man again rocked onto his heels. "Perhaps my time would be better spent auditing the records to ensure—"

"Actually, yes." Thornhill's look narrowed on me as if he'd decided something. "Let her try it. Let her show us what she can do with a pianoforte." His look was angry. Challenging.

Harford smiled. "Good, good. Now, won't you take a seat, my dear?"

He'd won. The bearded little clergyman had won—against Dr.
Thornhill. Although I had the fearful sense that Thornhill, in a
way, believed he had won too.

I sat on the familiar stool, Harford's pleased face nearby, and
lifted my arms that were heavy with metal chains.

"The shackles, Dr. Thornhill?"

"They will remain. Unfortunately they are necessary."

Harford raised his eyebrows but said nothing else. "By the by,"
he whispered, leaning close to my ear as Thornhill turned away,
"I'm terribly sorry it has gone this far. It was never meant to."

I stared at him, incredulous. Shocked. *He* had done this? He was
the one who'd set me up? "How long do you plan to keep me here?"

"Unfortunately, I do not have the means to get you out." He
looked strained. Remorseful. "As I said, it's gone further than I
ever intended."

I forced myself to breathe.

"And . . . about Beauchene. Terribly sorry for your loss. The
world will feel it keenly."

I stiffened on that stool, flooded with horror. Marcel, dead?
"When?"

His eyes widened. "You did not know?"

I turned back to the pianoforte, looking over the familiar strings
and soundboard as they began to blur. I'd misheard. This couldn't
be right.

"It was summer. There were articles in all the newspapers. He
was rather a well-known figure in the world of theater."

Months ago. Horror socked me, tidal waves of it pummeling me.
Drowning me. I pressed my lips together and stared down at the
keys, those perfectly even rows that were the same as every other
pianoforte I'd played for my entire life. I could play Mozart—no,
my hands wouldn't stretch far enough apart. A Schubert waltz? I
strained against the shackles until I trembled.

"Perhaps you'd like me to find Nurse Branson—I believe she
played in her church as a girl." Dr. Thornhill spoke up from his

spot a few yards away. "Since it seems this patient is unwilling . . . or *unable* to play."

I despised the man. Despised Harford for somehow manipulating me into this position. *Too far*, he'd said, as if he meant to destroy my life only a little bit instead of all the way.

I had missed Marcel's funeral mass. The burial. He was already in the ground, and I couldn't say goodbye. Because of Harford, who'd somehow lured me here, and Thornhill, who kept me trapped. My heart hammered with a sense of claustrophobia, of the walls of that dark larder that locked from the outside, closing in on me, on Bridget. I could do nothing about it. Nothing, but jump and do bidding like a trained monkey. Thornhill eyed me from the right, Harford from my left, expectation on both their faces.

I lifted my shackled hands, clenched my jaw, and rained my anger down on those keys. *Bang, bang, bang!* Dissonance resonated through my being, like a scream that ripped out of me. *Bang! Bang!* It was shocking and delicious and powerful. *Boooooooom.*

Then it was out, my fingers splayed over the keys, heart pounding. *Where? Where are you, God? Where have you hidden yourself when everything is so wrong?* I could feel Dr. Thornhill's pitying look, but his gaze deflected off my back. It wasn't about him. A performance was never about who was listening, but the one for whom the music was played . . . even if Marcel was not there to hear it anymore.

I flexed my hands, feeling the supple movement up my forearm . . . and then a surprising taste of freedom in every inch of my fingers. There was nothing to stop me from playing now—not even the chains.

I turned for just a moment and met Thornhill's eyes that sparkled with victory and I did not waver.

There was only so much about Paul they could lock up.

I looked back to the familiar ivories. Silence billowed through the room, and to me it was empty, the quiet onstage before a concert, and there was only one song on the docket. I closed my eyes, finding my way along the keys, and swept into the opening measures of Liszt's Hungarian Rhapsody no. 2 in C-sharp Minor. I pictured Marcel Beauchene—volatile, surprising, with periods of low, heavy notes and a few trills up high to balance out the dramatics. I played and played, stretching and adapting for the chains, but still honoring every inch of his life in this song.

What I'd always overlooked, however, was the ending. Rather than a warning of slightly discordant scales that reached a final satisfying harmony, Lizst's Rhapsody culminated in a frenzied climb that, in three simple chords, came to a solid and abrupt end. A final display of rapid color and a pop of finale chords—one . . . two . . . three . . . Then silence.

Shaking in the fading reverberation, I lifted my head and swept hair back from my face. How it echoed about this old place, with the double doors fully open and the pianoforte lid up.

A roomful of eyes watched me, each face displaying a different reaction. Dr. Turner's glowed—brilliant and eager and full of certainty over some unknown thing. Harford's face had softened, as if he'd experienced Beauchene's life through the song alongside me—not understanding the details, but compassionately sharing.

Then there was Dr. Thornhill, the great king of Hurstwell. He stood frozen halfway across the room, his aged face a mix of astonishment and pure anger.

No, fear.

All his anger today was borne of panic, I suddenly realized. He was trapped, with a patient missing and who knew what other secrets he didn't wish Harford uncovering.

I almost felt sorry for him, so vulnerable he seemed. I could see on his face that now, and only now, did he realize who I truly was.

And that it would not go well for me.

No one moved, and I was glad. It would take a few minutes to collect my scattered emotions and pack them away where they belonged.

At last, Harford spoke. He ran an appreciative hand over the polished body of the Broadwood. "I do believe you have underestimated this old instrument, Doctor."

Dr. Thornhill's face hardened, and I had the sense of impending doom, for Harford and his influence would eventually depart Hurstwell . . . but I would not. There was no maid to offer me fruit and peace. No Marcel to sweep in to my rescue. No Marcel Beauchene in all the world. For the first time in my life, I was utterly alone. I closed my eyes and tipped my face heavenward. *God, I begged. What do I do now? How do I escape this?*

But God did not give a response, and my heart dulled in despair.

At last, Dr. Thornhill spoke one sentence in a strained voice before taking his leave. "See that she does not overstep."

THIRD MOVEMENT

THE LOST TOWER

I was awake. Not just my eyes, but my soul, shuddering with warm awareness of the world around me, outside my head. Someone played the pianoforte. Music swam through my veins like blood warmed up to flow again, flooding my extremities with life and drawing me to wakefulness. I was alive after all.

Mostly.

I blinked, took in the small tower room, and waited, but no one else stirred, all those lumps of forgotten flesh. It meant nothing to them. Nothing. Couldn't even hear it, most likely. Not like I could. I crawled from the cot and moved toward the music, warm tears pooling in my eyes. The song came from here, the wall closest to my bed. I placed my palm on the stone and felt it, the soft, steady tones that soaked into my flesh and reached my very bones.

At last. Something beautiful. Something alive. I leaned against the wall, my entire body pressed up against its coolness, and my cheek rested there, drinking in life and rhythm, allowing it to invade the prison of my mind.

I'd been trapped for an eternity. The world outside me was dull and quiet. Insulated as a tomb. Nothing able to penetrate—except the music. It came from somewhere outside me, a world that still existed—oh, what unreasonable hope!

Memories unfurled along with the music. I'd had parents once—velvety soft and warm. I touched my cheek. The feather-light caress of my mother, with a voice like wind chimes. "How dear, how precious," she'd always said of me. Had my mangy self once been dear and precious?

And my father. I could still feel the gentle pressure of his hand on my head, a steady approval. It came often and washed my soul of the little nettles of life. I'd become disconnected from that girl, the one who was a beloved daughter with a life full of beauty, and been worn down to a rag. The discarded scraps of what was, a waste of space and humanity no longer useful to anyone. I was a body to feed even though the soul had fled.

Yet I could feel myself again—feel the warmth of my palms against that wall, the vibration of the music that tingled clear through to my fractured soul. It still existed. I still existed.

I couldn't stop awareness from unfurling of the colorful world outside myself—and that I was a part of it still—even though I knew this would lead to dull pain and disappointment. The music would stop, and I'd be locked up again, invisible and trapped in my own head with my voice rattling about my skull, telling myself the same gonging thoughts hour after endless hour. But for now I'd drink it up, eat it for dinner, and feed my parched soul, selfishly squeezing every last drop for my own pleasure.

Delicious. Succulent. Sweet and flavorful, inviting. Leaking through the stone walls. Unsettling. Comforting, though, too. And wonderful. Gloriously so.

It would stop, though. Music didn't belong here. Too beautiful for such a place. Yes, eventually, it would stop.

Or they would stop it. They always did.

Music is not a cure for broken bodies—you shouldn't expect that—
but a balm for broken souls.

~Vivienne Mourdant

Dead. Marcel . . . dead. When did those two words ever belong
together? Apoplexy, Harford had said, and somehow that made
it more real. Believable, at least. Marcel was not one to do things
quietly. A quick, dramatic ending would be his way.

Harford's aged hands spread the pages of a Beethoven sonata
across the Broadwood's music stand in the morning, the long,
narrow point of his nose in profile beside me. "I assume you can
read music as well?"

I stared flaming arrows at him, this man who had manipulated
things to go his way and gotten me into life's worst bind. All so
Harford could have the right sort of pianist for his harebrained
medical trials.

Grief closed over my head like the Red Sea whooshing back
over the dryness after God removed his restraining hand. There
truly was no plan now. My one last hope of rescue, my constant

guardian, was gone. It felt as though my last parental anchor had been cut loose, and I was adrift.

My glare deepened, but it didn't seem to penetrate his affable, easygoing nature.

"Right, of course. I've just never seen you play with it."

The music of that grand space had shifted. From my own private and richly shadowed nocturne to a silly minuet, the space seemed entirely new. Gaudy, almost. Then, there was Frederick Harford, with his devout mantle of peace and watchful blue-eyed stare that added an invasive little arpeggio.

"I've spoken to Dr. Turner and convinced him to let us try our hand with his chronic ward patients. I assume you will not mind." He paused, watching me. "Quite an interesting man, that Dr. Turner." His eyes gleamed with the mischief of an old man, but I did not return his smile.

With patients seated in rows to my left, Harford called out song after song—either a stimulating beat or a calming tune, depending on the group. I played the pieces I knew, eyeing the patients as I went. Their faces showed mild enjoyment, and some even hummed or tapped with the beat. But in the end, they all rose in their little group and returned to life at Hurstwell, just as trapped as before. Two became more agitated and had to be removed.

"This is useless," I mumbled, and shoved stray hairs off my face, scratching at the tickle they'd left.

"You don't know that."

"Look," I hissed. "I had a life of my own. One that would have actually changed lives and bettered circumstances. This is nothing more than some spa treatment for the senses. One that makes little difference. Heals nothing."

After eyeing me, Harford turned for a private word with one of the scowling nurses. Her frown deepened at whatever he whispered to her. "But Superintendent Thornhill has said—"

He spoke again, his voice infuriatingly soft, but the nurse seemed

to hear every word. She nodded, stepping back. "As you wish, sir."
Then she disappeared.

Yes, everyone did Harford's bidding. Every agenda of his was
carried out—he saw to that. Even if it completely ruined other
people's plans. Lives, even. Another wave of panic flooded my
being, and I gripped the stool, fingers curling into the fringe.

*God. God Almighty, you are stronger. Mightier than my father,
than Thornhill, than this odd Harford man and anyone else who
seeks to control me. Won't you intervene, Lord? I have rescuing
to do for you, lost people to find, both here and on the outside,
and I'm running out of time.*

A chair on wheels bumped the doorframe, and my gaze snapped
up, half expecting to see the answer to my request already. A new
patient was wheeled in, small frame slumped to the side, eyes focused nowhere in particular. Behind her, the frightened women of
Hurstwell looked back at me from the edges of the room, internal
pain evident in their faces.

I cringed. Yes. Yes, I had women to help in the here and now
while I waited. But what could I really do for any of them? What
lasting good was mere music when there was so much more to
their complex situations? Meanwhile, time slipped away like petals
on the wind. What of the more immediate needs—what of the
missing Rosamond? *What of Bridget?*

Then I turned to the aid wheeling in the patient I'd never seen
before—a young woman with one arm curled into her chest and
dark frizz matted flat on one side of her head. Her vacant stare
resembled many at Hurstwell, but her features were so small and
delicate, her flesh thin and almost transparent. There was something deeply familiar about her, something in her solemn little face
and elfin features, although I couldn't place it. I knew her, or had
at one time, and it made my heart ache all the more to look at her.
"Poor dear." My voice was small, my spirit deflated. "I wonder if
there's anything that can be done for her."

"Of course there is. For our first focused session, I've chosen the patient Turner believes most unreachable, incurable, because I must prove myself—and my methods—before we go any further."

I stiffened. "Dr. Thornhill is willing to let you have your way. You've quite won him over."

"It's you I'm hoping to convince, Miss Vivienne Mourdant." He waved the matron away and wheeled the girl to the side of the great instrument. Her arms, legs, and waist were strapped to the chair to keep her upright, and there was no indication of awareness behind her placid face. "She is unreachable, completely cut off from the world and without hope . . . according to her caretakers."

I looked away. I was staring. Pitying.

No, *feeling.* I felt this scene very much, hurting at the sight of those restraints tying her down, at the loss of life within a living body. I saw a piece of my childhood self in that young girl, something vitally broken and cut off and trapped—her bondage was merely more visible than mine had been. "Hello." I spoke softly. "My name's Vivienne. What's yours?"

No change.

"Would you like to hear some music? I'm a pianist and I'd love to play for you. Perhaps you have a favorite song."

"There's no use speaking to 'er, miss," said the aid. "She don't know a thing anyone says."

I looked into her eyes, willing her to connect with me, for her mind to register my questions or even my presence, but there wasn't a flicker.

"Play," Harford urged quietly, and I turned on the stool, directing my hands to take up position against the weight of my shackles, and my heart to steady its rhythm. With a calming breath, I began a Beethoven piece, picking my way through the sonata as best as I could with a limited reach, and strained against the metal on my wrists. I stole glances at the girl, and my heart sank as she remained unchanged. What had I expected, though?

I paused at the end of the second page of the score and looked at

Harford. He frowned, tugging on his pointed beard. "Try Mozart. That piece you played in Salzburg earlier this year." He flipped through his music but did not seem to have it. "Each patient needs either soothing music or stimulation, and it's up to us to determine which. Perhaps this one requires the latter."

Mozart's Piano Sonata no. 14 in C Minor. I settled my fingers again and began to play from memory.

"Now emphasize the beats."

I did, stiffening my fingers four times per measure to enunciate the tempo. Harford rested a hand on the girl's shoulder and tapped his fingers along with the song. I turned my attention to the keys and played on until his whisper broke my concentration. "Look."

I darted a quick glance at the girl, then a full look. The limp hand curled against her chest had begun flicking, fingers tensing with the beat. I played more, chills prickling my skin. Her head jerked in rhythm with the song, and I felt like crying. It wasn't much, but it was something. A flicker of life. Hardly noticing my shackles anymore, I poured myself fully into that piece, bringing out the richness of its spread up and down the keyboard, stretching to the full extent of my cuffs and feeling the tones all up my arms.

I finished the song in an easy ride up the keyboard with both hands and a closing chord, then turned and looked directly into the darkest brown eyes fixed intently on me. Meeting my gaze. Asking for something. Begging. She was in there, and she wanted out. The chills prickled all the way to my scalp.

"Hello," I said again softly.

She continued to stare. Alertness flickered in her features now and again, but she didn't speak. Perhaps she couldn't.

Canon Harford's voice came soft and private. "Her name is Violet, and I believe she liked your playing."

Violet. *Violet!* This was *Lew's* Violet. I saw traces of his serious little face in hers. She had his dark hair, his countenance, but her features were delicate. Decidedly feminine in a snow-white contrast of light and dark.

I took her cold hand in mine, pressing my thumb into the back of it. "Lovely to meet you, Violet."

Harford motioned to a nurse to come fetch the girl, but I held up my hand. "No wait, please. Just one more song."

32

Inside every quiet person is something very big, and whoever has the patience to gently coax it out will be rewarded with its splendid display of beauty.

~Vivienne Mourdant

I was on the cusp of something. The door had cracked open, and I needed to ease it wider. "Wheel her closer. I'd like her near so she can feel the rhythm."

Harford complied, bringing the girl to a stop directly next to me, facing the instrument. Fingers poised above the ivories, I took a moment to decide what I should play while the girl continued to stare at me, her pert little face intense as if compelling me to do or say something specific.

It flustered me. I couldn't think.

Then she grunted out a noise to go with her stare, imploring me. Directing. She gripped the arms of her chair and rocked forward and back, harder and harder with building frustration that had nowhere to go. Violet's groans increased with the force of her rocking, echoing about the empty space, and her distress infected the atmosphere, unsettling the others. Patients shifted on their chairs, whimpering and crying.

As aids flurried, I latched on to the beat of her rocking—even in distress, there was an internal rhythm, a tempo. I splayed my fingers over those keys and pounded out a quick-tempoed minuet, matching Violet's movements, honoring her natural rhythm. The song overtook the room, drowning out the rising chaos.

Even Violet latched on to the song and its beat. Her cries faded to pants, and soon her rocking grew controlled, almost productive, driven by the song rather than frustration. Her eyes were wide, but her jaw more relaxed. I stole little glances as I played, letting my hands find their way, and the tension began to crumble from her rocking body. Layers peeled away before my eyes, and I glimpsed the inner workings of God's creation—a heartbeat and pattern that tied everything together. An expression of his sense of order and creativity placed within humans—even the ones who were deemed lost in all other ways.

Even these, God. Even these people have at their core a rhythm, a natural pull toward order and beauty. Music beat an instinctual tempo in every human, trapped or free, broken or whole, lost or found.

Dr. Turner rushed in behind two aids who'd summoned him, but hovered near the doorway, gaze locked on his patient in a way that was protective. Alert. He glanced at me, then at her. She had stopped rocking and now only her hands fidgeted, endlessly moving here and there. I wasn't sure if that was an improvement or a backsliding.

I took a breath, studying her white little face so much like Lew's, and I knew what to play. Leaning near so our arms touched, I began again—this time, Brahms' Lullaby. She'd once been active and alert, Lew had said, but as their lives disintegrated, she'd moved further into herself, disconnected from the world. Something had changed her. But childhood . . . she'd been part of the world then.

"What are you doing?" Harford whispered as I began. "This is child's music."

"Trust me, won't you?"

Violet did not move against my arm, did not react to the song, but I forced myself through every note to the conclusion. Still nothing. Just a quiet calm. Maybe that was all I could hope for.

No. There was one other option.

"*Da wasn't English*," Lew had said to me once, "*and that's why he never felt at home there. He was from Connah's Quay, out along the coast.*"

Welsh. The man had been Welsh.

With a glance down at my patient's dark hair so near my arm, I positioned my fingers and began again—this time, the old Welsh lullaby that had become popular in London.

Sleep my child and peace attend thee,
All through the night.

I barely remembered the melody, but I'd had a Welsh nanny once, and I'd loved the sound of it on her voice. It had seemed impossible to fret with this song in the air. I worked my way through the simple melody, adding a small flourish with my left hand when I could manage it. I pulled it from memory, but every time the shackles rubbed my wrists I wanted to cry. It distracted me, took me out of the song, and I lost my place. I stumbled along, limping toward the ending as discouragement mounted—*D-E-F-E . . . No, how did that go? D-E-E. . . . D-E-E. . . .*

"Mmmmm." Violet's voice ground out a low F as if compelled to bring the song's resolution. Violet's eyes remained wide, her hands gripping the chair arms, but she was no longer fighting to be heard. No longer on the verge of outburst. Her rocking had returned but gentled into a steady rhythm as she stared intently at the keyboard, her single note ringing through the open room. She began to hum the tune—an erratic version in a voice clear and deep that came from somewhere in that slender, worn-out body.

What people say about closed doors is true. If the way is barred to you, simply find an open window to go through instead. Music was that window at Hurstwell, a way to sneak into the inner person that still existed, that beat with its own rhythm, where precious things were still hidden. Yet it had to be exactly the right song, something that engaged the patient's heart and memory, for music that didn't move them was simply noise. Knowing which song out of millions of possibilities meant knowing them. At least a little, and that too was a gift. Knowing these lost people.

The room held its breath. Dr. Turner crossed to Violet and gently released one, then the other restraint holding her to the chair. Her eyes darted about. Her hands, now completely free, felt about frantically. Then she yanked loose and sprang forward, pounding on the keys. It was chaos . . . but with a sure tempo—every strike.

A nurse and two orderlies rushed forward to pull her away and I shook my head. "Oh please, let her do it." I added a lower melody to the beat of her banging.

Dr. Turner bent toward me, hands on the girl's shoulders. "You don't mind?" His voice rang with the depth of his emotion.

I paused and smiled up at them. "If I did, I'd be missing the point entirely."

The way he looked at me then, with a tender kinship and unguarded affection, swept the last thing into place. He saw me, he heard the music—*my* music. His affection was borne of "because of" rather than "in spite of" and it was bigger than a tidal wave. Oh. *Oh.*

I could hardly breathe, sitting there in the glow of his admiration, that ruggedly handsome face that seemed more familiar than any longtime friend. I fell so deeply—not a flutter of romance as I'd expected such a thing to be, but a profound, weighted anchor for my floundering soul. A knowing. The sensation was rich and good, and it plummeted deep.

I looked down at my fingers, for I could not look at Mitchell Turner as he watched me, absorbing every nuance of my song.

Violet pounded out the rhythm as I played through the grand crescendo and finale, then she sat upright, shifting forward and back only a little as she stared at me. "Moe," she said. "*Mooooooe.*"

Dr. Turner's radiant face turned, taking in the whole of her, and I felt the wonder of a starry night sky in his gaze. Something in his expression had burst open, cobwebbed shutters giving way to a magnificent daybreak of the soul. This meant something to him—something more than the response of a lost patient—and I'd never felt such glorious sunshine in my soul. Not in ten thousand performances.

"More? Is that what you're asking?"

He gave a nod and I played again—a modern and delightful melody by Liszt. She rocked forward and back to this new tempo, attempting to hum along in her guttural voice, sometimes moving her torso in circles, then returning to rocking as she beat the chair arms.

It was contagious, this rhythm she thumped, and a few other patients began to respond. Leg tapping, smiles, and quiet laughter swirled together in the air of that room, joining in with our song and magnifying its rhythm.

Music and silence. Light and dark. When it came to darkness, you could succumb and let it consume you . . . or you could invade it with light of your own.

The nurse backed away and Dr. Turner ran a hand through his hair, leaving his fingers in the black masses as he observed the order coming to this room, led by the most lost soul of them all, whose rhythm had finally been recognized and drawn out. A smile lit my face as I tripped through the song I'd only begun to memorize for a coming performance, keeping the steady beat as Violet gave her entire body over to it, letting the music sink in as no controlling voice or tincture had been able to do.

I drew the song to a close, and Violet slowed her swaying, looking directly at the keyboard without a word, eyes wide but without the frantic flickering back and forth.

"Did you enjoy that, Violet?" My voice was soft. Cautious.

She didn't respond, but stared at the keys, eyes focused and alert. Dr. Turner knelt before the young woman. "You have a very good sense of rhythm, Violet. I had no idea. There is music inside of you." He looked at me as he spoke, that open, gentle face creasing into a knowing smile meant only for me. I couldn't help but smile back, lingering in the fading notes.

He turned her chair. With a whoosh of cool air they left, and normalcy swept back over whatever had just filled the room.

"Very good for the second day," Harford said, approaching from somewhere behind me. "Perhaps we shall continue tomorrow."

But my soul was filled. My heart hammered and my brain spun right to, *Wait until I tell Marcel.*

Then a fresh wave of grief rose up and pummeled me from the other side, knocking me down with the weight of a new reality. Death was the end of so many beautiful things, the ruination of foundational pieces of one's life. At times the great gaping loss was simply too much for one to reasonably bear.

"By the by," said the older man, once again leaning down to me. "Thought you might want to see what I dug up last night. I do hope you'll forgive my abrupt announcement yesterday. If I'd known you didn't know . . ."

I took the folded newsprint with a nod, waiting until the room had quieted and all attention was turned elsewhere. On the lower right side of the page were the announcements—birth, death, and engagement—with Marcel's name first on the list of deaths. I looked over every word of it until my distracted vision caught on an announcement farther down, with another familiar name attached.

Richard. *My* Richard . . . who was now someone else's Richard.

Distinguished shipping baron Richard Cartwright of Manchester was to wed one Georgianna Gaines of North Yorkshire on the 23rd of February in the coming year.

Yet another death, another loss. While I lay trapped in this place, the remnants of my life were quietly being stripped away.

I wilted onto that pianoforte, my cheek against its polished smoothness, and simply lay there, letting that wave roll over me again and again. Someone seemed to shuffle out patients and nurses, and soon I felt the stillness of an empty room. Of peace. A nurse would be standing guard just outside, no doubt, but one of them had seen my troubles and granted me the moment of solitude I hadn't even realized I needed.

Dr. Turner was the last to leave—I saw his shoes from where I laid my face. He stood, observing me with empathy I could feel. Then he too turned to leave, closing the door softly behind him.

I began to cry.

33

This utter fear of being thought peculiar has stifled any desire for originality among the English of every class. Therefore we've dulled ourselves into a society of sameness.

~Vivienne Mourdant

He should have brought a candle. Mitchell Turner knew those halls, but he should have prepared a light anyway—if nothing else, to see what the noise ahead was.

Footsteps. Someone coming toward him, despite the hour. The heavy darkness.

Then a short-statured figure came into the flickering light of a torch farther up.

"Canon Harford." Mitchell cleared his throat, pacing forward with relief. "What can I do for you, sir?"

"I heard you were looking for me."

"Yes. Yes, of course. Just a word, if I may." He gestured them toward an empty office down the corridor. Once inside, Mitchell sat down at the cluttered desk and invited his visitor to take the chair across from it. He blew out a breath, palms down on the mess of papers. "It's Miss Vivienne Mourdant, your pianist." He focused on the corner of that rough desk for a moment, properly assembling the question he wished to ask. "It seems you were already acquainted with her before. Knew she played the pianoforte."

"Oh?" The man's easy self-possession wavered just a bit. "Musicians are always somewhat acquainted in spirit, even before introductions. I can spot one in any crowded room."

"Of course." He clasped his hands before him on the desk, steadying himself. "But you seemed acquainted with her—as if you'd spoken to her before Hurstwell."

A pause. "I have."

"What do you know of her character in everyday life?"

"You believe me better acquainted with her than I am. I've seen her most often from a distance, with her onstage and me in the audience. I'm afraid we've only had one private conversation in all that time."

"Does it seem . . . odd to you that she's here? In an asylum?"

His mouth puckered as he considered his roundabout answer. "I believe it's an unnatural place for any living being, if you ask me."

Mitchell blew out a breath. The man could hedge Queen Victoria's entire garden with more to spare. "Let me be direct. Has she done or said anything in your presence to indicate she might be mad?"

The man rubbed two fingers together, watching Mitchell. "What do you believe, Dr. Turner?"

His jaw flinched. "I was given to doubts. Yet what I saw yesterday . . ."

"She is a magnificent pianist, is she not?"

"Indeed. But then the way she banged about on the instrument, as if having fits of some kind." He cleared his throat. "I've no doubt she is who she says, but perhaps also . . ."

Harford's expression softened. "Dr. Turner, you are no stranger to grief. To the up-and-down intensity of coming to grips with an unexpected loss. One can see it etched into the very planes of your face."

He looked down at his hands, the lined knuckles.

"I had the unfortunate role of informing her yesterday of a loss she knew nothing about, and it was quite a blow."

Mitchell let out a breath, the spinning world recentering again. "So then she isn't mad."

That little Harford man sat straighter, his long mustache and pointed little beard twitching. "I don't believe in labels, Dr. Turner. Boxes were never designed to hold people—they simply aren't the correct shape." He tilted his head to the side, studying Mitchell in a most unnerving way. "I suppose this is a requirement you have for pursuing her hand, yes? That she be considered sane in the eyes of the medical community?"

Mitchell gripped the chair, fighting his thoughts. Erasing the evidence of them from his face. "I never claimed—"

"Do not cheapen your affection, Dr. Mitchell Turner. Admit it plainly, and I shall have a great deal more respect for you."

He firmed his jaw. "I cannot outwardly claim any such interest—especially while she is a patient at Hurstwell and I am a physician."

Harford's gaze was steady. "You categorize almost as badly as your superintendent does. Boxes, boxes, everyone in boxes. This one a blue gown, this one in green."

"Those are a simple visual way to track who belongs where, and what their condition is. Green for epileptic, purple for chronic, blue for acute, and so forth. We are simply labeling facts, sir."

"You act as though God has painted with only one shade of blue. One purple. What shade, would you say, did he paint Miss Vivienne Mourdant?"

Red. She was burnished copper, flaming red—with hints of gold. Mitchell shifted in his chair. "I don't suppose you have much experience with madness, have you? Recognizing its signs and—"

Amusement touched the corners of Harford's countenance. "I've met very few so-called sane people who interested me in the least, for they are all the same—or they try to be, and what's the sense in that?" He leaned back a small bit into the chair. "I see the wisdom in your restraint, though. I do. Therefore, I will not push you in your pursuit of her."

"Thank you."

"I'll merely let your desires hurtle you toward her in spite of yourself."

Mitchell blew out a breath again. He was plumb out of words. Denials only tangled the web further. So did his desires, which surfaced at nearly every mention of the auburn-haired pianist.

The man's smile grew across his face. "One cannot help staring at the light, eh? Especially when he's been cowering in the shadows for so long."

Mitchell's jaw flinched. He looked down.

"It's quite all right, my good man. Allow yourself to be drawn to the light. You've a wick in you too. Perhaps together you can get it lit again."

"I don't need saving."

Harford leaned forward, one palm on the desk between them. "Perhaps it's time you quit choosing the darkness—quit lingering there. Whatever you believe you're paying penance for, it's costing you—and the people who need you—more than was ever intended."

Tension rippled through Mitchell's back, his shoulders.

"If you begin to think you are not worthy, too broken, you're focused on the wrong person. Not to worry, grief does that to the best of us. But don't be too long about it. You'll miss the mission he has for you—and the gift." His eyebrows rose. "Mayhap you don't believe you need her. But one glance at her today, and you'll see clearly how much she needs you just now."

At this, his barely suppressed longings surfaced like a whale coming up for breath. He turned his body with a gasp, forcibly strong-arming them down. *If you brought her to me, Father, I shall wait for you to open the doors. We'll come together the right way, or not at all.*

Yet he wasn't certain how long he'd mean that. "The ethical code of patients and—"

"*Hang* the rules. Isn't she more important than them?" Harford rose, fingertips on the desktop as he leaned over it. "She's been playing a solo far too long, and so have you. They're different melodies, but think how stunning they'd sound alongside each other. You know, my boy. You know what she is." With a long, sober look, the old man turned and disappeared through the door, leaving Mitchell alone in the moonlight streaming through the one tiny window.

Yes, he certainly knew what she was. More importantly, what she wasn't. The wind whistled outside, blowing through like the sound of desperate voices of the past. Memories tortured his still-raw soul.

"Please listen, Mitch. I'm not mad. Please. Don't let me die here. I'm not mad. I'm not mad. I'm not mad."

34

Music, when soft voices die, vibrates in the memory.

~Percy Bysshe Shelley

I twisted about under the sheets that night, and those awful shackles bumped the rawness with a jolt of pain. Scrambling to sit, I ripped a strip off the worn bottom of my sheet and wrapped it around each of the metal handcuffs to shield my skin from their cold, biting edges.

I was trapped now. Helplessly trapped and quite alone.

No hopeless cases, no hopeless cases . . .

Except Bridget.

Well, and me. Thornhill knew I was who I claimed, yet here I remained. Convincing them of my true identity would not free me, so I had nothing left to prove my sanity. Nothing. And with that, nothing with which to help those who needed me—including Bridget.

The sun would soon rise on day three—presumably her last. And because of Canon Harford's arrival, I was even more trapped than before. More closely watched, more deeply suspected. And there would be no Richard rescue. I dropped my head onto my hands and wept. *Oh God, I can do nothing. Have nothing.* I had the sudden aching sense of facing a huge chasm a mile long with nothing to cross it but the minuscule distance my legs could stretch. Consumed with my smallness, I closed my eyes and prepared to let despair sweep over me, drown me. I braced for it.

But instead, it was God's presence that washed over me—powerful, unexpected, immense. And very welcome. It flooded my being, my hollow lack, with an undeniable strength that was lavished on me, father to child, cradling me with comfort and courage.

I'm still with you, it seemed to say, and I felt it. Just as he'd been with me in the larder, and with Paul in jail and shipwreck and torture.

I spoke out in my heart. *She's lost, God. Bridget is lost.*

But she wasn't. Not to him. That answer came crashing like a second wave over the first, drowning out panic and covering me in an unusual calm. Bridget was found. She was within God's sight and in the very palm of his sovereignty.

I had been lost once. Enveloped in such darkness that I couldn't even see the floor that was holding me up. Yet God knew where to find me, when to do it, and how to overcome the thing I feared most. This is where he existed—not in the perfection, but in the cold darkness, in the messiest tears, in the deepest despair, on the dirty floor of my prison, ready to meet me with his presence.

I climbed out of bed when I'd given up on sleep—somewhere nearing eleven—and slipped through the priest hole to the only place at Hurstwell where I felt at home. There, streaked in moonlight, the beautiful Broadwood waited for me. I smiled and lit a candle, lifting the fallboard and stopping short at the sight of a note on the keys. It was on plain paper, not sheet music, and the writing was entirely different than the ghostly letter with the rose petals.

There's a small gift for you in the closet. The only thing of real importance you've ever asked me for. How could I not give it?

Blinking back my surprise, I rose and walked to the closet. It was the gown I'd packed from home hanging there, in desperate need of pressing but whole and soft and dearly familiar. I ran my hands over the deep red poplin gown with velvet trim that I had worn the night of that final parlor performance, then buried my face in it. It had been foolish to tuck it away in my satchel when I'd come here, but now I was glad. Pinned to the bodice was another note.

> You're not a blue gown or a gray,
> A patient or an aid.
> You are simply you.
> A flame as bright as day.

The small key for my handcuffs fell from the last fold of the note, and I snatched it up with a cry, jamming it in the lock until it clicked. I pulled them off like a madwoman, breathing deep and stretching my arms wide. Then, with wonder I slipped back into that gown from another lifetime, felt its smooth hug of my curves, and walked to the center of that sacred room, taking in its silent splendor as one made new. *"For once—for once—let me be more than a patient at an asylum. Simply let me be a human."* What ferocity I'd launched those words with, but he'd heard them. Tonight I was no longer merely a patient at Hurstwell—I was me again.

But I'd always been that.

Light in the darkness.

Indwelled by God, lamp for his flame to light a sin-dark world.

I jumped when a key rattled in the main door, metal scraping keyhole, and it swung open on oiled hinges. I exhaled at the sight of Dr. Turner standing there with a shriveled, aged man on his arm. They closed the door and slowly moved forward, the unknown man shuffling along the tile in stocking feet, craning his neck to look up at me. They were dwarfed in the grand room, these two men.

"How did you even know I'd—"

"Where else would you go?" He smiled down at me when they'd

neared. "Tonight of all nights. I did check to make certain, before bringing him down." Mitchell stopped before me with a small bow, indicating the man beside him. "I'd like to introduce Mr. John Michelson of South Leeds. Lately, of the men's ward of Hurstwell."

"Oh." I straightened, hand to my throat. Michelson. Anna's John Michelson? "A pleasure, Mr. Michelson."

They shuffled together to the visitor chair, where the man sank into the formal thing with his ratty asylum-issued garments and puffed out a rattling sigh. "It's a long way here."

"But hopefully worth the trip," Mitchell said.

"Indeed. Any word on my girl is worth a trip anywhere."

"Mr. Michelson here was brought in from the same workhouse as our Anna. I knew I recognized the name when I read it in her file. It seems they'd fallen into debt and landed here after the workhouse."

Yet the man seemed as healthy in mind as the doctor himself. "He's . . . a patient here?"

He shrugged, lowering his voice to keep the older man from hearing. "When they cannot care for themselves at the workhouse, the parish sees fit to send them here. Feeble bodies are the equivalent of feeble minds, don't you know."

"Hmm." I swiveled on the stool to face the watery brown eyes of the man now wilted on the chair beside me. What striking dark hair the man possessed. "You are Anna's husband, then."

A little light cracked through his features. "Annika. Her name is Annika Freidl, and she was the finest dancer this side of the channel. Nothing short of miraculous."

His hands trembled in his lap, and I placed my fingers over his. I felt the warmth, just as I had when his wife had done the same for me.

He looked at me, softening. There was a deep knowing in that gaze, a depth of sorrow as one who'd seen and lived much.

"You've been through a great deal together, haven't you?"

He nodded. "Many decades of marriage. Typhoid outbreak.

Arrest and gaol. Battles with barristers and solicitors, inquest after inquest, deep poverty and scratching out a living with our bare hands. Arguments and loving. Birth and death." His chin quivered, and he shrugged bony shoulders, and turned his face away. "The stuff of a long marriage." His weathered countenance attested to everything he'd mentioned, and much more that he hadn't.

"How many years?"

"It'll be fifty soon. November the second, two years from now."

He looked down at his hands, and I had the sense that he'd paused every year to remember the anniversary, even if he'd done it alone and in an asylum.

I turned to the doctor, chin low. "Do you think—"

"I'm already ahead of you. Wait here, and perhaps we'll find out." He leaned close. "You'll have to work your magic."

I raised my eyebrows, and he eyed the pianoforte without a word.

When Mitchell departed, I spoke to the old man of dance and music and everything that moved us, delighting in his keen mind and gentle spirit. He had a soulful face, and one could see he'd been handsome in his youth. Striking and memorable.

Then the panel opened and Mitchell returned, leading Anna by the hand. Her husband rose, holding himself up with the chair arms as his lady entered. The tremble began in his legs and reached his entire body.

Anna's nervous look swept the room, brushing right over John, Mitchell, and me, pausing on the great pianoforte. Dr. Turner settled her into the chair beside my stool and John Michelson took another seat, well behind her but with his gaze never leaving her narrow back.

The doctor smiled down at Anna. "I thought perhaps you'd like to hear Miss Mourdant play again."

The woman blinked, looking from Turner to the instrument without a word. Had he woken her? She seemed dazed. But then, she often did. Dazed, and slightly troubled by the invading world around her.

She had a wide nose and sunken cheeks, with white hair combed straight back, but her cheekbones were high and proud, her chin as poised as a pointed ballet toe. I played Rossini first, racking my brain for any pieces that had been used in a ballet. It wasn't until I played a piece by a composer I couldn't even remember that the woman began to stir. Something Russian.

Her stirring, however, was quite amazing. One foot slid along the floor under her wheeled chair, toes brushing the smooth wood as she lifted her leg with a deep arc to her foot. She held it inches from the ground, leg trembling, and the sight shook something in me.

As the music continued, she relaxed her foot and began to hum along, and she swept her arms into a great circle overhead, bending at the waist, first this way, then that, always flowing along with the song. It was as if her body knew what to do, her muscles carrying out the dance they'd been trained to do so long ago.

She was dancing. She was *remembering*. I watched the song sink into the forgotten places of her soul like a fishing line, returning from its depths with the associated memories hooked on the end. From this dusty, parched old mind came the precision of long-ago movements, learned routines, and natural poise. I watched in awe as her arms moved through the entire piece, executing slow, sweeping movements from her chair. As the notes crescendoed to a finale, she straightened, arms arched overhead in a pose of completion, then bent immediately forward in a low bow.

John Michelson and Dr. Turner clapped, faces glowing, and Anna sat upright to drink it in, bowing her head as if accepting a theater's praise. "Come, collect the flowers, won't you?" she said to me in her faint, willowy voice. "They enjoyed the show, didn't they?"

"You've impressed them."

At the sound of my voice, she blinked and her eyes focused on me. "Of course. That's what I do," she murmured, as if collecting her thoughts. "How grand. How perfectly lovely. It was always like this, every show. Every time." She was like Sleeping Beauty, having received her kiss—awake. Alive. Slowly returning to the world after a long slumber.

"Annika," spoke Dr. Turner softly. "Do you remember the story of the red shoes? You told me about them once. Were they yours? Can you recall those days?"

Tears budded in her eyes, and I took her hand, smoothing the dry skin with my thumb.

"I gave them the idea for that story, you know. That silly Russian boy always playing about my feet, wanting tales of the theater. He had red velvet curtains in his gaze, I tell you. Wanted to be a dancer."

"What boy was this?"

"Oh . . . you know. The one who wrote the music for it. For *The Nutcracker*."

"Tchaikovsky," I said. "It was Tchaikovsky."

"Yes, yes, it was." She laughed softly, her voice slow and garbled. "Just a lad he was. I told him the story of a ballerina. Way up on a balcony. Always wondered if that's where that little bit came from. It was true, you know. She threw her enchanted red shoe down into the alley to rescue the other dancer. Such a love story they had, that Ella Blythe and her hero." She sighed at the memory. "I told it all to him, and years later . . . Oh." She patted her lap, the arms of her chair, searching. "My music box. Where is it?"

"I'm afraid it's broken." I laid a hand on her arm.

Her face fell. "*She* gave it to me." Her voice was soft. Vague. "Such a dear thing. I left the theater, had my baby, and she came and found me. Gave me the box with the broken ballerina . . . so I'd never forget." Her chin quivered. "What has been broken, God can fix, you know. God can always fix." She blinked back moisture. Mitchell handed her a small square of linen and she dabbed her eyes. "Where have they gone? Where are they?" Her agitation multiplied as she searched the unfamiliar faces, dabbing harder.

Mitchell's low voice resonated through the emptiness as he rose, straightening his frock coat. "Anna, I have someone I'd like you to meet."

She grabbed my hand like an eagle's hold on prey, gaze flitting about.

"We've met," said John Michelson, rising with effort and fingering the hem of his sleeve. He shuffled around to stand before her chair and steadied himself holding on to the back of another one. "Do you remember me, Annika?"

She lifted her eyes, searched out his face. "Philippe Rousseau," she whispered, breathless. There were stars in her eyes, her long fingertips twitching on the chair arms. "You're . . . Philippe Rousseau."

I held my breath, studied the man, his gaunt old face and ragged hair and skin. We stood there, the four of us dwarfed in that room lit by my paltry candle stubs, and waited.

His face eased into the deepest pleasure. "That's right." The man gave a slow, intentional bow. "Might I play for you, my lady?" The clipped French accent—very slight now but becoming clearer—erased all doubt of who he was.

Anna gaped at him, her weathered cheeks glowing pink as her mouth hung open. I rose so Philippe could take my stool. Watching her face, John Michelson—Philippe—played a simple melody by Brahms, and Anna watched his hands. Then she turned her gaze to his face with wonder, and he stopped mid-ballad and watched her, longing palpable in his features. "Do you remember, Annika?"

"Philippe Rousseau," she repeated—slow and intentional, stringing out the words like pearls on a necklace. She smiled and leaned close, a flicker of lucidity in her face. "Would you like to know a secret?" she asked. "I used to carry a bit of a torch for you, Mr. Rousseau. Back in my younger days."

He leaned near, his face wrinkling into every possible emotion, and kissed the knuckles of her hand. "Me too, Miss Freidl. Me too." He lavished a smile upon her, then played again, a lovely ballad from the days of old. She leaned her head against his arm, and he slowed his playing to place a gentle kiss on her matted hair, then continued on.

I reached for Mitchell's hand, feeling the sudden urge for connection. He took it, so we stood that way, hands clasped, silent in the presence of true love. It was in the way of great classic symphonies—simple and unadorned yet underscored with a deep and subtle timelessness.

A distant noise tugged me from the moment, reminding me of where we were. Of the circumstances. I glanced up at the doctor. "You're not afraid of being caught?"

"Thornhill has made a sudden disappearance for the night. I've a feeling it has to do with Harford's presence here. But it's nearing midnight, and rounds will begin soon." He cleared his throat, pulling his hand from mine as he nodded toward the couple. "I should return them. It's best if no one notices."

When they had gone, I stood alone in that moonlit room and felt the sweeping romance of everything that had occurred at the beautiful pianoforte that night, all that room had witnessed. It still pulsed with sweetness I couldn't express. Not even in music. I remained until the candle stubs I'd brought melted down to nothing and flickered out, leaving me in the dark. My heart was too full to be afraid, though.

When I at last made my way back into the priest's tunnel, I went in eerie darkness, and the chill of the place wrapped tightly around me. I jumped at every noise. Every brush of cobwebs on my skin. The usual fear returned, clinging and tight. Choking.

But then there was someone else. Another body moving toward me, shuffling in the shadows. I paused, hand to my throat. One beat, two . . . Then great arms came gently around me, drawing me close, fingertips grazing my face. "Vivienne . . . Vivienne."

I was breathless. "Dr. Turner."

"Mitchell. And I have something for you." He was close enough to feel the words rumbling in his chest.

A collection of smooth, waxy pillars was shoved into my left hand. I ran my fingertips along the length of them and felt wicks at the end. "Candles."

"So you never have to face the darkness." He took my right hand and wrapped my fingers around what felt like matches.

I swallowed the lump that rose. "Why? You've already—"

"To thank you. To bless you as you have me, especially tonight."

"What on earth did I ever give to you?"

"Hope." He breathed out the word and I felt the layers of meaning. "Hope for some purpose in my life here."

"Oh." It came out more a breath than a word.

"It's quite silly to you, isn't it?" He spoke quickly now, stumbling over words that came directly from some deeply authentic place within. "Silly that I care so about Violet and Anna, all the patients. I realize I'm far too attached to this place, to the people. Thornhill has always said it's my weakness, allowing them to affect me so."

"On the contrary," I whispered into the darkness, "I should find you rather weak and broken if you were *not* moved by what goes on here."

His hand cupped my cheek, warm and tender, finger tracing along my temple and through my loose hair. He leaned his forehead onto mine, then as soon as my eyes fluttered closed, his lips searched over my face with butterfly softness until he found his mark and kissed me. Really and truly kissed me, man to woman, as I sensed he'd restrained himself from doing all this time.

There was no more restraint.

35

This is what I think art is and what I demand of it: that it pull everyone in, that it show one person another's most intimate thoughts
and feelings, that it throw open the window of the soul.

~Felix Mendelssohn

Music. A symphony. Color and light exploded through every cell
of Mitchell Turner's body, prisming vibrant color through the gray,
dried-up mud of his life. Good heavens, she kissed exactly as she
played—like she meant it.

He thought this small taste of her would placate him, but instead he could not get enough. Like a little sip of some sweet, flavorful concoction, he now wanted a deep gulp, hours spent hearing
her voice, being surprised by her, studying the little nuances of her
expressions. Tasting her lips.

He released her, keeping her face close so he could study her
intelligent eyes snapping with life in the dark. How unusual she
was. He was accustomed to patients at Hurstwell who walked
about with hard, brittle shells he had to burrow through without
destroying their unusually delicate centers. She was the opposite—
a core of strength bolstering her from the inside, and a softness,
a distinct femininity on the outside when interacting with others.
He'd never seen the like and never would again.

Which made the next part even harder.

He leaned back and looked down at her, that sweet, strong profile barely visible in the tunnel, wondering what it would be to vanish with her in the night and never return to Hurstwell. Temptation ebbed and flowed with her glowing face so near, looking up at him. He lifted one hand, running the back of his finger along her cheek, down her poised neck, indulging in the softness of her red waves of hair over her shoulder just for a moment. His sigh was deep and shuddering. "I shall miss you."

She caught her breath. Blinked. "You're leaving?"

He shook his head. "I'm the one who belongs here. The one who's broken, and quite beyond repair. I will not tie you down." He leaned his forehead against hers again, drinking in her scent. Savoring and remembering. "You have a whole world to light. A life ahead of you."

"Mitchell."

"Come." He couldn't bear hearing his name on her rich voice. "Quickly." He forced himself away from her, praying she'd follow. He felt his way along the dark tunnel, up the stairs to the clock tower where time thudded through his whole body, beat by beat. She rushed in behind him, stumbling into his back. He turned and caught her, panicked, and he momentarily forgot the reasons for what he was doing. Dahlia was gone forever, but he still had Vivienne, warm and alive, in his arms. Within reach.

Then the mechanism behind them clicked, and the clock began to bong, just as it had the first night they'd been up there. The night his eyes had been opened and she had danced to the beat of music no one else heard.

It was midnight. There wasn't much time.

Bonggggg. Bongggg.

With a faint smile, he swept out his hand and offered it to her. "May I?"

"Without music?"

He merely smiled and opened one palm. He heard the music now too. Or perhaps he'd merely stopped shutting it out. "Well?"

She stepped into the frame of his arms. With the clock bongs setting a three-quarter waltz tempo, they moved to the symphony of night noises—crickets, water pipes, and the sighs and groans of an old house. He kept his focus on her face, so white in the moonglow. It wasn't staring as much as it was her eyes not giving his leave to look away.

All at once she tensed in his arms, spinning to look up at the clockface. "The rounds. Twelve, three, and six. Who's on—"

He squeezed her shoulder, urging her gently back to the waltz as the final bongs died away, vibrating the air. "Trust me. Just trust me."

She met his gaze and they were once again swept up in the rhythm weaving between them. As his thoughts spun, heart pounding, they slowed to a swaying motion, her skirt like a clock pendulum once again as their song died away. He touched her cheek—he couldn't help himself. "God's plan for your life is bigger than this place. Make the most of it, Vivienne Mourdant. Fill the world with music. Light it up."

Her eyes were glistening, and he couldn't keep himself from glancing at her lips. How desperately he wished for one last taste.

A noise sounded nearby, outside the tower. He put a finger to his lips, listening. Someone was about. One more caress of her rounded cheek, a trace of the freckles there, and he released her for the last time, sending away from himself the only light that had warmed his days in a long time. "Harford's guest cabin is just south of the main house. Follow the path, and you'll find it. I'm certain he'll help you." He pointed her toward the rope ladder hanging down to the yard below, held out her velvet cloak that he'd laid on the bench beforehand. He allowed himself a final lingering look. Oh, how her eyes sparkled. "Don't be afraid of the dark."

She smiled, laying her hand over her hidden pocket where she'd slipped the candles. Then she spun toward the open window with a swirl of lush fabric and was gone, taking the warm glow of their evening with her.

36

Your internal rhythm will shift to match the song of your surroundings—unless the beat of your heart is strong enough to change your atmosphere instead.

~Vivienne Mourdant

I dropped to the ground from the last rung and walked into glorious, starry liberty, feeling the earthquake that shook Paul's jail occurring inside me, sensing the stones tumbling down around me. I walked out over the rubble to freedom. I was lightweight, as if tumbling down the sunny flower-strewn slopes of a meadow. I took three steps and looked up, up into the star-freckled sky, arms out and laughing as I spun a slow circle.

I was free. Could it be true? Giddy, I kicked the fluffy snow at my feet and laughed again. When had it begun to snow?

Then I froze at the sight of a lamp glowing in the building. That would be the end of the wards, wouldn't it? Chronic ward, third floor. A door opened and banged shut somewhere in the echoey night. Footfall sounded, and it wasn't far off.

Opportunity narrowing, I hoisted my gown and sprinted through the falling snow. I ran until my chest hurt and my legs tingled. Freedom was close. Freedom, and finding help for Bridget.

As Hurstwell grew smaller, I could see the tall iron fence in the far distance around the property, dark against the whiteness. I turned to the right and found a path, snow-dusted and bordered by stone. My eyes caught sight of the beautiful glow of candlelight in the windows of a cottage, and I made a hard pivot and stumbled toward it. I sidled along the wall and peered in through the frosted panes to be certain. There before the hearth sat Frederick Harford dressed in black, rocking in the firelight.

Glancing back at the speck of Hurstwell, then at the guarded gate, I prayed and stepped forward boldly to knock on the door. Footsteps crunched somewhere in the open yard behind me. Frantic, I knocked again. A voice came from inside. "Is someone there?"

"It's me, Vivienne Mourdant. Let me in."

"Good gracious!" The door opened and there he stood, his bearded face gruff but welcoming. "Come in, come in."

I stumbled over the threshold and stood shaking before him. My teeth chattered and words poured out of my nervous brain. "It's time this comes to an end, Canon Harford. Whatever your intentions were for manipulating me into this place, it has gone far enough. You said so yourself, so now you must end it and get me out."

He blinked at me for a moment. "I assume you've found her, then?"

"Who? Wait, you know about—"

"Rose. Yes." He waved me toward a three-legged stool before the fire. "That was the reason you were meant to come, of course. The reason he arranged all of this."

"He?" I stiffened, feeling the controlling power of my father even now. Somehow he'd managed to chart my course for me yet again. "He set all this up?"

"Well, he sort of . . . urged you toward the asylum through different circumstances. Then when it seemed you might quit, he made it a little harder for you to leave. I'm certain he never meant to leave you in there for long." He shook his head. "I had no hand in entrapping you here, I assure you."

"Exactly where *do* you fit into this little scheme?"

"Well, he merely suggested that I invite you to accompany me as pianist to perform my clinical trials—introduce you to Hurstwell and the patients—and hopefully one day, to her. It was all his idea when he heard of my research. And I admit, I was keen to locate Rose too."

Surprise coursed through me. "How are *you* connected to Rose?"

"Oh, I'm not, I'm afraid. Not yet, anyway, but I'd like to be." He fell onto a larger chair with a long exhale. "It has been many years since I've heard her play, but I've never before encountered such a rare gift. For a brief time, she stunned the world. She was something of a child prodigy, but then she vanished. To this place, apparently. He truly wanted you to rescue her, of course. It was his deepest wish to see her play again."

I stared. "If he wanted me to find her so badly, why didn't he simply tell me about her when he was alive? Bring me to the asylum himself? He never breathed a word of this woman—not in my entire life."

Harford shook his head. "If he'd merely told you about her, some patient in a lunatic asylum, how might you have reacted?"

"I would have done what I could to help." The words slipped off my lips quickly. Too quickly.

He said nothing, but there was a knowing on his face. Then I heard my own voice in my memory, speaking of playing in those very same asylums. *For what purpose? To perform for a band of hopeless inmates?* I shuddered. *Madness is a disease without a cure. Those people are broken in a way no one can truly fix.*

I turned away from Harford's look. "Well, it hardly matters after all. She has died, and I'm too late."

His features pinched, and he looked down at his hands. "I wasn't aware of that. 'Tis a shame. He'd have been heartbroken. It's good he isn't alive to find out."

I clutched my hands in my lap, forcing my brain to comprehend what couldn't be grasped. My father—he cared for no one. Loved nobody. "He was her guardian for years. If he cared so much for her, why not simply take her out and have her live with him? With us?"

His gaze shot up, searched my face. "Her guardian? He wasn't ever her guardian, and that was precisely the problem. He had absolutely no legal say in what became of her. He was merely a friend."

I narrowed my eyes. "We're speaking of my father, yes? Of Winston Mourdant?"

He released a breath. "Ah. That's the confusion. No, it isn't your father I was speaking of at all—it was Marcel Beauchene."

"Marcel?" My spine straightened, pieces of this wretched business slipping into place. All the maneuvering, the behind-the-curtain tactics. Yes—it couldn't be anyone else. He'd not only allowed me to walk into this mess, he'd all but planned it. My heart could scarcely take it in.

"He knew you were to become her guardian and he saw his chance. He wished to train her, to bring her out into the theaters, but he needed you, her guardian, to see her value and get her out. It became complicated when you wished to leave your position, though." The man lowered his bushy white head. "He came when you were sedated, after you admitted to them who you really were, and he told them something, signed something. Perhaps he claimed that he didn't recognize you. That you weren't Vivienne Mourdant."

"Well, then. Perhaps it was another man who signed for you," Thornhill had said, and his words smote my tender heart with the truth.

I rose, the heat from the fireplace suddenly too much. "So he set this up, just so I could . . . what, find this piano student my father had dumped here?" I shook my head. "But how did he even accomplish such a thing from outside Hurstwell? And why would Marcel even care what became of my father's ward? Why go to all this trouble, make this giant mess of my life . . ." I put my hands over my face, trying to make the pieces continue fitting. But they didn't.

"He believed she was a treasure. A gift to the world of music."

"So he sent me in like bait to fish her out. Except . . . now she's gone, and I'm trapped." I sat again on the stool and looked at Harford. "Do you have any idea what a mess he's left me in? I'm a patient here. An inmate. Even if I succeed in escaping tonight, I'll forever be trying to clear my name, to undo what has been done to me." I laid my forehead upon my clenched hands, trying to keep from shaking. He'd been one of the few in my life who valued me—but not enough, apparently. Not as much as he did her.

He'd made a sacrifice of me.

"I simply don't understand why—how—he could do this to me." I was shaking now.

A moment of silence passed with only the crackling of fire. "Do you recall what I said when we met that night, at the parlor performance? A light in the darkness—that's what I called you, but those words didn't come from me. It was Beauchene who first spoke them when he approached me about having you assist in the clinical trials." He let out a long sigh.

"After he'd seen Hurstwell for himself, seen what had become of Rose, he knew it was a wretched cave of darkness that needed to be thrown open, and you, Vivienne Mourdant, were the only one with a light big and bold enough to do it. He knew what you were capable of. So yes, he intended to release you into this place, let you see it for yourself and have your passionate way with it."

I hugged my knees to my chest, fighting the ache encircling my heart. The building tears. "But I'm not truly doing anything for these women—especially not her. They're all still lost, still stuck here. Or dead. There's simply nothing to be done. Besides, I'm just a pianist."

"That light shining out of you is not some sort of magical glow of your own, you know. It's *him*. It's God in you, and what candle

311

God lights . . ." He cupped my chin as a father might. "What God has set ablaze, no man can extinguish."

I blinked back tears. "But God provided a miraculous escape tonight, just as he did for Paul. Why would he do that if he intended for me to remain? Tell me that."

He did not respond. Instead, he rose and stretched. "I must retire for the night, and you may take the cot in the corner. Eat a little something—you look famished—then put out the candle when you're ready to bed down." He moved toward a separate little room across the cabin, then paused and turned back in the doorway. "By the by, Miss Mourdant. Paul didn't escape that night—the time the prison walls fell down. You should read the story again." With a wink, he disappeared into the shadows of the far room, leaving me alone with my troubled thoughts.

Sleep is rarely a friend of artists and creative types. Our minds continue to whirl and discuss and untangle long after our bodies have told us it's time to sleep. I stared into the fire, waiting for tiredness to approach, and finally settled in at the window with a melted candle stub and a worn Bible, flipping through for the story of Paul. But even as my fingers paged through Acts, I remembered what happened. Paul had gone on to do what he always did—right from where he was, he overflowed with words of God to his jailer, his cellmates, anyone who would listen. Some were touched by his light and walked toward it—toward God. All because he'd chosen to remain.

But how had he *known* God had wanted him to stay?

How did I know what on earth I was meant to do?

My eyes burned from squinting at the tiny print without the benefit of daylight, so I gave up with a huff and shut the worn volume. Stomach growling, I grabbed a jar of dried figs and dumped a few out onto my hand as I pondered. *Why, Paul? What made you stay when God miraculously released you?*

As I licked the sticky residue from my fingertips, Bridget's voice threaded again through my memories. *"There was only so much about Paul a person could lock up."*

Because he was already free.

More free than his fellow prisoners. Than his jailers. And he had chosen to remain in the prison to help set others free.

Faces swam before me, in all their bound hopelessness—first the patients at Hurstwell, but then the staff. Nurses, Thornhill, shadowed Dr. Turner. Was anyone truly free?

Not without me, my child.

The truth jarred me so suddenly I sat up straight and clutched my pounding heart. *"You were bound up in resentment, Vivienne. Shielded against being controlled . . ."* Mitchell had said that, and he was right.

But it was all different now. He'd said that too. I was softer, more aware. Loving. I'd learned what God had meant to teach me in this place, and perhaps now, despite Harford's words, he was releasing me. Maybe Harford didn't know what he was talking about. I'd gone through my desert, learned to love instead of resent, and now it was time to return to life as a better version of myself. To carry out the rescuing I'd always longed to do.

Won't you make a way, God? Won't you allow me to leave this place and rescue women for you? I've been preparing this symphony for years and have yet to be able to perform it.

Yet I felt no release. Sensed no solution. I reached for the last fig which was stuck to the bottom, but the whole jar came away from the table with it, my fist trapped inside. I stared at it in the dim light, that narrow-mouthed jar with the final fig and my hand still grasping it. Stubborn. Decided.

Trapped.

Then my heart burst open with awareness as gentle truth swept over me. The candle stub sputtered out and I stared at my hand grasping the last fig. I'd never been one for writing my own music. I only ever played what the masters wrote.

Except when it came to my life.

We're all of us told to walk in the light, but we don't. We simply wish to drag the light over to where we're already standing, so we may better see the path we've set out for ourselves. I dearly wished to set my own path. To take control for once in my life. But perhaps I wasn't meant to—not in the way I'd tried it, anyway.

Let go.

I stared into the dark, at my hand caught in the jar, and released my hold on the fig. The jar fell away, my sticky hand freed.

Freedom.

Release.

Then I did the same in my heart. *God Almighty, what is the song* you *have written for me?*

I closed my eyes and remained poised there in the silence of the night, waiting for the shackles to descend and clamp around my heart as I gave over control. But instead a sweet melody surfaced— one of Hurstwell and hopeless women and shadows that no one else dared venture into—and I knew it had not been Marcel or Harford or even Nurse Duffy controlling me, but *him* guiding me, gently beckoning me toward the pianoforte with the music he'd written laid out and waiting for me to begin. Now I was finally ready to play.

And it would be magnificent.

37

God sends you somewhere that makes no sense, because he alone knows what you will find.

~Vivienne Mourdant

Make today count. I repeated my old challenge to myself as the sun rose behind me early the next morning, casting long shadows across Hurstwell's open yard. I'd hardly said it—or lived it—since coming here, but it was time to start. Purposeful steps carried me toward the archaic building, into the chill of its shadow, but then I slowed. Getting out without being caught had been relatively easy, in the end. Getting back in and remaining unseen was its own problem.

I knew the corridors by this time, and when each would be empty. I'd have to stay alert and keep out of sight every minute, changing locations when the staff did. My heart pounded as I approached the place, and I crouched in the bushes, evaluating my options. Bare rose branches poked me. I was near the bench where I'd talked to Anna.

She'd be one of the first I'd help. Somehow.

It was then I realized I had no idea what I planned to do. Coming back here was step one, but hiding out in the corridors and unused rooms did the patients little good. What did I mean to do, help them escape? Bring them decent food?

A figure trudged over the snow-powdered walk ahead, and I shrank deeper into the bushes. She looked about—it was Nurse Duffy, her blond hair hanging limp from its crown of pins. I held my breath. The gardens were mostly bare this time of year, and she'd spot me if she looked hard enough.

Just a few more steps. I'd dash past once she'd turned the corner.

A solid arm yanked me back. A hand stifled my cry. "Thought to escape now, did you?" Thornhill's hot breath mingled with the chilly air around the left side of my face. His arm held me against him like a metal bar. "Troublesome creature, you are." He pulled me to my feet, wrenching the breath from my lungs. Smashing my ribs together. Obliterating all my plans. "I don't know why you've come, why you lied about who you are, but I won't let some chit bring this place to ruin."

Legs off the ground, I kicked and fought in a sudden panic. "You can't do this! I'm not mad. Not mad! I'll have your hide for this."

He stopped on the lawn, impervious to my flying limbs. "You'll have nothing. *Nothing.* There's no helping some people, and there's only one place for that sort."

Isolation. Again. Awash with fresh panic, I twisted and wrenched, screaming into the morning mist. The lonely moors echoed with my sharp cry, then he dropped me, hand flying across my face. The blow stunned me into silence and I lay on the cold ground.

Nurse Duffy was hurrying toward us now, clutching her shawl about her shoulders. Thornhill looked up as one beefy arm pinned me to the powdered grass, snow leaking through the back of my cloak and gown. I was panting. Despairing of freedom.

"Let me deal with her, Dr. Thornhill. I was looking for you— you're needed in epileptic. A bad reaction to the medicine. I'm afraid we'll lose another one."

He bared his teeth, huffing as he looked from me to the building just behind. "Wretched mess." Rearing back, he yanked my arms together and clamped shackles on my wrists. They bit into the wounds that had only begun to heal. "Fine then, get her locked up. And *don't* let her out of your sight until she's secured." He leaned into her face. "It'll be your hide if she's gone." He dropped a set of keys on the ground and rose, stalking toward the side door.

She remained still until he'd gone, then I edged onto my side and saw she was shaking. Her arm snapped out and she grabbed mine, daring me with a look to run.

I balanced on the edge of trust in God and bitterness toward this woman. "It was you, wasn't it? You who aided Marcel Beauchene in making me believe I was mad. In convincing them so I'd be locked away." Ire eclipsed the calm I'd just gained. The delicate trust. Now I felt only trapped and desperate once again. "A lot of trouble to go to over jealousy."

Her eyes flashed. "You've done it to yourself, you addlepated wretch! You've made them think it all on your own. You think I wanted you to stay here, around *him* every day?" She marched us toward the tower, her grip on my arm surprisingly strong. "I was the one on duty last night, and Turner asked me to look away. I agreed wholeheartedly the minute he told me his plan. You . . . gone for good?" She gave a huff of a laugh. "I was only too glad of it."

"Then why leave me those notes? What of the music in the middle of the night?"

But I sensed the answer even before she paused, turning to look at me with a curious mix of derision and shock. "You truly are touched in the head, ain't you? I can't write. Don't know how. And if I did, I wouldn't be writin' *you* letters." With a grunt, she shoved me through a door in the long stone fence and marched me toward the tall, ivy-choked tower. "And I can promise you, there ain't no music at night in that place."

Chills sent a forceful tremble through me. Where had the notes come from, then? And the song?

Rose. It must be Rose.

317

No, she was gone. Dead. And ghosts weren't real.

But there was more to this story. That truth beat against my ribs with the rhythm of my pounding heart. "Duffy, listen to me. You can't lock me in the tower. I have to help people. The women here. Even the staff is trapped in this place, aren't they?"

Her march continued. "You heard what Thornhill said. You've gotten yourself into a tangle. I can't just let you go."

I dug in my heels, leveled my most authoritative voice. "You're going to set me free. I have work to do. You know the people here need help, and I aim to give it. *Need* to give it."

"I'm glad you see it that way." She paused before the tower, taking a breath and shoving a key into the padlock. "That's exactly what I plan for you to do."

"How—"

"Up with you." She planted her hand into my back, shoving me into the darkness and coming in behind me. Inside, she fumbled with a candle and matches until she had one lit, and it cast an eerie glow over her wide-eyed face. She was still afraid of the place. Even with gaslights running up the stairwell, the place was dim and cold. Eerie. "Up, I said. On with you."

I climbed the twisting stairwell into the heart of the musty old tower, forcing myself not to shiver. "Someone will find me. I have people who care about me."

Chaos. The reckless noise of silence. That's the only song I heard in this place, and I was trapped in it.

"He ain't one of them. And I promise you, Mitchell won't be looking. He's near the tipping point, ever since his wife, and it don't take much at all to convince him he's slipped a little to the one side, that things with you aren't exactly as he remembers. It went the same with his wife."

I froze on the step. "What do you mean?"

"He's the one what found her, of course. Dead in the isolation chamber, with a bad reaction to the injection. No one caught it. He didn't catch it. She died alone, and he can't bring himself to let it go."

The story ripped through me again. "I don't think a man like that could ever forget," I murmured, my fingertips brushing the moist stones as we climbed.

"Remembering only tortures him." She was shaking now, staring intently. "A man like that . . . he deserves to forget. To move on, into the rest of his life. Into the warm embrace of a woman who's alive and willing to help him heal."

I turned, looking into her austere face. "And that's you, I presume?"

Her lips pinched white. "He won't come looking for you. Not in here." She leaned in close, shadows leaping over her face. "No one else will go looking, neither. That's why they call it the lost tower. Folks pay extra to have someone lost up here. Up where no one will remember they lived. These are the disappeared of Hurstwell."

The "D" file. The one in Thornhill's desk, with a separate little key. That's what it stood for—*disappeared*.

That would be me now. The notes of the place climbed to a heady pitch, frantic and dramatic, flying senselessly about.

"Not even Thornhill can bear to be in here. There's just a man to bring the food, and he won't listen to a word from you. He's heard it all. 'I'm the niece of the queen. I'm the daughter of the prime minister. I'm a celebrated artist.' But soon you won't have much to say. Drugged-up quiet like the rest of 'em, just waitin' their ride to the hill out yonder."

I shivered at the memory of tombstones, the crooked markers jutting out of an overgrown hill.

I grabbed her arm. "You say I'm to help." I was grasping at dust. "How can I do that from in here?"

"*She* needs you. That's who you'll help. Won't eat a thing. I done what I can for her, but she needs someone to talk sense into her." Duffy paused before a metal door near the top and fumbled with the keys. She turned and looked at me as she shoved one in the lock, and the door groaned open. "And since you've come back . . . Well, go on then. In with you."

I hesitated at the mouth of shadows, and she gave me a push, sending me stumbling ahead of her into the dark and shutting the door behind us both. I blinked and looked about, seeing a figure sprawled on the straw against the far wall, light from the barred window falling across the patient's skirt.

Everything else fell away in an instant, the chaotic notes of the day beginning to form a straight melody line. "Bridget!" I dropped to my knees and clung to the dear woman with one arm, hardly able to help myself, stretching the shackles so I could hold her. The thinness of her frame was alarming. I touched her face with one hand, pushed back hair tangled with straw, and studied her features in the stale room. "What have they done to you? What's happened?"

Nurse Duffy spoke from behind me. "Saved her, that's what I've done. Dr. Thornhill had plans to lock her up in the catacombs down below Hurstwell after surgery. He's afraid she'll be violent."

I turned on my heel. "What surgery?"

The nurse folded her arms. "The kind that means she won't be having no more babies. He thinks she's gone to hysterics, after her outburst the other day, and that's the way they deal with it." Her voice gentled. "Couldn't see how the girl deserved that. Only a good mother'd carry on the way she did over the loss of her bairn. She needs to go home and care for the others."

"You likely saved her life, bringing her here." Duffy's words of warning from that first night rolled over me. "Of all places to hide her . . . the lost tower. You told me you never go here. Yet you've braved it. Every day, if you're also bringing her medicine."

She shrugged, dropping her gaze. "Lot of good it does. Saved from the knife, but she won't eat enough to feed an insect. Don't like it here."

I touched Bridget's bony arm, her cheek where countless tears had dried. "Oh, Bridget."

She looked down at her hands.

"Now. See if she'll listen to you and eat something." Nurse Duffy departed, key clanking in the heavy lock as she left.

I turned back to my friend. "I wish you could see how much this world needs you. How much beauty is contained in you. Please, don't give up."

"I don't have a thing to give." Her voice was dull. "And I'll never be free."

I brushed the hair from her face. "No cell can stop you."

Her gaze lifted in the narrow streams of light and met mine.

"Just like your dear Paul, with a constant thorn in the flesh. A jail cell and accusers. But with a light that the rest of the world needs to see. And Bridget, the sun doesn't stop shining just because the clouds are covering it."

Her eyes glistened, wide and bright, then she wilted against me and wept. I held her, my hand smoothing up and down her bony back, willing her to live.

Something stirred deep in the shadows to the left and I jerked up, blinking to adjust my vision again. Another cellmate. This one looked animalistic, crouched for attack or retreat. Heart pounding a frantic rhythm hard enough to break my ribs, I looked closer, and the creature—a woman—inched out and lifted her face to me. The whites of her eyes showed, big and round, then she moved into the narrow stream of light from the high window, and suddenly the cacophony of Hurstwell's song reached a fever pitch. A blinding blur of notes twisting into a stunning symphony of clear order and brilliance and it was . . . the lost melody. Soft, satin tones with bright eyes and a complexion to match her name.

Rose.

I could scarcely believe the sight of her—the true flesh-and-blood melody that had been lost . . . and found again.

She was older, of course. How many years had this melody been missing from the world? Her smooth hair was a wild mess hanging around that dear heart-shaped face . . . and the little birthmark. The one on the edge of her lip. It spread a bit now as that ghostly face framed by wilted hair smiled at me, the song turning in smooth, rounded edges and gentle climbs up the keyboard to higher, sweeter notes I'd never before imagined. Never could have written.

This couldn't be. It simply couldn't.

Yet how very real she was, how warm her hand touching mine.

"What is it? What's the matter?" Bridget edged closer to me, looking into my face.

"Bridget." My voice was a breathy whisper as I stared at that face. Could Bridget hear it? Could she hear the haunting melody that swept this dark cell? "You see her, don't you?"

She looked in the direction of the woman, then back at me. "Of course. Why wouldn't I?"

I shook my head. "A ghost. This woman is supposed to be a ghost. She had a baby, and was married to Thornhill and—"

"Have you lost your mind? This isn't Thornhill's wife, and she's no ghost."

"But Clara told me everything—about the child, and Rose's death . . ."

"Clara?" Bridget's puckered brow smoothed. "Then you can rest assured none of it's true."

I clutched my skirt. "But there were notes. From Rose. Several of them. And she's been seen around . . ."

Bridget crossed her arms, looking more herself than ever. "If that don't beat all. She really had you going, didn't she? Clara was pulling your leg."

"You mean . . . she made it all up?"

"Why, don't you know? She's the grandest storyteller in all of Hurstwell. Except we all know what she is, and no one listens to her stories anymore. No one but you."

And I had tried to leave. The moth pulling away from the gaslight, a false glow meant to draw and ensnare. "The notes. They were from her?"

Bridget shrugged. "Saw her writing something a few times on them pages of music. Couldn't make out what, though."

"And does she play the pianoforte?"

"A little. They don't let her no more though."

But she had. *She* had been the one playing Rose's song that night, which meant she must have met Rose—heard her playing it long ago. My mind tipped and spun on a new axis, struggling to right itself. "But why would she do all that?" I'd been drawn to her, to that wonderful, cheerful spirit—she'd had light in her too. Or so I'd thought.

"To make you stay." She shook her head, and the truth settled over me. "Who do you think tipped off Thornhill, told him you knew something of his secrets? I thought you knew." Bridget gave a wobbly half smile through the shadows. "Here I thought you were the clever one. I suppose you do need me around."

I smiled wanly at her—then at Rose. Rosamond Swansea, my ward. The treasure I was sent here to find. What was the truth then—about Thornhill? About her? Why *was* she here?

Her lovely face simply watched me as it always had those many years ago, tipping sweetly to the side—a minuet of moonglow and roses.

The dreams. The nocturnal music played by this woman in the rose room. It was all real.

"Rose room." I blinked—looked at the slender form whose eyes still shone just as I remembered, with that shy, secret smile. "That was yours, wasn't it? You played there. You truly did." I hadn't dreamed it. She'd been at my home. Played the pianoforte. Spent time with me.

As I stared, the woman edged herself out farther and, with a tender look that harkened back to my most precious childhood memories, reached out and caressed my cheek with maternal affection, catching that birth-marked lower lip in her teeth.

38

My compositions spring from my sorrows. Those that give the world the greatest delight were born of my deepest griefs.

~Franz Schubert

Mitchell Turner had misjudged many a person in his life, many a situation, but never one so greatly as he had Dr. Thornhill. He stared at the news clipping flattened to the desk under his palm, mesmerized by the grainy sketch. Dr. Thornhill's relaxed smile graced the page, looking over at an intelligent woman beside him as if he still couldn't believe she'd married him. His hair was darker, his face narrower, but it was definitely him. Crowded before them were five children of varying heights, the oldest looking no more than ten or twelve.

He took a breath and forced himself to read the text again, the shock slightly less this time as he took the story in. The events of the 1859 asylum fire had resulted in numerous casualties, including the entire family of one of its doctors who all lived in a flat within the asylum—Dr. Timothy Alan Thornhill. The alienist himself, who had been away to participate in a special committee probing into English lunacy laws, was the sole survivor of his family.

An inmate from the acute ward, having earned certain freedoms from Dr. Thornhill as he worked toward release, had snapped unexpectedly and flown into a rage. The madman had been one of the doctor's success stories, one destined to be released as so many others had under Thornhill's skilled care—until he killed the doctor's entire family with a fireplace poker and set fire to the asylum with kerosene lamps. The building was a total loss, and fourteen patients were killed in the blaze. It had devastated the entire Southampton area to learn of the news, claimed the article, and the repercussions were felt throughout the community.

Dr. Thornhill's ominous warning spidered through Mitchell's mind. *"Someday you will stand back and survey the wreckage of what was, the utter devastation caused by a patient who only the day before seemed perfectly sane and deserving of every liberty he's been given."*

Those words echoed in Turner's head for hours, even through luncheon. Voices came from the entryway as he skirted it—several men he did not know were talking with Thornhill. He should join them as his fellow doctor, but Mitchell wasn't in the right frame of mind for passing pleasantries—not that he often was these days.

Veering away from the front hall where their conversation echoed, Mitchell ran fingers through his hair as he entered the kitchen, looking about for leftovers to scrounge from staff meals. Questionable meat and a few wilted vegetables languished on the sideboard, and he turned instead toward the few remaining teacups on the shelf. The rest were being readied for patient tea, spread over the surfaces as teapots boiled nearby.

"There you are, Dr. Turner. You're a difficult man to locate." It was Harford in the kitchen doorway, grasping his suit lapels. "A word, if you would?"

Mitchell turned and cleared his throat as he rummaged through the larder for a tin of something that wouldn't put him to sleep. "Of course. I'm making tea—would you care for some?"

"Please." He settled himself on a stool and gave a nod to one of the new aids who scurried about, pouring tea from kettles into a long line of cups.

"I'd like to know what you think of your superintendent, Dr. Thornhill."

Thoughts collided. Heat edged up under his collar. Mitchell glanced at the aid, who seemed not to be listening. He couldn't be sure, though. "I don't agree with every method he chooses, but what he does is born of hard-won experience." Mitchell's voice quieted on this last part. "He's a well-respected alienist, and he is dedicated to Hurstwell, whatever faults he may have."

"What makes you call him dedicated, if you don't mind my asking?"

"Thornhill takes more personal oversight of the place than most superintendents. He takes his one day off per week, but he has his fingers in every ward, knows a bit about every patient. It is more than a position for him—it's a personal mission." Mitchell poured their tea and stirred, dropping a bit of sugar into each cup.

Harford lowered his voice, leaning closer. "Do you consider him an honest man?"

"I've never known him not to be." Well, almost never. What of the use of those isolation wards, when he'd vowed they would always sit empty? And there was an oddness about Bridget Hurley's absence that never was properly explained. It was as if she'd vanished, and the disappearing act was somehow orchestrated and covered up by Thornhill. "At least, I haven't any proof he isn't. Why do you ask?"

Harford sucked in a breath and spoke in low, intentional words. "Well, I don't trust the man one whit. But my hands are tied—I have proof of nothing."

Turner's eyebrows shot up. "And why the suspicion of Thornhill?"

"I have my reasons. Most of which concern his treatment of your Miss Mourdant. I've been told she has been transferred overnight to a new establishment near London . . . for her own good. What do you think of that?"

Hair on the back of his neck prickled under his collar. Another glance at the aid. She bustled about, seeming oblivious to their talk. Heat again threatened to strangle Turner, and he looked Harford in the eye. Had Vivienne made it to his cabin? He couldn't tell from the man's face what he knew. Or had Thornhill caught her and sent her away as he'd claimed?

Mitchell broke the gaze. He couldn't get past the image of Thornhill's smiling family in newsprint. "I don't believe Thornhill is the villain you seem to think he is. He desires to do good, and he's lived through more than I've given him credit for. Perhaps he's been right more times than I thought too." This last part was quiet, almost to himself.

Harford's look was steady. "There's no villain so terrifying as one who's right. Whose logic is accurate, whose intentions are noble. But take note, it takes only one drop of poison to pollute an entire glass of water."

Poison—such as hatred. Fear. No one had more reason for those than Thornhill.

The question was this: Was Thornhill more perceptive than most . . . or simply more jaded?

Mitchell lifted his gaze. "If you should happen upon Miss Mourdant again—when your research takes you to other institutions, that is—you may tell her she has a friend here. I will always do what I can for her, and she may depend on that."

"Good." Harford lingered in the doorway. "For what it's worth, I'm glad she managed to change your mind. About her condition, that is."

"I've never—"

"Her intake form. You provided the second signature, of course, attesting to her insanity when she was admitted. But now it seems you've changed your tune, and I'm glad of it." A tip of his head. "Good day, Dr. Turner."

Shock clanged through Mitchell as his visitor left and the parting words sunk in. Second signature? Him? Utterly ridiculous.

Mitchell blinked at the empty doorway where the little man had exited, and the lens shifted on his view of the visitor. Wild accusations reminded one of the patients here. Perhaps Harford belonged at Hurstwell himself. The man had seemed a touch off since the start.

And yet . . .

Those locked chambers. The gleam of subdued rage in Thornhill's face. The unlikely passion with which he devoted himself to this place . . .

With a groan, Mitchell shook his head. It seemed there was a trace of madness in them all—including him. He was weary of sorting fact from fiction, madness from sanity.

He remained in the kitchen, head in hands over his unfinished tea, for many silent moments. When he lifted his head, it spun a bit, disorienting him. He saw her smile—Dahlia's. He could picture it clearly, with the world still slightly out of focus and his memories clear.

He had struggled in school years ago, until she'd come alongside him. His future had been bleak until she'd encouraged him that he'd make a worthwhile doctor. She'd given him everything he had, including some of the money to attend university . . . and he'd failed her in the end.

"Don't let me die in here, Mitch. Don't let me die."

On shaking legs, he walked up the stairs to the third floor, the chronic ward. He stared down the hall at the closed door of the chamber where she'd died, flipping through mental images of their past.

Her vivid nightmares.

Tears that wouldn't stop.

The baby that never had a chance to open its eyes.

A mother, his Dahlia, who could never fill the baby-shaped ache of her empty arms. His desperation to bring her back to life again when sorrow had sucked it away.

Then, Hurstwell. A place of healing that only seemed to break her further.

He walked past the roughly barred chambers to the one he hadn't been able to touch and began to breathe harder, as if he were running up the stairs rather than simply walking down the hall. He had been so wrung out in those days, weak with atrophied muscles he couldn't flex when they were needed by his own wife. He'd failed her. Failed to cure her, failed to be there when she lay dying and alone.

Some husband he'd been.

He quickened his pace and moisture began to sheen his face, his chest. He forced his legs to eat up the distance to the end of the hall and he barely paused before that door. He fit the key in and yanked it open, bracing himself for what he'd find.

His breath came in panicked gasps as he waited for his eyes to adjust to the dark. He blinked . . . blinked . . .

Empty. Just a loose sheet thrown carelessly off the edge of a stained cot.

"I'm not mad, Mitchell. I'm not mad".

He forced himself to walk in. To sit on the bed. He put his palm on the mattress and felt a surprising calm. A disconnection from reality.

"Dr. Turner. What are you doing here?" Thornhill's voice jarred him back to the present.

As Thornhill loomed in the doorway, his large frame blocking the light, his face was the same. Exactly the same as when he'd told him Dahlia needed to be in this place—told him, with sickening pity, that his wife was dead and he must come away from this cell. It couldn't have been prevented, he'd said. These things simply happened.

Liar.

Thornhill could have stopped it. *He* could have stopped it. Someone should have.

Harford's revelations returned to him then with a strange ring of truth.

"Where is she?" Mitchell's chest strained against his shirt with each breath.

The same dull pity softened the man's features. "She is dead, Dr. Turner. Your wife is—"

"I mean Vivienne Mourdant. Where is she? And is it true that my signature is on her intake form?"

Thornhill's face remained stoic as the seconds ticked by. "Who might that be, Doctor?"

"Vivienne Mourdant, who was supposedly transferred. I know for a fact she wasn't." He rose, shoulders squared. "What have you done with her?"

The pity in Thornhill's features deepened. "There is no one of that name registered at Hurstwell, Dr. Turner. There never has been."

Mitchell narrowed his eyes. Something electrified in him. He shook, skin clammy, and shed his coat, slinging it over the end of the bed. What game was this? "Bring her to me now, or so help me I will smash every stone in this place to find her."

"You won't find anything." His voice gentled. "And I won't allow you to damage—"

"The one you call Cora Fletcher. But you know that isn't her name, don't you? Knew it the minute you heard her play the pianoforte. Or perhaps before that." Everything seemed clear now. Too clear. "The truth, Dr. Thornhill. Tell me the truth about her. Now."

Thornhill gripped Mitchell's shoulders and forced him back onto the bed, as if to have a serious conversation with a burgeoning doctor.

"What are you doing?" He stood, but his legs shook. He couldn't breathe. Couldn't think. Life leaked out of him. Was he dying? Was he mad? He tried to push past Thornhill, but the man was like an ox, blocking his way and strong-arming him back. "I don't need confinement—I need the truth!"

"The truth, Dr. Turner, is that you are no more sane than your patients. I had the papers drawn up shortly after her death, after your outbursts, and you are in fact a legal patient here."

He sprang up, lunging for the door. "No!"

Thornhill stabbed a needle into Turner's flesh, and in a panic, Turner knocked it away. Cool liquid dropped on his skin and heat radiated from the injection site. Nausea swept through him in long, pulling waves. *Dahlia. She died this way. With an injection that was too much.*

He felt the bed beneath him, and he could picture it still—her white arm hanging off the edge. Her hair and pale skin. Images shuddered through him, pounding against his brain as caged animals desperate for release.

His moist fingers swept his hair off his forehead. It was as if he was happening upon her all over again.

"No one blames you, Turner. No one. But this is best for now. I'm afraid her death has broken you."

"No." Moisture gathered along his shaking limbs. "No!" A hole had been pierced in his lungs, and air was leaking out. This couldn't be his story. His reality. Wife dead, neglected and alone, and now him dead, or locked in an asylum. And not as a doctor. Not truly.

Then the door slammed shut.

But not before he weakly tossed the edge of his coat in the latch.

It was dark. Night. Turner's head still swam with the lingering effects of the injection, but the cool air of an abandoned corridor helped dissipate it. A good portion of the dose must have landed on his shirt and arm when he'd knocked it away, because he was recovering more quickly than he'd expected.

Quickly enough, he hoped, to be able to do what was necessary. He shook his head to clear it and waved on the man behind him. "Come quickly."

He urged John Michelson—Philippe—out into the dimly lit

corridor, an arm about his hunched back. He was liable to be caught by Thornhill at any moment, but suddenly Mitchell didn't care. Something had broken within him—something set free, perhaps. This had been no place for Dahlia, and it was no place for anyone who had any other option in the world. Rather than repairing the broken people who came to it, Hurstwell itself was broken.

Mitchell could practically hear the arthritis in the old Frenchman's legs as he hustled faster than was likely comfortable for him, but Philippe seemed to sense the urgency and did not lag. The halls were chilly farther down, the gaslights more scarce. Mitchell panted with the effort as his body struggled to recover but pushed through.

When they reached the service door on the main level, Philippe put a hand on Mitchell's arm. "I know what you're trying to do." Philippe looked up at him in the shadows. "I do thank you for it, but I cannot accept."

He paused, a hand on the wall to catch his breath. "You don't know what I'm offering."

"Yes, I do. You and I both know I'm not mad, but . . . no, I cannot leave. You, Dr. Turner, are the one who should be leaving. You're far better than this place."

Mitchell stiffened. "Yes, you can leave. You will." Gripping the man's arm tighter, Mitchell urged him on. His faint protests stopped nothing as they stumbled out into the night air, into the oddly welcoming light of stars set in a blue-black sky and the moon glowing down in approval. The old man shivered, and Mitchell threw a lap blanket around his shoulders. "Here, this'll do."

"Look, I cannot leave, I tell you."

"I'm betting I can change your mind."

"No, it is—"

They paused in the moist yard, and there, beneath a canopy of bare willow fronds, sat the rosy-faced ballet dancer without her music box. She sat straighter at the sight of them, and Philippe stiffened, his breath coming in little white puffs. His fight had stilled.

"So . . . success?" Mitchell smiled at the patient as Philippe looked up at him with shock.

The man's mouth opened, then closed upon whatever he meant to say.

"You'll be staying with Ella and Jack Dorian in London. I assure you, they're eager to have you both in their care."

Still, the man did not speak.

Mitchell paused and turned the man to face him. "Please, tell me I don't need to convince you further."

He shook his head slowly. "You had me convinced at the sight of her. If my wife isn't here, I've no reason to stay."

Mitchell froze, his grip on the man unintentionally tightening. No reason. No reason to stay.

"She moves, so has my home."

Mitchell looked back at the rising stone walls that had imprisoned him for so long, keeping him locked in one place. In darkness. There was a sky full of stars, bringing light even to the night outside that place.

Perhaps he should leave.

Could he? Dare he? He had nothing to keep him here either. Not anymore. But he didn't deserve to leave. Didn't deserve freedom.

A lump lodged in his throat as he led the man forward, toward the wife Philippe adored. Mitchell refused to glance toward the cemetery this night.

They sat on either side of Anna on that stone bench, and she relaxed, a mild smile crossing her face as she settled between them.

He wasn't looking at the cemetery, but he shook. Leaving felt so foreign. So impossible. Yet the notion tugged at him. Guilt fought back.

He passed his hand through his hair.

A gnarled old hand grabbed his, patting the top, then tracing the thick veins, the knuckles. Then music rustled from deep inside her chest, wavering through the quiet night as it had those stormy nights when she'd been the one afraid and he'd sung to her. *Amazing grace, how sweet the sound.*

He stilled, focusing on his breathing.

That saved a wretch like me.

Mitchell glanced up at the rambling old structure that held so much pain.

I once was lost . . . but now I'm found.

Was blind, but now I see.

Just beyond the trees, a full moon shone round and bright against the inky sky. A light amidst the darkness. Amazing grace.

"Come, it's time to go." He rose, stretching his tense back and helping the couple rise. "You'll be to London in a few hours, and life will be far brighter for you. I'm sure of it."

Philippe laid his hand on Mitchell's arm, tired old eyes looking up into his. "You wouldn't have us go alone, would you? Escaped patients of a mental ward . . . and at our age. Won't you escort us, Dr. Turner?"

The man knew not what he even said. What those words did to him.

Mitchell took a breath and released it. "Yes. Yes, I will go with you." One final giant band released from around his chest, and he took a deep, fresh breath, turning his back on Hurstwell. Perhaps for the last time.

39

Music comes to me more readily than words.

~Ludwig van Beethoven

The low notes of that rapturous lost melody climbed in pitch, in intensity, driving toward some unseen climax but always dancing around it. I touched Rose's face, her hair, and she did not pull back—she only kept smiling at me. The moment was breathless—surreal. "Who are you?" It seemed ridiculous to ask when I knew the answer, had seen her portrait, but I wanted her to say it.

She didn't, though. She only continued looking at me as I withdrew my hand, her head tilted with the same sweet affection I remembered. Then she reached out and caressed my arm, thin fingers running down the length of it, grasping my hand and turning it over to trace the length of my piano-playing fingers. Her smile broadened.

"What is she doing to you?" Bridget asked.

I could do nothing but stare at this time-faded version of my lovely childhood memory, full of wonder and dawning horror at the sight of her . . . here. "What is your name? Who are you?"

She nodded and smiled reassuringly, as if she'd heard something

337

different than I'd said, smoothing long fingers over my hand as she cradled it.

I drew near to her in the dark until I could smell the straw in her hair. "Helena?" I pointed at her chest and repeated my mother's name as clear as I could. "Helena Garvey Mourdant?"

She blinked, as if the word registered through the fog, but she shook her head. "Roe." She touched her fingertips to her chest as her rosebud lips struggled to form the sound.

"Rose. Yes, you are Rose. Rosamond Swansea, yes?"

A slow nod.

I turned to the woman behind me. "Bridget, do you know anything about her? Who she is, where she came from?"

She shrugged. "Had a mother and father once, but they're gone, from what I can tell. Doesn't talk much, and she doesn't seem to understand, neither. Any talking we've done has been with our hands, like two people speaking a different language. Figured maybe she was a Celt or something."

I reached out a hand, caressing her dirty cheek, feeling the roundness I so remembered in those moonlit meetings at the pianoforte. Rose—*Rose*—had played in my home. In my mother's pianoforte room. And her portrait—Mother's portrait—hung in Seaton Hall.

She had to be. Had to be my mother.

But . . . *not*. Now that I sat face-to-face with the woman, there was a marked difference. Something in the bearing and nature that wasn't quite the same as that portrait. Freedom and a youthful joy had been captured in that portrait, and Rose had always, even in our long-ago encounters, worn a quiet calm that made her seem almost shy. She was the same now. And the little birthmark on her lip—I saw it clearly before me, had seen it in the rose room all those years ago, but it hadn't been in the portrait. The artist, I had assumed, had deftly covered up the supposed flaw, but perhaps it hadn't been there to paint at all.

"I do know she's like me—come from a mother who weren't

married." Bridget heaved a sigh. "Makes life difficult on a person, that. Never quite sure who you are—or whose you are."

"You managed to get all this from her?"

"Over time. Taught her to dump the tea they were giving her, and she's been a lot better company since. We've had a few talks. Well, I've talked and she's . . . you know." Bridget's hands floated around.

I couldn't take my eyes from the woman in the shadows, couldn't block out the symphony of past mingling with present. "Not Helena?" I asked helplessly, pointing to her.

She shook her head, vigorously this time, and leaned forward like a baby bird, trying to make a sound come out. "Mud . . . her. Mudher."

Mother. *Mother.*

"Helena was . . . your *mother?*"

A single nod. Knowing flooded my chest so hard, I could barely keep up with the rush of it. Like twins they were, the same sweetness of spirit in nearly identical bodies. Rose was so like the portrait of Mother . . . but her own person too. My mother would always be lost to me, but she'd left behind this fragment, this small piece of herself—her eldest daughter. I took her hand, laying it against my cheek. I pointed to myself, then to her, and said, "Sister."

A smile glowed across her face, a kerosene lamp with the wick slowly turned up to light the room with a soft glow. Her fingers traveled over my features, and I let them, enjoying the gentle feel of them. This was my sister. My *sister.*

"Why did you disappear? Why are you *here?* And why can't you speak?" I took a deep breath. "What happened to you?"

I wasn't certain what she understood—her lovely smile remained in place and she said nothing. Then, seeing my frown, she traced five long lines in the dirt and a treble clef. With one fingertip she colored in four notes on the lines, a single bar of music, then pointed at them.

I hummed them, but it wasn't a familiar melody. A shrug.

Yet, how eager she looked. Her message was urgent. Something important. Shoulders tensed, she pointed at the single measure of music, then at herself. Again I shrugged, and her shoulders drooped. She drew them thicker, deeper, making each note clear as if on ink and paper, then blew out a breath, grabbed my hand, and stared hopelessly at the floor.

40

To copy the truth can be a good thing, but to invent the truth is better, much better.

~Giuseppe Verdi

Control. It was all about control, starting with one's own expression. Superintendent Thornhill did not look up at Leizel Schumann as he casually replaced a book on his office shelf. "I regret that I cannot be of more help to you, Mrs. Schumann." His smile was slow, untroubled. Compassionate.

Nothing like the chaos raging below the surface.

Her gently accented voice echoed through his office again. "You will search again, *Herr Tornheel*. I'm quite certain my husband is here. That woman . . . de patient with de red hair . . . she know my name."

It wasn't Mrs. Schumann's slight frame that made his neck ache with tension—it was the four men in black suits standing just beyond her, hands clasped behind their backs. He smiled again and rubbed at the kink in vain.

The lunacy commission had kept out of his affairs thus far, and he'd taken for granted that such would always be the case. They were simply far too overworked to check up on every single country asylum across each district in England and wouldn't have ever bothered with one little madhouse way up in the moors . . . until the meddling.

Most visitors were handily put off, but Leizel Schumann, the tiny pillar of confidence with a firm voice, had returned—with her small army of support dispatched by the home secretary. All because of one red-haired patient who had a habit of causing trouble. Once alerted to a problem and provided with proof, Thornhill knew the lunacy commission would not look away until it had seen everything there was to see.

Or at least, what he allowed them to see.

The question was, what proof had she given them to entice them here? What exactly did they already know?

He forced himself to look only at her pert little face. "I'm sorry, but there's no record of an Otto Schumann at Hurstwell. You're welcome to search the entire filing cabinet yourself." He stood stiff and tall, leaning against the desk drawer that held the all-important files—the ones of patients who had needed to disappear. Ones whose madness had gone overlooked by other alienists—hidden by deceptive masks of sanity—and thus eluding the constraints they required.

"Actually, we'd like to search the wards again—on our own." A tall gent from the commission with an even taller hat stepped forward, eyeing the superintendent. "Unless you have objections."

"Of course not. Why would I?" Yes, yes. By all means, leave this office. Go tromping about the wards without him and stay out of his way for a moment. Opportunity was so close, he could nearly smell the fresh air of it. A few moments to himself and he'd have everything set to rights. He'd designed it to be this way—tracks easy to cover, secrets ready to tuck into shadows.

They began to funnel out. Backs faced him, and he waited grimly, clutching the desk. Leg braced against the drawer of secrets.

Then one turned. "By the by, Thornhill, what of that tower out back? It wasn't part of the tour you gave us."

"Because there isn't anything to see out . . ." His courage tapered as he noticed Sam Barnhill just behind the gents—Sam, who slipped daily trays of food under the doors of the dazed and drugged patients in the lost tower. He stared at Thornhill, steady and knowing.

Thornhill cleared his throat. Straightened. "It's storage." A shrug and a smile. "Mere storage." That was the truth. "It should probably be taken down, actually. It's a crumbling mess, and not fit to set foot in at the moment." A light laugh. They weren't truly patients stored away out there, were they? No treatment was offered. No rehabilitation attempted. No, they were something else entirely. Yet he felt the burn of dishonesty as he neared its flame.

It was a necessary evil. For now.

The men looked at one another and turned again to move into the corridors. Thornhill gripped the edge of the desk. One . . . two . . . three . . .

Silence. Blissful solitude.

He exhaled. Spinning to the desk, he fumbled for the key to the lower drawer, fitting it into the lock and yanking it open. Calm. Keep calm. Grabbing handfuls of files, he tossed them into his cold hearth and struck a match.

He held back only one—a file marked "Schumann, Otto." He flipped through it as the fire surged to life, wanting to be sure of what he remembered before disposing of the paperwork.

The man had been brought in unconscious and bedraggled by his three brothers, and even without any documentation to be had in the middle of the night, he'd kept the man as he had all the others. Within hours, papers had been drawn and two medical signatures—one forged as necessary—appeared on them. Then the volatile, powerful Otto Schumann had been locked safely in the tower, away from everyone he might hurt.

Who knew how many lives he had saved this way?

Well he knew the broken, twisted mess that often lay in wait behind even a placid face, just waiting for the right spark to ignite it into fatal explosion. Only the family knew, and so often no one believed them until it was too late. He, Dr. Thornhill, would never doubt them. He knew better.

Another stack onto the fire, one by one. His fingers paused at one folder he hadn't glanced at in years.

Thomas Thornhill. Thomas, the amazing elder brother so full of life . . . and fear. How Thornhill had hated the way people judged his brother, afraid of his outbursts because they didn't know him. Didn't know how truly wonderful and friendly and vivacious he could be.

Most days. Then others . . .

No. He would not go there. A shudder passed over him, and the instant memory of the smell of smoke. The screams. It had cost him his family to believe in his brother. His *entire* family. No one should ever be forced to face such a loss. With a hard flick of the wrist, he tossed Thomas's file on the fire too.

Goodbye, big brother.

It was brutal, quite extreme, but this was the only way that made any sense at all. Yes, one day all of England would come up-to-date in their understanding of these silent bombs of patients. They needed to be handled carefully—neutralized with firm treatment and tonics, and locked in a place far from the rest of the world.

He stared at the doorway where Mrs. Schumann had stood, recalling the details of her husband's admittance. The men who'd brought Otto Schumann—men who looked nothing alike—were obviously not his brothers, but Thornhill had steeled himself against doubts. One look at the unconscious man stirring on the table, the gashes across his giant body and the dirt and blood under his fingernails, and Dr. Thornhill knew the men's account of Otto and his violence was true. It mattered not how the men truly knew the patient—their story matched what Thornhill's eyes observed, and that was enough. Better safe than unutterably sorry later.

He stood for a moment before the files in the fire, watching them all burn. Satisfaction mingled with fear in his chest as the blackened papers curled. What was right wasn't always legal—and Timothy Alan Thornhill had always operated on a higher moral plane than the law.

After a moment, he strode out of the room and listened for footsteps. They'd be on the first floor or perhaps out on the grounds, searching all the patient work spaces. The laundry, the kitchen, the butcher shop. He had only a small measure of time to do something about the lost tower, but what? Free the least harmless? Topple the tower on them all?

No. Too barbaric.

He thought briefly—madly—of the tunnels. Of the waterways running beneath the tower, which sometimes flooded if the rains had been bad, as they had this past year. The week had been unusually warm too. The water would have thawed. The tunnels would be filled with it, and no one trapped down there would stand a chance. He shuddered at the thought of human bodies shoved into the dank tunnels, but hopefully it wouldn't come to that. He had other options to consider first.

But for *her* . . . Cora Fletcher—no, Vivienne Mourdant—a permanent solution would need to be found. It was the only way—one life to save countless others. She mustn't be found. Mustn't topple his house of cards.

Thankfully, there weren't many people who even knew to search for her.

Head down, shoulders back, he moved into the hallway and turned sharply toward the back hall. An hour. Just an hour was all he needed, maybe less. But they were there, gathered in his front entry like a wall of black stone. Watching him. Waiting. He gripped the tower keys in his right fist.

The one in a black derby stepped forward, hands in his pockets. "Might you recommend a suitable inn for the night? We'd like to go over our findings tonight and start our journey in the morning."

He blew out a breath. "Of course. There are several." They were leaving. *Leaving.*

But one formidable gent stepped forward, his long, open great-coat flapping about his legs. "I say, Thornhill, I don't suppose you could let us into that tower before we call it a night, could you? The others are ready to leave off, but I thought we might peek in, just to be thorough. I never like to leave a stone unturned."

Thornhill's heart slammed his rib cage, and his skin went cold. No, hot. "Well, if you insist upon it. I cannot attest to its state of cleanliness. I'm afraid I'll have to suggest entering with handkerchiefs over your nose. No telling how bad it is at the moment."

The little party stepped forward expectantly, ready to follow Thornhill.

He eased a smile over his face. "Right this way, if you please." Through the dim corridors and into the kitchen he led them, pausing at the butler's pantry. "You'll excuse me a moment while I turn on the gas for the place. I'm afraid it's been shut down since it isn't in use."

Lie, lie, lie. He could barely catch his breath. Fumbling about the shelves and broom handles, he felt about for the copper pipes with valves on them and gripped the biggest one. With one yank, the gas—and every light in the place—blessedly shut off. "Oh, bother." He exhaled a lungful of air. Darkness, the ultimate cover, blanketed them. He was safe.

"What is it? What's happened?"

"I'm afraid this happens on occasion. The gas valves interfere with each other at times, and it seems tampering with the valve for the tower has shut them all off."

Bumps and clangs and voices sounded above. The patients would be unsettled with the sudden plunge into darkness. It couldn't be helped, though.

"Well, turn them back on." The unseen man's voice was demanding, the edge of panic evident.

"It isn't that simple, I'm afraid. Any one of the staff is liable to start lighting candles and other lamps, and if I turn the gas on just now, the entire place could—"

"He's right, you'd blow the roof sky-high," came another voice. "I suppose we'll just return on the morrow and see what's to be seen in broad daylight. That's what I thought we should do from the start, anyway."

Thornhill held his breath. It was perfect. All too well arranged. God's blessing upon his little operation.

He lightly smacked his cheeks to keep alert. Calm. It was all working out. They'd leave, and he could safely do what he must to the tower and everyone in it. Given a whole night to deal with the issue, he'd leave nothing for them to find. He felt about for matches and a candlestick, lit them, and waved the men back down the dark corridor.

Thornhill gave a light laugh. "I do hope you'll forgive the mishap and not write it up in your report. I plan to repair the system when I have the funds. They're always limited, as you can imagine."

"We won't hold such a thing against your institution, Doctor." The inspector tipped his hat. "Good day, sir."

With scrapes of shoe soles and flaps of coats, the men descended into the darkness toward the waiting carriage. Thornhill exhaled a few quick breaths. They were leaving. Leaving. He itched to start, to run to that tower and take care of everything.

Soon.

But they stopped. Turned. Pointed at something toward the other side of the building. "Do you see that?"

"What? What is it?"

"Light. In that empty old tower."

Thornhill jerked around to look and there it was—a tiny flame dancing about in a high window. The alienist ground his teeth. He pivoted back to the men, but he had no more words to offer. No more diversions. For all the locking up he'd done, all the patients he'd managed to control with cells and restraints, there was one thing those walls could not contain.

Light.

41

I am convinced that there are universal currents of Divine Thought vibrating the ether everywhere and that any who can feel these vibrations is inspired.

~Richard Wagner

I clutched my candle, staring into its tiny flame that lit up our cell. *Thank God for you, Dr. Turner.*

I had cried out when the world went suddenly dark. I couldn't help it. It had been so swift, so unexpected. Wails had come from all around, echoing against stone as if the dead were arising all at once and making an escape. The women in my cell made frantic little noises, shuffling around.

I clutched a pair of cold hands—Bridget's or Rose's, I suppose—and forced calm over my mind and body. It was all right. Just a malfunction of the lights. I was not alone, not in immediate danger, and this wasn't the larder. Just darkness. Nothing to fear. Not really.

Then I'd felt something hard in my pocket. A memory had arrested me.

"So you never have to face the darkness."

Eyes closed, mind focused, my breathing began to normalize

as I clutched Mitchell Turner's candles now. "It's all right, it's all right." I spoke to myself as much as everyone else. The familiar smell of animal fat had never been so comforting as its light glowed smooth and warm through the cell.

I passed a few candles from my pocket through the bars connecting our cell to the next, then held my candle out to light theirs. "Here, hold steady. Now pass some on. Let's have some light in this place."

As the few candles I had in my possession circulated down the hall, the nearest cries and moans turned to soft voices. Tense whispers. Our section of the tower was lit with a soft glow that increased as the handful of candles were lit all down the way.

I sighed. "It's all right, we have some light."

I turned to pass my candle to Bridget so I could move about freely, and she grasped the hand that held it out, smiling up into my face with a knowing look.

I returned her smile. "At least I'm not wasting it out in broad daylight."

Her eyes shone and one eyebrow rose.

I moved toward Rose, who had huddled around the twist in the tower wall again, and sat before her. "Are you all right?"

She nodded, and I urged her out, coaxing her to sit beside me on the straw. When I tried to speak to her, she merely shook her head and re-drew the single bar with four notes, pointing at each one.

I shrugged and shook my head. "I wish I understood."

Her face was pained. She jerked her finger at the first note, so I looked down. "That's a *D*." I put my hands up in a gesture of helplessness, but she brightened. Leaned forward. Then she pointed at the next note.

"*F*? No, *E*."

She nodded hard and pointed at each note again.

I read them aloud. "D . . . E . . . A . . . F." I frowned. "D-E-A—" I jerked upright. "Deaf. You're deaf."

She grasped my hand, her tender face looking up into mine with gratitude. Relief. She smiled. Music had become her language. How long had she been secreted away here, that her brain had been stripped of everything else?

I touched her ear, tucked tufts of hair behind it. "You cannot hear, can you?"

She merely looked at me, her eyes wide and staring in the dim cell. Just as she'd watched me when we played together, sat together in my childhood. We'd never spoken. Only played. And this was why.

Also why she'd been locked up, perhaps. But there had to be more to it than that. Had to be.

I leaned close so she could see my lips and spoke slowly. "How do you—"

Something banged. Metallic groaning and creaking, then a door slamming open. Men's voices. Footsteps.

"What's that?" Bridget whispered.

I grabbed her hand, heart pounding as we waited.

"I'm positive." A man's voice echoed up to us. "I saw lights about halfway up, and they were moving. I vow to you, there's someone in this tower. And either Thornhill doesn't know about it or he lied. Which means this is sure to be a find."

I shot to my feet and put my face to the tiny, barred window, straining to peer out.

"What is . . . what *is* all this?"

The footsteps slowed, shuffling through the grit of the main floor.

"James, look, there are *people* here. Not a person, but . . ."

Their voices mingled into one low discussion as they moved about.

"Mrs. Schumann, I think you should come in here," a firm voice called out. "Take a look at these faces. See if there's one familiar."

Movement. More shuffling.

"No," said a clear feminine voice. "He isn't here."

My heart thudded. "He's here! Go up!" My voice echoed off the rounded stone walls, bouncing about to every part of the tower.

A murmur of low voices, then the footsteps pounded, echoing a hurried march up the steps. They were coming. All of them were coming.

Police? Asylum doctors? Who had Leizel Schumann persuaded to bring her to the tower? Soon a light bobbed along the stairwell, bouncing off the grimy walls. I clutched the bars.

Then they were there, on our landing. The slender veiled woman paused, looking in each cell until she came to ours. "There. She is there, de woman who knew my name."

"Come, let her out, haste!"

They unbolted the door from the outside and it swung wide with a rusty groan of old hinges, and I was facing them, standing in the light of their lantern. Shoulders back, I walked from that cell and held out my hand, brushing straw off me with the other. "Gentlemen, Mrs. Schumann, I am Vivienne Mourdant."

One man blinked at me from behind spectacles. "The pianist, Vivienne Mourdant?"

I gave a single nod.

The other men shrugged, apparently not having heard of me.

I turned to the petite woman watching me from behind her veil, at her features pale with strain and determination. "Come, I will take you to your husband."

They let me pass toward the upper stairs, blocking my exit to the lower—likely so I could not escape. Crowded together, we moved up the stairs with me in the lead. "They call it the lost tower, because it's where people go to be lost—who *need* to be lost. I don't know why, though."

"My husband, he has enemies," said the German woman in a poised but trembly voice. Her gloved fingers clutched the handles of her bag. "They vish to quiet him because he disprove their research. He more clever than them, and they don't like."

We reached the top of the tower and the smell assaulted us. The stench I remembered from the other visits. "Mr. Schumann?" I called out.

Metal scraped on stone. A voice growled. Leizel Schumann shoved her way to the front, standing on her toes to peer in the barred window. "Otto. Otto!" She turned to us. "The keys, give me keys!"

A roughly shod man, one I'd seen about the asylum, stepped forward and unbolted the six latches all the way down the door and flung it open, flattening a handkerchief against his nose and mouth.

"Madame, is this your missing husband?"

The little woman burst into the chamber and threw herself upon the man in chains. With a groan he melted around her, swallowing her small form with his giant one and raining down kisses upon her head, her face. She burst into sobs and buried her face into his chest, heedless of the grime and odor.

Somehow a pleasant sweetness came over us all as we looked on. The prisoner continued to fold his wife close, hands making gentle paths over her back as if to ensure she was real, every inch of her. Words filled the chamber, clipped German speech, impassioned statements and questions pouring over one another and alternating back and forth in a most lovely duet.

I blinked as my eyes warmed, tears pricking the corners.

Then a door banged. Boots clomped up the stairs. I backed against the wall, watching. Listening.

Thornhill appeared, bursting upon the scene with all the rage of a bear. "What is the meaning of this? Who let you in here?"

"You said to show it to 'em." The scruffy asylum man stood back, dark anger over his unshaven face.

"The outside. I said the *outside*."

One of the men in suits crossed his arms over his chest. "You've likely already surmised that we've found the nonexistent Mr. Schumann."

The burliest gentleman grasped Thornhill's arm. "Let's continue this talk in your office, shall we? Perhaps have a look at the records for the rest of these patients."

His face went red. A vein rose on his neck. "I'll do no such thing. This is none of your concern."

Another man took Thornhill's other arm. "Just a talk, Dr. Thornhill. For now, just a talk."

Several of the men moved down the stairs with Thornhill while two others stood across Otto Schumann's doorway, watching the scene unfold. "We'll have this sorted out, Mrs. Schumann. I'd expect your husband to be released into your care, unless my suspicions on the situation are wrong."

"What I'd like to know is where this *Turner* character is. He's signed off on most of the patients in this place, but he's nowhere to be found."

"Dr. Turner?" I asked. "He's head of the chronic ward."

"You wouldn't happen to know what's become of the man then, would you?"

I shook my head, worry surging through my veins.

A hand gently took my arm. "And how is it that *you've* come to be here, Miss Mourdant?"

I turned to the bearded man watching me from behind his spectacles and took a deep breath. Then I told my story of coming to this place, of the music being all wrong, and of the unexpected symphony that is Hurstwell.

Hurstwell, my prison. My rescue. The dark asylum that needed light.

REPRISE

If only the whole world could feel the power of harmony.

~Wolfgang Amadeus Mozart

SIX MONTHS LATER

So many people despise the boring days, the uneventful seasons. They must not have experienced difficulty and so cannot properly value normalcy. They overlook the simple brilliance of Mozart in favor of the more surprising works of Liszt. But there's a sweetness to the Mozart days, the ones where everything happens just as you expect, just as it did the day before.

I'd made a rhythm of my life. I watched the sun set at my childhood home, playing my own pianoforte, then at daybreak I watched the sun rise in the windows of Hurstwell, and witnessed a beautiful dawn coming to the place—and to my sister.

Harford had gently nurtured life back into her, drawing out her natural ability to read music and people. She had easily picked up

25

the threads of his research, having an almost instinctive sense of how to match a person's rhythm and use her music to draw them out. She would one day take the reins from him completely, and in that work she would shine.

As a result, so would Hurstwell.

When I passed the large, empty office where she was now established with her own pianoforte from our shop, I slowed in the doorway. I looked upon the slender figure of my childhood vision, her long hair now freshly oiled and hanging down over her back, as her song was unleashed upon the old instrument like a gentle wave upon the seashore.

Bridget brushed past with a smile and a begging of my pardon as she led a gowned patient into the room, settling her beside the musician for her session. Rose paused to smile at the newcomer, her nature as warm and welcoming as she'd once been to a lonely little girl.

Bridget left them and paused to lean against the wall beside me. "A wonder to think she can still play, after all these years."

I nodded. "She's a bit rusty, but it isn't something one forgets."

"Think she'll hear again? All the way, I mean?"

"Probably not. But that may be to her benefit." It had slowly come out that the loss was due to my father, her stepfather, when he had boxed her ears years ago for botching a performance. The problem grew worse until it was nearly complete. She was afraid of what might become of her if her musician stepfather discovered her affliction, so she hid it. Continued composing and playing, pretending she could hear him when he yelled. Nearly lost her sanity keeping up the charade.

She lived in mortal fear and finally lashed out in anger, attacking him with the depth of her terror when she could not hear a word he said, and he had her removed to an attic room of our home for several years, and then to Hurstwell when people began to ask questions. He paid to have her and her lovely music locked away in the forgotten tower as one whose value had expired, so no one would ever know what had come of the enchanting stepchild of Winston Mourdant who had once been a budding performer.

"She's playing Beethoven right now. His final symphony, written in his worst season." I watched her flowing fingers climb and descend the keyboard with the effortlessness of a waterfall dripping over rocks. "Imagine, a deaf musician creating music he cannot hear."

I wondered if this final piece might have been less brilliant if he could have. Some prisons bring great freedom.

"How does she do it? How can she play?"

"She plays by feel." I put my hand against the doorframe and felt the vibration. "She knows by the vibrations of sound on walls, on furniture, if she's hit a wrong note, and she plays most everything from memory."

Together we watched her smile at the patient as she played.

"Say, you've not dusted the keys of our old instrument in a day or two, you know. Ought to make sure it still plays." She gave me a friendly jab and returned to her duties.

Her suggestion triggered my desire, and I was soon sitting at Hurstwell's beautiful old Broadwood, bathed in the pale yellow sunlight streaming through open windows and lightly blowing curtains. I swam in the clear waters of Mozart, my heavy soul beginning to lift. I had found such freedom—even before my release from this place.

After a pause, I closed my eyes to acknowledge the presence of God filling this room, filling my soul, and followed the direction of my overfull heart toward the song that had once lifted to the rafters of our old church in Manchester.

> I wandered in the shades of night,
> Till Jesus came to me,
> And with the sunlight of His love
> Bid all my darkness flee.

Warmth spread through my body, even in the chill of early morning.

> However dark the world may be,
> I've sunlight in my soul.

Footsteps. Music swirled up within me and eclipsed the song I played as I realized at once who it was. That low, gentle voice, the steady steps. I slid my hands off the keys. As my fading notes rang through the room, I felt him approach and I paused, feeling the oddness of his presence within a fully lit asylum. In this place of light and sunshine and rich wood instruments.

Then he was standing just behind me, his aura calming and exciting at once. In the ringing silence, he pulled up a chair on the left. Out of the corner of my eye I glimpsed his profile, kind and sturdy, and its masculinity nearly overwhelmed me.

I turned to face him, saying not a word. Drinking in Bach's cello solo that filled the room in its subtle, unobtrusive way. How handsome he was, swathed in sunlight and warmth of spirit with a new calm, a peaceful levity, while the slight stubble on his jaw and those rolled-up sleeves remained so familiar. He hadn't even bothered to change his appearance to call upon me—for I knew that's why he'd come back—and I adored him all the more for being so wholly himself.

His steady gaze lay upon me, radiating appreciation, tender affection, then he magnified it with a crooked little smile that lit up every corner of my heart.

"Play," he said, and I did, allowing another verse to spill from my heart.

> I cross the wide, extended fields,
> I journey o'er the plain . . .

But suddenly I wasn't journeying over them alone. Mitchell Turner's fingers found the lower notes, adding depth to my higher ones, joining his melody with mine. His rich baritone filled in the words echoing about the chambers of my heart.

> And in the sunlight of His love
> I reap the golden grain.

We continued, and I shivered at the textured melody flowing from the instrument, the very rightness of these harmonies playing together. Through the last two verses we played, then the refrain, his hand crossing over mine and climbing the notes in an intimate, intermingled piece that lay gently over the pair of us and lifted to the God we praised together. We climbed and crescendoed, and I closed my eyes, drinking in the most richly woven piece I'd ever played. One I'd never known existed.

As the notes of our duet faded, I waited a beat, then glanced over at him. He was watching me with bright appreciation, just as he had when I'd played for Violet.

That crooked little smile again. "Hello."

"You came back."

"How could I not?" He looked down to our hands, then back to my face. "Your music has pierced me and lodged within. I could not get it out of my head."

With a smile I leaned close, nestling my face into the steady frame of his shoulder. He tipped my chin up with one finger, and after allowing himself a moment to gaze at me, to delight in the freedom to be so near, he kissed me. Kissed me with as much longing and warmth as he had in the dark tunnel. Chopin and Bach mingled in a breathless new piece, a duet sweetly carried out with a magnificent depth I could feel in my soul.

I opened my eyes and looked at him, right into that countenance I had easily grown to love, and he spoke. "I'm a broken man, Vivienne. Cracks and fissures at every angle."

My smile widened. "Then we shall be the perfect fit." I kissed him again to seal my words and delighted in the taste. The very authenticity of his lips on mine, the stubble brushing my chin and nose. When at last we pulled apart, he let his fingers trail over my cheek, my hair, tucking a strand behind my ear where a flower had once perched that had drawn his attention.

"So you are free now." It was a statement from him rather than a question. The lunacy commission had swept through Hurstwell and reevaluated each patient at length—I was one of the fortunate ones released quickly. "What will you do now?"

"Rescue women. Give a voice to the silent. In some form or other."

"Nothing to do with Hurstwell, I imagine."

"On the contrary, I shall be here often." I curled my hands around the edges of the stool. "Harford has been given temporary reign over the old place to run his clinical trials and bring whatever healing he can to the patients who remain. I have promised to help—for now, at least. There's another musician who will take charge, actually."

"Indeed?" His face brightened. He looked pleased at all of this. His eyes continued searching my face. "Hurstwell has not managed to dim you. Not at all. And I'm glad of it. No, in fact I think you have lit up Hurstwell instead. It seems quite different—so full of music."

I closed my eyes and listened to the faint sounds of Rose masterfully playing a Schubert piece. Oh, how it lit the air with beauty. Changed everything. No matter what you do to them, there's only so much you can lock up about a light like Rose. A musician like me.

And nothing you can lock up about God.

Arise, shine; for thy light is come, and the glory of the Lord is risen upon thee.

Isaiah 60:1

AUTHOR'S NOTE

When I set out to write about the Victorian asylums, I found myself not wanting to spend time in that world. Not wanting to journey into it with my heroine. So I decided to join it with another intriguing story idea that had been bouncing around my head—the origins of music therapy—and I was pleasantly surprised at what I found. In short, music therapy is not at all what I thought it was: a sort of "bubble bath" for the senses, meant to calm patients and bring order to a chaotic situation. It's much more complex and beautiful than that.

Music therapy syncs with the natural rhythm at the core of all humans and taps into the beauty and personhood found there. I watched many videos demonstrating how music brought back lost memories in fragmented minds, accessed surprising depths in chaotic patients, and connected those considered lost to the outside world. I admit to crying through most—or perhaps all—of these videos. I hadn't given much thought to how fundamental rhythm is to our ordered world, how deeply God has built it into everything, but reading about music therapy made me want to give up writing and go learn this profession. When the therapist is skilled enough to truly see their patient and thus know exactly what to play, a connection is made that realigns the order, the natural rhythm, of all created things.

Canon Frederick Harford (whose name was Frederick Kill Harford, but I dropped the "Kill") was a real man who brought music into hospitals and even asylums. He later founded the Guild of St. Cecilia with other musicians to continue the work. He died not long after founding this guild, but his work in music therapy echoes like Vivienne's songs well beyond his lifetime.

Victorian asylums, I found, were also not what I'd expected. They're often presented in literature as places of abuse, especially toward women, and wrongful imprisonment. The data shows, however, that far more men were placed there than women, and that many institutions did act with kindness and charitable intentions toward patients. The one dreadful part of asylums was the wide swath of people placed into them, often for life, because of conditions that people simply did not understand. Stroke victims suffering confusion or loss of clear speech. Women entering menopause. Children born deaf or mute. Mothers with postpartum depression. People with epilepsy, mental illness, even situational depression.

I'm beyond grateful for resources, including music therapy, that shine immense light onto conditions we misunderstood so we can see the problem for what it is—and see the people beneath.

A MIDNIGHT DANCE

Can Ella Blythe change the fate
of her own doomed love?

1

He was so very *blue*. That was all my scattered mind could gather as he sailed past the window of Craven Street Theatre. Blue and sparkling under the glow of streetlamps that shone down the alley. I ended my three-point pirouette in demi-pointe with a soft landing in the quiet of the old abandoned room of the theater and stared again out the window, but he had vanished. Curiosity drove me to abandon my solitary practice as the second act carried on below, and I ran to the window for a better look.

Breeze from the broken window cooled my skin, rolling in pleasant waves over my too-warm body as I stepped out onto the balcony and looked down upon him, straining to see. He was a shining streak in the night, halfway down the alley, gauzy cape billowing behind him. A dancer, in full costume. How curious!

As the muffled music crescendoed below, several colossal ogres of men barreled around the corner of the Lamb and Flag Pub, jeers trailing them in the night. They cornered him with harsh, echoing laughter that vibrated off the walls. They meant to rob the man. I crouched out of sight behind the doorframe, hardly breathing.

A man with one suspender holding up his dirty trousers smashed a gin bottle on the brick, advancing with playful thrusts like a sword. I shivered, anticipating the plunge of glass into flesh, but I could not look away.

Run!

But that dancer was trapped as a cornered pig, poor fool.

Why wasn't anyone coming? Another dancer, a passerby, a confounded bobby, for pity's sake? But everyone around was safely cocooned in the theater, and there was only me, way up here. The Almighty possessed a sense of humor, he did. Ella Blythe was not one for high places—especially approaching their edges.

I stepped out onto the balcony and forced myself to look down as I clung to the rail, my breath coming in thin gasps, prickly panic climbing my skin. I yanked off one beloved scarlet ballet slipper that had been my entire reason for sneaking in here tonight and held it up, but the men were too far away. Climbing upon the low brick railing, I poised myself and focused on the stair landing a little to the left and a few feet lower. One glance down and my vision blurred at the sides, the familiar panic cinching my ribs. Moisture tickled my skin.

Fear be hanged—it had to be done. I sprang and crouched into a soft landing, still gripping the precious red slipper.

I rose, and with a final goodbye squeeze, I whipped the shoe at them, satin ribbons rippling behind it. It struck the face of a pursuer and crumpled in the street. The sloshed assailant stumbled back, bracing for an unseen attacker in the darkness beyond the streetlamp's reach, then lurched off. The others hesitated, and in that brief uncertainty, the blue wraith slipped into the safety of the shadows.

I sank hard onto the stair landing and exhaled, trembling as I shoved hair off my face. Drunk as they were, it hadn't taken much to scare them off—just one of the enchanted red shoes. I slipped the other one off and clutched it close, then stole back inside to the forgotten old materials room, where I could be alone until I'd collected myself.

I pressed my face to the window glass, half afraid to see, but no one moved about in the alley. Only the strains of the *Nymphes des Bois* sounded from the ballet performance in the main auditorium, all the familiar sights and creaks of the old theater surrounding me, and my tension began to unspool.

The rest of London may have forgotten about this old room hidden away in the theater's side wing, with its dust-laden crystal chandeliers lying on their sides and silk faille draped over painted wooden clouds, but to me it was a sanctuary. A haven for my own private dances.

But there were footsteps in the corridor, echoing over hard flooring outside the room. Heart fluttering like a million trapped butterflies, I leaped behind a silk-draped ladder and crouched, barely daring to breathe. The door squealed open and there he was, filling the doorway, filling the room, his crepe de chine cape fluttering against his solid frame.

I didn't know anything about men. I seldom spoke to them. His presence here in my private sanctuary was unsettling.

He strode in like a lion, glancing about for his prey. Awed at my close proximity to him, I looked into his magnificent face from the shadows, the sculpted and dimpled features highlighted in the dim light. The grease paint tried to cover the ruddy glow of his skin, disguise the deep vibrancy of his expression, but it could only do so much. He moved on, then turned back, his roving gaze resting on me cowering like a little fool behind that ladder. I hadn't any idea what one was supposed to do with oneself in such a moment. Should I go to him? Smile and make introductions? How vulgar.

Well, I *was* in a theater just now. The rules were a bit different here.

He moved the silk aside like a curtain and smiled down at me. I wasn't prepared for the glorious sunshine that radiated from his masculine features. I rose, eyes still on him. Merciful heavens.

"Ah, here's my gallant rescuer." Rugged and warm at the same time, the man stood before me, my rescued shoe close against his chest.

My poor heart. It thrummed like a drum about to pop.

"I wanted to come up and thank you . . . and perhaps defend my masculinity." But his deep voice proved it aplenty. "I was in desperate need of a small drink before my part comes back in the third act, you see, and the theater's supply sprang a leak this morning. I hated to run into the pub this way, but there is nothing for it when one is dying of thirst and every spare hand is needed. Not unless I cared to scrape up what's leaked onto the cellar floor, which I didn't."

I worked my jaw as his voice echoed about the room, but my head was a scatter of random letters that refused to form words.

"That, of course, left me in the rather awkward position of dashing to the pub in costume during my off time in the second act, falling in with a pair of men deep in their cups, and thus being rescued by a . . ."

"Girl."

"Ah, you *can* speak." He folded his arms and looked intently into my face, his presence softened by dark, glossy hair that all fell over his forehead in one boyish twist. "So tell me, dear rescuer, what brings you so boldly into this haunted part of the theater? And how ever did you learn to spring and land like a cat?"

"I'm a dancer."

He raised his eyebrows in a way that somehow wasn't mocking, bless him. "Are you, now? That explains this." He held up my rescued shoe—that precious red slipper I desperately needed back. My hand itched to snatch it close. "I might have known it with a mere look, though. You wear dignity like a royal cape, even when you're afraid and hiding. Like an exotic wild animal, perhaps."

I had no answer for such a response. No one had ever looked at me and labeled what they saw as *dignity*.

"Which company do you dance with? Who is your manager?"

I stiffened. "N-no company. No manager." So many questions. I hated questions.

"You're a *petit ra*—forgive me, a member of the *corps*."

Miserable, I shook my head again. I was not even one of the lesser dancers onstage.

"I'm curious, then, what makes you call yourself a dancer?"

I looked at him solemnly, chin edging up. "Is art only validated by the presence of an audience?"

His eyebrows shot up, eyes flashing, and I knew I'd won his admiration—and that I was in trouble. One good look into his compelling eyes, I couldn't stop staring, couldn't keep my composure. They were magnets at the soul level. He moved closer, as if drawn, and I backed to the wall.

He slowed his approach. "Forgive me, but I simply don't know what to make of you. I've never heard of anyone willing to take on the label of a dancer without any of the spoils of the trade."

"I've never admitted it before."

"But you practice."

"Every day."

"Hmm." He shifted down onto his right knee, gaze still holding mine. "May I?"

I nodded, and he slipped the shoe onto my foot. Butterflies—oh, the butterflies. How beautifully that red slipper fit. It struck me again as his solid hands wound the laces, the small kindness wrapping itself around me.

I looked away. "Why must you stare? Haven't you seen enough?"

"It's just that . . . well, these do resemble a rather famous pair of slippers. One might wonder how you came to have them."

"Oh?" I focused my gaze on the floor beside him. He knew these shoes, of course. He had to. They were legendary.

"I'm speaking of the missing ballet shoes of the extraordinary Delphine Besseau." He watched my face.

"Oh." I tried to act properly astonished, but he'd gotten it wrong. It was *Bessette*.

He looked at me as if I'd stolen them, which I hadn't, thank you very much. Not exactly. Three weeks of extra wash I had done for the pleasure of having her slippers, my hands rubbed raw just so they could hold the gleaming satin shoes at last.

Mrs. Boffin, Craven's laundress, had scrunched up her face as she handed them to me only an hour ago, jamming a hair cloth back over her wiry wisps. "What do you want these for, anyway?"

I paid the woman my extra wages to filch them from that old underground dressing room long since abandoned, since everyone seemed to have forgotten about them, so that made them more mine than anyone's.

"Ain't none of my nevermind, but you ain't no dancer, Ella Blythe," she'd declared. "You're a regular churchgoer. A good girl, you are."

Good, indeed.

Supremely *good* was precisely how I felt as I slipped my foot into that other shoe, heart beating the rhythm as if it was already inside me, tapping away. Was dancing truly so divorced from God that they could not both be woven tightly into the fabric of the same girl? Something inside me resonated so deeply with the immensity, the vibrant beauty, of both. I had quite a weakness for beauty. Such as this man—the sight of him pulled at the core of me.

He tied off the slipper and rose, gaze still searching. "Did you know, she died in a tragic gaslight fire in this very room, a dozen years ago or so."

I knew.

"The room has been gutted and rebuilt, of course, but it used to be her private practice room, and was the place where she died. It's where people have claimed to see her ghostly figure, which is why you'll seldom find anyone in it."

I shuddered. "How awful." I knew the story, of course, but it still affected me with every telling. All but the brick shell had been pulled down and rebuilt throughout the entire theater, yet I could still sense the uniqueness that remained in this room. I always had.

"It's said she's looking for her famous red satin ballet shoes . . . and for poor Marcus de Silva."

"Marcus *who*?"

"De Silva. The man who supposedly killed her, of course."

My heart skittered, mind turning that name over. "How do you know all this?"

He laughed. "How do you not? Everyone in the ballet world, especially at Craven, has stories about being haunted by poor Delphine's ghost. She is known for her tragic end, and for her red slippers." He sobered, something odd flickering over his features.

He went back to studying me again in that terribly unnerving way. "Ones that look exactly like these." His gaze dropped toward the shoes, then at me, head tilted in question. Our gazes tangled and held, and I couldn't breathe. He lifted one hand as if to poke me. "I've never seen her, though. That is, until . . ." His fingertips brushed across my face, a whisper-soft movement.

I shivered again, then ducked away, flustered and speechless.

"Very well then, you're not a ghost." He continued to watch me, a sparkle of wonder dancing on the shiny blue surface of his face. "Care to try the shoes? I hear they're special—the secret to her legendary success."

Normally I'd refuse, but moonlight softened my reasoning. It cast an intoxicating glow over this man who saw the ballerina in me, melting my insecurities. He moved so close, his breath warm on my cheek, and I felt suddenly, for the first time, that I could not fail.

The evening's encounter with this stranger was brief but significant, sinking deep into my memories to remain forever bottled there—a most precious experience that would never quite seem real once we left this place. "All right, then." I took his hand and we moved toward an open space. He pulled me directly toward his solid frame, hands resting on my waist, and with a thrill I finally understood why the finer set of London declared dancing immoral.

I could smell whatever made his glossy black hair wave so perfectly across his forehead and feel his breath across the part on my scalp. I felt his heart beneath his shirt. The moment was dreamlike, separate from my fruitless days in the washhouse, and I could not turn away from the gentle frame of his arms, the promise of my first *pas de deux*—a partner dance that, for once in my life, included a partner.

Yet the minute we stepped into the muffled rhythm, moving through the familiar paces—*relevé, attitude* leg lift, *cambré* to the right—my defenses melted in the cool moonlight. This was not carnal—it was art, and it was sacred. My feet arched easily into tiny *pas de bourreé* steps forward, propelling me into a spin with foreign hands bracing my waist. He was self-assured but in an easy, gentle way. I became aware of my every curve in a manner that made me feel more alive, more comely, than I ever had before.

We danced through discarded scarves, thick cobwebs, and broken chairs, then he spun me with a lavish release, and the distant music of the second act twirled me up in its magic. I arched my back and glided into the familiar precision of ballet, feeling that glorious stretch again in my calves. I lifted the warm air with my arms, and I was off, spinning and gliding, my patched skirt flipping against my legs.

I twirled over and over, the world fading easily away around the face that held my focus with each turn. As the music below crescendoed and faded in its finale, I finished with a small spring, folded down, and rose with a gentle curved back, chest high, arms overhead. When my vision centered on his painted face, the astonishment there was absolute.

And utterly gratifying.

His clap split the silence as I caught my breath. A giant smile broke over his face and he stepped toward me, glancing at the shoes. "Perhaps they *are* enchanted."

I pushed stray hair away from my eyes. "As I told you, sir, I am a dancer."

That gaze was back on my face, studying. Assessing. "Indeed." His reply sank into the silence.

I sat to remove the slippers and replaced them with my well-worn work boots, wondering how I could possibly return to the washhouse at five the next morning.

He crouched before me, face vivid as if wanting to say more but not possessing the right words. I wasn't about to offer any information—he'd already gotten more out of me than most anyone ever had.

"You're quite blue." I nodded toward his costume, desperate to divert the focus.

"As the North Wind should be. Come to think of it, they'll be expecting me onstage with the third act, so I should take my leave. Such is the life of a dancer. It's a terrible flurry of—"

"Of wonderfulness." The words slipped out on a breath.

He paused, eyeing me. "Would you care to see it?"

My mouth hung open. "The *ballet*?"

"Come." Grabbing my hand, he pulled me out the door, into the dark corridor, then up narrow steps that led high into the rafters. "The third act will begin presently." He stopped me in a narrow passage and pushed open a tiny peep that looked down over the lavish royal-blue and ivory auditorium glinting with gold trim and muted gaslights, over the upswept hair and top hats and smartly glittering jewels in the audience.

I'd never seen it this way, so full and alive. "It's magnificent."

"I used to watch from up here at times. Just keep quiet and no one will know. And watch out for Delphine's ghost." He winked.

"*North Wind!* Get your sorry hide in here." The harsh whisper jolted through our quiet moment and the dancer sprang up. I cringed at the way the manager spoke to the stranger who'd been so kind to me, even though this level of rudeness was far too common in theater.

He paused and cocked a half smile, seeming to sense the longing he'd magnified in me. "How's about this? I'll put in a word, and we'll see where it gets you. One day we'll be dancing together on that stage. I vow it. Keep that focal point as you spin through your days, and don't stop dancing." With a salute, he spun in a whirl of sheer organza and crepe but quickly turned back, grabbing the doorframe. "Oh, and keep those shoes close, love. Wouldn't want anyone else knowing you have 'em."

Then he was gone, lighting like a gazelle down the stairs.

I stared down at the red shoes in my hands, fingering the perfect stitching along the soles. *Enchanted*, he'd called them. But as I flexed the tingling hand he'd squeezed, I wondered if maybe it wasn't the shoes.

Settling noises sounded throughout the auditorium as the intermission melted away, musicians cuing up, then the orchestra eased gently into the third act. Two callboys parted the heavy blue curtain, and I plastered my face against that little peep, my nose pressed into the rough pine-scented wood around it. The music thrummed and so did my heart, matching beat for beat, then the dancers leaped onto the stage from both sides, two by two, trailing flowered ribbons and spinning pirouettes. Color. Beauty. Artistry. Symmetry and grace. My heart unfurled as a blossom in spring.

The lead ballerina in bright red twirled into the center, her skirts whirling into a filigree flower around her. Amalia Brugnoli, favorite of the great choreographer Armand Vestris, had captivated my imagination since I'd glimpsed her through a window one day in the rehearsal room. Now here she was, dancing before me with acrobatic bursts and the most complex footwork I'd ever seen. I squinted at her tiny slippers—how was she doing this?

Everything about her was strength and perfection, from her smooth chestnut hair to her paces. Astonishment and jealousy wound in equal parts through my veins, thick with angst. With desire. When she landed in an *arabesque* and tilted to the right, the music rose to dizzying crescendos, and suddenly *there he was*— leaping with bold precision onto the stage, springing forth and spinning in the air, his powerful legs propelling him across the stage again and again.

His legs scissored above the other dancers, and he landed with a double spin on one knee, arms overhead, and swept back into the air with an effortless leap. I sucked in my breath. If ever I'd imagined that ballet damaged a man's masculinity, he disproved that notion in three beats of my heart. He was all muscle and control, skill and artistry—and such *power*. It oozed from him as he overtook the entire stage, the other dancers merely a background to his stunning performance.

And to think, I'd been in his presence—dancing alongside him.

I withered to the floor when the curtain shut, siphoning off my view of the most magical sight I'd ever witnessed, its intensity still sitting hard against my chest. Ballet was so much more real, more stirring and magnificent, than I'd ever realized. I was alight with more happiness than any devout member of St. Luke's Church had any right to feel inside a theater, but I couldn't help it. I straddled two worlds, my heart evenly divided.

I danced my way home through Covent Garden's crowded streets and up the Strand, clutching the soggy program I'd managed to rescue from the gutter outside Craven. When I reached our home on dirty old St. Giles, I paused amidst distant shouts and banging doors to look through the paper for the name I desperately had to know.

North Wind . . . . . . principal dancer, **Mr. Philippe Rousseau**

I gasped, cold fingers over my mouth, and read it over and over. Principal dancer. I had danced with the *principal dancer*.

I looked up at the tiny square window with its four panes of greenish glass, the wealth of moss slicking the walls of our building in this little Covent Garden side street that clung by a thread to respectability. A single errant flower dared to grow between the building's stones, and I plucked it, spinning that rare show of color between my fingers—beauty amidst poverty. *"One day we'll be dancing together on that stage. I vow it."*

Impossible as it seemed, I ached with a crushing desire for that promise to be true.

When I climbed the stairs, barely remembering to skip the broken one, dear Mum's warm smile greeted me, then Lily's sisterly scowl.

Poor Lily was a pretty, dimpled thing two years older than I, who'd been built for a life of pleasure and amusement, but fate had stolen her real mum years ago and left her stuffed with us in this little flat, a life that snuffed her dreams of men and gowns and coquetry. Her mum, a longtime costume designer who'd worked in the theater when mine was dancing there, had once dressed her daughter in fine leftover ribbons and paraded her about London. I was seven when her mother died, and Lily nine. Now here she was with us, stirring her specialty—*soup de scraps*—in a pot over the fire, charging me with her look for every minute of work she'd had to do in my absence.

I pinched back a grin as I clutched the precious shoes and program under my cloak. I met Lily's stare with a smile and spun her around with my free arm before bending to kiss Mama. "Happiest of birthdays, Mama. I'll finish that cake, I promise. But first, a gift for you."

Grinning so hard my cheeks hurt, I knelt before this gentle woman and placed the sacred shoes in her lap, ribbons spilling down over her knees. Weeks of extra work and secrecy . . . all for this.

And it was worth it. She blinked, mouth falling open and hands framing her face as tears swelled in her eyes. She dabbed them with the corner of her apron and lifted the slippers as if they'd been the crown jewels. "Oh, Ella. Child. Are they . . . ?"

"The very ones."

"Oh, but how—why . . ."

I shrugged with a little smile. "Merely returning them to their rightful owner."

ACKNOWLEDGMENTS

I'll admit, this was a difficult book to write. It had a darker, more limiting setting that I had to creatively work around. It would have been more than difficult without lots of brainstorming help from some very important people. Allen Arnold especially helped me "shine the light" on this dark book.

I'm incredibly grateful to God for coming alongside me in this book. From the planning and note-making stage on, every new stage I reached, I felt like he was already there, waiting for me to catch up, enjoying the dance through the pages together. This process was incredible and difficult and eternally valuable to me because of his presence in it. Talk about making something out of nothing, shedding light on a dark situation—or novel—no one compares. No one.

Rachel and Angie—you wanted to be in one of my books so here you are . . . until I can work you in as two of my characters one day. You girls are the absolute BEST encouragers, brainstormers, and what-if friends. This book took shape largely because of your help and all those brainstorming sessions. You're creative, endlessly kind, and lots of fun!

My dad talked me through just about every plot point from the initial stages of planning this book, helping me sort through what worked and what didn't. There's no one else to whom I can just prattle on about every angle of every idea, who will then come alongside me and help me sort through them.

Two other women were HUGE helps in shaping this story. Susan Tuttle, my wonderful critique partner who helped me untangle the mess I made of this story in my head, has listened to me talk about this story endlessly for over a year now. Her buoyant spirit toward every project often helped buoy mine. Thank you, Susan! Also, Jennifer K. was just about the best cheerleader I could ask for as I wrote this story. Her invaluable insight, her background in music therapy, and her gracious friendship really saw me through the draft of this book. I'm thankful for you, friend!

My wonderful Revell team has gone above and beyond in cover design, polishing manuscripts, and introducing my books to readers. I'm so grateful for their talent and their gracious help for me and many other authors. You all are a stellar team, and I thoroughly enjoy you!

My grandpa. Honestly, I don't think I'd even know how to write about the value of people without watching him. He was one of those rare men who saw value, not just potential, in everyone he met. Really—everyone.

I am also eternally grateful to friends like Rachel and Faith for watching my children and giving me writing breaks to finish this novel. Of course, my husband, Vince, is the superhero of all this, and I couldn't do it without him.

Joanna Davidson Politano is the award-winning author of *Lady Jayne Disappears*, *A Rumored Fortune*, *Finding Lady Enderly*, *The Love Note*, and *A Midnight Dance*. She loves tales that capture the colorful, exquisite details in ordinary lives and is eager to hear anyone's story. She lives with her husband and their children in a house in the woods near Lake Michigan. You can find her at www.jdpstories.com.

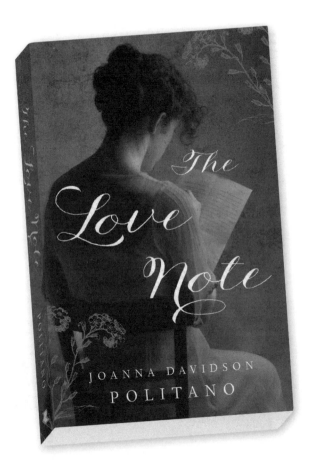

Lynhurst Manor is a house built on secrets . . .
and the arrival of **Aurelie Harcourt**
might reveal them all.

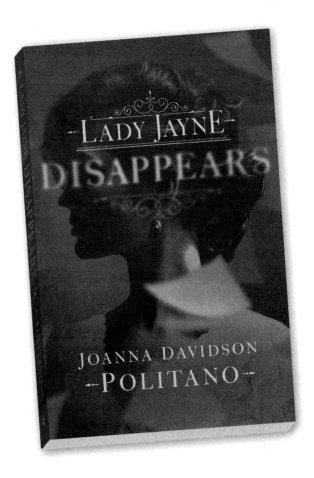

Welcome to Trevelyan Castle, home of the *poorest heiress in Victorian England*.

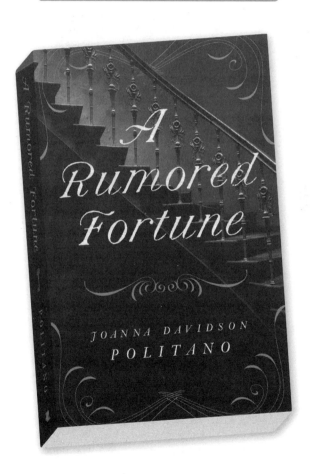

— MEET —
JOANNA

JDPStories.com